Through Forests and Mountains

Through Forests and Mountains

by

Margaret Walker

Through Forests and Mountains
Copyright © 2021 Margaret Walker

ISBN-13: 978-1-950586-71-4(Paperback)
ISBN:-978-1-950586-70-7(e-book)

BISAC Subject Headings:
FIC014000FICTION / Historical
FIC032000FICTION / War & Military
FIC047000FICTION / Sea Stories

The Book Cover Whisperer:
ProfessionalBookCoverDesign.com

Address all correspondence to:
Penmore Press LLC
920 N Javelina Pl
Tucson AZ 85748

DEDICATION

To

Rev. Neil Flower

PERMISSIONS

The following publishers have kindly given their permission to use quotations from copyrighted works.

Extract from Women and Yugoslav Partisans by Jelena Batinić. Reproduced with permission of The Licensor through PL Sclear; copyright © 2015 by Jelena Batinić. Published by Cambridge University Press.

Extract from Disputed Barricade by Fitzroy Maclean reprinted by permission of Peters Fraser & Dunlop (www.petersfraserdunlop.com) on behalf of the Estate of Fitzroy Maclean; copyright © 1957. Published by Jonathon Cape.

ACKNOWLEDGEMENTS

'You can't reason with a fascist. All you can do is shoot them.'

Thus said Jana, a female Yugoslav Partisan, in Chapter Twenty-Two of this novel. The actual quote came from my father-in-law, and he was referring to members of the Gestapo and the fascist collaborators in Northern Italy. Gunner Doug Walker was an Australian soldier who was captured by the Germans at the First Battle of El Alamein and went on to fight with the communist Italian Partisans in Piverone, north of Turin. Because the war was started by the German fascists, the Nazis, and supported by the Italian Fascists and smaller fascist groups across Europe, such as the Ustasha, resistance movements during World War 2 were often organized by communists, who were anti-fascist and allied to communist Russia, an ally of Britain. Though he disliked communism, Doug and the other Australian and British soldiers who fought with the Italians subordinated their ideological differences for the sake of defeating a common enemy.

Through Forest and Mountains is about the communist Yugoslav Partisans, the resistance movement that most endorsed the role of women. My birth mother came from Tar, in Istria, and travelled on a Yugoslav passport. In Sydney in the 1960s, it was through my adoptive mother that I first heard about the women in Yugoslavia who had fought alongside the men, a story that has captivated me ever since.

I have Jelena Batinić to thank for her excellent and very readable academic study on the subject, *Women and Yugoslav Partisans* (Cambridge University Press 2015). In 1985 I spent a wonderful two weeks in Yugoslavia at a time when the country was opening up to tourism. To me it seemed fresh and new, its people warm and welcoming. On a recent trip to Croatia, I purchased *Po šumama i gorama* (Through forests and mountains, Zagreb 1952). Subtitled *The Poems of the Fighters,* the book reveals the spirit of the original Partisans and their deep desire to rid their land of the fascists who occupied it. I was captivated by these poems, and listened avidly to the less dominant voices of the men and women who had written them. In all cases, when I have used them in the novel, I have credited the author. I hope my translations have done them justice.

The exciting escape of the Yugoslav submarine *Nebojša* in 1941 in the face of the invading Axis forces was recorded by John De Majnik in his book *Diary of a Submariner* (Asgard Press, 1996.) He was a wireless officer on the vessel, and the mission was led by Đorđe Mitrović who was not the boat's captain at the time.

I always wondered what happened to the real captain. This was the question that inspired the novel.

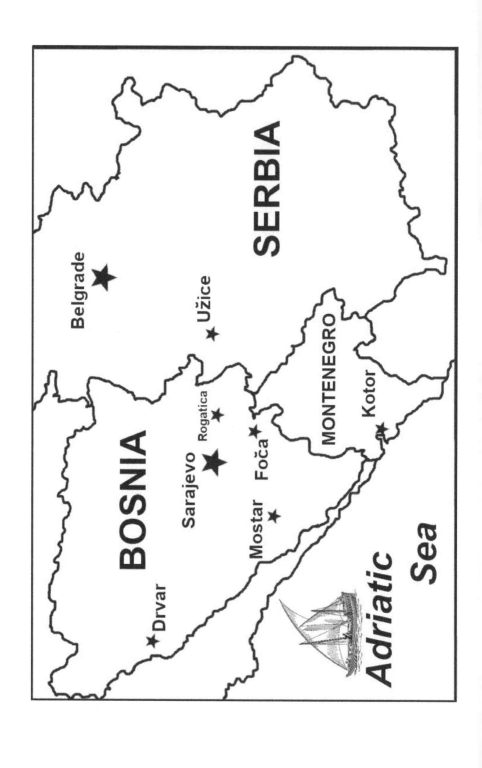

CHAPTER ONE

At the hour of national crisis he was brought down like a bull by a terrier, and his memories returned to him only slowly, the good and the bad, but mostly the bad. There was shouting in which he had joined, then a weakness outside his experience and the confusion of not understanding why the slipway was rising to meet him. As is usual with accidents that occur in public places, there was also a crowd that gathered from nowhere to watch in horrified silence. He remembered the woman who stepped out from the onlookers to bully him kindly: 'Put your head between your knees, Captain, before you knock yourself out.' He remembered his reply: 'I'm not going to faint,' just before he did.

So he couldn't recall Miloš Lompar, aged seventeen and frantic with remorse, attempting to staunch his desperately bleeding shoulder with a rag stained with lubricating oil, nor Commander Filip Kolarov (whom everyone expected to be the hero) recruiting five sailors to transport him from beneath the blood-stained propellers of the torpedo boat and into the waiting ambulance without dropping him. Upon his arrival at the hospital, the rural surgical ward, which dealt mostly with tonsils, appendixes and adenoids, at once increased in self-importance thanks to all the excitement, and he was hustled inside with as little delay as a starting pistol. From a morning that had threatened mundane routine, his shattered shoulder had given the ward meaning and purpose and, by the time of the afternoon ward-round, it was all back together again and reposing below its soft white pillow, as contentedly as if it belonged to the hospital and not to him.

This general sense of achievement originated in a surgeon, white-coated and elegantly balding, surrounded by a retinue of medical students who beamed in unison every time he opened his mouth. Adjoining them stood a scrub nurse and a ward sister who looked like she had ironed on her scowl that morning. Before their eyes, Dr Rastoder had performed veritable miracles of surgery, keenly assisted by at least two of those present—possibly more—and had only had to consult the textbook once.

'Awake at last!' he chirped. He smiled. His audience smiled. 'Eighty stitches! And that's not counting the two severed tendons I repaired, or the puréed muscle or the skin graft. You have a great deal to be thankful for, Captain Marković. You're lucky you didn't lose your arm. Damned lucky!' he stressed with a very personal determination.

Marković sensed a conspiracy and, in confirmation, one of the students twirled his moustache.

'How long...?' he began.

He pushed himself into a sitting position with his left hand and was at once overcome by a wave of dizziness. On a wheeled table to one side he saw the hazy remains of a blood transfusion, a throbbing jug, the ghost of his dead mother, and a glass that replenished itself with water. At the very end, in proud isolation, a urine bottle grinned at him, half-full.

'You've been unconscious for five hours,' returned the doctor. Acknowledging the urine bottle, he added, 'More or less.'

Marković grimaced. His mother eased him back onto his pillow and then floated away, and the mountain of snowy bandages on his right side settled comfortably down beside him. He watched the crowd observe this with pride.

'Wiggle your fingers,' ordered the angry ward sister.

He wiggled his fingers and a shudder ran through the shoulder.

The scrub nurse glanced apprehensively at the surgeon.

'Perfectly normal,' he purred. 'Touch your toes.'

The medical students tittered.

'Just my little joke.'

'Can I go home?' asked Marković. As they seemed so cheerful, he allowed himself hope. 'I need to get back to the apprentices.'

'Those two who landed you in here?' Dr Rastoder inverted his eyebrows and proceeded in a voice of doom. 'There are more immediate things that you need to know. An infection from any wound that extensive is inevitable. We expect one quite soon; don't we, Sister?'

The ward sister nodded grimly.

'You're not serious?' exclaimed Marković.

'I'm afraid I am, Captain.'

'But I've heard about trials of...'

'Penicillin? Rumours, at this point. Your one stroke of luck is that Yugoslavia's not at war with Germany yet. In that case, there would be the possibility of catching an infection from someone brought in fresh from the battlefield.'

Marković levered himself up cautiously. He stopped. He checked both sides. Reaching one arm beneath the injured shoulder, he hauled it up beside the other one and searched around for the exit.

The surgeon cut him off shrewdly.

'Don't even think about it.'

'I can't stay here.'

'You're no good to anyone dead.'

'It's only a shoulder!'

3

'You wait,' declared the surgeon.

'Next patient,' said the sister.

The team moved on, and the medical students beamed back like a round of applause.

The frustration of his predicament and the pain made him grumpy, of course, and, by the close of that first day, as dinner was served with regimental efficiency from the other end of the long ward, there was no one in it who wasn't heartily sick of his clenched teeth and thunderous face. When, at lights out, the same sister who had stood by his bed during the ward-round pinned on her veil like a helmet and marched towards him with his night's morphine flashing from her syringe, he glared at her with such indignation that she declared, in a tight-lipped tirade, that she'd met a lot of patients like him. Oh yes, she had.

'Take a good look around you, Captain. The worst tonsils, appendixes and adenoids of my acquaintance are models of virtue compared with *you*—God give me strength! And you needn't think you can expect pain relief to order later on when you can't sleep, so you'll have the injection when I tell you—and do something about your manners while you're at it.'

As bad luck would have it, the instant he had accepted the shot and she was massaging it in, he fell asleep in full view of the whole ward, and everyone said they hoped he stayed that way.

The next day was visiting day. The hours were from two o'clock until five, on Wednesdays and Sundays. No illicit visiting was permitted, except when compassionate grounds intruded upon the mental health of the ward sister, to whom the disruption of her routine occasioned great anxiety. Before the double doors could be flung open to gift-bearing relatives, the beds must be made to perfection, the floor must be swept clean of every cowering microbe and the surgeon

must complete his rounds. Pills, elixirs, injections, and ene-
mas must be distributed and their associated smells dispersed through the open windows.

At the very end of the day's queue, as if the act of waiting
might atone for their guilt, in slunk two gangly boys. Accompanying them was a commander with a sharp eye and a reso-
lute bearing that invited trust. Indeed, a head or two had already turned at the click of his boots on the floor, though he
had cloaked his agreeable features with a severity appropriate to the occasion. Marković could see that he regretted doing it, but the boys were completely fooled. They had been
very careful to dress in full uniform, to comb their hair and
shine their boots, but the perfect presentation could not obscure the terror on their faces nor their quaking knees.

As the trio approached the bed, the officer came to a halt,
removed his hat and placed it beneath his arm.

'Lompar!' he commanded.

At once one of the boys handed forward a small bunch of
flowers, missing half their petals. At the sight of his com-
manding officer sprawled on the bed undressed and unshaven, he mumbled an apology only distinguishable as such
by the flush of shame that preceded it.

'Ilić!'

The second youth now produced a package of waxed
brown paper, which he unwrapped to reveal a small nut cake.
He saluted feebly and stammered as he stepped back, 'Miloš
and I are very sorry, sir.'

Marković smiled wanly and acknowledged them without
criticism, for he could see how miserable they were, and he
was only grumpy.

The commander waved the youths away.

'All right, dismissed!'

The boys fled. At once, the atmosphere lightened and the
officer sprung upon the crisp white sheets and positioned

himself comfortably on the bed, flipping up the back of his jacket where it subsided too far into the springs.

'I knew you'd want to see them, Anton,' he began—bounce, bounce.

'Oh, don't sit on the bed, Filip, for God's sake!'

'Why?' Now that he didn't have to put on an act, he slung one leg across the other, and the bed chortled a little creak in response.

'Because that old nursing sister will kill me. You're not allowed to sit on *her* beds.'

'Really?' Filip released his long limbs and extracted a chair from beside the bed of the elderly man next to him. 'May I?' he enquired, engaging the fellow in such a charming smile that the man looked suddenly shy, as if few people had ever taken the time to acknowledge him. 'Thank you.'

He settled himself comfortably on the chair and tapped a rhythm upon his hat.

'Which old nursing sister? They all looked nice to me.'

'Boadicea. The one wearing the armour. She hates me.'

'Nonsense.' He flourished a cavalier hand into the depths of a canvas satchel and announced, 'Housekeeping!'

'What a pleasant fellow you are!' grumbled Marković.

'I am on *your* side, Anton,' returned Filip genially, 'even if you have already made an enemy—though, personally, I doubt it. Now, the Chief, out of the generosity of his heart, has packed you two shirts, your most threadbare trousers he could find—he believes old clothes are suitable for convalescence—your toothbrush, some odds and ends, and a razor to cut the cake.'

'To shave.'

'To cut the cake. Poor Petar's mother insisted he bring it. You won't be able to use the razor to shave, so beguile one of those nice nurses to do the honours. Girls love that sort of thing. Makes them feel like mothers. Let them bring out your legendary charm.'

'What legendary charm?'

'*Intimacy,* Anton, that female equator you haven't crossed yet. Now observe! You need a shave and that was a good-looking nurse who just slipped behind those curtains across the aisle. She'd be an ace with a razor, I bet.'

'I can shave myself.'

'Then here's a shirt. Get her to help you dress.'

'Can you leave if you're going to provoke me, please?' said Anton, attempting to make himself comfortable with his single arm.

Filip grinned at him, poised like a barge pole above the mattress.

'It's true, then, what they say about hospital beds being the delusion of a Spartan mindset?' he asked.

'My shoulder hurts,' said Anton in reply.

'It's your own fault.'

'It was not my fault.'

'It wasn't your boat.'

'In that particular case, Filip, it didn't need to be.'

'You still haven't told me what you think of the bed.'

It did no good arguing with Commander Kolarov. While he breathed, he would pursue his theme of sympathy being detrimental to recovery, and the ward, which had tensed for a clash of opinions, settled back down, pleased that no one had ruffled its professional façade by arguing about whether sympathy might be helpful.

'The wonder is,' conceded Anton at length, 'that you're expected to get better sleeping in one.'

This answer relieved Filip of a social burden, and even the elderly man in the next bed expressed his mottled pleasure with lips crinkled by the absence of teeth. But Anton was disappointed because he would have liked some sympathy from Filip and it looked like he wasn't going to get any. He lay on his bed between the convivial commander and the sensitive old man and thought about the pleasure of his own company, as he often did.

He had regular features, similar to the vast majority of his compatriots who agreed, to a man, that he looked good in the right light and the right mood, but could appear fractious when the sun disappeared behind a cloud. Anton said his feelings were none of their business, and this was generally true except for the present circumstances. Yet, he had made no attempt to adjust to the hospital, claiming in his defense that he didn't care what people thought of him. By contrast with the two rows of men and boys all washed, dried and thoroughly institutionalized, he stood out by his refusal to acquiesce peacefully, which no amount of soap and water could remedy.

A faecal odour floated from behind the curtains. The pretty nurse withdrew with a bedpan and hurried from the ward. Filip frowned.

'I hate to see you like this, Anton. Smile. Be grateful. Tell them a joke. You can look like the grim reaper, but if you make them laugh, they'll love you.'

'I would appreciate some sympathy, Filip.'

'You won all hearts yesterday when you fainted on the slipway.'

'Go to hell.'

Kolarov laughed.

'Not today, my friend. Got the incident report to write.' He pulled out a pencil and paper from the same modest satchel, crossed his legs and began scribbling. 'What happened?'

'I'm not sure.'

'Then you'd better think of something quickly for the sake of bureaucracy. I put the boys through this, this morning.'

8

'You weren't too hard on them, I hope?'

'Me?' replied Filip, his head still sunk in the paper.

'I thought they looked pretty scared.'

'Well, one look at you would be enough to scare anyone.' He tapped the pencil on his teeth and continued writing. 'If you must know, there were safety procedures that everyone overlooked, including you.' The commander was not given to reprimand, but the blistering white bandages reflected the sun into his eyes and circumstances had wrung it from him. He paused in his writing and placed his hands open in front of him. 'What were you even *doing* there, Anton?'

'The boys were curious.'

'Petar, who hadn't removed the fuse before you started lecturing him on engines and Miloš, who insisted afterwards that he heard you shout "turn it off"?'

'Well, why did he start it in the first place?'

'Because he's seventeen and he's wondering what might happen if he flicks that switch. That's what seventeen-year-old boys do. You shouldn't have left him and gone off with Petar to explain how propellers work. Miloš panicked when your sleeve got caught; Petar said that he forgot about the fuse, and so did you.' Kolarov shook his head, most particularly at Anton. 'Disregard for protocol, Anton. This is when these things happen. Now that we've lost a man we can't afford to lose, I realize the advice is a bit long in the tooth, but you always have to learn the hard way.'

'You really think I'm that bad?' Anton muttered.

'You know I don't,' replied Filip. 'You're one of the most capable men I've got but, right now, you look like a bear with a sore tooth. And I'm sorry about the boys, but you picked a bad time to be their friend instead of their leader.'

'Why? You've had some more news from Belgrade?'

Filip tossed aside his pencil and drew his brows together.

'Well, you heard about the prince, that he capitulated to Hitler?'

'Yes. And?'

'And you knew that the alliance with Germany had not gone down well in the capital. Prince Paul's long gone. General Simović saw to that, and now they're ranging the streets singing "better war than the pact." The fellow on the wireless said he'd never seen such jubilation.'

'We're at war?'

'Not yet, but the staff at the German and British embassies have left Belgrade, so it's coming. Hitler knows the strategic value of the country and, after the capitulation of Romania, Bulgaria and Hungary, he expected us to agree easily. Our show of defiance will have let that famous rage of his off its leash.'

'But are we ready?'

'No, we're not ready! We've been treading on eggshells to keep their eyes off us. Now the Nazis will wipe Yugoslavia from the map.'

He spoke calmly but the underlying tension in his voice conveyed its own urgency, and through the window to the west, the grey limestone peaks trembled at his words from the water to the sky. What a desperate place was a hospital when the enemy would come over the mountains!

Anton pushed himself up until their eyes were level.

'Listen, Filip, I've got to get out of here.'

But Filip only rose and replaced his hat.

'The minute I hear anything further, I'll tell you.' He patted the bed affectionately. 'You just sit tight and get better.'

He headed towards the exit. On his way out, he met the pretty nurse who was struggling to load the cleansed bedpan into the top level of a cupboard. With a gracious smile, he took it from her, slipping it in easily and, out of the corner of one eye, Anton caught him winking at her.

Margaret Walker

*****

By the third day, he was managing to rumble around the ward without dizziness, to the distress of the other patients who wished he'd push his throttle in and not appear so menacing: one hundred and ninety centimetres of bone and muscle, as dense and dark as the trunk of a black poplar and just as communicative. Since regaining consciousness, he'd scarcely exchanged two words with anyone except the old man beside him, whom he'd found hiding beneath the bedclothes in anticipation of a visit from his wife.

However, early on his fourth morning, while watching out the window for Germans, his wolf-like reflection in the glass so alarmed him that he ensconced himself in a secluded cubicle in the bathroom and, with Kolarov's threats of female intimacy ringing in his ears, attempted to shave with his left hand. In order to avoid cutting himself, he was forced to proceed so carefully that an hour wore away in utter concentration, until a white veil swished into his cubicle and he glanced up to see the senior sister frowning down at him. She watched without speaking as he scraped cautiously around his neck, all the while exhibiting that female exasperation for his sex that assumed he would make a mistake merely because he was male.

Finally, she slanted her head to one side and remarked, 'All you had to do was ask, Captain.'

'You are disturbing me,' he informed her.

They had supported his injured shoulder with a sling and he had put on the trousers that Filip had brought. One arm he managed to ease into a shirt and he had draped the sleeve of the other over the bandages and fastened three buttons up his chest. Thus attired, he fancied that he looked on the road to recovery. The nurse and her caustic quip had soured that achievement. He was all lather and inexperience.

11

'You are going to cut yourself,' she said.

'I am not going to cut myself, sister,' he replied coolly, wiping his face with a towel. 'And now, if you please, I'm certain you have better things to do with your time.'

'I do, as a matter of fact, but it took me a while to find you. Your commander is waiting by your bed.'

So certain was Anton that Kolarov could only be there to inform him of catastrophe, and that the nurse had deliberately delayed the announcement because she was a ball-busting man-hater, that he pushed past her before he broke his own rule and swore at a woman in public.

Sure enough, he found the commander pacing around the bed, unable even to sit.

'What?' demanded Anton. 'What?'

'Thank God!' Filip motioned him aside, brushing a ribbon of sweat from his forehead. 'Where can we talk privately?'

They returned to the cubicle. At the sight of the commander, the sister departed politely.

'The Luftwaffe has bombed Belgrade,' Kolarov reported. Punctuated. 'Early this morning. Easter Sunday. With civilian casualties in the thousands. For our jubilation, Hitler has sworn to teach the Slavs a brutal lesson.' He paused and Anton heard the suffering in his voice. 'They didn't even target the military.'

'Where then?' asked Anton in a taut whisper.

'Homes and businesses. The whole city's ablaze.'

'Do we mean that little to him?'

Disbelief was in his voice, yes, but a growing recognition of something that was merciless as well.

'It's intimidation, Anton. Don't credit Hitler with any sophistication.'

'And how did we respond?'

'Not well. A few dog fights. I told you, we weren't ready, and there is the sense also that some of our positions were betrayed.'

'What about the naval base? I haven't heard any planes. How soon will we be attacked? What about my boat?'

'The *Nebojša's* dived at Tivat, but nothing's happened yet. She's sitting on the bottom of the bay.' Kolarov checked his watch. 'It's half past eight. She's been there for an hour and a half. Late last night Naval Command was warned by the British about a possible attack here this morning. All craft have been ordered to change their positions daily, as long as they have the fuel to do so. Other than that, we wait to see if and when the army surrenders. When, I think, sooner than if.'

*****

After Kolarov had left the ward, Anton felt bereft. He stared at the two long rows of beds, some empty, a few occupied, and experienced a loneliness he had not felt since he was a child at the end of a long summer's outing. Something had delayed his family—the bank, the tram, he couldn't remember now—and, by the time they'd arrived, everyone else had gone home except him. Distressing for a man to recall the small hurts of boyhood.

The German attack on Belgrade had profoundly shocked him. As a member of the military there should have been some action to take, yet he could do nothing.

'Destroy Paris,' he thought bitterly. 'Slaughter French civilians without provocation and see how the world reacts.'

Once, as a student, he had been to Paris: a new city then, only seventy or eighty years old, but already the darling of the Western world, as dedicated to style and indulgence as London was to finance. Paris was not to know that to Serbs, Belgrade had had the same reputation for pleasure, and he doubted whether it would have cared. Paris was a teenager and just as self-involved. The Nazis would not ravage a city younger than the age of consent, but their ideology justified the destruction of a Slavic population.

The morning sun flooded the long ward and Anton sat on his bed with his head in his hands contemplating with increasing despair the fate of his boat. Since nine o'clock, he had heard the drone of bombers and, in reply, the sharp report of anti-aircraft fire. He knew the planes would have to have come from Italy. The Italians had long coveted the Yugoslav coast and were undoubtedly taking advantage of the German invasion to launch their own. The bombers would be targeting ships anchored in the bay and he doubted whether a civilian hospital would be evacuated.

Lunchtime came and went. The sun began its swift descent upon the crags around the water. Three o'clock struck and Anton watched the minutes glide on until a quarter past, when the day-nurses, anxious but professional, would gather in their small glassed-in office for the handover to the evening staff. As his case arrived, they would discuss its particular features, his treatment and his progress. Quickly they would move on to the next patient, one or two men after him, then the last one, close their books, smooth their veils, and seal his doom for another night.

His shoulder would not heal while it was condemned to be here, for healing is holistic and his heart was broken. Briskly, he seized the satchel from beneath his bed, sat with it on the sheets and thrust the flap open with his foot. He shoved in his few belongings, ignoring the insistence of the evening nurse, who came bustling up, that he wait for the doctor.

On observing that he had no intention of waiting for anyone, she repacked his satchel with hydrogen peroxide, iodine and bandages and begged him to return tomorrow. But he

14

had made up his mind and her plea fell on deaf ears. As she chased him down the ward, he threw the strap over his shoulder and left without a backward glance. He could imagine her expressing his medical sacrilege in outrageous adjectives.

CHAPTER TWO

It is called the Adriatic Sea, Jadransko to the locals living along its Dalmatian coast although, for most of its four hundred kilometres, their view of it is obscured by islands. A thousand isles from Rijeka in the north to Dubrovnik, many looking as large as another country, just across the water. One might suppose them ruled by a type of offshore feudalism, like a chapter from Grimm's Fairy Stories—*A King in a Far Away Kingdom*. Not so far away, in this case.

Like the karst landscape of the coast, the big trees are long gone and the islands appear a rubble of limestone and dirt, green in parts, where some scrubby vegetation has managed to take root. They look sterile, though they are fertile in number. They crowd the coast and sweep onwards, further and further south. Perhaps they are seeking tropical lands of constant sun and warm rain to return them to life.

Just as you start wondering whether families can survive here—for there seems little but plunging limestone mountains as bare as a wart—suddenly, between the slender coast road and the water, appears an olive tree by a stone house. It's just a little house, a squat rectangle and an attic room accessed by an outside staircase, a few roofing tiles clinging to its rafters. To feed his family, the owner has removed blocks of limestone to construct artificial garden plots of earth he has carted from elsewhere. Further along, another enterprising farmer has coaxed a grove of cypress pines into life to complement the Adriatic and its barren cliffs. You can just make out his house beyond them. The complex is perched on the barest peninsula, so intact that it seems a world unto itself.

Everyone has boats here, peeling, painted wooden things as small as a bathtub, and sometimes a cabin that's a mere triangle to keep off the sun. The road hurries past them, around the cliffs, until the journey becomes tortuous and you dread the thought of someone coming at speed from the other direction. Finally, here is beautiful Dubrovnik, shining from the coast like a blue jewel, and the islands cease for no reason that is apparent.

Even now you must proceed further south, on and on, until you arrive at the Bay of Kotor. The nineteenth century British adventurers termed it a fjord, though in a geographical sense it isn't. It is a narrow stretch of water, and the big ships are forced to execute a three-point turn in order to leave. The mountains soar around it like sea birds, wheeling and plunging into its depths and, on a sunny day, there are three colours only: yellow, green and blue. Sun, mountains and sea in endless combinations. The sun rises late over these mountains and sets early, blushing the peaks with rose. By two o'clock in winter, it has sunk behind the highest rise and the long mountain-induced night has begun. In the hinterland rises Mount Lovćen, pine-clad and dark, which gives the country its name: Montenegro, Black Mountain.

Kotor itself is a small town at the far reaches of the bay, enclosed within two triangles. The first is the peninsula on which it is built, and the second is the much vaster triangle of its ancient defensive walls that leap up behind it, almost perpendicularly, from the water until one is breathless just from looking. In April 1941, a submarine waited at the quay at Kotor attached to cleats by ropes as thick as a man's arm. The main base at Tivat, where the *Nebojša* usually docked, lay ten kilometres to the west, and a third naval establishment, at the tiny town of Kumbor, was set back from the entrance to the Bay of Kotor, as if to act as a falling lock on a gate to a distorted harbour.

*****

Anton walked along the road home, blessing the fresh air, and the soul of the shy old man in the next bed accompanied him. During the night he had died of pneumonia, having caught a cold from another patient, and his final visions of this lovely world were of nothing more holy than starched white sheets and stethoscopes. Now his body lay cold and stiff in a mortuary smelling of bleach. *Why did I let him go to that hospital?* wailed his disconsolate widow. *What danger to him were two gangrenous toes? They should have let them drop off naturally.* He had had surgery and now he was dead, and, in revenge, she had been the only one to antagonise the ward sister more than Anton. Her cries of venom echoed across the bay and up the mountain on the other side until everybody, from the baker to the cobbler, knew that her husband had passed away and that there was a special place in hell reserved for surgical wards.

An hour since, the sun, which had presided over this drama, passed west behind the mountains and, in the artificial gloaming, Anton watched his boots kick up pebbles and saw his trousers crease as he marched—left, right, left, right. He was sorry for the widow and her husband, but felt quite a different person now he was out of that dreadful hospital. He wasn't grumpy any more. Breathing deeply of the salt air, wonderfully free of institutional smells, he reflected that, of all the sins in the hospital, the worst had been an improperly

18

made bed. That ward sister had a fetish for bed making and it was rumoured that she and the sister in charge of the medical ward across the foyer outdid each other in the pursuit of perfection.

Left, right, left, right. The sling cut into his neck. With the endorphins from his dramatic exit declining at each step, the satchel grew heavier, and the ten-kilometre walk home now appeared a symptom of temporary insanity. He had covered about five and was starting to feel dizzy again when he was overtaken by a farmer with a horse and cart, who took pity on him. When finally he arrived at the naval base at Tivat and sank, fully clothed, onto his bed, the startled cook, who had rushed up to feed him, observed Captain Marković in such a profound slumber that she had to summon the Chief Petty Officer to determine whether he was alive or dead.

At first, the daily dressings were no problem. Anton got one of his crew to do them—that gentle fellow, Viktor, whom he had noticed replacing a baby bird fallen from its nest in the spring winds.

'Wash your hands, Viktor, and come and have a look at this shoulder for me.'

'Aye, aye, Captain!'

Viktor had laid the hatchling carefully back into its nest, jumped down from the tree and stuck his hands under the pump while Anton unbuttoned his shirt and gingerly peeled back the soft cotton dressing from the tender skin. Two neat rows of stitches ran down from his shoulder and branched out over a craterous landscape as pale as moonlight.

Viktor examined them with fascination.

'Looks clean, sir, just a bit bumpy.'

'Thank you, Viktor. Would you mind doing some nursing for me?'

'Nurses are girls, sir.'

'Of course, they are. And how is that young lady of yours, by the way?'

Viktor bit his lip.

'Um, very well. Do you think I'd make her a good husband?'

'A husband?'

'That's what her father said.'

'Then, I'm sure you would. Hand me that bottle of hydrogen peroxide and the iodine, would you?'

How hard could it be to look after a wound? Viktor bustled around and made just the right degree of fuss. The status of Anton's shoulder as the prize trophy of the hospital meant that it attracted attention like ants to honey, and he had found that difficult. He wanted the nurses, that radiant doctor and his chorus of proselytes to go away and leave him alone, to let his body manage itself as it had always done. Who was that sister who had handed over the bottle of hydrogen peroxide, the iodine, and several rounds of immaculate linen, and insinuated with pointed irony that he might need them? She had the presentation of a laundress. She and that ward sister had made a good pair.

He was over the morphine by now. He could handle whatever pain nature threw at him. He just needed to be out of hospital and in a familiar environment, to smell the sea and to know that he could lose himself in it. In that respect, he was eminently calm. In fact, he could even have been a nurse himself, so well did he understand his own body. Things had been progressing very well. True, he could not yet use the arm, but he could be patient when it was in his best interests. Once he had reached the startling conclusion that the arm, like a car, was a mechanical invention, he expected it would work, in time, as well as any other machine that had been put back together. He did not anticipate problems. He believed in biomechanics, but the list of things he couldn't do was ever expanding. He could eat but not cut, and was too proud to ask for help, so he ended up dispensing with cutlery and picking the meat up with his fingers, just using the fork for vegetables. He could dress himself slowly and shave, also slowly, by propping his useless right shoulder on a pile of books and just using his fingers. That worked effectively every second day. He couldn't write well, but he could write. He couldn't make his bed, but when the cook volunteered to do it for him, he graciously declined with the excuse that neatness reminded him of hospital. Worst of all, he was unable to accompany the *Nebojša* on her two day patrol to Albania to search for Italian convoys, unless he remained on the bridge of the submarine.

Every day, after the motherly Viktor had finished his regular tasks, Anton asked him to change his dressings. The bottle of hydrogen peroxide had suffered an unfortunate spill the day before yesterday. In the meantime, he thought he'd just use the iodine. If he was desperate, he could send the boy back to the hospital to replenish the hydrogen peroxide and let him take the motorbike as a sweetener. Better not to return himself. He might lose his temper with Boadicea.

'Viktor, when you've finished, please?'

'Yes, sir, nearly finished greasing the propellers. Won't be long.'

'Then give your hands a good wash and come over when you're done.'

'Yes, sir.'

And the day after, it was loading the torpedoes.

'Wash your hands, Viktor.'

'Yes, sir.'

And cleaning the officer's wardroom in the submarine.

'Have you washed your hands, Viktor?'

'Yes, sir.'

'You sure?'

Through Forests and Mountains

'I'm sure, sir.'

And then the boys had played a game of football on their day off.

'Already washed them, Captain!'

The first indication of trouble came at the end of that week, the day after he and Viktor had decided to remove the eighty stitches with scissors and pliers. Beneath the bright morning sun, forty cuts and forty yanks stung the same tender point in his gut forty times, until he was either going to vomit or faint again. With barely enough time to wipe the sheen from his forehead and clutch his abdomen like a seasick whale, he panted, 'Thanks, Viktor. We'll take the other forty out this evening.'

When he woke up ten hours later, he noticed a faint pinkness, just swelling the flesh around his neck where the stitches had been. All day he ignored it while the bustle and fear created by the Axis advance accumulated at the naval base and he tried to keep the sailors busy at their tasks, as if Hitler's threat to invade without mercy was the least of their worries. By the following evening, his shoulder had begun to throb slightly, though intermittently, and he went to bed with an unusual exhaustion, which he put down to the dire situation of a country that had delayed its preparation through fear of provoking an enemy.

After an eight-hour sleep as solid as the dead, he had awoken to a yellow seeping beneath the bandages and, when he got Viktor to carefully remove the layers, he found that the swelling appeared to be trying to divide the two halves of the wound, which had been securely together the previous day. He had a vague memory of his mother speaking of pustular wounds, and issuing warnings about the smell, but sniffing cautiously, he couldn't smell anything. Two days later he noticed that the swelling had extended and now included a regular throbbing, a small but unremitting suggestion of

22

trouble. The next day it was worse, and he dispatched Viktor back to the hospital.

Viktor roared in on the motorbike, upset the gravel on the circular drive and, parking at a safe distance from his misdeed, checked to his right and his left for witnesses. Not seeing any, he tiptoed into the surgical ward, clutching the small brown bottle that he hoped might replenish itself. There, he was accosted like an escaped criminal by the scowling senior sister and her conspirator in ablutions from the medical ward. From their disapproving faces, he was evidently in a great deal of trouble. After merely simmering as they first laid eyes on him, they boiled over when they heard his humble petition because they knew perfectly well whom the hydrogen peroxide was for. Under their combined attack, poor Viktor broke down and confessed the developing situation with the infected shoulder.

Upon locating Anton back at the naval base, he blushed a sort of mildewed pink, and launched into the recitation he had rehearsed all the way home.

'I'm so sorry, Captain, that I told them. I knew you didn't want me to. But sister said you must go back to the hospital right away. She said I had to come and get you. She said I should put the sidecar on, like while the bike is still warm, sir. Please, Captain,' he stumbled miserably, 'it did seem that sister wasn't very happy with me, her and that other one. So I'll just drop you off, and maybe wait outside this time.'

Anton grimaced. The wretched shoulder was throbbing again. With every pulse, it pounded the pain through his traumatised tissue and he could just detect the slightest smell from beneath the bandages, like a wraith floating up and across his neck. Probably Viktor couldn't notice it, but he saw his face and winced.

'No, Viktor, it's me she isn't happy with.'

'Will you go, Captain, please?'

23

Through Forests and Mountains

'Try to not to worry, Viktor, you've done well. I just need to speak with Commander Kolarov first. You see over there? He's looking for me.'

Viktor walked away with a very worried look crumpling his young face.

Anton swung around, 'Yes, Filip, what is it?'

'Bad news heading our way.' Even the authority he wore so easily and his popularity could not hide the dismay on his face.

'Bad news? What?'

'You have been ordered to surrender the *Nebojša* to the Italians.'

There was a pause while his heart grew silent until he could not hear it at all, and then he said, 'When?'

'Late today, tomorrow.' Kolarov spoke in an abstracted fashion, his eyes searching Anton oddly. He flicked his fingers at the wound bulging beneath the shirt. 'What are those pink lines running up your neck?'

'They're nothing. Nothing. I asked you—when?'

'Today, they think.'

'What are our options? The way the mood is at the moment, my men will go down fighting.'

'I know. Yes, I know.'

'Look at Belgrade. They'll want to be just as defiant here.'

'I know.'

'This is our people, our land, our fight,' insisted Anton.

'I know.'

'Then what can headquarters be thinking, blithely telling me to surrender the submarine?'

Anton could never decide afterwards if the defiance in Filip's eyes was the desire to fight or the knowledge of what resistance might cost them.

'Listen to my suggestion, Anton, and tell me what you think.'

So Anton listened.

'...and the Italian navy has laid new minefields,' Filip concluded. 'They're supposedly waiting at the mouth of the bay, but I'll have our barricades open before we get there.'

'You want to escape? You're going to run the Italian blockade? You'll never do it! You're asking those boys to commit suicide.'

'No, I'm not! I'm giving them the choice, to stay or go. Some want to come with me and join the Allies, others want to fight as partisans. I'll ask your crew first and see whether I can get sufficient numbers to man the submarine. Two torpedo boats want to go with us. We'll try to make it to Egypt.'

'I can do that!' cried Anton urgently, but he was feeling hot. The stress? The shoulder? He saw Filip looking at him with concern, as if he had some foreknowledge of a very definite nature.

'Anton, you're sick. Go back to the hospital.'

'No! I'm coming with you. What is this talk about sufficient numbers? I'm needed.'

'Look at your neck. Something's clearly wrong. Fight another day. There is other naval staff here. There are civilians, mechanics. I'll get the numbers I need. We're not surrendering that boat to the enemy.'

The rest of that day passed in wretchedness. As proficient in medical neglect as he was, there was only so much denial even Anton could maintain and, despite the cool spring afternoon, he recognized that he felt warm and dizzy, had a pounding headache and a heart that fluttered fast and lightly. And all the while, that blustery pain from his shoulder failed to dissipate.

The *Nebojša,* his boat, was waiting at the key at Kotor, seventy-two metres of iron rocking as calmly as if it had no forewarning of its fate and could not hear his heart thudding in his chest nor sense his attempts to conceal it. He was hot, and the still depths swept around the flanks of the boat, reaching out to cool him. Eddies of water rose to the surface and dispersed in circles as delicate as flowers. Kolarov had his crew and Anton had travelled across from the naval base with them, even now unsure of events, and strangely detached from them. It was not his boat anymore and, along with that renunciation, it was not his body either. He looked upwards into the lowering skies, and the mountains hovering above the town seemed to fall on him. The bastions of the old wall scaling the heights were scarcely discernable against the grey limestone; the rain that had plagued them for weeks lingered in the damp air.

Talk of what Kolarov was planning had got out and already a considerable crowd had formed at the dock outside the Sea Gate to farewell the submarine on its bid for freedom. Many of them knew Anton as its captain; all knew that Kolarov was its ex-captain. Anton greeted a few absently and watched, through blurring eyes, as they stared back at him. They could see his clothes, still thick and padded with bandages. Yes, they'd all heard about his accident.

The arrival of the commander from town caused a ripple of excitement through the crowd and a tense foreboding about the planned escape attempt. Anton noted the sudden spark of interest, even delight, as Kolarov strode along the quay and approached the gangway. Clearly the belief in his martyrdom was already strong, for how could he have stayed, and to what purpose? To put his own safety above that of those who looked to him for leadership? To observe with a resigned face the takeover of his land? No, for this respected and popular officer and his crew were doing the only thing possible, and offering themselves as a sacrificial gesture for the freedom of their people. Anton observed several women weeping as, with each step along the gangway towards the tower of the vessel, Kolarov reinforced their belief that this was the end, and that he and the men he was leading were bidding them a loving farewell, to meet a fate already spelled out.

It was six o'clock. The sun had disappeared beyond the high peaks and night was falling. Anton raised his head and saw the rain clouds crowning the mountains, and suddenly it seemed that he could see beyond them, to a place that was restful and pain free—where his country had been liberated, where threats did not exist, where he needed to be. So the boys wanted to fight as partisans, did they? By doing so, they were carrying on a centuries-old tradition of mountain warfare. Fighting for their country in lightly armed bands was not a new idea. One only had to look at the Bay of Kotor and its coronet of mountains to feel that Kotor itself had been built at their foot with the express aim of being a backdoor to fighting Byzantines, Venetians, Austrians and Turks. No plain to cross, no river to ford. One hundred metres out the back of the town then straight up to freedom.

Anton would meet them directly above the town, towards the heart of the black mountain, where armies faltered, where tanks couldn't follow, where canons were unable to aim. Even if the enemy knew, as he did, where to hide, they could not follow him with any speed and, once there, he would be free. So, he would not ascend the old road that slowly zigzagged up the mountain beside Kotor. Instead, he would go straight up, beside the defensive wall, in order to scale the mountain as quickly as he could. All this he thought as he became increasingly detached from his body, like someone standing on the edge of his own grave.

The crowd had forgotten him. He turned and entered the town through the shadow of the Sea Gate, crossed the rectangular cobbles that comprised the square, and plunged directly into the maze of limestone dwellings. It was a very old place, Kotor. As he stumbled past, saints peered at him from ancient chapels: Saint Luke, Saint Paul, Saint Anne, Saint Michael, Saint Francis, Saint Joseph, Saint Nicholas, and the bones of Saint Triphon. He must have been a frivolous fellow, for on the walls of his cathedral was a laughing icon.

Anton's boat was leaving without him and it wasn't funny. Soon the town would sink into slumber; there was nothing here for him now. He looked up to the mountain that he must climb and the bleak fortresses along its wall. What would the sentries have seen from their watchtowers? The bulwarks have protected the town from the Turks upon the peaks; little wonder the wall was still standing and the townsfolk had not stolen its stones to build their houses. But now, the Italians had come by sea because their allies, the Germans, had invaded his country—bountiful, heartless Italy licking its lips in his meandering streets.

At the close of the town, Anton tripped up a step below a mediaeval arch and stopped, breathing rapidly, leaning against the cold stone blocks. The street led steeply upwards, for the houses, too, must climb the mountain, and steps had been fashioned beside the rough cobbles to aid the residents. The dwellings jutting above him made angles that dived and leapt, their shutters closed against the drizzle, strung with wet washing, damp cats and trees leering like ghouls. He lurched on until he found the path he was looking for that veered precipitously to the left and the commencement of the climb, beside the wall that had stood for a thousand years.

He climbed, and the town quickly became an ocean of tiles that sunk below him while the bay grew and its recesses swelled and dominated his view, sweeping around shores and inlets and ancient churches on islands built at sea level, scarcely troubled by the small tides. The rain that had been threatening all day still held off, but the clouds lowered over the high peaks, draining the water of colour. In the last of the

28

twilight, he looked down and saw the submarine move slowly past the point on which sat the chapel of Saint Elijah, following the wake of its accompanying torpedo boats. The hull was barely discernible against the grey water, the conning tower looked like a squat tree lapped by nurturing waves. From this height, it cut the water quietly and he could only make it out by searching for its wake.

So it had begun, and they would live or they would die. Word would filter back to Kotor. In two hours at the most everyone would know. Had it all been for nothing? Was the brave commander dead? But the boat seemed happy to be striving for freedom, and strangely, Anton could tell this, and be pleased for it. Upon the bridge stood five tiny figures. Already he could imagine the rest of the crew and its associated civilians, tense but busy, waiting without sight within their circular steel tomb.

Suddenly he wanted to hold it back, along with the essence of himself that was alive within it. But it had gone. He had lost it to the night. The camouflage created by metal, weather and darkness would be the boat's salvation, but not his. *I am no one*, he thought. What I am *no longer has significance because what was* me *has departed and left me behind. I had not intended it to be this way. This was not what I wanted.*

Twilight had faded now over the bay, blue to gold to rose, to grey to black. Why was the water black? It seemed to Anton that it should be alive and brilliantly blue, that this beautiful bay so fiercely fought-over through the centuries ought to welcome him home, even as he left it. For he was slipping away, and he had doubts that the dawn would break in the east. They said that the world was temporary, like the fall of the leaves, but the leaves would return in the spring. It was he who would leave the world. He staggered on because putting one foot in front of the other was easier than stopping to explain to himself this overwhelming sense of his own mortality.

'The Italians are expected later today', Kolarov had said. 'Their civilian population at Hercegnovi at the mouth of the Bay is preparing to welcome them with open arms.'

Surely, he was unable to think anymore and he had begun to shake. Who was this population of which Filip had spoken? He didn't know them. Or, if he did, he couldn't remember now. All he knew was that his boat was gone and there was nothing left for him to return to. Once his brain cleared and his shoulder ceased its poisonous march through his body, he was leaving, to fight as a partisan. He and the others. Over the mountain.

The path ascended steeply through a succession of acute angles beside a low wall. He faltered in the dark, memory alone guiding him. At each angle he paused, breathing hard, waiting until his heart calmed enough for him to continue. It had at last begun to rain and the initial soft mist had hardened into drops. It soaked into his clothes and penetrated down to his skin. A piercing cold. Even his bones shivered, yet at the same time, he sweated, and the wound throbbed a sickly warmth, like blood on ice. Once, he'd tripped on the irregular stones and, where he could, kept to the inlaid rocks to each side, but that brought him closer to the low wall and increased the sense that he would fall over it. He retreated to the middle, tripped again. At the point of the wall where it loomed over the town so directly that it looked as if he could drop a stone onto it, he was forced to halt, clutching his bursting chest, before stumbling upwards again.

At last, more than two hundred and fifty metres above sea level, he reached the Castle of Saint John and searched for the hole in its wall that he knew was there. He searched and searched but couldn't find it and, while he stood perplexed gazing up at the high peaks wreathed in cloud, he was overcome by such a sense of peace, such a vivid comprehension of the unfolding of time, that he ceased striving. It was perhaps the divine that had touched him, and he began to argue with it to stop distracting him, for he was not giving up, not even at the door of eternity. So love stood aside and he saw the hole immediately, plunged through it, fell over, rolled down the hill, picked himself up and willed his legs to continue.

It was not, in the end, that he'd found what he had been searching for but rather, in his desolation, that something had found him. The little church of Saint John lay protected by its years, secure even against time in its quiet crevice, grass on its roof, a fir by its apse. And, as the last of the twilight hurried away behind the mountains, Anton careered down the path towards it and collapsed beneath the lintel of the porch.

In the morning, the priest discovered him there.

CHAPTER THREE

The Yugoslav ambassador stood on the beach at Dover, in fog so thick that he couldn't see the street he'd walked down. The yellow lights of the town were nearly obscured and the bombed areas to the south, which had taken the worst of the cross-channel shelling, had disappeared into the murk. The pebbles that passed for sand swept a ditch to either side of his feet, and he swore under his breath that no place was as noxious as an English beach in the fog, and why had he ever come to this country? Surely, spies leaned from every wall of white mist and seduced his anxious brain with whispered threats to his daughter's safety.

He had taken the train here, not for any more practical purpose than because it was the closest point to Belgrade. How many thousands had been killed in the bombing and was she amongst them?

It was one of those dreary days that were chill and bleak tending towards evening and the silence stretched in all directions. It was the fog, of course. Within it, the ambassador felt so completely alone that it seemed a portent of his ultimate fear for her: that she was nowhere. He had alighted at Dover Priory station and walked through the town, passed the remains of the Pier District, Snargate Street and the

Wellington Dock and on towards the Prince of Wales pier itself. Seventy-six miles to London, but only twenty-six to
Calais, in France. To his left was the single gaping break in
the Georgian townhouses, planted by some canny German
shell. Now he stood on the beach by the rickety old pylons
and berated himself bitterly for allowing her to leave England.

Of course, he hadn't understood. He was only her father.

It was back in 1939, and instead of sympathizing, he had
tried to reason with her as she dragged her suitcases past
him down the narrow stairs, hitting an inlaid table and a rural scene in Royal Doulton on her way.

'Mara, don't go. Think of the political situation in Europe.
Think of your mother.'

'*Mum* would have understood,' she said, her eyes welling
with tears. She shoved her hat on her head and dragged her
beige overcoat around her shoulders, the one the ambassador had ordered for her from Belgrade because all the English ones were too short, while below in the street strolled
dozens of personable young men five inches shorter than
her, on average.

'Then what if I get you a job?'

She ignored his offer.

'I want to go home, Dad. It's all very well for men, you are
expected to be tall, but I feel like an apologetic giraffe in
London!'

'That's not a good reason to put yourself in danger, Mara.'
For this is how it seemed to all fathers, surely. But she had a
reply for everything—every objection he could conceive—until he had raised the white flag through sheer inability to
compete with her creative output.

'I'm tired of seeing everyone from above and I'm sick of
hitting my head,' she protested. These things were important
to her, he should understand. 'I spent *all day* shopping and

found only one pair of anonymous lace-ups that fitted. Some shrivelled shop assistant actually swore at me last ski season, because there was nothing on her shelves in my size. My shoulders are as broad as a bus, the curve from my waist to my hips would dwarf a racing circuit... and everyone would feel sorry for the cars.'

'But, Mara, aren't they just clothes?'

'Dad, you're not listening.'

The last straw had been that wretched Minster of Foreign Affairs, whom the ambassador was forced to meet with regularly; he had no hair, was the height of a sheep and had a nervous habit of rolling his lower dentures over his gums. He had gazed up at Mara's towering six feet and asked, 'What's the weather like up there?'

With war clouds gathering over the continent, Mara had shot him a look of horror and demanded to return to Belgrade forthwith. The best English schools and a degree in languages from the Royal Polytechnic would be her passport, she declared—English, French and German being employable subjects. She would stay with her aunt until she found work and a flat of her own.

'This country is a nightmare!'

He was forced to concede defeat; even so, the ambassador wouldn't let her go alone, and he wouldn't let her go through Germany. His compromise was to sail to Athens, where he could personally put her on board the Hellas Express that travelled through Kosovo to Belgrade. Through a cloud break in her existential crisis, Mara had at last relented. So it was here, amidst luggage racks, broad vistas of Scenic Greece, a gas heater, a toilet with the Willow pattern on the bowl, and a little old lady knitting socks, that he waved her sadly goodbye, praying she would be safe.

Now, perched upon the Dover pebbles, he stared out across the shrouded waves that swept coldly around the pier, past the ghostly Western docks, past the idle railway line. They sat silently in wartime. No passengers clambered onto the cross-channel ferries anymore. No more day trips to France. No more boat-trains from London to Paris. No Boulogne sausage of lung, tripe and sweetbreads. And no help for the ambassador of a defeated country, an army that had collapsed in only a week and a half. He turned to his secretary whom he could barely see through the fog. 'Find her boyfriend!' he snapped, and ground his toes into the pebbles. 'He's Croatian. He's a journalist.'

The secretary, a modest scholar from the Belgrade suburbs who, in his spare time, liked to compare copies of the gospels in Glagolitic and Cyrillic texts, balanced precariously upon the pebbles while the ambassador bellowed at him over his shoulder.

'Damn this apology for a beach! This is what comes of mixed relationships.'

'Sir?'

'Well, why couldn't she go out with a nice Serbian boy? If only my wife were alive.' He turned to the trembling scholar. 'What was the latest report?'

'From Belgrade, sir?' stammered the secretary in view of the ambassador's evident distress. 'Or Zagreb?'

'Belgrade!'

'Ah, well, there is a poster: Death to fascism! Freedom to the people!'

'That was the trouble with him,' seethed the ambassador. 'He was a fascist!'

'Hitler, sir?' The man swiped his brow.

'No, the boyfriend!'

'If you have his particulars, I could....'

'Zagreb. He lives in Zagreb and his name is Miroslav Novak. Mara dumped him because... as I said, because he admired fascism.' His voice broke and he drummed his knuckles into his coat. 'But he's got more chance of finding her than we do. How can we reach him?'

'Well, I could try the telephone. Failing that, the wireless. The army perhaps might allow us to radio. Then there could be a telegram. I'll have to check the restrictions.'

The ambassador subsided.

'Thank you. Please, do what you can.'

CHAPTER FOUR

The British Minister of Foreign Affairs had one rule for his life: not to allow his personal prejudices to affect his judgement. Naturally, this applied only to Britain, America and France. Other countries suffered the full partiality rap, and the top two on his list were Italy and Yugoslavia. The Italy that had joined forces with Nazi Germany belonged to a different country entirely from the Italy of food and culture, in which the minister owned a villa (resplendent in both) not far from Florence. His beautiful villa! His beautiful Italy! Unfortunately, he couldn't get to either because of the war.

That annoying young secretary of the Minister of Trade had obliterated his idyll, that school boy who had never taken his mortarboard off and always let everybody know it.

Italy is our enemy? The Minister of Foreign Affairs had had to listen twice.

'And Yugoslavia is our ally, Minister.'

That country of hotheads and peasants? Yes, yes, theoretically, the minister knew this, but the Italian people and the glorious countryside were not the enemy, surely?

'Italy is an Axis power, Minister. You remember the pact between Hitler and Mussolini? You remember their racial

37

laws? They have committed themselves body and soul against us.'

'But might it not be that only Rome has slipped up?' the minister suggested.

'The whole country is behind Mussolini. The women are throwing themselves at him.'

'What about my lovely housekeeper, Gianetta?'

'Your mistress, too.'

Poor Italy! The minister had always felt sorry for the Italians, having democracy thrust upon them by their own *Risorgimento*. The timing hadn't suited them, clearly. This was why they had succumbed so easily to a dictatorship. In the manner of an indulgent parent, he exonerated the violence and corruption associated with Mussolini, and exhibited genuine concern for the welfare of that sunny nation that generations of Englishmen had come to love. So, when he had met the Ambassador for Yugoslavia in the halls of Westminster one day, about two months after the German invasion, his sympathy for the ruins of the man's country was tinged with overt suspicion that anything east of Trieste was nothing but barbarism and slivovitz.

He began by inquiring about the illiteracy rate. Following that, the assassination of Alexander, the King of Yugoslavia in 1934 and the minister's insistence that the death had in no way assisted Italian land claims along the Dalmatian coast. He ended by discoursing on the *coup d'état* in Belgrade last March that had deposed Prince Paul, and the quality of the dandelions that the local inhabitants of Belgrade had been forced to eat recently to avoid starvation. Were they the same as those that grew in the embassy garden in London?

This was all very provoking to the ambassador, and the minister droned on, largely because he liked the sound of his own voice although, at one point, he mistook the tall ambassador for an oak tree carved into the ancient woodwork of the Hall. Eventually, the minister realized that he was speaking to a heavily accented gentleman and not to a branch above his head. The ambassador, for his part, strained his long neck to look down at the Minister of Foreign Affairs. He saw the shadow of his lower dentures waving upon the floor and realized that the man was looking particularly nervous and unhappy this morning. That made two of them.

He therefore began a polite conversation about the weather and had the pleasure of not having the articulate minister congratulate him, as usual, upon his improved use of the definite article.

'Sun shines gloriously upon grass.'

"The" Ambassador, "the" the Minister of Foreign Affairs had instructed him countless times. "'*The* sun shines gloriously upon *the* grass."

'Thank you, Minister. My daughter is *the* linguist, not me.'

The ambassador then spoke of his concern for the young King Peter, recently arrived in London, the rapid collapse of the Royal Yugoslav military and the return of the British Embassy staff to London that had preceded it. Then, right at the end, he'd accidentally dropped the hint that he had received permission to contact, in Zagreb, a certain Miroslav Novak. He'd given instructions for him to try to locate the ambassador's daughter, who had not been heard of since the bombing of Belgrade. The search for Novak had taken the ambassador's secretary two months.

Tuscany is nearer Zagreb than London, realized the Minister of Foreign Affairs. But what was he thinking? England was at war, the Yugoslav ambassador was mourning his daughter, whom the minister, despite all his prejudices, sincerely hoped was alive somewhere under the rubble. The traditional route across the channel to Paris, through the Alps by train to Turin and thence to Florence and his villa, was barred to him, but could he charter a plane to neutral Lisbon and proceed from thence to the occupied territories? Or should he exploit the minister's communication with this young man in Zagreb? It was galling. *Dear Gianetta, so warm and accommodating.* At some point in his musings, he realized what a pipe dream it all was. The reverie had turned into something to keep him warm during the blasted fog of these islands, the muck that passed for food in these days of rationing, and his arthritis. You could pass a soccer ball through his knees. The only thing he could do was to humble himself before the ambassador and endeavour to improve his attitude towards Yugoslavia. That done, he might point out that Zagreb was only a day's ride by train from Florence. If he made it worthwhile to Miroslav Novak, could he report on the condition of the villa that was so dear to his heart and his Gianetta (ditto), so that his knees could depart in peace from the wretched British fog that was dividing them?

He went to his bed musing upon these thoughts and, after the maid had woken him, he washed and dressed, had breakfast and a shot of whisky (like Churchill) and asked his driver to take him to Claridge's Hotel, lately the residence of the Yugoslav Government in exile. The minister liked to wear tails to meetings, even though he didn't have the height to carry them off and they made him look like a dumpling. Dumplings were unfashionable in these days of German aggression. Winnie the Pooh, perhaps, was a more patriotic analogy. As he stepped from the car, the tails dragged on the wet pavement. He brushed a wet leaf or two from the wool gabardine, sashayed between an arch and a pillar, and knocked.

He could only describe the receptionist who opened the door as Himalayan.

'Good morning, Miss Dragomirović,' he began and was delighted to have her beam down at him in congratulation from her halo of mountain mists.

'Minster, have you been practising? That was perfect.'

'Smith, Jones, Black, Brown, Dragomirović!' sang the Minister of Foreign Affairs. 'I wonder, my dear, whether it might be convenient to have a word with the ambassador? Just a quick one.'

'Well, he has had quite a lot to occupy him this morning, Minister.' The receptionist shook her curls out. 'But I can just knock on his door for you. If you would like to take a seat?'

The minister obeyed, but had scarcely combed his recalcitrant tails back into place when the door leading to the ambassador's suite of rooms thundered open and that gentleman himself burst from his office in a distracted storm. The minister rose and intercepted him, and the ambassador stared at him as if they had never met.

'Have you heard from your daughter?' began the minister.

'No!' shot the ambassador. He stopped. He had just remembered who the minister was. 'Pardon, Minister, for my rudeness.'

'Not at all, not at all! You haven't yet had a reply from Miroslav Novak?'

'This morning I had a telegram. Tomorrow he is travelling from Zagreb to Belgrade.'

The minister hesitated.

'Indeed, indeed. I hope he soon returns with good news of your daughter's welfare. Would he...I wonder could he...he is he able to perform a small request for me? You see, I have a villa in Tuscany run by a dear friend, whose welfare I am quite anxious about. I am in a position to recompense Mr Novak for his trouble... but I really would like to know the condition of my villa. Since the war, of course, travel to the continent has restricted my access. If, once he has returned from Belgrade, he could possibly do a day trip to Tuscany and send me some news, I would be so grateful.'

The minister stared at the minister then turned to the receptionist.

'Marija, telegram to Zagreb, please. Take Minister's name and address.'

The minister thanked him heartily and neglected to correct his grammar.

The following morning he was woken by the maid with his tea, his whiskey and a telephone call from the Consulate of Yugoslavia.

'Good morning, minister. Marija Dragomirović speaking. Ambassador wishes you to know that villa is fine.'

CHAPTER FIVE

The minute he had sent the telegram, Miroslav Novak knew he had made a mistake, but by then it was too late. He had blurted out the required information, irritated that the knock on his door from the telegraph office had interrupted a lofty train of thought; by the time he remembered the money, the delivery boy was off down the street on his bicycle and Miroslav had missed his opportunity.

Naturally, he knew the villa *La Casina*—a convenient mule ride from Florence, superb views over the Arno. Everybody knew *La Casina,* but not everybody knew Gianetta, although Miroslav had heard that she was bunking in with an elderly Italian general right now and appeared more than comfortable. Imagine that old Brit expecting his villa and his mistress to wait for him in these stimulating times! *La Casina* was not the first piece of foreign-owned property to be requisitioned by Mussolini for the Ustasha. Condemned by Europe following the assassination of the King of Yugoslavia in 1934, this Croatian fascist terrorist group had been imprisoned with regret by Mussolini, who only realized how handy they could be once the Nazis put them in charge of Croatia in 1941 and he could coerce them into handing over the entire Dalmatian coast of Yugoslavia to Italy.

Through Forests and Mountains

Miroslav was an Ustasha supporter and a very beautiful young man. Curious passers-by, not always Italian, often commented upon him. Since he had been a student in Zagreb and observed that its trade unionists didn't rate beauty very highly, he had moved to the far right, and liked to tell his admirers that his politics favoured the cause of the Croatian ultra-nationalism that the Ustasha represented. There was some truth in this but also some flattery for, with the Ustasha's ascendency, Miroslav's time for glory had arrived. It was a shame about Mara and the difference in politics that had separated them. His ego had never quite got over their split, and it was easy enough for him to interpret the request from her father to inquire after her safety in a light very positive to himself.

Telling himself it was a waste of effort to worry about his error (but not about the money), he packed a travelling bag and made his way to the Zagreb Main Station, where he boarded a train for the twelve-hour trip to Belgrade. This was not the first time he had been there since the German bombing; the party was sending him again anyway.

It was already the beginning of June. Miroslav was an investigative journalist with a string of high profile exposures to his name. Following the invasion of Yugoslavia, when the Ustashas had been ordered to co-operate fully with the new German authorities, he had gone the extra mile, not because he was their keenest recruit but because the excitement of the invasion had died down and he was bored. He had accepted instructions from the High Command to protect German supply and communication lines throughout Yugoslavia by investigating the anticipated activities of resistance groups in the capitol. The Germans added that they did not expect any.

Since their invasion two months earlier and the Greek offensive following it, they had fully exploited the country.

They helped themselves to Yugoslav timber and copper, chrome and bauxite from the mines in Bosnia, Serbia and Macedonia. Barges shunted up the Danube from Romania through Belgrade to Germany loaded with oil and wheat. Nearly fifty trains a day chugged leisurely through the east of the country and across the ravines of Greece to Athens, to supply German armies in North Africa. In the process, they ravaged Greece, delivering all Greek crops, cash, shares and timber directly back to Germany and leaving the inhabitants to starve.

'Oh, shop till you drop,' mused Miroslav, laying his long legs on the seat in front of him and pulling out a newspaper. 'What a busy little lot the Nazis are.'

He sighed with pleasure at the thought of a lovely long train trip. He had deliberately picked a carriage in the sun and, as the locomotive moved out from the platform and picked up speed, shadows from the station's girders dappled its seats faster and faster, scurrying across the leather one after the other, until finally the train had left the station behind and was chugging sedately through the suburbs and on into the open countryside. Having risen only twice the entire trip (once to go to the bathroom and once to shut the window to keep the smoke out) he dawdled through rural scenes untouched by war: pigs and pastures, sleepy villages, fields full of grain, peaceful acres of livestock. Over the mountains he travelled, through the murmuring forests and back down onto the plain to the shattered city of Belgrade, its rubble-torn buildings, broken water mains and mass burials. Never mind. The Germans would find somewhere comfortable for him to stay. They always did.

He smiled when he thought of Mara. Find her? He'd like nothing better, although he hadn't passed that titbit on to her distracted father. They had loved each other once, and part of him insisted she see reason and come back to him.

Through Forests and Mountains

Miroslav was an efficient mixture of stealth, logic and force. He could control himself with regard to Mara if he had to. He'd been very angry when she'd left the relationship, of course he had, but the bombing of Belgrade shortly afterwards had salved his wounded pride, due to the assumption that, with so many thousands killed, the odds were that she was amongst them. Served her right. But what was that tiny spark on the outskirts of his reason that suggested she was still alive, fanned into a flame by that telegram? Had it not been for that, he could have let her go. Now he just grew angry once more.

How like a typical woman she had behaved! He never apologised, she complained. He lacked empathy. Why was he always criticizing her these days? Where was the Miroslav she had fallen in love with? Well, he could have countered those accusations by pointing out that, since meeting her, he had become more the man he wanted to be, not less, so why was she complaining? And then, just when his needs became paramount, she had allowed her emotions to rule her head and had left him. For that he despised her. Once he had her back, he would convince her that her intuition, or whatever rubbish she called it, was not in her best interests.

By the time he arrived in Belgrade he felt stiff and not as relaxed as he might have been had his thoughts not been on the way Mara had treated him. Where once he would have emerged into the old barn of a station set up by the Serbian kings and out into the crisp evening air where taxis, horses and carriages awaited, now he was forced to alight into a temporary structure the Germans had built following the bombing. *Stupid Germans, to bomb the very thing you needed.* He loped off to the High Command, who assigned him a room in the Hotel Moskva not far away, an elegant hive of latter-day intellectuals that, at present, also housed the Gestapo. Here he ate, washed and fell pleasantly, if superiorly, asleep. He dreamed he was a king and he woke up bathed in the scent of finer things that lingered through shaving and breakfast. Even the coffee grounds in the bottom of his cup seemed lined with velvet.

But first things first. He decided that the Germans could wait, and began his trek by admiring, but ignoring, the swastikas fluttering in the morning breeze along the public thoroughfares, relics of the German Victory Parade following the fall of the city. More than two months after the *blitzkrieg,* mountainous piles of rubble still spewed out across footpaths and into the streets. Walls tottered as gravity bore down upon them. Shattered neo-classical architecture, seared by incendiary bombs, seemed already two thousand years old. Every German he met looked confident and cheerful, every Serb guarded. They watched him, a stranger, and asked themselves who he was and what, by his attentive eyes, he might want, but Miroslav felt far above victory parades and refugees displaying extravagant emotions. He had a few jobs to do, and he ticked off number one: to take the half hour walk to the apartment building Mara had shared with her aunt. It didn't look like he'd be able to catch a tram.

The structure that had once risen to four storeys had been reduced to about one and a precarious half. He almost walked straight past it until he remembered that the tram tracks had run along the street outside. Eventually he located it by re-imagining the structure as it had been originally. Yes, some of it remained, but the lowest floor had lost all its windows. Gaping wide from the wooden frames, they lay open and exposed, and the spring rains had transformed the blasted furniture, carpet and sawdust into a casserole where dinted reds and dirty moss greens emerged like vegetables from a stew. It smelt of rats and sewers, and the only life was the result of seeds that had blown in and sprouted, so that grass and dandelions now grew in what had once been a living room. Some enterprising refugee had even planted a row of potatoes in a sunny corner, but the back of the building had completely caved in and was now only a mound of broken floorboards and plaster.

Miroslav wandered around this shell until he found a small bunker, haphazardly erected between the back lane and the entrance to the cellar. Two sticks supported a line of washing hung out to dry—underwear, shirts, nappies and clothes for small children—but it gave him no indication as to whether Mara was there or not. In fact, upon poking his head in, he disturbed a young mother attempting to force some herb stew, so mangy that it looked like she had gathered it from the gutter, down the throats of two toddlers. The children were both crying with hunger and dismay at the sickly green mess and, moved to an unfamiliar pity, Miroslav had murmured an apology and hastily extracted a bar of chocolate and a packet of biscuits from his bag and given them to her. He guessed that he must have a weakness for children, as well as for rural scenes from railway trains.

For the remainder of that day he sat at the tram stop across the street until finally, after four hours, he was rewarded for his persistence by the arrival of the aunt herself, the sister of Mara's father. Plastering a look of concern across his face, he jumped up and accosted her with an anxiety that belied the patience he had so recently exercised. *Was Mara all right? Was she still there?*

The aunt regarded this young man, whom her niece had wept so many tears over, with a guarded eye. *Yes, Mara had survived the aerial attack but no, she was not here now.* As far as the aunt knew, she was still in the city that afternoon. There had been talk of....

'Yes?' asked Miroslav eagerly.

Margaret Walker

'Well,' concluded the aunt, stepping into the bunker, 'you're young and nationalistic, Miroslav, what do you think?'

Stuck-up old cow, thought Miroslav, thanking her with a benign smile. *You know what I want to hear.*

That carrot had been enough for him, though. He could have waited for Mara to come home, but the mysterious talk had lured him in, and he decided to stroll back in to the city to think. What had there been talk of? Where could he hear such talk?

For several days he loitered around that cafe the university students frequented, dressed smartly casual as always: a sports jacket and tie, nothing overly conservative because he preferred his dress choices to reflect his self-image rather than the expectation of others. Once, he even went in, ordered coffee and sat down with his newspaper in an attempt to listen in to the conversations and gauge the mood of the city. In the pre-war years the place had been a hotbed of inquiry and intrigue, fomenting discourse against the corruption of the throne and the nationalist politicians. However, it was Miroslav's opinion that the more conservative citizens of Belgrade were happy with the way things were, and that it was only its youth who wanted radical change, hinting that the status quo might not have the interests of Yugoslavia at heart, merely those of Serbia. By their coffee and their talk, they hoped to support change. As far as Miroslav was concerned, Hitler and Mussolini had brought about all the change he needed.

Eventually, tired of waiting, he thoroughly combed the grounds of the Belgrade University, the shell of every library and newspaper office in the city, and then returned to the café, strolling down the other side of the street. This time he was in luck. A small crowd inside were listening intently to a male speaker, some standing, some sitting, and he thought he glimpsed Mara on a chair towards the back. The shop had lost its front glass and someone had boarded up the window so that little light entered the café, and Miroslav could not clearly see to whom they were listening with such intensity that its force was transmitted to him, even across the narrow street. Curious, he risked a closer look. The crowd, all young people, scarcely took their eyes from the speaker.

He remembered the days when Mara had looked at *him* in that fashion and his crotch tightened with something he recognized uncomfortably as jealousy. He got out a pair of binoculars and shuffled up a lamppost, aware that such an action might provoke an angry response in these desperate days, but he felt he had to find out who the speaker was. The shadows blocked his vision and he jumped back onto the pavement. Circumnavigating a large arc so as not to draw too much attention his way, he glued himself to the wall of the restaurant next door and could just make out the accent of the quiet but precise speaker. Croatian, North Croatian, mountains? He never heard a raised voice, yet every ear seemed to hang on his words. Who could he be?

After a further fifteen minutes, the group in the café began to disperse. Miroslav still did not have his answer but, before he was able to observe any longer, Mara herself stepped out onto the street, right in front him.

His hiding place was hopelessly compromised, so he moved to head her off and only succeeded in frightening her.

'Miroslav!' She put a hand to the breast he had once fondled. 'Where on earth?'

'Good afternoon, Mara,' he forced himself to say pleasantly.

She stepped back, in surprise he hoped. 'You did give me a scare. What are you doing here?'

'You wouldn't come to Zagreb to see me, so I came to Belgrade to see you.' That was a reasonable opener and he laughed at his version of events. He knew he was handsome when he laughed and noticed, with a perception entirely his own, with what hope her eyes shone when he did so. 'Are you pleased to see me?'

'Like a rash!' She angled her head. 'Still love yourself as much?'

'Not as much as I love you. Come on, come for a walk.'

'Miroslav,' she sighed, shoving a lock of hair behind one ear, 'it's over.'

'Not for me, it's not,' he said with another beneficent grin. 'How about that walk?'

Mara hesitated, and it was apparent to him that she was distrustful of his desire to please.

'Just a walk and that's all,' she answered. 'A short one. To the fort and back, then I'm going home.'

Miroslav cast a distasteful glance at the rubble-strewn streets.

'To that wreck? Come home with me. No one's bombed Zagreb.'

'I'm not going to Zagreb or anywhere else with you.'

She stepped away from him. It pricked his self-regard and he observed the tatters in her clothes and the marks of the bombing on her shoes. Still, though a ladder trickled down one stocking, he grudgingly admitted that the fashions of the day suited her. In the summer's day, she walked tall in a pert silk blouse and straight skirt. Yes, she was a tall girl, and on her collar-length hair, she sported a quaint little straw hat with a flower pinned to the brim that made her look even taller. No makeup other than a provocative mouth of red lipstick. That alarmed him.

He flapped a cursory finger in her face. 'Been collaborating, have you? Who gave you the lipstick?

'Knock it off!' she threw back. 'You're the same old super-cilious Miroslav, you're just losing control earlier than you used to. I wish you'd go away and leave me alone.'

'To the fort and back, you said.'

Miroslav was very intelligent but not very wise for, in every situation, the urge to control soon overpowered any pretensions to discernment. Even his ghost would have had mass, had he had a soul, and people frequently distanced themselves from his physical presence because they sensed in his smugness and in the entitlement that gilded every word he uttered, the tyrant-like attraction to power of a teenager. Though he was twenty-seven, he did not perceive this child within, and that was what made him dangerous.

He watched as Mara searched around her, and realized at once that she was looking for support from the crowd in the café; but they were disappearing into the shattered streets. He ought to have resisted the desire to put her down.

'I'm hardly capable of gang rape, Mara.'

She sighed.

'You haven't changed.'

But he did not wish to force her at this early stage, so he made a brittle joke of his blunder, with his pride in his pock-et.

'Correction. It's not me; it's the company I keep. Look, Mara, I'm sorry. Will you take a walk with me to the fort?'

He grasped her hand, noticing that his apology had soft-ened its resistance to him, and they stepped out onto the two-lane street, narrowly dodging a German tank that made no move to avoid him. The Germans seemed to be the only ones who had petrol or food these days. On every corner they hovered, well fed with the crops they had stolen, carrying their rifles, making their jokes, driving their tanks. Miroslav ignored them, pushing his way past random pedestrians and onto the main thoroughfare that sloped down to the river Sava.

In a handful of minutes, the fort guarding the confluence of the Sava and the Danube rivers rose to their right, above its terraces of stone and brick. It dated from Roman times, but, in the most recent battles, it had defended the city against the Turks—inevitably the Turks in this part of the world. Beneath the summer sun the grass on the slopes was bare and dry; only oaks spread their branches to shield their eyes from the intense blue heavens. Behind them squatted the King Alexander Bridge, just one of many that the Royal Yugoslav Army had destroyed in an ultimately useless attempt to slow down the German advance into the city. At this moment the Germans themselves were rebuilding it. So many bridges had been built and demolished over the centuries as a logical consequence of Belgrade's defensive position on its two highways: the River Danube flowing north to Budapest, Vienna and Germany, and the River Sava, that went west to Zagreb and Slovenia.

More men than usual were fishing from the broken piers along the Sava. Families had to eat. One or two boats were tied up, and, as they strolled past, Miroslav saw the thick river scrub along the oncoming banks of the Danube.

He got straight to the point.

'You left me too abruptly, Mara. I'd like to see more of you.'

'You frightened me,' she said.

'I need you.'

'What about me?' she blasted back. 'What about what I need? You were so critical. You were becoming verbally abusive by the end and I don't think you even realized it.'

She kept accusing, as he knew she would. She could natter away for hours; and in their early days they had often spent entire afternoons just talking, until it really wasn't about him anymore and, as their relationship developed, it had got to the stage when it needed to be. That was the great irony about his relationships: he couldn't grow without another person, even if he destroyed them. He had been a prince while he had had Mara, and every day his wealth had grown. Since she had left, he felt stunted and was fearful of his future.

Her voice faded from his consciousness. He lit a cigarette, walked to the edge of the river, took a few puffs, walked back.

'Far be it for me to argue with you,' he said. 'I need you and we can talk about that later. In the meantime, tell me who you were listening to in the cafe?'

'I don't know.'

'That's no answer, Mara.'

'It's true. I don't know his name. Nobody does.'

'How do they refer to him then?'

'I believe he has a *nom de guerre*,' she replied and, at his piercing mandate, she hesitated. 'And I don't know that either.'

Miroslav bided his time, counting the seconds by tapping his fingers on his thigh.

Then he said, 'Yes, you do, Mara. You also know that an assumed name implies an illegal past.'

'I don't know anything about his past.'

Miroslav was no taller than Mara, but he could puff himself up like a turkey when it was necessary to claim the innate superiority that he believed was obvious to everyone.

'All right then,' he said, 'I'll tell you. Illegal in this country means communist.'

'Yes, I know!' She swung around and shouted at him, 'Look, Miroslav, if your purpose in finding me was to pump me for information for your nasty little political party, you're barking up the wrong tree!'

'We're more than a political party now,' he retorted. 'We're in government.'

'What? That pack of gaolbirds? And whom do we have to thank for that miracle?'

'Herr Hitler, Signor Mussolini and our very own leader, *Poglavnik*. "Ready for the fatherland!"' He gave a Roman salute—he looked like Hitler when he did it—then grabbed her hand again. 'Now tell me his name!'

'No!'

'You're so stupid.' He flung the hand away. 'Just like a Serb.'

'I'm not stupid. I had a job until *your stupid friends* bombed us.'

'It doesn't take brains to be an interpreter, Mara. You're only good at languages because you can't stop talking. Very soon it won't be safe to be a Serb anymore, and I could have protected you. Poor you. The other day, or rather a month or so ago now, it hardly matters which, the Ustasha began their program of eradicating all Serbs from what was once Bosnia, now Greater Croatia. As a Serb, it would be dangerous to sit in a café these days in Zagreb, like you've just done with your communist friends.'

'But Croatians aren't killers!' protested Mara.

'Mara, Mara...' Miroslav swatted a fly, 'killing is not a suitable word for what we're doing. The Ustasha have a dream of an independent Croatia, and nationalism is seldom bloodless. In any case, Darwin has proved that some races are superior to others, so it's an entirely natural concept. You can observe throughout the animal kingdom that all species produce some offspring unfitted for survival. Therefore, if the two million Serbs currently living in Greater Croatia were divided into thirds, we would only need to exterminate seven hundred thousand. Those who are unfit. That's half the survival rate for infants up until the last century. About one in

three. The other two thirds will flee to Serbia proper or convert from Serbian orthodoxy. What causes war, Mara? You've
never considered it, so I'll tell you. It's quite simple. It's the
survival of a race and, in the case of the Germans, a specific
need for land. The sub-humans who live in lands Germany
needs are not Aryan, they're Slavs. As well, there are forty
thousand Jews in Greater Croatia. We have our work cut out
for us. You don't create a superior country unless it's ethni-
cally pure.'

Mara staggered backwards.

'You're planning to kill other human beings who have
done nothing to you?'

'Not killing, I told you, purifying the fatherland. An honourable thing.'

'And where does that leave you?' she choked. 'You're
Slavic, too.'

'Oh, Croats aren't Slavs, Mara. We are honorary Aryans,
thanks to the Third Reich.'

'You're insane.'

'If I'm insane, then so are Hitler and Mussolini who, between them, control the entire European continent.'

'Not Britain! *Not Britain*. You tried and you couldn't!'

'There's no need to repeat yourself, darling.'

He drew from his cigarette as nonchalantly as if people
were fish on hooks, but the fishermen along their path kept
on fishing, and his smoke was like the train he had come in
on, a pleasant distraction. He blew it away from her, but he
could equally have blown it into her face. All his actions, like
his words, held a dichotomy of purpose.

'Goodbye, Miroslav,' said Mara. 'You've been caught up in
this whole fascist European craziness and I don't want any
part of it. And I'm sorry for what you're doing to Croatia.'

She turned to leave when suddenly he snapped. Letting his cigarette drop to the pavement, he grabbed her by both arms and shook her until her head spun.

'*What's his name!?*'

'I'll never tell you!' she shouted, struggling in his grasp. 'Let me go! You spoil everything!'

His performance had attracted the ire of a group of fishermen. One of them, roughly the same age as Mara's father, reefed his rod and walked casually across to them, a gigantic man, easily two metres in height, as broad as a bull, although not that remarkable for Belgrade. What was unusual in those troubled days was the look of imperturbable infallibility on his face. A study in stoicism. He planted his feet on the footpath as if they had grown out of it and, without a word, waited in front of Miroslav until the flush left the younger man's face and he brought his rapid breathing until control. Gradually, Mara felt Miroslav loosen the grip he had on her arms and move one hand down to hold hers in a mock relationship that did not fool anyone. Eventually he released her completely.

The fisherman broke his silence. Without a change in his demeanour he asked, 'Can I walk you home, miss?'

'Yes,' whispered Mara. She brushed Miroslav's touch from her skin. 'Thank you.'

The fisherman picked up his rod and bait, saluting his friends while Mara cowered in his shadow.

As they left the river, she heard Miroslav's irate tones shouting after her.

'This isn't the last you'll see of me, Mara! Have a look at yourself. You need help. And, as for your communist friend, you can save your breath. I'll find him.'

CHAPTER SIX

'I have to leave, Auntie.' Mara, still white and shaken, sat on the steps leading down to the cellar. Into the warm summer evening the cold air from below wrapped itself around her ankles. 'I can't stay here.'

'Still as possessive as ever?' her aunt replied.

'Worse. They shouldn't let people like Miroslav loose on an unsuspecting public. Now that he's got his puppet state, he sees no reason to curb his instincts and I can't tell if what he's saying is the truth or a lie. He will, without conscience, cherry-pick his information and then subjectively interpret it. Typical journalist.'

'And what do they call this puppet state?'

'Just the Independent State of Croatia. No fancy title, you see. Makes it sound more legitimate. But they've lost Dalmatia to Italy, and the Italians have taken Montenegro as well.'

'I've heard of the Ustasha,' said her aunt. 'But I didn't realize that the party was so popular.'

'I don't know that it is, but the Croatian Nationalists on its side are rejoicing in self-determination under whatever guise, and it's supported by Hitler and Mussolini because they're all fascists. I can't work it out.' Mara paused. 'Do you know what I did today, Auntie? I heard a talk given by the General Secretary of the Communist Party.'

'Oh, Mara!'

'Don't sound so shocked. He didn't talk about communism. He's come up from Zagreb, too. Today he was giving instructions on how to restrict supplies to the occupying army.'

'He gave this to a group of distressed refugees?'

'But that was the odd thing. No one was distressed. Well, they might have been when they walked in. I saw a few, but everybody calmed down. He was so practical. And he made it sound do-able—as if he knew us personally and what we could achieve, and how best to organize things. You know, to fight as partisans against fascists like Miroslav.'

'What's his name?'

'I don't know, but his war name is Tito. Listen, Auntie,' she went on excitedly. 'I really think this is going to work. And I'd like to spend some time with them, if they'll have me. They could use my language skills. I could be an interpreter.'

'Mara, be reasonable,' begged her aunt. 'Consider your safety. Consider your father.'

'What he can't know won't hurt him!' snapped Mara. 'I am not responsible for the restrictions on the mail.'

Her aunt sighed.

'Don't be your usual headstrong self, please. We'll find you somewhere safe from Miroslav.'

From the shell of the apartment block, they heard a baby wail. Half a roof protected the young family from the elements and they had strung tarpaulins across the remaining space as an attempt at privacy.

'And here we are living in the cellar!' exclaimed Mara. 'There is nowhere safe anymore. Germans control the city. German tanks drive down our thoroughfares. Germans tell us what we can do and what we can't.'

'Miroslav might go back to Zagreb, Mara.'

'Not the way he was talking. He was sapping me for information.'

Mara's aunt was not like Mara, nor was she like her father. When she got upset, she reasoned calmly.

'You don't know anything to tell him, do you, Mara?'

Mara looked right and left, then she faced her aunt and dropped her voice to a whisper.

'Look, Miroslav's no soldier. It would have to be organised resistance that he's interested in tracking, and *that* was what they were talking about today.'

'That's exactly what I feared! What on earth will happen first?'

'Well, they want to sabotage the eastern railway between Belgrade and Niš.'

'The lines?'

'For six or seven kilometres; but it's easy to repair broken lines. What they want are the trains themselves. You achieve two things: you weaken the enemy and supply yourself with food, fuel and arms.'

'Women don't sabotage trains or fight in armies, Mara.'

'I said I could be an interpreter!'

'So you did, but for whom? Captured Germans?'

'Maybe not them... oh, I don't know!' Mara threw her hands into the air. 'There must be something I can do. I can type, for instance.'

'It's war, Mara. They will want women to knit socks and jumpers.'

'In the summer? Will it last that long?'

'That's what they said about the last war. It won't last long and then, what did the women do? Knit socks and jumpers. They'd want nurses, but you're too squeamish for that.'

'I want to help!'

Mara was well aware of the crease down the centre of her aunt's forehead. It rose and fell depending on her stress levels. These days the crease looked like the earthquake that had destroyed Dubrovnik. Beneath the pot of herbs, ham bones and potatoes she had been trying to cook, her fire was dying. Mara shoved a piece of broken rafter beneath it and watched the embers stir and bristle. Sparks flew up and the fire regained its vigour, then began to die again. She slid a piece of newspaper beneath the wood and puffed at it abstractedly. Out it burst.

Her aunt watched her.

'Have you found a way to contact your father yet, Mara?'

'No,' Mara replied quickly. 'Listen, can you teach me to knit?'

'Those peasant girls have been knitting since they were five, Mara! *Have you found a way to contact your father?* I'm sorry to repeat myself but you must tell him you're alive, at least. He'll be beside himself.'

Mara deflated.

'I'm sorry. Poor Dad. I should have asked the Secretary today if he knew who had a radio. He would have known, of course. I just didn't think of it at the time.'

'Please, sweetheart, put it high on your list of priorities. I think your mother would have told you that.'

'I feel awful already!' snapped Mara. 'Don't make me feel any worse! I'll find a way to contact Dad, all right. Please leave it with me.'

Such a harsh judgement was not fair. Mara had not done anything towards contacting her father that would justify reacting so defensively towards suggestions that she might. Yet, the aunt had known the nights when her niece cried herself to sleep over her mother. She'd seen her stumble, puffy-eyed, up the stairs the next morning, still defensive, still not doing anything to ease her father's worry. Now that they lived in the cellar, nothing could be hidden.

'Mara, why do you procrastinate like this?'

'I don't! I don't! Please let me do it! What we need to do right now is get Miroslav off my trail. Then I'll do something about Dad. I will. I promise.'

From long experience, the aunt merely emitted an exasperated sigh.

'I hope you marry a man from the army, Mara, who won't put up with your nonsense like I do.'

'I like a man in uniform,' said Mara.

*****

It took a long while for Miroslav to master his anger after Mara rejected him. Though he knew he was justified, nevertheless, the emotion hampered his actions and ruined the clear sightedness that he employed to such good effect in his investigations. She had wounded him. She had gone. Once again he was sinking. That connection between the anger and his depression—now that was the rub.

In order to deal with the problem that threatened so often to overwhelm him, he wrote Mara three and a half pages of abuse on good quality paper with his brand-new fountain pen. By her actions, he informed her in his clear hand and concise style, she had betrayed their friendship. Meticulously he outlined the emotions he had experienced as he watched her walk away under the protection of another man. One, he had been profoundly disturbed. Had he been a woman, he would have wept—a measure of the depths to which she had plunged him. Two, had she noticed that along the shore that day were numerous witnesses to her heartlessness, poor men fishing for the salvation of their families? She hadn't noticed, had she? Because she had only thought of herself. Three, it had taken him a great deal of time and effort to subdue the

Margaret Walker

heartbreak she had caused him, knowing that she had ruined the future he had planned for them. Had she given him time to explain? No, she had not. For all this, she was responsible. *I believed you were my friend, Mara,* he lamented exquisitely. *Yet, despite your cruelty, I would have loved you. Come back to me.*

He posted the letter. It soothed him somewhat. It inspired hope. All would be well. The post box was red and shiny. Despite the ruins of the city, it had authority. He was sure the pages would reach her. His ego assuaged, he could turn his mind to the detection of groups resistant to the German occupation. Already the meeting with Mara had brought him dividends.

Miroslav was a methodical investigator. He was well aware that looking for the *nom de guerre* of a communist in the conservative Belgrade suburbs was a waste of time. Therefore, he returned to that great haven of revolutionary spirit, the university, and strolled around, listening in on every conversation, lecture and tutorial he could without drawing attention to himself, for a further three days. What had the Germans said? 'These people would rather have Bolshevism than us.' If it could be said that the Germans struggled with concepts, then they struggled with this one. Well, the corruption of the Leninists in Moscow was no secret, so the question was, what attraction could communism have for the young people of Belgrade? In promoting the equality of the sexes and universal suffrage, it may have driven further nails into the coffins of the hated Empires of Austria-Hungary and the Russian Czars, but it was also clear that, in the fight against fascism, the students felt that they were moving towards a future cleansed of the political crises, assassinations and regional power struggles that had characterised the Kingdom of Yugoslavia.

Through Forests and Mountains

So much for the theory. On his third afternoon, Miroslav was rewarded. Beneath the commonly seen poster: 'Death to fascism! Freedom to the people!' he listened in to a band of communist irregulars and discovered that the leader of the communists was called Tito.

*****

June wore away and, at the beginning of July, to Mara's great relief, her aunt found them a room in the house of a distant cousin on the outskirts of the city. It offered a measure, if not of safety, them at least a respite from the fear of knowing that Miroslav might turn up at the remains of their home any time he felt like it.

CHAPTER SEVEN

Anton never regained the weight he'd lost during those desperate weeks in the mountains above Kotor and, in the months that came later, sleeping in the open, under trees, in barns and burned out villages, he looked as gawky as an adolescent, all arms and legs, with his adult years yet to commence. Everyone was thin then, on a diet of herbs and bark, but no one was quite as thin as he was, who had had a head start in the weight loss stakes. He had noticed, in addition, white hairs at his temples that hadn't been there before, and it was not those that distressed him but the knowledge that he was vain enough to notice them. The injured shoulder had its good days and bad days. Sometimes it worked and other times it just managed to creak its way to the end of a march, giving him so much pain at night that he couldn't sleep. Since April, when he had discovered himself lying on a bed of straw between a cow and a donkey with an old woman glaring down at him, he had come to accept that he and his injured shoulder were doomed to a long and unhappy association.

The woman was dressed completely in black, including a black headscarf. Over the course of that first day, as he lay sick and confused, she had stalked into the sloping stone barn half a dozen times and scanned him purposefully from top to toe, perhaps with the intention of eating him, for her reconnaissance was accompanied by observations of a cannibalistic nature.

'This one's not done yet.' She paused, chewed a finger and steeled her brows of old leather. 'But he's a bad colour.'

Anton had been wandering around the edges of consciousness for most of six long-sighted leers but, upon her seventh, he managed to hail her.

'Where am I?'

The woman scowled crossly. 'Shut up and stay still!' she ordered, doubling over him like a folded page so that he saw the random teeth clinging to her gums and felt the squall that had driven them hard over. She was fervent in all she did, even to controlling the elements.

'You don't care about your survival, man!' she hissed accusingly. 'And you should, for death always comes in threes. First himself, then you. Who will be the third?' She seized Anton's right hand and cast upon it a salutary inspection from his fingertips to the lifeline on his palm, which she forlornly construed to be growing shorter by the minute. 'Cold,' she muttered, thrusting it down. 'Wicked, wicked man.'

She was working herself into a fury based upon her conjecture that it was his intention to depart, and she tried to determine whether he had indeed given up the fight. Had the eyes of his heart opened already? Were his sighs too deep for words for was it, indeed, the Holy Spirit that pleaded for him? There would be little hope after that.

Above the cow, icons of dubious holiness rollicked and swayed, so blackened by methane that no aid could be expected of them, except as charms for milking. The widow clicked her tongue at their dispassionate gaze.

'Can he live?' she enquired petulantly and one saint alone nodded back, the bashful one who had argued with God.

66

Margaret Walker

Would you destroy the righteous with the wicked? For the sake of ten, I will not. 'Is it likely?'

The saint gave her his affirmation and began to pray with a mighty rush of wind that shook the barn and worried the cow but relieved the woman, for she took from an earthenware jar two poultices of garlic wrapped in old linen and proceeded to bind them to the soles of Anton's feet and knot the ends. Burning and boiling, as hot as a cauldron, their acrid smell smote the donkey, who wiggled backwards as if hit. Then the woman knelt down and began to plaster large leaves in a cloying green humidity upon Anton's shoulder and halfway up his neck. No shirt, no jacket, no bandages, no boots, no socks, and he was too ill to care what she had done with them.

The priest found him at the church, all dead meat and nobody owning him.

'Where is your mother?'

Anton blinked at her demand.

'Dead,' he said.

The woman smacked on the last leaf and crossed herself ferociously from forehead to belly. 'Eternal rest grant unto her,' she snarled. 'And your father?'

'Dead,' he repeated. 'Last war.'

Her face plummeted at these dismal revelations, for immediately she construed his chances of survival to be equally remote. 'God have mercy!' she spat, twisting her head to and fro. 'After all my hard work!'

Hair flew from her headscarf. In her fury, she breathed heavily and her breasts, in the sack that she wore, slid up from her belt and cast themselves upon it again and again, like surf against a dyke. Yet, in the midst of the tempest she halted, apparently struck by an idea, for a sly blush tarnished the wrinkles on her face. 'I'll get that priest back!' she barked, as Anton lapsed once more into unconsciousness. 'To cover myself. And it won't hurt you either.'

So saying, she slapped the cow and stormed out. The cow raised affectionate brown eyes from her mouthful of hay and went on eating. Shortly, her mistress re-entered the low structure bearing a drink that smelled worse than the shed Anton was lying in. Gathering his head with one arm, she buffeted it against her breasts until he woke, and then proceeded to force the concoction down his throat, until he choked and coughed and the tears ran down his face. Then she mopped him up and began again, until the cup was empty. Anton squinted at her through watery eyes while she stood observing him, one hand on a scrawny hip. In her free hand she held the empty cup and, for that single suspenseful moment, she controlled her mounting fury. Then suddenly, she hurled the cup into the straw and, from where it landed, a cloud of flies rose into the air. Mortified, she swiped away at their flight path until their indignant buzz perforated the air and they deliberately flew backwards. That made her even angrier.

'Don't you dare die!' she snarled over Anton's head.

'I'll be fine,' murmured Anton and fell asleep.

The woman withdrew, with renewed curses about mortal men and other defiant things.

Late that afternoon the orthodox priest arrived, bringing with him scents of frankincense and myrrh. His towering black presence filled the outhouse with authority and Anton experienced a fleeting sense of Christmas, like the family in the manger. The cow and the donkey were sent out to pasture and the priest set himself up with his small communion set. Lying motionless upon his straw pallet, listening to the man drone his solemn words, Anton fled from consciousness one moment and returned to it the next. His arm seemed to have stopped hurting and, at first, the absence of pain worried him, with its implications that perhaps he had already crossed a threshold. Yet, he felt no inclination to reassure himself what side he might be on, nor even to demand life. As the priest continued to intone the prayers, he ceased to worry at all. He was not unhappy. He felt no inclination to resist. It occurred to him to wonder whether he was truly dying, but not even that worried him, and he let himself be carried along on the ebb and flow of the ancient words, feeling the imprint of the man's fingers drawing the cross in oil on his forehead. After that, he drifted away, and when he woke up the sun had set, the cow and the donkey had regained their accustomed places on either side of him, and the priest had gone.

Like a feverish spider, the old woman hurried back into the encroaching shadows, her preoccupation with saving Anton's life whipping her once more into a tempest. Casting backward glances at the night, she again forced the vile herbal brew down his throat. Anton was sorry that she did it, for he did not share her fear of what the darkness held, and the bitter tisane made him want to vomit. It poisoned the solace that the priest had brought and his dream of a quiet dissolution.

Let me die in peace, you stupid old woman.

But, by the time she had returned a third time, the dizziness had increased, his abdomen had begun to throb with pain that radiated into his legs and his throat, and he couldn't find the words to tell her that, finally, he understood. He rolled to one side to escape the increasing agony in his hips, then to the other, arching his back to pull away as it encroached upon him until, to the right and the left, he remained one ball of pain and escape proved futile. After that, the thing became unstoppable. Surely that priest was just outside the door and Anton could call to him to return and take him away from himself, out of the fug and the animals and the torture, to some place where he could breathe. But the priest was not outside the door. He was nowhere. He wasn't coming to rescue him after all.

Such a sense of desolation overcame him. He was suddenly as upset as a child that the man should have left and not stayed to hold his hand, to tell him that all would be well. But the old woman was there. She had taken her station by his side and he reached up, thinking that his dead mother had come to comfort her child. She caressed his hand and he clutched it so tightly that her fingers cracked, and she laid his hand down again upon the blanket that was covering his body. The cow shuffled, the donkey snored, and he writhed between them. Though their warmth filtered through the straw and around him, he felt cold and clammy, with a heart that was leaping to escape his chest.

It's going to burst, he thought, *and this time I will certainly die, and I could give some thought to death if only I could escape the pain.*

Beyond the shed, obscured by trees, a trail led into the valley. Through the angle of the door, the night around it was lighter, and Anton saw that the *vily* had come out from the woods to dance in the silvery moonlight. The nymphs had become obscene since last he'd seen them, their buttocks swollen, their breasts grown monstrous. Like erotic infants, they beguiled him to suck. *Rather you than a serpent,* they crooned, but he turned his head away and said, *I don't know who you are.* To escape them, he closed his eyes and, in a second, he had a nightmare of his old girlfriends, all yellow skin and discolouration, begging him to pray for them. *I can't*, he said, *I'm sick.* Beside him, the old woman was praying, and he wanted to ask her which of his girlfriends she could possibly have known, to make her beseech the Lord with such fervour. But the words wouldn't come out. He tried and it was no use.

The dead were roaming the earth that night. They had laid aside their consecrated stones. He mustn't let them in, so he called to the cow, but the cow was eating hay. He begged the donkey, but the donkey was asleep. He looked around and by his side was a black dog with one side of its face all bloody. And still the woman prayed, until finally, at the quietest hour of that night, the point of least resistance, he heard those dead calling his name, arranged outside the door of the milking shed from the greatest to the least, and knew that they had come for him.

But later, so much later that he couldn't count the days, there came a time when the world decided to keep him and, in the hush of a spring morning, he knew a sense of continuance. Down the side of the hill through the morning mists, he heard the donkey braying. He was embraced by the soft air of the mountains. He slept.

The old woman came and milked the cow and the sheep over the head of his straw bed, where he had tussled with death and won. With the methodical rhythms of the elderly, she lifted the heavy bucket with one uncertain hand, then the other, and disappeared with it, only to return and stand looking at him. A wisp of hair escaped her scarf and floated on the dawn breeze. He waited for her to speak, but she remained silent and he was grateful, because it didn't disturb the utter hush of his new life.

Then she said, 'Drink.'

'I don't like it,' he replied in a voice much softer than he remembered.

She shook her head.

'Water.'

'Yes, water,' he said.

After water it was vegetable broth, and then kefir. In the weeks following, he worked up to bread and cheese and herbs, which was all she had; later some ham appeared, a gift from a neighbour who had heard about him. After about two months, he was well enough to help her lightly around the farmyard but, before that, it was days of lying on his pallet, looking out the door at the ever-changing sky, then sitting propped up on the wall, watching the mountains as if he had never seen them before. No duties, no books, no company but the old widow. When he asked about her husband and why she wore black with such stern resolve, she enquired, did he not remembered her? Finally, he recognised her as the wife of his fellow patient, who had departed to his afterlife following the removal of his gangrenous toes. That memory was a long, long time ago.

The widow kept a couple of sheep as well as the cow and the donkey and, seeing that he looked bored but was not yet well enough to walk any distance or lift a load, she taught him to spin their wool. So, as the summer spread its verdure around him and the mountain sky turned an intense blue far above, he would sit in the yard with a spindle in his left hand, teasing the fibres out with his right and spinning the thread, with his arm in a sling.

He wasn't too bad at spinning, he considered. The widow ticked him off a couple of times when the thread became too thick, but he was a quick learner and flattered himself that his was the equal of any she had threaded on the loom that took up nearly half of one of the only two rooms in her cottage. During one week when it rained without ceasing, he had sat by the open door, watching the drips pour from the lintel, and spun enough fine thread to finish the cloak she was weaving of undyed wool for a woman in the parish even older and more ferocious than she was.

The widow had constructed a garden bed upon her rocky acre by removing the limestone rocks strewn heavily upon the ground, and adding soil that had taken her many hours to cart from further down the mountain, fertilized with cow dung. In this artificial garden she grew potatoes and maize; occasionally he saw the elongated green stems of onions and garlic. She had a single pomegranate tree, herbs she gathered from the hills, milk from the cow, but she also milked the sheep and, from the two, made a traditional cheese that she sold in the markets at Kotor.

As Anton slowly recovered, she taught him other things, and he began to think that, in another century, he might have been a farmer and had a farmer's wife. There wasn't a great deal to cook, and it wasn't as if he was expending any energy, but he learned the different ways she had of preserving the milk she kept, of gathering vegetables from her garden, and how to distinguish between the herbs and grasses that grew wild on the mountains.

Though time had stood still in his world, there came a day when summer was already well advanced, when the troubles of his fellow countrymen once again began to play an active part in his imagination. He thought a few things. One, what had become of Kolarov and the *Nebojša?* It was as if they had ceased to exist and this feeling troubled him because he was neither psychic nor superstitious, although he was a sailor, and he wanted to believe that all were alive and his submarine was resplendent somewhere upon the surface of the ocean or below it. Two, if Belgrade had been bombed and they were at war, why had he not seen any German soldiers? Why had they not come burning and plundering, as he heard they had in Poland? There were several possible answers to that question. He realized, after thinking hard about it, and with a brain that was still not up in the saddle, that Filip Kolarov had said specifically that Anton was to hand the submarine over to the Italians. Yes, now he remembered. So where was this occupying force? One morning he asked the widow which day it was (he had forgotten) and had she seen any Italians? As the crow flew, they weren't that far from Kotor. *Yes*, she replied. She had seen strangers in uniforms. *No violence?* he asked.

She shook her head.

Then he recalled that the Italian Queen, Jelena, had been a Montenegrin Princess and he wondered about the politics connected with that. He determined that, when he had spun the rest of the basket he was currently working on, he would visit the priest and enquire, priests being renowned, as everybody knew, as repositories of gossip and intrigue.

'Could you milk the cow for me before you go?' called the widow.

So, he milked the cow and afterwards visited the priest on unsteady legs in that light summer morning. He had a memory of once being assisted down the hill he now walked up, towards the ancient church of Saint John at Špiljari and when, a little breathlessly, he reached the top, he thought he could even remember the wall itself, eclipsed in his memory by the night and the infection that was calling him away.

The priest had finished morning mass and the peasant woman who had assisted him stepped aside as she left, to allow Anton onto the porch. Centuries of incense and windows like puzzle pieces had waylaid even the exit of the Holy Spirit, and now the holiness of the old building intruded in him, along with the chill from its stone walls. He pulled his jacket around his shoulders and wandered up the nave, where he spied the priest, like a wily old ox, bustling around to one side of the transept.

In common with most sailors, Anton respected the sea and, from his first childhood memories, recognized a similar circumspection connected with priests. Now, caught between the ancient whispers in the church and the mountain silence beyond, he experienced a very odd hunch, bordering on a certainty, that this priest possessed two sources of information for everything from farming to families, from politics to

74

partisans. There was the obvious one, but a second ran parallel to it and had a foot in both worlds. But Anton was not at sea now, and he tried to explain away this intuition as venerable priests in the still mountain air developing an uncanny ability to discern thoughts.

He approached cautiously.

'Good morning, Father.'

The priest lifted his head and stroked the beard that fell to his chest. 'Ah, yes. You are... forgive me... Anton Marković. I remember now. And you're here to ask about....'

'My boat?'

'Yes, yes,' repeated the priest. 'Safely out. Safely out.'

'To Egypt?'

'That was it, was it? Egypt.'

A sparrow wedged its way into the narrow window and sat perched on the grill, laughing at the saint's icon. Anton had never considered Saint John to be the humorous sort, yet here he was on his wall, all robes and haloes, winking a knowing glance back.

'Did they make it?' he asked the priest.

'All the way to the pyramids? Well, well, well! I can't tell you that, young man. But Egypt, yes, yes, Egypt, was it? I've heard nothing to the contrary.' He stowed his heavy Bible away on a shelf and without turning, he said, 'The widow did a good job on you, I see. You seem much more amenable.'

Anton was taken aback. *More amenable to whom?* he thought. The priest, the widow, the celestial crowd of witnesses, of whom St John and the sparrow were the first, who had measured the faults in his attitudes, criticisms, soliloquies, and considerations against their virtues and were happy to declare that he'd finally tipped the balance? Oh, why did priests always speak as if life was a series of graded apprenticeships? He was at a disadvantage and the priest had the upper hand. It was his church, Anton had come for his knowledge, and having Anton submissive before him, he now had decided to congratulate him on the improvement in his personality. The options for reply seemed limited.

'I'm still alive,' Anton protested.

'But not quite ready. I heard you, every step of the way up the hill. When you can creep up that slope without a sound and melt into the forest, I will tell you that over near Cetinje there is a man to whom you will want to speak. Not yet, as I said. When you've recovered.'

'Do you have a name for me?'

'Nikola Mugoša,' replied the priest. 'We haven't risen up against the occupiers yet. But we will.'

'We?' A ticklish wind whispered across the old stones of the chancery. The priest rubbed his back and Anton rubbed his shoulder. 'Aren't you too old to be fighting?'

'You don't know your scriptures, son,' returned the priest smartly. 'Wasn't Moses eighty when he the led the Israelites across the Red Sea?'

'I don't know. Was he?'

'"Arise! Let us go back to our people and to the land of our birth, because of the sword of the oppressor."'

'Moses said that?'

'Jeremiah.'

Anton didn't argue, and the lack of self-determination depressed him momentarily until he realized that he didn't care to argue. Perhaps he would just wait, as the priest had suggested.

As he retreated towards the porch the old man called, 'You'll find those sailors that you were looking for with him.'

Anton stopped.

He had forgotten about his crew? It was not like him to forget, but it seemed that he had. The priest realized this by employing his powers of mind reading, but this was ridiculous, surely. To add insult to injury, he probably knew that a man like Anton would neither declare a metaphysical contest unfair nor accuse an old priest of unkindness, when it was consideration that had motivated the update.

Or was it? Would Anton allow him this small victory? Old as the man was, Anton could not imagine him decrepit. He looked as everlasting as if he could build houses until the day of his death, and then accept the inevitable (of which he had had prior warning, of course) and suddenly depart. *Who would have thought that the old fellow would survive as long as he had? Oh, he'd known about his death for some time but he had a bargain with God to wait until the timber was seasoned.*

Anton swivelled around.

'Which sailors?' he demanded.

'That poor boy whom you worried sick, for a start.'

'Viktor?'

The priest brushed a spider from his cassock. 'He's just about to become a father. I married him a fortnight since.'

At Anton's look of dismay, the priest added, 'Gentleness is the secret to success, as my wife, I'm certain, will tell you.'

Anton faltered. 'I think he may have mentioned something concerning marriage,' he said.

'If you'd not had your mind on other things, you might have picked up his undertones.'

'Is that a rebuke?'

'An observation.'

'And what if I'd returned to the hospital that day, as he wanted me to?' Anton demanded. 'What then?'

'With septic shock? Oh, you'd be dead by now, undoubtedly. That ward sister didn't have the same determination to keep you alive as the widow.' The priest adjusted his cassock, and it seemed to Anton that, in so doing, he was creating the pause that he required for consideration, for, immediately after, he lifted a finger and struck it into the thin air. 'It was revenge! I'm certain of it! She's never forgiven herself for allowing her husband to go to hospital and she blamed the place for killing him. She was out to prove them wrong about you, her and her herbs, although personally, I think she achieved the miracle by force of will. Had you died in hospital, it would have been your will against theirs. You were outnumbered and you would have lost. Don't think they would have blamed themselves. But in the milking shed, the widow won. Right spheres have been restored and I notice that much of her bitterness at her husband's death has dispersed.'

Even in the short time Anton had spent within the church, the morning had lost its first freshness. As he stepped outside, a chorus of cicadas burst into the air with that abruptness that made him recall that it was summer and that he was alive. Living, he had defeated death with all its wormwood and gall, although he deserved to be dead. Perhaps. It just depended on whom you spoke to.

From the stones of the church, he had allowed eternity to sink into him and, when he left, he understood that timelessness awaited him in the world, too. And yet time had passed. Three months. Soon it would be four—out of his whole life—and what had he done with them? Nothing. Yet, he had no regrets. He was not resentful, nor did he, in any degree, embrace change, even as he discovered himself morphing into a model of rectitude. And that was only the priest's opinion. Therefore, he resumed his steps and did not demand more information. Today, he decided, he would exist for the moment alone. A lizard sunned itself on the wall by the church, the sparrow, tiring of its holy watch, flew off to a little house with a red roof and green shutters. Anton returned to the farm, completed the chores awaiting him, ate silently with the widow, swept his straw bed free of bugs, replaced the two homespun blankets, and sunk into unconsciousness upon it, as tired as a young boy after a busy day. Long before, the sun had sunk behind the cliffs, swathing them in night, a close relation of the death he knew he had avoided. A sweetness intruded into his dreams and he recognised it as gratitude. The knowledge that he was grateful disturbed him and, in the dead of that night, he awoke to a troubled conscience. Finding no one to consult, he enquired of the cow, but the cow was dreaming of spring pastures and did not answer.

*****

The time came to leave, as he knew it would, at the end of July, when he sensed that his recovery was complete. He was ready for a world that had changed from the one he had known; where the mountains he had come to love would be his protection against an enemy as yet unknown.

In the same manner as she sensed the change of the seasons, the widow was prepared, even before he came to tell her.

He'd learned over the months that she didn't rank sentimentality very highly, so he simply asked, 'What can I do to thank you?'

'Liberate our people,' she replied.

He nodded.

'I'm sorry about your husband.'

'That hospital killed him,' she said savagely. Then she gave him a package containing clothes once belonging to her husband, a blanket and his knife in its metal sheaf. 'In this way, he will be part of the fight.'

CHAPTER EIGHT

July that year was shorter than other Julys. Before her father had taken the family to England, when Mara's mother was still alive, the long summer holidays had lasted an eternity, in the way they always seem to, for children. Rambling weeks of reading and walking in the countryside, swimming, freethought with her legs up her bedroom wall, afternoons blossoming with friends and daydreams. Ever the Anglophile, her father, made sure that there was date cake with lemon icing in the cake tin, tea with scones at four o'clock and, in the evenings, a nice stodgy dinner from cook. Romantic notions of rural life in her own country obscured the reality, and so she was unable to appreciate that, for most men and women, life was a daily grind of subsistence agriculture from the cradle to the grave, with hunger an ever-present storm on their horizon. Now, Mara's anxious July days tumbled over one another towards August. Each day she slid her head carefully beyond her door, scanned to the right and the left and, not spying Miroslav, ventured forth only in the shadow of a protective gentleman who might chance to walk past. A long walk towards Belgrade's main avenue, flitting in and out of safety like a sparrow. She had already startled several men this way and not one of them had the reassuring dimensions of the fisherman who had rescued her on the banks of the Sava.

Despite the bombing, despite the occupation, the Terazije was still the centre of the city's life and here, amidst the rural vendors selling farm produce and live poultry at black market prices, the peasants in their colourful costumes, the students, the elderly gossips, smells of Turkish coffee, plums, apples and poppy seeds, Mara felt a measure of anonymity. She shopped frugally from her aunt's dwindling supply of jewellery, among the altered faces of wartime and their covert financial exchanges. She jumped aside to avoid a German staff car replete with well-fed officers. By closing her eyes and wishing very hard, she tried to make them feel guilty, but their hearts were so hardened that their faces were flushed with success and, beneath their uniforms, their stomachs bulged with appropriated food. Perfidious souls and black paunches, thought Mara, sniffing the wind as they belched by. *That driver has been eating cinnamon, the major bratwurst and sauerkraut, and the general beside him the one little ewe lamb that lay in the poor man's bosom. You are the man! said the prophet Nathan.* Mara ground her teeth until she thought she saw Miroslav leaning against a bus stop, smoking and observing her tantrum with his meticulous attention to detail. *I hate the way you judge me.*

She ran away and hid behind a stall selling potatoes until he had stubbed out his cigarette and left, before following him at a safe distance to the railway station, hoping to see him depart. The horrible temporary German structure stood beside the ruins of the old station and Mara experienced a pang of nostalgia for that beautiful day when she had arrived home from Athens in a trainload of potential boyfriends. Only at the last minute, as the smoker stepped onto a train, did she realize her error. The man she'd seen was older and thinner, not the man she knew who was devoted to self-love and violence.

The young people and university students who had met in the café that auspicious day when Miroslav bounded back into her life, unlike him, held no notions of the self-aggrandisement of war. They had a job to do. On 4 July 1941, the communist party, whose audience they had been, called for a popular uprising against the occupiers and, as July turned into August, Mara heard talk of a proposed antifascist front of women, a new organization to support the fighters.

Was Mara interested? Yes, very.

'Women,' she enquired incredulously, 'involved in the war instead of just waiting at home for bad news?'

'Which is what women generally do in wars,' added the girl who had told her, 'or knit socks for the troops.'

'I can't knit.' Mara chewed her lip thoughtfully.

'And you're not a communist either. I've been involved with the party for ages.'

'Really? What prompted that?'

'I went to university in Belgrade, Mara, not London. Young people here are tired of the old empires and monarchies. What good have they ever done the proletariat, or women for that matter?'

'Is that why the Nazis hate communism?' asked Mara.

'Communism contradicts their plans for expansion and the exploitation of Europe. The two things are mutually exclusive—Marxist theory.'

'But I thought that Marx and Engels were bourgeoisie, who invented the idea of communism safe and snug in middle class England.'

'They also conjectured it for the Western Europe they knew, which consisted of bloodsucking aristocrats.' Her friend gathered her argument together and then launched it unashamedly and with some vigour. 'Working people don't want what you want, Mara. That's the first thing you need to understand. You just think that, if everyone was like you, they'd be happy.'

'Yes, and why not?'

'Well, you aren't epic, are you?' The young woman attested this enigma confidently, as if it should settle the matter and, as is usual with paradoxical arguments, Mara had trouble replying.

'What do you mean by "aren't epic"?' she asked after a pause.

'I mean that you've got education and money but no one will remember you for anything. That's the difference between you and the proletariat. These people belong to the land like a sock in a shoe. Now Germany and Italy roll in and take this land, *by which they define themselves*—I am stressing this for you, Mara—and I'll tell you exactly what they will remember during this war: their fields of grain, their granite mountains, the sunset catching the leaves, the flaming sumac bush, the fireflies at dawn, the clouds plunging into the Adriatic, the spring waterfalls.'

'I remember when I've read a good book.'

'I know.'

'Does that mean I can't join the resistance effort?'

'Dunno,' mused the girl. 'They want communists and peasants, and you're neither. I don't mean to depress you, Mara, but to add insult to injury, the communists have taken organization to a new art form and you'll need to do what you're told.'

'I can do what I'm told,' Mara assured her, nodding her head vigorously. 'And I won't tell my aunt about the communism, I promise. Or the peasants.'

'She already knows that you went to hear Tito speak.'

'I haven't told her anything else, honestly. What she doesn't know won't hurt her.'

'Then don't tell the communists your father's the ambassador in London either.'

However, upon enquiring, Mara learned that a party of women from Belgrade was travelling to Drvar in Bosnia to observe the first women's conference organized by female Bosnian party members. They aimed, from the very start of the conflict against fascist Germany, Italy and the Ustasha, to get the women to support the men in the ways women traditionally did: cooking, and the making and laundering of clothes. Those who could read could be trained to type, others would complete a nursing course for the soldiers at the front.

So Mara turned up, with enthusiasm glistening from every pore, certain that there must be a place with the travellers for her, although slightly daunted by the threat of an institutional organization that was not a tertiary campus. Vera, a woman who could have been in her late forties, considered Mara, noting the lines of determination around her mouth, looked the ambassador's daughter up and down, and wondered if she could cook, knit or sew.

'I can't cook and I can't knit,' interrupted Mara, anticipating her reply. 'Or sew. Except to sew buttons back on my blouse.'

'You look like you can read and write.'

'Yes,' Mara answered warily. 'I studied languages.'

'What do you speak?'

'English, French and German.'

'Maybe when we have a radio transmitter we can use you.'

'But I heard about you from our group at the university and I want to help!'

She's going to say no!

Vera tightened her lips and glanced impatiently across to where other women were sorting sundry items. Her distraction made it clear to Mara that she had a list of things to do pinned to the inside of her skull and was itemizing each one with only half an ear to Mara's polite plea. Her invisible list completed, the woman once more gave Mara her attention and asked briskly, 'Which of the Serbo-Croatian dialects do you know?'

'I'm pretty good at understanding most things.'

'Any Slovenian? There's a party coming.'

'I understand it.'

'Then I suppose you can take minutes for us.'

Mara brightened up.

'Though I'm not a communist,' she pointed out.

'This is greater than politics,' replied Vera. 'We are looking after our fighters.'

'Our army?'

'Our fighters.'

'Not the army?'

'The Royal Yugoslav Army, Mara, surrendered after only eleven days at the beginning of April,' said Vera, only briefly disguising her disgust.

'Yes, yes, I know that. It's just that when you said "fighters", I immediately thought "army".'

'Our task is to rise up against the Germans and the Italians who occupy our land. All over the country, local fighters have begun to do that.'

'Communists?'

'No, not only communists. Local men like the *hajduks,* the outlaws, who took to the woods in the days of the Turks, and the border raiders. You know the old stories, surely. As we speak, men are burning down German warehouses, derailing their trains, capturing trucks with fuel and food, guns and cannons, uniforms and medicines. Not a large army. Just normal people. The call to rise up has come from Tito, and it's time for the village women to get ready to support them. Tito. Do you know who I'm talking about?'

'Yes, I heard him speak, here in Belgrade. He's the secretary of the Communist Party, right?'

'That's right. So we itemise what we think they'll need and organise the women to help.'

'Where?'

'Everywhere.'

'Doing what?'

'A woman from the villages would not have to ask,' Vera added bluntly.

Vera, thought Mara, could certainly cook, knit and sew. You could tell by the way she took control without shyness or apology. All this partisan warfare stuff, apparently, began with the ability to knit socks from the age of three. *I can't knit,* Mara mused miserably. *That's why I'll never be able to organise as well as her, but I hope it doesn't mean I can't belong to the resistance. She's probably been herding cattle since she was five and bossing the bulls around if they didn't co-operate. I wonder if she can milk a cow. Of course she can. I can't milk a cow.'*

She brushed her reservations aside. If she was to make this work and not be accused of spending the war behind a book, she needed to stop being so squeamish. Mara: Bachelor of Arts, languages. Employment history: interpreter for American embassy. Life: sheltered. Habits: clean. Leisure time: considerable.

'When do we leave?' she enquired timidly.

'Monday morning,' replied Vera, 'at five.'

'How are we getting there?'

'We walk, Mara, like we've always done. Ten days.' When Mara stared at her, Vera regarded the girl's pale complexion, her good shoes, the shoulders that would buckle under a scythe, and added, 'Possibly eleven. Even this early in our battle against the fascists, we must get the women behind our men. We have two months of good weather—not long— we have clothes to make, socks and jumpers to knit, food to organize, nurses to train. Anything the village women can do needs to be mobilized now before the winter sets in.'

Stirred on by this taut, almost savage, organization, Mara found herself in an unfamiliar world whose edges, just slightly, were stirring with anticipation. The breeze ruffled primaeval instincts at the outskirts of her world that she was casting aside. This was something special. No one in England could walk for ten days without falling into the sea.

On the morning of their departure, she farewelled the city as the dawn cast amber ripples across its traumatized buildings and felt her soul swell with adventure. She was about to depart on an important mission with directed women, who knew what they were doing, who had not allowed bombs to daunt them, nor occupation to intimidate them. Bidding her aunt a tearful farewell and brushing aside her final efforts to reflect upon what she was doing, she walked across to the point by the Sava where she had had that fateful conversation with Miroslav. Five women waited to be rowed across the river beneath the remains of the King Alexander Bridge and to commence the first part of their trek along the Danube on the other side.

The boat rocked as they stepped in. The two men at the oars rowed strongly, flickering up drops of water that caught the first sunbeams as they fell. Mara wiped a trickle from her face and turned around. There on the riverbank, with his stone heart bleeding before her, stood Miroslav. Given the chance, he would expose his wound until he expired of it. None of the other women noticed the internalization that was draining him, because no one knew him as she did. Yes, she knew she'd hurt him; she knew he believed he needed her, but not for the first time, she wondered how someone so vulnerable could be so frightening.

*****

Mara spent much of the first day securely in her head, either bragging to her friends in London about the achievement of walking four hundred and fifty kilometres or wishing she was in England and could catch a train. What was the problem, really? *Nine hours of walking each day; fifteen hours to sleep. I can do that.*

Bent on escaping the suspicion of the occupiers, the women walked quickly. At first, their speed and the distance they were determined to cover across the flat landscape seemed interminable: fields of ripening crops, clustered villages, dusty track after dirty street, earth around her ankles, a brief shower of rain and then mud on her shoes. Nevertheless, Mara congratulated herself upon her splendid acceptance of suffering until twilight, when she discovered that she had already held the party up by five kilometres. By that stage, her left hip stung in a fiery circle around the joint.

At a village called Putinci, fifty kilometres from Belgrade, Vera found a house that could put them up for the night and, as Mara watched the wife idly scratching beneath her armpits, she opted for a bed of straw in the yard. There, beneath the stars, she fell into a repose so absolute that she remembered nothing until she was awoken the next morning to a breakfast of maize porridge and a handful of walnuts. Observing with his astute peasant's eye that Mara's background had not included epic marches, the husband asked her would she care for a shot of his apple rakija to get her moving again. She thanked the man and, inspired by the first proletariat impulse of her life, replied yes, please, but only if the others could have some as well. Then it was back on the road and blisters on her feet.

'Take your shoes off, Mara,' urged Vera.

'You mean walk in bare feet?'

'This is not London. Look, all these women walk barefoot.'

'Don't they have shoes?' asked Mara.

'If they could afford them, they would be careful not to wear them out.'

Despite her own tiredness, Vera massaged Mara's lower back each night, which, though it was slowly strengthening, nevertheless threatened to arch into a cave and prevent the hip from functioning at all. As the fourth day on the road drew to its close, they crossed the border from Serbia into Bosnia and Mara began to feel that at last they were getting somewhere. Excitement buoyed her up and, early on the fifth day, she began to see little towns of one, two and three storeyed wood and plaster houses nestling amongst hills, their roofs pitched as high as ski slopes in preparation for the winter snows. Animals watched them from within rickety handmade yards: cows, pigs, big black boars, chickens, dogs and ducks. Nearby, hay was stacked in peaked domes about two metres high. Very seventeenth century, Mara mused romantically, relaxing into the scenery. But the people themselves seemed mired in poverty and, as they came closer, she saw that the houses were not well kept: dirty white walls, doors angling off hinges, beaten earth floors. Mara watched the women nursing their babies from the porches and thought how pretty they looked in their embroidered blouses and headscarves, until she grew closer and was dismayed by the blighted reality.

'What a pretty place Bosnia is!' she exclaimed, pausing momentarily to admire the vivid green countryside. 'But why is it so poor?'

'Taxed by the Turks, bled by the Austrians,' replied Vera. 'Bosnian poverty is a shameful legacy of the great empires and religious division, but you're seeing the wrong things. They're getting their families through each day. It is through exactly this type of woman that we will win this war. We will ask them to help by doing what they've known how to do every day of their lives.'

It was the situation of one particular woman, however, that caused Mara most concern. She wore a long dress over pantaloons that billowed to her ankles. On her feet were coloured slippers.

'Why is that woman wearing trousers?'

'She's a Muslim, Mara.'

'Muslim!' exclaimed Mara.

'What's the matter with being a Muslim?' said communist Vera.

'Oh, you know, Serbs and Turks and things.'

'She's not a Turk. She's a Bosniak.'

Mara had caught sight of the woman in her enveloping clothes coaxing a plough through a fallow field. The air was moist with the showers of the previous days and the earth pliable. The woman, moreover, was adept at her task, drawing the wooden implement as it was intended to be used. The shock, nevertheless, of coming across a female engaged in heavy labour caused Mara to cross quickly to the side of the road closest to her, based on the incongruous philosophy that those further away had moved there because blatant staring made them feel guilty.

'But she's drawing a plough, Vera! Think of the weight. Honestly, I can't believe she's doing that. Where's the horse?'

'They probably can't afford one.'

'Then where's her husband?'

'You will find, Mara,' replied Vera with something of the exasperated teacher in her voice. 'That everywhere women do a lot of the agricultural work.'

'Muslim women?'

'All women.'

'And everything else, too, probably!'

The woman paused from her work to smile at the travellers and Mara made sure she straightened herself up, so as not to appear chained to a piece of farm machinery. She acknowledged the smile because she didn't wish to appear prejudiced, and felt cranky at Vera, who had implied that she was.

'If it was me,' she answered that lady primly. 'I would make sure my husband did the heavy stuff.'

'Most likely, Mara, you would do no such thing.'

But Mara was not to be suppressed.

'They ought to stand up for themselves, poor things! Tell those lazy husbands that men and women are equal! I'll bet after this she'll have to go and suckle the baby!'

'Yes, probably.'

Once the long climb into the Dinaric Alps commenced, Mara began to believe she would soon cease to have any legs at all. They would be left behind on the long, long trek, beseeching their mistress to be allowed to rest while she tramped on without them.

'You must develop a rhythm, Mara,' advised another of her companions. 'Talk less. Stay in the shade, if you can; keep your face out of the sun. Rest briefly and then continue. Lean into the hills. Relax down them. Drink whenever there is a stream. Here is an orchard—eat. You don't have to ask. Bosnians are very hospitable, and we are on party business. We are getting the women behind the men to liberate our people.'

What good was such advice for a body lacking years of adaptation? When one of the women again admired the scenery, through waves of exhaustion, Mara could not immediately reply. As far as she could see, the landscape had been relentlessly beautiful for days. However, in order to be polite, she remarked that the orchids were lovely in Belgrade this year. In truth, while the orchids and roses and apple blossoms attracted the bees in the crowded city, the lonely hills of Bosnia rolled above the horizon like waves down a river in flood. Finally, right at the horizon, she saw a purple peak. This much she remembered.

In the end, the most effective method she had was to recall the advice her mother had once given her regarding childbirth. 'It will begin and it will end.' Except that by then she had walked herself into a semi-coma. The day that had begun as apples and plums waiting to be harvested ended as a soaring mountain backdrop blackening with the sunset, and she couldn't remember anything in between. Day and night. Fruit and shadows. Thoughts rumbled through her brain that perhaps this was what death was like. One obliteration after another, until suddenly she would be surrounded by a deep hush and a fresh breeze blowing her into the light of eternity. She would see her mother again, dressed in white, saying, 'It's not time yet, Mara. Go back. Your father needs you.' At once she would watch herself from above and observe, with detached pity, how everyone below was weeping, 'Oh, why did we send Mara to Bosnia when she was just about to die?'

But when the ten days ended and she was not dead, they crossed the river and commenced the final march into town. She was almost surprized when the green country lanes and rural fragrances gave way to the odours of a town: markets, hay, dung, beasts of burden, old timber and the awareness that men and women inhabited this place, as if one could smell them breathing. Drvar was a town on a river plateau in the west of the Dinaric Alps. The area had been a victim of the initial atrocities against Serbs by the Ustasha forces and the focus of a strong and early Partisan formation that had liberated areas from the hated fascists. For Mara, who had

92

not the personal reasons that stimulated the local women, the journey to get there had been the anticipation, mixing with the communist women and the knowledge that she was part of something new. Actually being there quickly resolved into a sense of isolation and disappointment.

Admirably purposeful and determined even after ten days on the road, the women of her party deposited Mara beneath a tree like an urbane exhibition of possible interest (they would return later and put her on display for a small entrance fee) and disappeared to find friends and party members. Only Vera remained, rummaging around in her rucksack.

'When will you be back?' asked Mara.

'Not long. Rest.'

From where she rested on the ground of the main street, the telegraph poles rose taller than the hills, shaved bare by the timber industry. The streets were unpaved, which Mara had expected, and there was a factory and old railway for lumber that unfortunately didn't go anywhere near Belgrade. Houses rose up to three stories, peaked rooves with attic windows, a wealth of chimneys. In their shadows squatted bungalows, and everywhere the walls were white, giving Drvar the pretentions of an overgrown village. The sun had passed the meridian, the midday meal was over and, in the early afternoon, the summer heat hovered silently over the town. Behind them, a flock of sheep slept in the shade at its straggling entrance and presently a group of barefoot children stepped from random houses to stare suspiciously at the strangers. A small boy spat at them and even the little girls wore headscarves.

Mara shook her head.

I don't know why they wear those.

'It's very quiet here,' she observed.

Through Forests and Mountains

'The mornings are busier,' replied Vera smartly. 'Never been to the country before, Mara?'

'Holidays,' Mara whispered. 'Skiing and swimming.'

Vera didn't need to reply. She nodded so loudly that Mara knew exactly what she was thinking.

Any strangers were news and a few local women had joined the group of children. They wore the ubiquitous skirt to mid-calf, blouse and vest, and that white headscarf she had seen everywhere on the walk down from Belgrade, which enveloped the face and caused even the youngest and prettiest girls to appear miniature mothers. They eyed Mara warily, a city girl by her clothes, as, she supposed, they might observe any stranger who looked at them as if she was questioning everything about them, which she was. They scarcely moved except to rearrange busy hands by transferring a baby from one hip to another, by securing a spindle into a belt or by inspecting a carded fleece.

Drvar seemed a collection of villages, all joined up, so that the sheep found a comfortable place in between. Dwellings ran along the road in ripples of heat and silence, as undisturbed as a graveyard. Mara cast her eyes one way, then the other. An oxen yoked to a cart emptied its bowels in the dirty street and a horse waved a fly away with his tail before neighing his discomfort. He had the biggest, yellowest teeth Mara had ever seen. He looked like he'd been chewing tobacco. Nearby, a dog dozed in the sun, the sides of its mouths fluttering as it dreamed, and an artless chicken clucked its way across the street.

That chicken, thought Mara, has not considered the consequences of its actions. No city chicken would be that guileless. Immediately, the dog woke up: a sudden rush of legs, a squawk! A collection of feathers fell to the ground and the dog commenced circuits between the buildings with the bird in its mouth, joined by two naked toddlers and a housewife

94

shrieking behind, thumping indiscriminately at it with a tea towel. Buoyed up by the excitement, the dog showed no signs of slackening his pace. He tightened his grip on the terrified bird that, with a last despairing cluck, succumbed to sheer terror and gave up the ghost, whereupon the dog lost interest, dropped the chicken and loped away. The housewife, who had joined the pursuit with a measure of hope, screamed an obscenity at it, retrieved the corpse and began immediately to pluck it, still fuming against the culprit. She was shoving handfuls of feathers into a pocket of her skirt, stooping to retrieve the ones fallen after the initial attack, when she stopped, leaned down and, apparently realizing that the bird still had a heartbeat, wrung its neck in one abrupt action.

This episode was observed by two desultory housewives, one big and one small; a study in insight, like a lighthouse and a lookout.

'That dog's done her a favour,' said the first. 'The chicken wasn't laying anyway.'

An inebriated man wavered towards the excitement, belching across the street and picking lice from his clothes until he had pulled the shreds of his shirt from his trousers. He took the convenience of this freedom to relieve himself in a warm yellow stream up a wall but, upon perceiving that he was being watched, made a cursory attempt at dressing, which he performed with the obsessive regard of the drunken perfectionist.

'You know what his problem is, don't you?' said the second woman. 'It's his mother. All his life, "tuck your bloody shirt in!"'

'Listen, Vera.' Mara motioned her aside. 'I don't mean to be rude or anything, but...'

'Yes?'

Through Forests and Mountains

'But how are these people going to beat the Nazis? I mean, Germany is a big, organised, um...educated sort of place really, isn't it? Very aggressive. You're a positive person... I can appreciate that, but do you think things here might improve... like, a bit? I mean, what do the communists propose to do in Drvar, exactly, tell them that men and women are equal? That's ambitious in a place like this.'

'Mara.' Something had happened to Vera. Her face had disappeared behind one of those wretched headscarves. She had become one of Them. 'Mara, you are allowed your opinions of other women and I have often heard you express them. You also know a lot about languages and I can tell from your face that you have worked out their dialect. Nevertheless, you must be self-controlled in how you reply or we will lose this battle before we start. Do you understand me, Mara? The party cannot afford to alienate these villagers. They may not come from Belgrade like you—they certainly don't come from London—they may well be illiterate, but they are very good at looking after their families and we are going to ask them to look after ours. And in reference to your comparison between Drvar and Germany, fascists don't preach the equality of the sexes.'

The two local women had shrewdly pricked their ears to the conversation.

Mara didn't notice.

'I'm sorry, Vera. I simply cannot imagine living like this.'

'Like what?'

'Well, like not being able to read.'

'That's a generalization. How do you know...'

'I can read,' interrupted the first woman, stepping aside to let a herd of pigs pass by.

Vera stepped over to the woman and shook her hand.

'Good day,' she said warmly. 'My name is Vera. We are so looking forward to having you at our conference. I hope you will come.'

'I have heard about it.'

'Excellent! That's the most important part accomplished. Now tell all your friends, won't you?' Vera turned to Mara. 'Welcome to Drvar, Mara. These ladies might even teach you how to knit.'

'She can't knit?' said the woman who could read. 'I'll teach her how to knit.'

But do you have nits? Now I know why they wear head-scarves. Protection from head lice.

Later that day, when Mara had shaken off her despondency and the sense of expectancy around her had at last begun to excite her, one of the communist women approached her, leading by the hand a girl aged about fifteen or sixteen, blank eyed, her gaze disinterested. Long ago the child had passed hopelessness; now all that remained was despair. Like most of the women, she walked bare foot and her clothes were dirty, stained in places with ash and grime, ill fitting, as if she had put them on a week ago and lost weight in the days since. Her long hair hung lank and unwashed and she had an attitude about her that suggested she did not care if she lived or died, for both were the same. She spoke not a word and Mara wondered if she could speak at all.

'We don't know her name,' confirmed the woman. 'She is Serbian. The women from Slovenia picked her up as they walked through the remains of her village in the Krajina region of Croatia. There was not a house standing, not another person alive, as far as they could tell. They discovered this girl beneath a pile of men who had been shot but, before the bullets, every man had been blinded and their eardrums pierced. The women said they could tell that it had been done before death by the large amount of blood. This child was found beneath one of the men who appeared to be shielding her—maybe he was her father. The women and children they had herded into the church and burned.'

'The Germans?' Mara whispered.

'The Ustashas,' stated the woman.

'The Ustashas?' repeated Mara.

'You've heard of them?'

'My boyfriend is a fan.'

'Well, well,' said the woman and reviewed Mara with a stern eye.

'My ex-boyfriend.'

'All right, then,' the woman added, turning to leave. 'She's in your charge. Look after her. See if you can find out her name.'

But Mara had scarcely heard a word. She took the girl by the hand and sat down beneath her tree. Pulling out her comb she began slowly to smooth the tangled locks. She took water and washed the girl's unseeing face. She tried to get the thin, silent figure to eat and drink, and at night she slept closely by her side on a straw bed in a barn. At the end of a week, she discovered that her name was Aleksandra.

CHAPTER NINE

Miroslav Novak finally sent his telegram: To the embassy of the Yugoslav Government in Exile. Stop. London. Stop. Regret to inform ambassador that daughter is collaborating with enemy. Stop.

*****

Marija Dragomirović was watering the pot plants when the ambassador for Yugoslavia staggered into his office looking like he was suffering from apoplexy. Behind him waddled the Minister of Foreign Affairs.

'Which enemy was he referring to?' blundered the ambassador, mopping his brow like a bowling ball in a sauna.

'We are at war with the Axis powers, ambassador.'

'Mara's not collaborating with Germany!'

'Italy then? That boyfriend of hers seemed to know all about my villa.'

'She'd broken up with him!'

Far below the ambassador, from the point at which his vest button strained after dinner, the minister steeled himself in anticipation of a further onslaught. The calm British response, he declared to himself in some desperation, was appropriate when dealing with heated Balkan emotions. His

99

head ached. His neck was strained because he had been forced to look upwards a great deal. At some point in the emergency, he suggested that they might both sit down for, by this means, their two heads would be no more than a couple of inches apart. He suggested the velvet couch. The ambassador adjusted his trousers upon his knees and the minister swished his tails beneath him. They sat.

'What can you tell me about your daughter's boyfriend?' the minister asked politely.

'She met him in Belgrade at a press conference,' answered the ambassador. 'She was interpreting for the American embassy staff.' He shook his head distractedly. 'I got her the job through my contacts there, and they met, shortly after she arrived from London. Miroslav was a journalist, born in Zagreb. Charming and attractive, but possessive, involved with a Croatian fringe fascist party active since the thirties—the Ustasha. Have you heard of them? They had been in Italy, supported by Mussolini. Mussolini and Hitler paraded together through the streets of Florence in an open car in 1938. That's why he knows about your villa. It's close to Florence. He probably requisitioned it for them. A foreign owned property in his country—you couldn't use it. It would be ideal.'

The minister wondered how the ambassador could expose the truth in so brutal a manner. Then he upbraided himself and wrestled with his baser instincts alternately. The poor man was distraught. Nevertheless, his own hopes of retrieving his property were looking dismal, and he wasn't the personification of happiness either. How much had his villa cost him in lira and what would be a similar amount in dinars? Everyone knew villas in Dalmatia went for a song. He could buy one on that coast to show solidarity with the ambassador, but, he thought in dismay, Florence was so convenient from London! How could he even get to Dalmatia, and wasn't it in Italian hands at this stage of the war? At least, if he bought a villa in Dalmatia, he could offer it to the ambassador for the winter breaks, when he wasn't using it himself. But he could bet that the bloody allies would bomb them both if they thought the Italians or the Ustashas were encamped there. Damn, why hadn't he bought in neutral Portugal? Or Spain? Why? Why? Why? Well, he knew why. It was because the government there, before the Spanish Civil War, had been allied with the Communist Party.

A very dark look clouded his face.

'It may be, Ambassador, that the boyfriend was referring to the Communist Party of Yugoslavia.'

'The Communists?' The ambassador drove his fists up and down his waistcoat while behind him, Marija Dragomirović hurried away with her watering can. 'That's preposterous!' Although he did not appear convinced. 'The communists and their Russian ideas are not in favour at all in Belgrade. In fact, they are illegal and, even if they were not, there is nothing in their philosophy itself that Mara would ever be attracted to.'

The minister relaxed. Finally, they were on common ground.

'The British government is virulently anti-communist,' he said.

For a second, the distracted ambassador calmed and appeared in his own world. A germ of hope, perhaps?

'And yet,' he mused. 'It is left wing and Miroslav was right wing. Ultra-right wing. Communism and fascism. Could it be her reaction to him, I wonder, or is that even what he was referring to? "Your daughter is collaborating with the enemy"'. Communism would be the enemy to him and quite possibly to the Yugoslav Armed Forces as well. "The daughter of the ambassador of the Yugoslav government in exile is working for the communist party." That would make headlines. He knows that neither His Majesty's Government nor Yugoslavia would support anything remotely Bolshevik.'

Beyond the window and its floral bouquet, London got on with the war in its own dogged way. The same well-worn hats, the same step from a splintered front door, the same walk down the pock-marked street, bomb crews, blackout curtains, ration books, courage and stoicism. The ambassador watched them, heartsick and weary.

'Mara isn't interested in communism, Minister. It's organized resistance she'd want, not the politics of its leaders. She probably thinks she can disrupt German supply lines or some equally absurd notion. That would,' he said sadly, 'be just like her.'

CHAPTER TEN

Nikola Mugoša was happily married with six children, and had perfected the swagger of the Montenegrin chieftain with all its verve and splendour. He stood head and shoulders above any soldier in the Italian army occupying his country and was twice as heavy. He boasted a comfortable moustache, a comfortable belt, equipped this evening with a collection of historical armaments, and looked supremely comfortable in the security of his home, his family, Anton, the priest, and the small congregation of would-be partisans who were listening to him.

Concerning the mountainous region he inhabited, he was a mine of information, and he neither knew nor cared about anything outside it. In his head, which rose like a globe from his shoulders, was marked every blade of grass, every rock, every root and every leaf on every page of what amounted to a local directory, upon which he exhibited a running conversation on his walks, as if he were the intimate friend of all of them. No one who knew him doubted that this was so. Though a solid member of the Orthodox Church, he was not superstitious. He feared neither witches nor demons. He refused to carry a charm against the evil eye, although his years in the countryside had given him a healthy perception of all enemies, seen and unseen. He was a genius at the problem at hand and a cornucopia of all possible solutions. Like the loquacious patriarch he was, he varied his days between exhortations and sudden strict silences that bore down upon all present the importance of giving him their undivided attention.

All his best qualities had come out once he signed up as a young man in the Great War, and they had not appreciated being put out to pasture in the twenty years since, for he was a born war leader. As soon as the Axis powers invaded his country in 1941, Nikola Mugoša was in his element. How long, however, he would have lasted in a regular army these days remained a matter for speculation. He had little concept of institutionalized corruption, beyond the regal wrangling in Belgrade between the wars and, in his opinion, the recent and rapid collapse of that hierarchical pyramid called the Royal Yugoslav Army proved his point. But it was not as the leader of a regular army that he found himself now, and the politics of a kingdom that had not survived a quarter of a century had raised their head above his periscope only marginally before being swamped by circumstances. Now that that situation had gone the way of all flesh, it was up to natural generals like himself to forge the new path.

But he was not yet at war with bugs and lice. Like everyone else, he was accustomed to a normal number, and scratched occasionally and, for a soldier, he was far too fond of food. In the months ahead, he was to spend long nights under the stars eating grass casseroles with birch bark, waxing lyrical about second helpings of spring lamb.

'Did you often eat lamb, *druže*?'

'Pork, comrade, if I was lucky—if the fascists hadn't stolen it first.'

Only once in those early days had he tasted fresh lamb, but what a once it was! Should you arrive at his house at any time of the day or night, his first request was always 'are you hungry?' There was a story about Nikola that a party of men had arrived in the small hours, having covered seventy kilometres in twenty-four hours, and he would not let them sleep until he had fed them, though they might reasonably have been expected to be dead on their feet. He was an experienced man, however, in the ways of his countrymen. In spite of their obvious exhaustion, he knew that long distances tramped over mountains and through forests were customary, and it may well have been that, after walking for a day and a night, his visitors would truly have preferred to eat rather than rest. They never got the choice, however, with Nikola and perhaps they knew this before announcing their arrival, thumping on his door three hours before dawn. By the time they had been fed and watered and the usual familiarities got through, the entire household, comprising Nikola's wife, his elderly mother and his three children not yet married were awake and alert to the mood of the conversation. Everyone around the hearth wanted to learn what had transpired beyond their village. The two dogs, not including the snarling one chained in the yard, were kicked from around the hearth to make way for the guests. Most of the town had never gone further than thirty kilometres away from home, except for one or two of a more communist persuasion who had sharpened their muscles in the Spanish civil war. It was expected that, after Mussolini in Italy, Franco in Spain and that Nazi lunatic who hated everybody and everything and who had once been termed the German Mussolini, that Yugoslavs would need the experiences learned in Spain to prepare themselves for the present strife at home.

But the answer that Anton most needed from Nikola Mugoša was this: how did he expect to win a war using only labourers, farmers and shepherds?

Through Forests and Mountains

As in everything else, Nikola had a prompt and confident answer.

'We will win because we are right and they are wrong.'

'And if you fail?' asked Anton.

'We will not fail, although one has to expect a few trips along the path. Do not disasters happen in the normal course of a farming year? Do you give up your life on the land for a hailstorm or a dead cow, when it rains at harvest and the grain re-sprouts and is eaten by mice? You don't! You pick yourself up and get on with it! The principle governing our fight is the important thing, not the fighters necessarily. Factors in our inexperience will not deter our eventual victory over the fascists.'

'The Italians?' asked a voice in the crowd.

'And the Germans,' corrected Nikola. 'Italians and Germans are fascists. And Franco, of course, in Spain.'

'Spain is a long way from home, Nikola, and Franco won.'

'I am not responsible for the Spanish, and now that I have straightened that out, who's hungry?'

Anton was always hungry, and after he had eaten, and drunk what wine Nikola provided, he outlined his situation. Nikola listened while Anton flexed his injured arm as if the action could distract the man from probing more deeply than the physical.

'I'm navy,' said Anton. 'I've never served in an army before.'

He was only here at the suggestion of the priest, was he not, and to see his sailors? Although his illness had addressed parts of his psyche he hadn't known he possessed and the awareness of their existence disturbed him, he didn't want it broadcast, in addition to his litany of other troubles. His country no longer existed and, with the Yugoslav surrender, his job had dissolved. His boat was in Egypt, and the remaining three of the four submarines that the Yugoslav navy had possessed were in the hands of the Italians. Where was the road forward for him? This rustic group in a stone house led by a farmer, to whom the faint intimation of need that remained from his illness resonated as clear as a bell? His black eyes, customarily so focussed, fell to the floor. He wished the guy would get the agony over with.

'What was your rank?'

'Lieutenant commander.'

'Then you are accustomed to command.' Nikola indicated the sling. 'How well can you shoot with that arm?'

'Well enough,' answered Anton. 'It's only the shoulder. I can use the forearm and fingers if it's supported. I can use my left arm now almost as well as my right.'

He was about to demonstrate when there came a shy knock at the double doors of the living room. He turned eagerly towards the sound. Nikola's wife opened the left door, revealing Viktor, a girl about six months pregnant and Miloš, standing sheepishly beside them, on the top step leading down into the room.

As if the struggle with life and death had not been enough for Anton, Victor's reaction upon seeing his captain, watching from one side of Nikola's belly, gaunt and superficially taller, but alive with interest, almost undid him.

'Captain...' began Viktor before being strangled by emotion and shuddering to a halt. He ransacked the pockets of his vest for a handkerchief while two large tears splashed down beside his nose. His young wife rebuked him with a playful smack on the arm.

Anton stepped across the room. The two men embraced and then Anton slapped Miloš on the shoulder.

'Well, how do I look?' he smiled at the youth.

'Good.' Miloš knocked his knees together and mumbled as he regarded the sling, 'Um, are you better, Captain?'

'Getting there. What happened to Petar?'

'Petar's in Egypt with the Allies and twelve of our crew. They made it.'

'That's wonderful! Wonderful,' said Anton. His heart was full and his eyes were shining. 'Come in, then. Viktor, let's find your wife a chair.'

They returned to the warm company and the abundant room, fearful lest their momentary departure should suggest to anyone present that Nikola was less than welcoming or his larder depleted. Legs of hams were suspended by hooks from the rafters, olive oil from Nikola's trees and wine from his vines waited in hopeful vats. On a table by the range lay plates of bread and small sweet cakes, cauldrons of sauer-kraut, pickled vegetables, peppers, carrots and potatoes. His wife, who was pouring jugs of kefir, was like the sturdy beams that supported the floorboards of the rooms above, her welcome as broad as the arched, tunnel-like ceiling of bricks that led to the hearth and the open kitchen range upon it. In a corner waited her spinning wheel and loom, and parts of Nikola's extensive (and famous) collection of old Montenegrin weapons had been secured to the wall beside them.

'Where's your Turkish medals, Nikola?' cried a voice.

'Put aside for my old age.'

'Then sing us a war song to get the party going! We've got to keep fighting or we'll be working in the fields with the women.'

'Quiet! Quiet, all of you! This is bigger than that.' Nikola was accustomed to having all eyes on him. Not to have it was the only impatience he ever showed. 'Now listen: what is the aim of Germany?'

'*Lebensraum*!' somebody drawled.

'No! Yugoslavia was never intended for German living space. They need Yugoslavia for their supply lines between Germany, Austria, Hungary, Italy, Greece and Croatia. They need to transport oil from Romania through us. They need to move troops. They need the railways to supply their armies in North Africa. They need copper and aluminium from our mines. They need timber and crops. They need arms. Our aim must be to break these lines of supply and communication.'

'Then what do the Italians need Montenegro for?'

'Their ego!' cried a voice.

'That's right,' agreed Nikola. 'So they will be easy to get rid of.'

Nikola Mugoša was an efficient mixture of history, strategy and mountain philosophy. With every eye upon him, he lectured the ensemble with antiquity and experience behind him in equal measures, binding the two together with skill.

'You can't fight in Montenegro without knowing its history,' he was fond of saying—he said it now. 'That's why the Germans and the Italians will lose.'

'You just said we'll win because we're right!' someone shouted.

'They are two different things. The first Montenegrin principal has always been one of surprise. That's why we don't need superior numbers. We guard the passes, melt into the forests, hide in the mountains. We give our enemy no time for knowledge of the land, for rest or reorganization. By these means, they begin to fear us. *That* is knowing your history. It's the moment the Germans and Italians discover that might is not right. We have changed the way they think and now they know that they can lose. We have the advantage because it's our land. We fight without pay, without leave, without fear. We put personal feelings and hardship aside for our people. We don't face our enemy in battle. Instead we exhaust them by constantly harassing them. Surprise is our best weapon. Night is the time when we strike; ambush is our defence against superior numbers. This we can achieve because we live in a land of mountains. The Montenegrin doesn't take shelter. He marches through rain and snow. He bears thirst, hunger and every deprivation. He requires the minimum of sleep. In the cause of his land he relinquishes all feelings of personal safety and comfort. He does not seek shelter from the rain or the cold. He neither begs for mercy nor fears death. To the Cross, while he breathes, he is faithful. This, my friends, is why, though we are outnumbered, we will still win.'

When Nikola had finished, his audience was impressed. Nikola had intended it that way and welcomed their warm congratulations, although sundry ones were still scratching and murmuring, 'I tell you, Nikola, you'd never get away with this in the Royal Yugoslav Army.'

When at length he was persuaded to sing one of his own songs about the old days, in which were as many glorious defeats as splendid victories, the evening ended in harmonies. They wove in and out of the fields of ripening maize and brushed the moonlit mountains.

Anton went to bed on a corner of the floor, wrapped himself in his blanket and was handed a packet of pyrethrum for the bugs.

*****

When the Italians proclaimed, on the 12th July 1941, that Montenegro was to be, in all but name, a part of Italy, there was a general uprising that profoundly shocked the occupiers, who considered that they had been lenient towards the Montenegrins. The Montenegrins, for their part, were not surprised. Everybody knew that Italians took themselves more seriously than any situation warranted and, as a consequence, got upset really easily, particularly after an anonymous graffiti artist painted horns and a pitchfork on the portrait of Mussolini that hung in the town hall of Cetinje.

Margaret Walker

The uprising the following day, the first such movement in occupied Europe, had lasted from the middle of July until the end of August and was half way to its conclusion when Anton arrived. It had much in common with the Dance of the Eagles, the national dance of Montenegro, in which young men and women jumped as high as they could and swivelled around in the air until they were completely exhausted. Likewise, beginning with enthusiasm, the uprising against the Italian occupation was briefly and wildly successful and then trailed off as a result of issues regarding organization and ideology. Traditional fighters, like Nikola, felt that the remains of the Royal Yugoslav Army would have been wiser to stay out of it. The officers, however, who had returned home to Montenegro after the surrender of Yugoslavia with their weapons locked and loaded, believed the contrary, and would have preferred to manage the impetuous Italians without help from tradition. Though the Italian army out-numbered the forces of the tiny Balkan nation by at least twice, they could never have occupied Montenegro in the first place, had it not been for the Germans. This observation was resoundingly pointed out.

By the end of August, the uprising was starting to unravel. Nikola was not impressed and bombarded his small band with the direct assault they had all been expecting. 'Frontal attack? You're joking!' he had bellowed when informed. 'What sort of *hajduk* led that?'

'Not a guerrilla, Nikola. A communist intellectual. A local, but studied in Belgrade.'

'Unbelievable! They think they know better than their own history. This is what comes of higher education.'

Imbued, as he was with Montenegrin folklore, Nikola could not comprehend how any army hoped to combat the Italian occupiers with modern techniques and vague promises concerning the liberating effects of communism. In the

111

first week of October, he and his youngest son Boško were caught attempting to dynamite by moonlight a convoy of Italian trucks departing from Cetinje to the capital of Podgorica. They barely escaped when a cloud (sent by God, declared Nikola) obscured the moon and they were able to descend rapidly into the forest and lose themselves amongst its blackness. Thereafter, they spent over a month living between the trees and a *baza* on Nikola's property, an underground pit commonly used to escape invaders, and dating from the Turkish occupation.

In November, the double doors of Nikola's substantial farmhouse were nearly knocked from their hinges by two Italian soldiers hammering on the wood. Nikola's wife creaked one side open and peered out over their heads towards the chill wind from the fields. She waited without a word, forcing the soldiers to speak first.

'Where is your husband?' they demanded.

'I don't know,' she replied, blank faced and recalcitrant.

'He's been seen coming back here for food.'

'Then if you find him, let me know. Winter's coming.'

The Italians regarded the farmer's wife with contempt.

'You're his wife. You ought to know.'

'You Italians know nothing about Montenegro,' she replied to the soldiers, though she'd barely open her lips to give them the time of day. 'He's taken to the woods like they all do. He didn't tell me where he was going.'

The two men stretched their legs until their rifles scraped the ground behind them. One general had told them not to use force and another had said, force is the only thing these people understand. So they shrugged and walked off.

'Peasant!' they barked over their departing shoulders.

Nikola's wife wiped her hands on her apron.

'Feeling's mutual,' she said.

Margaret Walker

The Italians left in a confused state of mind, and stole two pigs from Nikola's yard. They had grown fat from this land, but that snarling dog had stood between them and the sows and, when they had left, Nikola's wife found the animal in the yard with its throat cut. After that, she kept the other two dogs inside whenever the patrols passed by. Due to being far from home and not having the requisite tools to make ham and sausages, the Italians ate a lot of roast pork and made themselves sick.

It took until Christmas for anything less diluted than mutual wariness to be re-established in the land, notwithstanding that the Italian Queen was a Montenegrin princess. Subsequently Italy proclaimed that fifty Montenegrins were to be executed for every Italian officer killed or wounded or, in the case of a soldier, ten. This, of course, was hardly fair, as Italy had neither conquered Montenegro alone nor regained control after the uprising without help from irregular forces from neighbouring countries.

In the middle of November Nikola gathered his rifle, his son Boško and his brother Slobodan, and a selection from his famous arsenal store and took off into the woods a final time, over Mount Lovćen by night. With him went Anton.

CHAPTER ELEVEN

'Have you seen my girlfriend?' enquired Miroslav of the elderly woman tending the potato plants. 'She used to live here.'

Without straightening up, the woman creaked around to glower at the handsome young man, who had addressed her in a Zagreb accent.

'Love her that much, do you?' she mumbled. She rubbed her crooked spine in an arc of increasing circles until her two feet were below her knees instead of her chin, and returned him that baleful stare.

'We lost contact after the bombing,' explained Miroslav. He put his hand to his heart and winced. Feigning integrity was so unprofessional.

'That was a long time ago.'

Miroslav brushed away an imaginary emotion.

'Please...' he begged. 'Look, she's about my height, collar length brown hair. Lovely smile.'

'Half this building died,' spluttered the woman. Her back was killing her—these wretched potatoes—but she had to eat.

'Oh, dear. I'm so sorry. But I feel very strongly that Mara is still alive...'

The woman belched. 'Oh, her? Well, you're a hypocrite if ever I've seen one. You don't deserve her. Try that old man asleep on the tram stop if you must. He's in contact with more people than me. I keep to myself.'

So I see, thought Miroslav acidly.

The man she referred to looked like he hadn't washed in a year and he smelled worse. Miroslav leaned over him and tapped the gently snoozing shoulder. Its owner groaned and rolled over, and Miroslav inhaled the sharp tang of methylated spirits.

'My girlfriend lived in that building with her aunt,' he began. 'Mara? Do you know her?'

'Gone,' drooled the man through bloodshot eyes. 'Got a room in the suburbs. Dušanovac. Other side of the church. She comes by here and feeds me.'

'Mara feeds you?'

'Her aunt.'

'When?'

'When I'm hungry.'

'Why?'

'She's a good woman. Now piss off and let me sleep.'

CHAPTER TWELVE

Anton thought that first night walk would be like an escape by submarine. He would cast off his moorings, depart from port and set his face to the open sea. Though it was black beyond the harbour, he knew the darkness well, and the breath of a cold sea caressed his cheek. The track behind him would be the wash from the propellers and the brushing of the undergrowth ahead, the bow cutting the dark water.

Yet, the forest called to him to accept a more menacing welcome and, had he been alone, perhaps he might have proceeded with caution, but Nikola and his sons plunged in without hesitation. The dense velvet held no fears for them and Anton had no choice but to follow. The moon was full and, beneath it, the forest was veiled in a grey mist from the tops of the smaller trees down to the floor of leaf mulch and decay. A thin grey mist in that expectant wood, so evenly distributed that it seemed a curtain about to part. The moonlight was strong and swept the path in swathes of pale lemon, but upon the tree trunks it appeared white and flushed the wood. Enough light was provided by its beam to see but, even without it, one could navigate if one knew these woods well. They were not mysterious. There was nothing to fear, yet. But here was a dead trunk, black amidst the undergrowth. Behind it, as he passed, he heard a snap, a rustle, a scurry. He started. *What was that?* But all quickly returned to quiet. It was, after all, nothing.

Anton knew, because he had been brought up on the old stories, that there was a heart of the forest, and in the heart was a house, and in the house was a witch, and the witch knew he was coming. But he was not a child; he no longer feared witches. He followed Nikola, Slobodan and Boško, and heard the call of a night bird sail towards him on the wind. They were descending a hill that led towards a softly tinkling watercourse hiding in a hollow. For an hour or so, hearing it but not seeing it, they followed its turnings while the rocks they trod on were uneven and the brush encroached on all sides. No harbour light, no lighthouse, no warning bell. Anton was not aware how he walked on without falling, and they must not make a sound in this occupied territory. But the enemy didn't know it as they did, and that was a comfort. Their safety and the safety of those who have helped them depended on their silence.

Upon the cliff to their right, he saw a single light, the last house of an isolated village. Then even that vanished and the night lapped them gently. He was glad now that the darkness was total and that the slightest noise he might make could not bring the retaliation of the enemy down upon them. He was panting, for their pace must be fast to escape this last dwelling that bound them to all he has known. Once, as a naval cadet, he had sailed across the Atlantic, and now he conjectured that this great expanse of forest resembled it. He might have his ship's clock, his compass and his sextant, but they wouldn't help him tonight; he must follow those whose land this was.

They had been walking for about four hours and he had begun to swing with the rhythm in his hips when they reach the ford of the autumn stream. As they descended, the temperature had been dropping and now he heard again the faint jingle of water to his right. They forded the stream and commenced the climb up the mountain beyond. The trees thinned and, through the branches above, he saw one star, then two and three. Finally, the trees parted until he could see the whole of the Milky Way above him, so glorious in its vast silence that he could only gaze at it in amazement, though he had seen it many times before when it tremored above the pulse of the waves. He was reminded of the widow's milking shed, where he had battled death and won, and he sensed again the child in the manger and fancied that he, too, was following a star. His comrades had gone before him and, regretfully, he took his leave of the galaxy and the marvellous eternal. Too soon, the dawn hurried the night away; he observed the first lightening of the sky and farewelled it with regret. The eternal no longer interwove itself with the world of men, and the sense of things to do and routine to fulfil oppressed him momentarily.

During the night they had descended to a district of low hills, a carpet of scrub, the ever-present limestone, faded green, emerald and grey. It had a feeling of isolation Anton had not experienced in the trees, but Nikola was not fooled. He pointed across the lonely terrain to a field of maize left late so that the grain could harden. They saw a wall of cypress pines, their green washed out by the grey of early dawn. Further still, barely distinguishable from the landscape, was an arthritic fence and leafless trees reduced to brown bones, a farmhouse; all lank like seaweed or the moss that lives under a rock. Unwelcoming to tired men.

'Not quite,' whispered Nikola, reading Anton's thoughts. 'But let's see if he's still got that dog.'

'Which dog, Tata?' breathed Boško, close behind him.

'Bob the dog—the one that likes me.'

Far across the deep gloom of the fields an amber light sprang into a window and they crept through the wet mist towards it, hushed because of the dog, wary of Italian troops.

'Bob doesn't like you, Tata.'

'Shh, shh, shh! I'm going to make friends with him before he lets the whole neighbourhood know we're here.'

They pushed through the maize, thankful for its cover, brushing away damp stalks and sliding into puddles of liquid mud, hearing birds, rats and smelling the damp morning. A raw day. The cold seeped into their bones. Winter was almost upon them and soon the snow clouds would descend, thick and white. As the sun rose, the outlines of a substantial smallholding appeared out of the mist: a barn, hayricks, ploughs, a harvester, all bathed in the same vaporous flood. A two-storey stone house, red-roofed, with an attic window and a long, low barn slung by its side, a couple of outhouses. A kitchen garden, bare trees, apple, pear and plum, two rows of grape vines pruned close after the harvest. The light they had seen earlier glowed brightly from one pane of glass in a downstairs window, perhaps from a thick candle placed upon a stand.

Abruptly, there came a whine and an urgent trotting around the corner of the barn, and there in front of them appeared the biggest dog Anton had ever seen, almost up to Nikola's hips. He looked like an enormous, menacing sheep —fleecy, brown, anxious and single-minded. Nikola stooped down and reached for the animal, quite a stunning act of bravery.

'Ooh dog, dog, dog,' he crooned. 'How's a boy, then? How's a boy? Dog, dog, dog. Atta boy.'

The dog sniffed uncertainly and emitted a low growl.

'I told you, Tata, he hates you.'

Nikola ignored his son. 'Good boy, good boy, who's a good boy, then?' He extended his arm to be sniffed until, all at once, the dog lost interest and ran away around the corner of the yard. 'There, Boško, I told you so.'

'If that's liking you,' declared Boško. 'I'd hate to see what he does when he hates you.'

'That dog was always antisocial. Come on, let's go.'

He ran up to the window and rapped upon the glass. The light that had burned so brightly was suddenly rooted upwards and shot crazily around the pane. The sash was wrenched open and a face of massive proportions stuck out of it like a fender from a ship.

'Nikola!' it cried. 'What...?

'Don't ask what I'm doing here, Erik,' stomped Nikola. 'Just let us in! We've got the Italians on our trail.'

'All the way over the mountain?' slurred the huge face in the early morning. There was sleep around his eyes. 'Those lazy buggers wouldn't do that—too cold. There's no one, Nikola, who can exaggerate like you.' He opened the front door. 'All right, come in and let's hear it.'

They trudged around to the entrance and entered a large, square farmhouse kitchen, barely warmer than the fields, wherein they found Erik's wife on her knees attempting to encourage a fire from the embers of the previous night. The uncertainties of the farming life and the hegemony of men had baked her features into a mask of resignation whose expression rarely altered. But, upon seeing Nikola, a grey curl smiled from beneath her headscarf and Anton saw that her apron was still stained with the sweet plums of yesterday. She rose and regarded Nikola with fondness.

'I'll get your breakfast,' she said, as though he had lived there for weeks.

'Your wife's a wonderful woman,' remarked Nikola to Erik.

'You can address me, Nikola,' she said.

Nikola gave her a bear hug, from which she emerged breathless and red-faced.

'It's good to see you, Katarina.' He stepped back. 'Here's my two youngest, Boško and Slobodan. Look how they've grown!'

Katarina viewed the two young men who overtopped their father, but between them, equalled his girth. Slobodan was twenty and his brother Boško two years younger. Though reared in the shadow of their boisterous, father they were not as dominated by him as appearances might suggest. In fact, they knew him too well to take him seriously, and those who paid close attention to the replies, considerations, suggestions and repudiations made in his presence were aware of this. The boys and their father often appeared as three equals with different ages, because Nikola, having used up his determination to be the perfect patriarch with his first four offspring, had tired of the effort by the time it came to the youngest and had adopted a more relaxed attitude.

Katarina laughed.

'We'll have to extend the roof,' she said. 'What have you been feeding them?'

'Ah, there's nothing to eat any more. Bloody Italians live on their stomachs.'

'So I see.' Erik laughed his jolly laugh with a humourless face.

'Look, we were living between the *baza* and the forest for a month, before things became too hot.'

'So now you're on the run? That's just like you.

'Well, I'm not ending up in a prison in my own country.'

'They would have shot you, Nikola, and made sausages out of your carcass.'

'So, now you understand.'

Erik regarded the boys ruefully.

'Boško didn't have to come, at his age.'

'Well,' replied Nikola. 'I had Slobodan to consider.'

In the midst of the joyful reunion, Anton slumped exhausted onto the cold floor, clutching his wet blanket around his shoulders.

'Here, give me that!'

Katarina whipped it up onto a chair before the struggling fire and, opening a press on the wall, tossed him another one.

'Anton Marković,' introduced Nikola. 'Army recruit.'

'Navy,' shivered Anton.

'What did you do, desert?'

'He's only got one arm, Erik. Can't you see?'

'I have two arms, Nikola.'

'Well one's grazing the top pasture. We hope it will come home for milking.'

'What happened?'

'Accident in dry dock, Katarina. Thank you for the blanket.'

Katarina shooed them all to the table where she laid bread, ham, cheese and milk. Anton heaved himself off the floor and did as he was told, watching her bustling around and taking him in, summing him up, desperate with curiosity about the arm.

Any minute now... he steeled himself for the inevitable. She was going to use him to prove herself in some way— country knowledge, motherly skills, or, most likely, that experience was better than education, a popular topic amongst capable, uneducated women. He thought, as he had so often with women, that evaluation was all a game to them. Still, she didn't seem unkind, and he proceeded, as he frequently did to his regret, to play by her rules.

She bustled around, large and energetic, encouraging them all to eat and drink, stopping too frequently in a position most suitable for observing his arm. From the other side of the table, Anton was certain she'd stopped too long in one position, so that the vest covering her white blouse remained raised, as if she had taken a large final breath in order to ask her questions and seemed unsure when to let it out.

Finally, the vest dropped and she said, 'Can I have a look?'

He sighed silently, thinking that he knew perfectly well what was coming. He removed the sling and his wet jacket, unbuttoned the damp shirt beneath and pushed it down his shoulder from the collar.

Katarina cast a keen eye over the dip in the triceps, the trough that carved out the skin around his rotator cuff, the jagged lines where the eighty sutures had been ripped from the flesh, the scars of infection, and a look of triumph brightened her face. He was transparent to her. She could see everything straight away. *Here it comes.*

'Why did you take the stitches out?' she demanded.

'Can't remember,' said Anton.

'How did it get infected?'

'I don't know.'

'Oh, come on!'

'All right, perhaps Viktor didn't wash his hands properly.'

'Who's Viktor?'

'One of my crew.'

'No hospital, then?'

'The Germans invaded.'

'They invaded the hospital?'

'No, they didn't.'

'You discharged yourself, didn't you?'

'Yes.'

'If you were my son... '

'I'm not your son.'

'...I would tell you that your behaviour was not in your best interests.'

'I've already been told that.'

'Who'd like some ham?' interrupted Nikola. He waved the plate around. 'Put your shirt on, Anton. Poor Katarina! It's all your fault, Erik. You're just not very exciting.'

But Katarina was not to be denied her moment of glory. She prodded Anton's shoulder where she had spied a tiny black dot upon an island spot of raised skin.

'You've left half a stitch in your arm. Give me a minute and I'll get it out. Keep on eating. It will distract you.'

She hurried away and returned with a pair of tweezers, a bottle of slivovitz and a needle of audacious proportions. It was probably just as well that it had been a long march and Anton was too tired and hungry to watch while she examined the tender new skin, as fresh as the dew, upon his disfigured shoulder. Such items, as well as the slowly healing nerve endings, were best left alone. Really, the half stitch could have remained without incident for the rest of his life. It was hardly a medical emergency, in the opinion of a man who hated being fussed over.

Eating as he was bid, Anton was suddenly catapulted forward by a burst of pain. He gagged on the mouthful he was eating and spewed breadcrumbs all over the table.

'Shit!!'

'Got it!'

Katarina held aloft the tiny thread between her tweezers. She sloshed slivovitz on the dent she had made in Anton's shoulder then handed him the bottle. 'You'll feel better now.'

'I felt better before,' muttered Anton darkly, but he scoffed two mouthfuls of the fiery spirits and sat with his eyes closed, feeling it course through his system and calm him.

Around the kitchen table all eyes were turned upon him, as he hunched over the scrubbed wood, clutching the bottle of spirits as if alcohol was the only thing that understood him. Nikola, ever the pacifier, laid a silent hand upon his shoulder—the other shoulder. Beside their father, Slobodan and Boško were trying not to laugh, while Katarina calmly reinstated her authority in her own kitchen.

Erik patted her on the bottom.

'That's enough, woman. All the man wants to do is sleep.'

*****

Erik put them up in the barn loft above his horse and his donkey. Within five minutes Nikola and his sons were asleep and snoring on their beds of straw. Anton was not slow to follow them, floating like driftwood into the silent day. When at last he woke up, the sun had set and night was closing in. For a while, he watched the shadows creep up the wooden beams above him and then, as sleep at last dissipated, he realized that he was alone. Even now, months after his accident, sleep could still hold him so firmly that he would wake like a child, not knowing where he was or what had happened.

The day had been mild, for the cattle were wandering in for milking without a care in the world, but the mellowness of that late autumn evening was fragile, and in its hidden corners the premonition of winter brought a bite to the air. Anton climbed down the ladder and rumbled across the farmyard, finding Boško and Slobodan in the kitchen, consuming more ham and bread, apples and plums, and a bottle of wine. Katarina had subsided back into her usual stoicism, and motioned him to the table without a word. Nikola and Erik, fed and watered, stood by the fire deep in congenial disagreement.

'You think he's going to organise farmers into an army?' Erik was saying, waving an errant arm around, as if to say that every farmer knew the odds of success in such difficult conditions were low, so why waste resources trying? 'I can just guess what'll happen all over Yugoslavia, little *odreds* of excitable peasants, each revolting in their own way against the Germans and the Italians, sundry Hungarians and Bulgarians demanding a piece of Yugoslavia, and internally, the Chetniks, the Ustashas and the communists.'

'You have a complicated brain, Erik,' retorted Nikola. 'To organise resistance you've got to think simple and take risks. One, decide upon your enemy; two, disrupt his supply lines.'

'Yes, yes, yes, you are repeating yourself, Nikola, but how are you going to communicate that? *Communicate.* You know? This is a big country. Without communication, organised resistance doesn't stand a chance. And how are we going to do that? We don't even have electricity outside the cities.'

'You think we should just keep it local then? That's very frustrating.'

'I have no doubt you would find it frustrating, Nikola, but I did not want to be the one to point that out.'

Nikola adjusted his considerable weight, leaning towards Erik so that he looked as if he knew what he was talking about. Of course he did. Erik just didn't realize it. This bone of contention had played a significant role in their friendship.

'All right, Erik,' he said at last. 'Just tell me what you've heard on your side of the mountain and I'll tell you what I've heard on mine.'

'I have heard unconfirmed reports that a party of Royal Yugoslav officers were landed on the coast of Montenegro at the end of September from a British submarine,' replied Erik. 'But no one here has seen them. We *have* seen communist-led partisan bands in the hills who are fighting the Italians. They're loosely aligned with the officers from the Yugoslav army, but I believe it's all a bit informal. If you want real organization, Nikola, you must go to Užice in Serbia. Six

days' walk north. Since the Germans invaded Russia, occupying troops have been thin on the ground here, and the Partisan High Command has been running the town like busi-
ness-as-usual.'

'Communists also?'

'Yep.'

'What's the difference between the two groups?'

'The Užice mob have been fugitives since the last war.
Underground, you know. Illegal. I'd hate to see you involved
in Bolshevism, Nikola, but I know that you'll get the support
you need in Užice, until the situation here calms down and
you can go home.'

'Can you tell my wife that?'

'I'll find some way to tell her. What about your boys?'

'What about them?'

'Well, they can stay here, if you like, so you don't need to
worry about them.'

Nikola only gave it a moment's thought.

'You'll have to ask them,' he replied. 'They're men, not
boys.'

But he knew all too well what his sons would say.

CHAPTER THIRTEEN

The woman who could read had been as good as her word. She was teaching Mara to knit with two bone needles and a ball of three ply wool. By their side sat Aleksandra, absorbed and wordless, and almost certainly able to knit herself.

'I learned how to knit during the last war when we had to knit socks for the Austrian troops,' the woman told Mara.

'How old were you?'

'Four. Try to keep your tension correct. How many stitches do you have now?'

'Twenty in this row, nineteen in the last one, eighteen in the one before, but I think I'm back to nineteen.' *I've dropped two stitches, picked one up and cracked a nail. Some miserable sheep in a blighted paddock has been shaved bald for me to fail in front of this woman. Do they eat sheep here or just knit them? Lamb, that's right. They knit lamb. Let's work out the proportion of lambs per sheep, enough to eat and enough to knit. You just need not to eat lamb in the spring, so there'll be plenty left to knit.* 'Sorry about my tension. Is that better? I can't believe you knitted socks when you were four.'

'Yes, and on four needles, not two.'

'You were four?'

'I had four needles.'

'Oh, you poor little thing! That's cruel. Couldn't your mother have done it for you?' *Bugger, I dropped another stitch, picked it up and made a hole in the fabric. Maybe my hands are too big for knitting or my eyes are short sighted or something.*

'You need to watch your work, Mara.'

'I need a coffee.'

Along came Vera in her headscarf—*I am never wearing one of those, never*—she was perusing a letter.

'I've got a job for you, Mara,' she said with her eyes on the paper. 'You see, once you become known, people remember your skills. Someone has name dropped. They're asking if we can supply a teacher to take the evening classes of young village women who are keen to learn reading and writing. That's you, Mara!'

'Where?'

'Oh, in Užice, south of Belgrade. It's not actually on our way home but we could detour to drop you off. It was the first of the territories liberated from the Germans, and it's doing quite well. That is the crux of the letter. We'll walk half the way back with you, and then you and Aleksandra can continue east. You don't want to go to the city, sweetheart, do you?'

Aleksandra shook her head.

'Then we'll find you a guide from one of the villages for the last part of the journey, Mara.'

Mara was mildly disappointed.

"Teach?' she asked. 'But I was hoping for something a bit more exciting.'

Vera cocked her head and the scarf drooped over one eye.

'More exciting? What, nursing?'

'Well, no, not exactly, but...'

'How do you think you would react, a girl like you, to blood on the battlefield?'

'What do you mean, "a girl like me?"'

'Does your family sacrifice the pig at Christmas?'

'What pig?'

Beside her, she heard the other woman laugh.

'To make ham and sausage,' Vera pointed out. 'All the village girls see animals slaughtered regularly, Mara, in particular the Christmas pig. You're going to get upset if you see a dead human being. There's much more blood than a pig. It isn't pleasant. You would be a good teacher. You're friendly, you like to talk. And you'd be comfortable in Užice, with winter coming on.'

Above them the first autumn leaves were yellowing on the branches. Their green edges, already bordered by a brown line, would soon blossom to burning gold, then fade and fall. Thinning cover, the pale sun, the harvest slowly drying and fermenting. Then months of harsh winter until spring reawakened the land. Mara knew exactly what Vera was implying; what the fall of the leaves foresaw for the Partisans. Mara had never experienced a hungry winter in the country. She'd no idea of the amount of blood when an animal or a human was killed. Who would pick up her pieces when she fell apart?

But, 'If they can do it, I can!' she stormed, rather unnecessarily, as before her Vera awaited her reply with complete composure. 'I wish, I just wish, that I could prove to you how much I want to be a part of this. You forget that I'm a Yugoslav, too. It's my land just as much as theirs and if I want death to all fascists and liberty to the people, I must just get over seeing a bit of blood, even if I can't knit and can't milk a cow! You know, the first time I met Tito he was giving instructions on sabotaging enemy trains, and I wasn't the only

woman there.' The final six words—*naturally*, thought Mara
—were the most important.

'You want to blow up a train?' responded Vera flatly. 'You
need to do what you're told, my dear.'

'That's what my father was always saying,' replied Mara.
'And I'm tired of hearing it.'

'Has he got no one but you? No other children?

'No. Mum died a year before the war.'

'Of what?'

'Pneumonia. And she's buried in London, but Dad's got
her heart in a little bottle of slivovitz. He's going to bring it
home, when this is all over.' She wiped away a tear.

'They why do you want to fight? Your father doesn't want
to bury you, too.'

Here followed a long pause.

Then, 'We're at war,' announced Mara. 'I'll have to take
my chances, the same as everyone else.'

Vera remained silent, but Mara could see that, in her
view, the discussion was not over. Finally, she said, 'Tito's a
very practical person. He will expect any forces under his
command to be disciplined and well-organised. If he allows
women to fight—*if*—he would make sure you are fed well and
have had enough sleep first. You'll get that at Užice.'

'Read you loud and clear,' said Mara.

'All right now, the letter goes on to say that they are desperate for teachers. You come from the city and you might
not be aware that some of these villagers are rather backward. So, you see, Mara, it doesn't matter that you can't knit,
after all,' Vera concluded with a penetrating glance to where
Mara stood, looking at Aleksandra, who shuffled her feet because she perceived that Vera was talking about her.

'And how are you going to turn the peasants into communists, Vera?' asked Mara to divert the focus from Aleksandra's illiteracy.

'There's two things going on here,' Vera responded. 'Tito's got to sort that out. I just can't tell, at this moment, what his priorities are. It is true that communism and fascism are diametrically opposed, but the politics of anti-fascism, which to me means communism, is not what the villagers here care about. They just want their land back. Striking a balance is our problem.'

'And what about the Germans?' demanded Mara. 'They might want Užice back.'

'It appears that they've gone to invade Russia. This, of course, is why we were able to drive the Germans from Užice. The enemy doesn't have the men to control the countryside now.'

To say that the prejudices of a lifetime had been swept away in a week would be an exaggeration. Mara had gradually, but not yet completely, developed a grudging admiration for the canniness and worldly-wise attributes of her teacher. Once she had laid aside her insistence that pretty countryside didn't mean tourist brochures, that sheep didn't smell, that pigs and mud were clean, that sewage systems in the city meant that human waste was fragrance-free, and that food came from shops, she was in a position to appreciate that she was not living in a social state and that things didn't automatically appear because the government had ordered it.

Wool was spun so that families could be clothed, grain ground to make bread, and crops stored to sustain men and women during the harsh Bosnian winters. This knowledge itself was extraordinary. If someone was sick, they got better, more or less alone, or they died. No one had sophisticated doctors and surgery was not an option. Not only this, but the woman herself seemed as adaptable to change as Mara hoped she herself would be in a short space of time, and this appeared to be a common attribute amongst the other women.

Margaret Walker

Whether it was a relief that the communist party was providing a genuinely new experience for countrywomen or because the experiences of invasion and occupation had overcome their reluctance to be involved in something outside their world, the meetings held in Drvar to provide support for partisan fighters had proved unexpectedly popular. Like a flock of swans, the hall of The Worker's House was a white ocean of headscarves, all turned in the direction of a speaker. Word had got around, and women had attended from the town, but also from the surrounding villages and farms. Meetings were packed to overflowing. Perhaps it was the knowing that she had been wrong that had occasioned Mara's conversion to humility, but not to knitting. Maybe she would be better at milking.

CHAPTER FOURTEEN

It had taken Miroslav a fortnight to locate Mara's aunt, and he had just spied her underfed figure disappearing into a doorway as Mara was leaving Belgrade. He had watched the women's passage across the Sava with a depression that gnawed at him like the rats in the sewer. The rodents lifted the grate and peered into his depths, saw Charon crossing the stream with the dead, heard the bone man clanking beneath the brick-lined arches. It felt wearily like an old friend. He was reassured that gifted, extremely intelligent people like him frequently battled the same black sludge.

Naturally, he had not come across the women's expedition by accident. He had followed that woman—the one who looked like the leader, whom he had seen Mara with—to her home one afternoon before locating her again early the following morning and experiencing the shock of seeing Mara depart with her. They could not be heading south. By crossing the river, he assumed that they would be walking west. By their rucksacks, boots and blankets tied about them, they looked like they were preparing for an overnight stay. In a village? Could they be going as far as Bosnia? (Sorry, Greater Croatia.) You didn't have to cross the river to walk to Bosnia, but there was that formidable mountain range to cross, and the river route was marginally easier.

Miroslav ground his teeth. He felt the sting of tears behind his eyelids, but he shook himself and straightened up. He was not an animal without intelligence. It was horses who required bridling, was it not? He would not let this disappointment destroy him. What he had expected of Mara was reasonable. She had disappointed him, not the other way round. Though he had written to her, explaining how he felt, he found it extraordinary, looking back, that she had forced him to do it at all. It wasn't merely that she had wounded his pride. One simply didn't deny Miroslav what he requested. Nobody did. How dare she? *Calm, calm,* he told himself. *Don't be a woman. Control yourself. Start again.* He could easily find her. They would soon be together again and his head would be straight on his shoulders. On foot, Mara couldn't go fast, and her journey, to wherever it was, would be observed by many witnesses. She had to be somewhere. He reasoned to himself that locating one person in Yugoslavia was easier than in Italy, or England, or even Germany, whose massive populations rendered all manhunts, rat hunts instead. People bred like rats in those countries and finding one person could take months, if not years. Now in Yugoslavia, by contrast, the population was far less dense and any small group like the one he had just observed must meet regularly with the established settlements in order to eat and sleep. He would ask at every village. Someone would have seen them. Alternatively, he could ransack the mail at Mara's new address to see if, by a miracle, her aunt received anything sent from farther away than Belgrade. Of course, he could simply follow her now, but he had business to attend to for the Germans. He needed to compose several communications based on the snippets of information he had picked up, concerning local resistance groups and the soirees he had overhead at the university. He would keep his ear to the ground. He could work and stalk at the same time.

Miroslav never lost. Even when the unendurable happened, he spun the story in order to remain the winner, to fortify the dam that held back his demons. In fact, he looked forward to trailing Mara again and he loved a challenge. So she was off on her adventures? Excellent. The whole thing was just great fun. Such an overused word, but appropriate in his case. He would wait by the aunt's mailbox until he had definite proof of her whereabouts. That could take a long time, but what was deduction if not a game? What good patience, unless it was rewarded? Ultimately, they were the same thing.

*****

Operation Barbarossa, the invasion of Russia, had commenced on 22 June 1941 and, while the Germans were otherwise engaged, the Communist Party of Yugoslavia called upon all Yugoslavs to rise up against the Axis powers and their allies who occupied the country: Germans, Italians, Ustashas, Hungarians and Bulgarians. The uprising took the Germans by surprise and at their most vulnerable. They had not expected reprisals of any kind and, other than rounding up all Jews within a few days of their invasion, they had allowed the local inhabitants to go about their business. Overstretched with their march towards Moscow, they had even given up manning many of their garrisons in the towns of Serbia. The countryside remained relatively free and people could come and go as they pleased.

The partisan attacks that took advantage of this lull began that same month, with the intention of disrupting German communication and supplies and plundering them for guns, ammunition, vehicles, clothes, food and medical supplies. The stores of the old Yugoslavia were looted. In Belgrade, the telephone office was sabotaged, the German press office burned and the railway station attacked. Enraged, the general staff had a job of it to repair the tracks before the supply trains could continue on their journey east to Greece, to supply Rommel's army in North Africa. While they were thus engaged, eighty trucks carrying oil and ammunition within Serbia were also blown up. An uprising in Slovenia slaughtered an Italian garrison and the telephone office in Zagreb was destroyed, much to the chagrin of the Ustasha who thought that they were in control.

Whether it was genuine surprise at the behaviour of an inferior race or anger that the Nazi war machine had been halted, the behaviour of the Yugoslav people had provoked the following response from the German High Command on 13 October 1941: 'For every German soldier killed, one hundred prisoners or hostages are to be shot, or fifty for every one wounded.' The definition of a prisoner or hostage was the following: Jew, communist, nationalist, democrat, and "sundries" were homosexuals and Gypsies. The definition of an attack upon a German was also modified to include ethnic Germans living in the north of Serbia, the Bulgarian military in the country and all those who were collaborating with them.

Despite their legendary efficiency, the Germans were not precise in how many people they killed until after the proclamation was made, when their maths suddenly improved. Within a week, in Kraljevo, Serbia, 1736 men and boys were shot for 10 Germans killed and 14 wounded = $(10 \times 100) + (14 \times 50) = 1700$. In nearby Kragujevac, the same week, 2324 men were killed for 10 Germans dead and 26 wounded = $(10 \times 100) + (26 \times 50) = 2300$. The discrepancy in the predicted death toll and the actual one was noted, but, happily, more hostages were killed, not less, so that the Ger-

mans did not lose face. The error distressed the more educated, for it forced them to acknowledge that women may
have been among those who had broken the new law so accurately proclaimed.

When he heard how good the Germans were at mathematics, Miroslav went for a run. He ran all the way to the
house where Mara's aunt lived, as he did most days, and he
tried to coincide his arrival with that of the postman. He did
so, mostly, at this time but not always, depending on his duties for the Germans and the articles he was writing to send
to Ustasha Headquarters in Zagreb. This continued for many
weeks and he was finally rewarded for his tenacity with a letter addressed in her handwriting. He wedged it into the elastic of his track pants and kept running. Once he got back into
the city, he sat in the park and read:

Dear Auntie,

Now, I don't want you to worry about me, I am
well and really (really) happy. I spent a profitable time
with the communist women in Drvar and am now
teaching not so far from you in Užice. When I say 'not
so far' I actually mean to say, in Serbia, not in Bosnia.
These village girls outside the town are a bit behind in
their studies and I am teaching them reading and
writing. So that's quite respectable, isn't it? I have a
dear little friend called Aleksandra, a victim of this
horrible war, and she is in my class.

I am the happiest I have ever been and you will be
pleased to know that I am still not a communist, even
so. Yet, in the purpose and comradeship of these
women, I have found the substance that was lacking
in my life. For the first time, I believe in something
more important than myself: the liberation of my

country. I wonder these days how I could ever have believed in my previous, privileged existence, or that materialism and romance alone could satisfy me. My clothes, which went up in smoke at Easter, have been no sacrifice. I am happier and freer and more determined without them. (Don't worry, I'm not running around naked or anything.) I am better dressed, because the heart on my sleeve is a far more alluring garment.

Užice has its own postal service, Auntie, but I'm not certain how this letter might be delivered within the occupied territory at Belgrade. I have tried anyway. The woman in the post office raised her eyebrows at my request but said nothing except, "All right." Perhaps the fairies will deliver it. These days it's better not to ask, but I hope you have received it and are reading it right now.

As the days go by and my knowledge and compassion grow, I have discovered that the old Serbian poetry from my school days has its personification in these village girls I am teaching. Initially, Auntie, I was very dismayed at their illiteracy and their peasant manners, until I discovered the zeal with which they long for the thing denied to girls in village life: a proper education. They have become the embodiment of notions I had relegated to theory: literacy, self-determination and universal suffrage. It has been a revelation, really; and I have ceased judging their embroidered blouses, dark skirts and bare feet, the way I used to. The summer heat has dried the grass beneath their feet and the cicadas cackle their jittery song, but the leaves will soon change and I'll have to see if I can get a warmer coat. I only have the one Dad got me while I was in London.

Through Forests and Mountains

I'd never met a peasant at school, though perhaps, as a child, whilst driving with my parents through the Serbian countryside, we had bought autumn fruit from their stalls. Was there not that other time, on a holiday in Slovenia, when a whole party of black clad women appeared from nowhere and offered us poppy seed pastries? It grieves me to think that I had been oblivious to their existence until our country was invaded. I might have existed in a bubble. And now here we are, united by a single goal, and I am discovering that they have the same desires as I do. It has been quite a revelation. It is true that at this particular locality they are mostly Serbs and mostly orthodox, and only about one quarter ardent Communists. But I have heard talk of similar partisan groups from all quarters of the country, no longer Serbs, Croats, Slovenes, Bosnians, Catholic, Orthodox, Muslim but united as Yugoslavs to drive the oppressors from our land.

Tito is always at the coalface, a superb organiser. I don't worship him, he is too practical a person, and I get the impression that's not what he wants, but I am immensely proud to be one of his heroes. This is what he said, 'What is theirs, we don't want. What is ours, we will never surrender.'

I will put up with anything to be part of this fight, Auntie, even the mosquitos.

Your loving niece,
Mara.

When he read this, Miroslav felt justified in his decisions, and he had the Croatian Ustasha party to thank for not having to allow unwelcome morals to rule his life anymore. The deletion had come as a huge relief. He had often taken himself to task for worrying about the rules of the polite society he had been brought up in and that had whispered over his shoulder for much of his life. One should not, one could not, one would not.

But what if one could?

What if he could arbitrarily stab anyone along the street who, like Mara, had upset him? The woman who walked too slowly in front of him, the elderly person he could not overtake, the fat man who ate too much, the veteran on his stick, the date who wouldn't sleep with him, the fool who couldn't talk, the Jew who charged interest, the gypsy who begged in the square, antifascists murmuring in a closeted café, Serbians: stab, stab, stab—such pleasure—and no one could rebuke him because ethics and morals were not part of the new order. Self-gratification and winning instead were his ardent bedfellows. Each fed off the other. Violence was only the knob that turned them. We are at war, after all, he reasoned. They are my enemies.

Out in the Bosnian territories, in what was now Greater Croatia, he had been particularly interested in the villagers whom a party of his Ustasha colleagues had pushed off a cliff merely because they were Serbian. He had gone out just to watch, in order to determine the results of such a fall, and had been disappointed to note that, from his view, swathed in low bushes at the very edge, he was unable to see them drop. He was reminded of Galileo's experiment from the top of the Leaning Tower of Pisa to determine whether bodies of differing sizes landed at the same time. Whether, in this instance, the theory of the great scientist was proved true, Miroslav could not tell. The bottom of the gorge was partially obscured by the trees that protruded from the rocks along the descent. By peering very far over he could just catch the disappearance of arms and legs into the branches, but the bottom itself was not the level plain required of science and he could only judge the success of his interest by the juxtaposition of limbs on the ground. None had taken much longer than any other to fall. Probably Galileo was right and physics could again be triumphant, but it was disappointing almost to have had the opportunity, but lost it due to the difficulties of the terrain.

Not one of the villagers had run against the rifles urging them towards the edge, not one. Miroslav detested the hope that defined humanity, even in the most desperate of situations. *If I don't run, perhaps they might spare my life.* Thus they had all been rounded up like sheep at the point of a bayonet and herded over the cliff to their deaths. What incompetents! He experienced no empathy for the villagers. He thought they were all rather stupid. They dressed like peasants; he had never seen such uniformity of white headscarves, caps and waistcoats. They walked like peasants, old before their time, bowed over by years of hard work and childbearing. They disgusted and depressed him, but the lack of a good view had depressed him more. He had peered over the cliff until he had vertigo.

He wondered whether they would have tried so hard to live if theirs had been the fate of the Serbian villagers in the Krajina region who had been blinded by the Ustashas before death, by way of amusement. Miroslav hadn't been there but he had heard about the idle gesture from the victors, who had intended to kill them anyway, Serbs or gypsies or Jews. Whatever. *Now that would be an experiment worth trying. Is life so precious that one would strive for it even after such a fate as blinding? How does the immediate absence of light affect the human desire to survive? Does one succumb to the darkness as to the prompting of the evil that lives there? Is one, in fact, different in the soul by the blinding of the eyes?*

Margaret Walker

Miroslav had heard of buckets of eyeballs extracted from victims merely to see what a bucket of eyeballs looked like. Well, he supposed that, if the Germans could make lamp shades from human skin, the Ustashas could have a stamp collection of human trophies—and why should they be scalps only? It was said that that particular village had possessed a single blue-eyed girl amongst the brown and that some Ustasha corporal had left her alone, to make it obvious to the wretched child that her real father had been some passing traveller from a northern climate who had wooed her mother for the night and passed on anonymously. The next day they had found her dead by the road, after the rest of the village had been blinded and slaughtered, and Miroslav conjectured that the cause of death was some fever brought on by the knowledge of the circumstances of her conception, and that she couldn't live with that knowledge.

One night after too much alcohol, someone from the Ustasha rank and file had had the bright idea of holding an In-House Extermination Competition. They'd done it years before, the man claimed, after the spring floods, when the maize re-sprouted and encouraged a mouse plague. *Let's hold a mouse trap competition!* someone had said. That had been in the days before the connection between entertainment and human extermination had been established. Now, it would be far more entertaining to discuss extermination of people instead of mice, because gangplanks baited with ham over pits of water could only be built so big, and what if the beggars could swim? Wouldn't that spoil the fun? Something more ambitious needed to be in the pipeline. A human extermination competition. There was something in that. Heads got together. Good ideas were shared, just no more water, please and, whatever the solution turned out to be, lace it with sadism.

And they believed him! What a pack of idiots!

143

Through Forests and Mountains

So, here was Miroslav's dream presented to him on a plate: a political party without morals. Having to re-evaluate one's motives constantly and to perform by the arbitrary standards of the society he had grown up in not only frustrated him, but made him resentful. Of course, the Nazis had no morals, and he had initially been attracted to Mussolini because he had read how the dictator turned a blind eye to the violence in Italy while still retaining power and popularity. How did *Il Duce* get away with it? Either the Italians loved opera too much or they honestly believed Mussolini didn't know, and his innocence in itself was attractive. Seriously, self-deception was an Italian invention. Then, he thought, the Serbs they pushed over the cliff had proved the adage about hope. Well, he knew he had power now, he did not have to hope for anything and therefore could never be said to despair, but were not the two emotions horns on the same goat? He just needed to keep his head together.

By the time he ran home to the hotel, panting and sweaty but flushed with the rosy hue of exercise, his happiness hormones were sky high. He felt like a millionaire and he knew he looked good. He took the steps to his room three at a time and, as he leapt the last triplet, there was no one in this world who would not have scraped the floor to do his bidding. King Miroslav! *Il Duce, der Führer, Poglavnik!* The leader! He washed, changed his clothes, swept a comb through the robust mane he was too vain to oil, and then went looking in the restaurant on the first floor for a drink and something to eat. He just loved waltzing around the headquarters of the victorious powers as well dressed as only he knew how to be. For Miroslav was a natty dresser. His suit was pressed, his tie a sober black silk, but so beautifully fine that women often asked him what he called its colour. He wore the gold cuff links his grandmother had given him for his first communion so long ago that he had almost had them melted down when he and God considered parting company. (This was when he had commenced journalism and become aware that most journalists were atheists. He was happy that he had not committed either sin, because the cufflinks reflected his perfect teeth when he smiled and he knew that the Ustasha needed to exploit the importance of the church to the Croatian identity in order to stay in power.) Then, resplendent with his own self-importance, he proceeded to his scheduled meeting with the German Military Commander of Serbia, General Böhme.

He found the general enjoying afternoon tea on the balcony and writing a letter home to his wife in Austria. The general was very fond of his family. Every second day found him assuring them by letter of his affection and making solicitations after their welfare, in the way that only a well brought up Austrian could express, and the gentle love note he was penning to his darling Gretel and his children Marta, Herman and Rolf had softened his stern features. Only yesterday, he had had to shoot every able-bodied man in a village south of Belgrade after a scurvy rogue of a Slav had killed a corporal in his regiment, and the sight of shrieking, wailing women had upset him so much that he had to have a bath, a shave and a manicure afterwards. The knowledge that his emotions depended on such small luxuries as these was an expression of weakness that no Nazi should allow. Today, however, the soothing effect of loving words was enough, and he was peacefully considering the correct phrase he should use to enquire after his sons' sporting achievements when Miroslav strolled into his verbs, as smoothly as a bachelor to a dance.

The general raised his eyes over his glasses at the handsome young man.

'Ah, Miroslav,' he mused. 'Miroslav, Miroslav. That's an unfortunate name. Have you perhaps thought of changing it to... something decent and honourable... something German?'

Miroslav paused. 'No, general.'

'Ah, that's a shame. Then what is your surname?'

'Novak, sir.'

'And what does Novak mean in Croatian?'

'It means 'recruit', sir.'

'Does it, indeed? That's an improvement on Miroslav.'

'Miroslav means "peace and glory".'

The general guffawed. He loved his own jokes, but in laughing, he had made an ink blot on his letter, in the middle of his most amorous expression.

'Not in German it doesn't,' he remarked sourly. He returned to his epistle and his face assumed a mystic look. *'Liebste Knödel, Süßester Apfelstrudel, höchster Schokoladenbrunnen....* And what choice tidbits do you have for me today then, Miroslav Novak?... *Nachtisch meines Herzens.* Oh, yes,' he crooned. 'Yes.'

'There is a resistance leader, General,' replied Miroslav excitedly while the general strummed adjectival phrases to himself, 'who is holding meetings within the city. A communist, I'm almost sure of it.'

The general yawned and stretched. 'Is he real?' he enquired without interest. 'You've seen him'

'No, general, not yet, but I know someone who has.'

The general laughed. 'Oh, give me facts, not riddles, Miroslav Novak, please! And I thought you were more intelligent than your barbaric Ustasha. What's his name?'

'I don't know his name yet, general, but he has a *nom de guerre.*'

'Of course he does, of course he does.' The general adjusted his cufflinks. He was bored. 'I almost believe you. These Slav leaders are figments of their own poetry. By the way, I had dinner with your Prime Minister Nedić today, the one who says he's looking after his Serbs.' He laughed and the tone had a sweet mockery to it. 'That should please you. He is concerned that the methods of your Ustashas against them are too brutal.'

Miroslav barely registered what he was hearing. It also distressed his recent world-without-morals choice.

'The Germans have trouble with brutality?'

'Well, we don't want your Serbian victims swelling the ranks of the resistance movement. If his route from Belgrade to Athens should become obstructed, the Führer would not be happy.' The general looked perplexed. It could have been his gout; it might have been his hernia—both had been playing up—but Miroslav fancied that he had encountered a philosophical problem relating to the disruptions of his ideology of war, for which he was struggling to find a solution. 'I do not know why we should have had so much trouble with these wretched people. They just won't recognize authority. They blow up their own bridges and railway lines to stop us. I don't recall having these problems in France. Have you seen what they've done in Belgrade? That warehouse they destroyed? No one saw the attackers enter and no one saw them leave. But we must blame someone, I expect.'

'Why don't you blame the Jews?'

'The Belgrade Jews are long gone, my young friend. Belgrade has the pleasure of being *Judenfrei* now. No, we'll blame the resistance movement and deprive Serbia of a few more villages. That should please you.' Abruptly he snapped with frustration and his face no longer looked poetic. 'How shall we deal with these Bolshevik bandits so efficiently?'

'I didn't think they were all communists?'

'I don't care!' bellowed the general, all thoughts of love letters flung into the afternoon air. 'Any offensive will be treated as if they were. Mark that, Herr Novak. *Any* offensive. The very existence of insurrection against Germany offends me, yet we are forced to find a more humane way for my troops to execute Serbs. Simply lining them up and shooting them into trench graves *is not working.*' He thumped his chair. 'We are upset, one, because they defy us and, two, because we are forced to kill them in a manner that is taking a psychological toll on German soldiers.'

'It's not the communists, general,' said Miroslav carefully. 'It's the country. Its people have been disappearing in and out of mountains and forests for centuries. If you want to beat them, you need to change the way you think. '

'Germans are superior, Miroslav Novak, and Slavs are subhuman. They are *untermenschen,* but even such sheep will follow a leader. So give me no more history lessons. Get me a photograph of this Tito, so that I will know who to kill!' At Miroslav's look of astonishment, the general drummed his fingers on the table. 'Ah, you are not so clever as you think you are. We already know who he is. All his plans will be about disrupting our communication lines. Our *vital* communication lines. This is where you come in. I will arrange a rendezvous point for one of our wireless operators from which you can send me information about their plans, so that we can be prepared.'

'This is not a regular army, general. I don't think...'

'So that we can be prepared,' the general repeated.

Learning when to disagree and when not to was an art. Miroslav smiled at the general and wondered if he could try again to dissuade his thinking from the superiority of German warfare.

'Naturally, General Böhme. It would be a pleasure. You must be aware, however, that there are local groups resisting who are acting alone all over the country. Some are allied to the communist party of Yugoslavia, some are not.'

'I'm only going to say this one more time, Herr Novak, and then I will not say it again. The fifty to one hundred shot for every German killed is a general principle for all lands of the thousand-year Reich, not just Serbia. The people of Yugoslavia can torture themselves all they like by asking 'what if'?'. What if we do nothing? Will the Germans shoot us anyway? How are your skills at geography, Miroslav? It may not have come to your attention, but Germany and Italy are densely populated. Czechoslovakia is not. Poland is not. Yugoslavia is not. Hitler has proclaimed a war based on racial principles. The extermination of the Slavs is not too difficult to achieve due to their low numbers. Do you think Britain would complain if we slaughtered the Slavs? As you are aware, we have already started. No, Britain wants the Slavs to fight us because it would help Britain, but if the Slavs resist the Germans, they will in effect, be killing themselves.'

'I like your sense of irony.'

But the general's face flushed and he furiously polished a brass button on his dress uniform to reduce his blood pressure.

'Slav land is necessary for the German people to survive and flourish! To expand eastwards. It's not open to discussion or to your jokes! Reichsführer Himmler called this war a racial struggle of pitiless severity, in which twenty to thirty million Slavs and Jews will perish, due to military action and crisis of food supply. You are aware, no doubt, of the so-called republic of Užice south of Belgrade, the first of our territories this Tito boasts to have liberated from our overstretched forces, where the communists go about their daily business under our nose.'

'Užice?' Miroslav squared his shoulders in order to appear unruffled beneath his excitement.

'They use our armaments factory to produce guns to conquer the unconquerable Germans? The audacity of it!'

'The Ustasha are more audacious, General,' soothed Miroslav. 'We control far more territory than those rebels.'

149

Through Forests and Mountains

'No, you do not!' stormed the general. 'Your Ustasha is driving the population into the hands of the communists, who are the only ones who seem organized. You and those incompetent Italians are making life more difficult for Germany. We came to Mussolini's rescue in North Africa *and* in Greece. Now I have had to request regiments from France, Greece and Russia just to control Yugoslavia. The 342nd, the 125th and the 113th to this wastrel of a country. Do you realize how much I resent having to do that? I hate this country! I feel like I'll be stuck here waging war against Yugoslavs for eternity. How dare they resist us! I will give them reason to fear me. Go to this communist republic—this Užice—before I destroy it; and, mark me, I will do so, as brutally as I can. You speak their language. Do whatever you have to, but bring me back a photograph of this communist leader, this Tito they all talk about, so that my soldiers will know who to arrest. And when they arrest him, they will bring him to me and kill everybody else.'

'You're asking me to spy for you?' asked Miroslav in a subdued voice in view of this tempest. 'I'm not a spy, I'm an investigative journalist.'

'A very good one.'

Miroslav contemplated, but only for a minute.

'I'll go to Užice with pleasure,' he said, thinking of Mara. 'And aside from that, what do I get out of it?'

'The wireless operator I promised you,' answered General Böhme flatly. 'And the glory of serving the Third Reich. One treats one's country and one's family with the greatest respect.'

He returned to his letter.

CHAPTER FIFTEEN

Užice was not a village but a large market town of old squares and stately buildings, with a regal history and glorious Old Town ruins as proof. A river wound through it and craggy mountain roads descended from the forest above. It dominated the main road and rail communications of western Serbia and, whilst in Partisans hands, brought to a halt all enemy movements. The retreating Germans had thoughtfully installed an arms and munitions factory that now turned out four hundred rifles a day for the Partisans, each marked with their red, five-pointed star on the butt. This star, in many variations, was well evident in the town and included an electric version over the large modern bank building occupied by Tito and the general partisan staff. Accompanying the star, the slogan 'Death to fascism. Freedom to the People' was evident everywhere. Whether they liked it or not, the residents of Užice found themselves the focus of a political revolution whose fervent adherents had taken the opportunity offered by the temporary German weakness to promote communism. Gone were the hated empires of the Tsars, the Hapsburgs and the Ottomans. In this new world, power would be in the hands of the people or, at least, a few of them.

Through Forests and Mountains

Mara strolled past such a star in red graffiti on her way home from the markets. Some young communist had scrawled it on a wall. The afternoon was very cold and, although not officially winter, a glacial wind whipped off the high peaks and straight down to where she strolled, huddled in her coat. She picked up speed. There hadn't been a lot to buy this late in the season—a sausage, a few potatoes, sauerkraut newly jarred, a loaf of bread—and the strings of her shopping bag ran up her arm as she shoved her hands deep into the sleeves of her coat to warm them and clutched her upper arms against her chest.

She rarely gave Miroslav a thought anymore. She imagined him back in Zagreb, a long way from Užice, reaping the benefits of Nazi support for his horrible political party, the Ustasha. At the time they had met, late in 1939, during her first job with the American Embassy, she had not been looking for his sort of love. He had been merely a journalist at the back of the press conference, the attractive one with the keen smile and the pen raised high, his questions of such relevance that silence fell upon the room of media and embassy staff whenever he spoke. This drawing attention to himself was certainly deliberate, and it was not hard for her to locate him afterwards and offer to assist with a few points of language that had translated poorly for the media crowd at the back of the room.

She had been so relieved to be back in Belgrade. She knew that she'd been criticized for leaving London, but this joy of living in a city of people of her own height was something that the smaller English women would never understand. Their platitudes wearied her: 'just be yourself, Mara', 'keep your shoulders back', 'Gloria has big feet, too, you know.' Now here she was in her real home, and she would never forget the thrill of disembarking the train and at once

Margaret Walker

feeling physically comfortable. Belgrade, best city in the world!

Miroslav wasn't *that* tall, but he was just tall enough, and she was flattered by the attention of this insanely good-looking and articulate man. She had never failed to come away from their meetings enriched and stimulated. As the months passed and their relationship developed, she had discovered that he could give her the answer to every problem she brought him. She knew he must be right, because he scarcely had to consider his answers before launching forth on every female problem known to man. She began to deliberately turn to him, reading aloud to him her letters to her father, asking how to live with her fussy and anxious aunt, her problems at work, her grief for her mother, dead only a year then. In public, her friends told her what an attractive couple they made, and what a lucky girl she was. Without knowing it, she fertilized his ego, while he supported her until they could scarcely do without each other. And, underneath it all, the serpent in the garden whispered in her ear, *he needs me.*

Somewhere he had lost control. Fuelled by his obsession with the rise of fascism in Europe, he had become initially instructive, then bossy, then controlling of her, then critical and, by the end, verbally abusive. The question that tormented her was: was abuse just another definition of fascism or would he have been like this anyway? Had their relationship remained platonic, would the trigger never have been there? Would he have continued just an attractive and intelligent friend? Perhaps their very intimacy hastened the change and, in the end, their breakup. He had not yet raised a hand to her. But she was becoming more and more aware that that 'yet' was in her future, so she had done exactly the same as she had with her father, made up her mind and left. Miroslav had been furious. He had lost her, but he had lost, as well,

153

and he hated losing. She was like an end that he could not tie off and the free flowing strings worried her.

'Death to Miroslav. Freedom to Mara!'

She couldn't escape the feeling that she was being watched, even in Užice, and no doubt this was the lingering effect of Miroslav's possessiveness—his belief that she was his. She needed to reinforce the mantra that she belonged to no one but herself. As she was well acquainted with most of those she saw from day to day, she had at length convinced herself that this disquieting feeling of observation could be attributed solely to her imagination, unless it was a feature of the utter stillness of the countryside. One became turned in upon oneself and discovered senses previously unknown.

So it was not until nearly the end of November that she at last discovered a possibility of contacting her father. A British engineer who had been working in Belgrade, a fit man with a purposeful gaze (and ears like a Pixie, thought Mara), arrived one day in Užice with his radio set and operator. Mara was not aware of the radio until the day after he arrived, when she happened to be passing the arms factory. He was chatting to a fighter as both of them admired it with their looks of cool male approval. *Tito did what? That took some nerve, but I like his style!*

She could tell that the officer owned a radio set by looking at him—that country sixth sense she had recently acquired. Peasants, she discovered, were invariably correct in their estimations of someone, via the selection process by which anyone different from them was named as such. A lone man in a foreign uniform. Can you see his radio set? No, it's too big. But I know he has one. Men like him always do. *Men like what?* No further comment, merely knowing peasant glances.

Although the Englishman was speaking in Serbo-Croat, Mara picked up his accent the second she passed him.

'You're English!' she yelled in English, immediately feeling homesick for the foreign country she had disowned with so much relief. The fighter saluted and walked off.

The officer turned to her.

'You can speak Serbo-Croat to me,' he replied politely in that language.

He's English, thought Mara dreamily. *Of course, he is polite.*

'*Ali ja mogu govoriti engleski,*' she said, switching languages. 'But I can speak English. I learned it at school—in England.'

'Then, how do you do, young lady?' He extended his hand and Mara shook it. *(They're so lovely, the English.)* 'Do tell me you enjoyed your time in England.'

'Absolutely,' lied Mara. 'But welcome to Užice, by the way. My name is Mara. What's yours?'

He leaned towards her confidentially, but not so close that it would intrude upon her personal space. Perfect.

'Hudson,' he replied. 'Bill Hudson.'

Mara smiled.

'Well, Mr Hudson, and what is an Englishman doing here?'

His handsome brow creased but behind it lurked the allure of the secret service.

'Do you want the official version, Miss Mara, or an edited account?'

A truck reversed into the loading bay in front of the underground sheds prior to transporting the day's load of rifles. They moved aside to let it pass.

'Wouldn't the official version be secret or something?' enquired Mara, rather wide-eyed, in view of the not entirely concealed suggestion of collaboration behind Hudson's features. *Men,* she thought, *they only want one thing. But this guy seems really interesting (apart from that). I'll bet there's a lot he's not saying.* She turned her face towards his and beamed with the ardent expectation of the adolescent.

'Let's say, secret to certain parties,' replied Hudson returning her trust with such a charming smile that Mara immediately melted. 'I'm a captain. I am here on the business of the Government.'

'Yugoslav?'

'British. Special Operations.'

Mara gasped. 'Wow! You mean spying?'

'Not in your case,' he laughed. A British laugh, warm but reserved. 'We're here to help resistance movements in occupied Europe. To find out what's going on.'

'But I need help!' blurted Mara.

'Really?' He regarded her with fond interest, in the way one might regard a lost child. 'And what can I do for you?'

'Well...'

Just what happened at that point, Mara could not afterwards tell. A rush of memories overwhelmed her, provoked by his English voice: her father rising from his desk to greet her, that tobacco pouch in his pocket that always smelled of sultanas, his big hug as he pulled her against his vest, the way his moustache tickled her as he kissed her goodnight.

'My father is the ambassador to Britain!' she cried, swiping aside one measly and embarrassing tear.

'The ambassador?'

'Dad is the Yugoslav ambassador... in London!'

And with that, the sluice-gates opened. A great flood of emotions rolled down Mara's face right in front of this intriguing British officer who, she was sure, would not welcome female tears in any form. But here she was wrong. As she stood there weeping desperately in front of him, her hair splotched down her face and her blouse puffing out of her coat, he just put his arms around her and let her sob her heart out on his jacket until the large wet patch turned the khaki the deep green of eucalyptus, stroking her hair and allowing his finger to rest over one tender ear lobe a fraction longer than was necessary. Happily, they were the same height.

'I just walked out and left him!' wept Mara, sensing his thighs through her bag of potatoes. 'Poor Dad! All by himself. Mum died and he didn't have anyone but me and look what I did!' She wrenched a torn lace handkerchief from her pocket and blew her nose hard, and Captain Hudson waited compassionately until she was calm and able to detect the faintest suggestion that he had practised this with other women.

'Why did you leave, Mara?'

'Because England is a horrid quagmire full of dwarf-sized men and I hated it!'

Here followed another squall.

Captain Hudson adjusted his tie.

'There is some truth in that,' he admitted.

'But I'm so sorry, now that I can't contact him.'

Hudson leaned forward.

'Perhaps I can contact him for you?' he offered kindly.

'Oh!' cried Mara. 'Oh, could you? Could you?'

'Not directly, but my wireless telegraphy operator and I have set up the radio link here. I'm not trained as an operator, but I can send a simple message to London through Cairo.'

'They'll let you do that?'

'I'll do it for you under my name, but you must refer to me as Marko after this,' he added. 'Except in private.'

Mara felt deliciously conspiratorial.

'Marko,' she breathed. 'Golly. When shall we send it?'

He smiled at her and she was suddenly filled by a sense of absolute reassurance. Everything would be all right. Providence had brought her this lovely man and he would tell her father that she was safe, so she could finally close her eyes like a tired child whose parents had arrived home. They would pay the baby sitter, close the front door, and peace would descend upon the house, sending her to sleep without a worry in the world.

'Why don't we send it now, Mara? Now is as good a time as any.'

He led Mara and her shopping around to the front of one of the larger buildings, which she knew held officials of some nature—the court, the finance department, she couldn't remember exactly what—and she spent the ensuing five minutes so excited that the tears that threatened to flow freely under the influence of his accent once again bided their time, gently reminding her that they wanted to return. Mara told them sternly to desist, but back they came after six minutes and she wiped them away, hurrying behind Hudson up the main stairs, hoping that someone she knew would see her with him and quiz her all about her adventure later. She felt very important. They entered the foyer and he jogged down a small flight of steps to a lower level swathed in shadows—a long, echoing corridor, musty, smelling of old leather, printer's ink and machinery. He stopped at a door and knocked. No answer.

'Good,' said Hudson before briskly entering.

Mara fell behind him into the room and told herself to calm down. She had not met a friend to whom she could reveal her astonishing adventure—*gosh, isn't it amazing how these things happen?*—but little Aleksandra would smile quietly, as she always did. Within the room, Mara saw two beds neatly made—that made her pause but, seriously, did it look as if there was room for a woman? She sniffed; it didn't smell like it—and a wooden box, about the size of a small table, lay upon a desk. Some papers lay neglected around it. Hudson opened the box, seated himself upon the chair and began fiddling with a piece of wire that ran along the wall and out the window, closed and locked to hold it in place.

'Antenna,' he explained.

Mara was speechless with anticipation. She sat down upon one of the beds. She wondered whether it was his, and what he would look like asleep.

'Wouldn't it work better on a hill?' she asked.

'Užice is higher than Belgrade.'

The box was full of minute but connecting articles, neatly packed. The only two things Mara recognised were a small Morse Code key and a pair of headphones.

'We'll have to send it in code, Mara, so we'll keep it brief. What shall we say? To Ambassador Yugoslav Government in exile, London. Mara is well. Teaching. Sends... Greetings? Best wishes?'

'Love,' suggested Mara, a thoughtful finger to her chin.

'Simplicity itself, my dear.'

'Thank you, Captain Hudson,' breathed Mara.

He cranked up the transmitter. It had a handle and sounded like a cross between an aeroplane and an air-raid siren. He wound and wound, half a dozen rotations, until a light globe went on, and then he put the headphones over his ears, checked the book beside him and placed a finger over the key. Mara watched him eagerly. Tap, tap, tap.

'When will my father get it?'

'You can imagine him reading it right now,' he said, abstracted with his task. 'That will give you sweet dreams.'

She watched his clever finger dotting and dashing the short message and was gripped by conflicting feelings: the pleasure of the strong and tanned digit tapping away for his country. The bravery of men who knew Morse code and went off to battle the enemy afterwards, as if the two must always go hand in hand. Her father's relief at hearing from her.

'That's so clever, Mr Hudson.'

'All part of the service.' *Dash, dash, dot, dash, dot, dash, dot, dot, dash.* 'And I've just written Mara.'

Within the small room, it was warm. Casual scents that she had never noticed out of doors wafted pleasantly between them. He was wearing some sort of aftershave that reminded Mara of the bath salts she had enjoyed in London. Peach? Ginger? Paris in the Springtime?

To draw her attention from these wayward thoughts, she observed, 'Tito is always so immaculately presented. Do you know, he wears rings with diamonds? Fancy that in the middle of a war!'

'To thine own self be true,' reflected Hudson in his debonair manner. 'I could suggest that Tito was deliberately creating an exotic persona, but it's unlikely that the chicken designs its own egg. In his case, it's just the nature of the beast. And,' he admitted modestly. 'I can't think unless I'm tidy either.'

'Then I don't know what you would have done after Belgrade was bombed,' blurted Mara with her foot in her mouth. 'It was Easter Sunday and my aunt and I heard the planes coming over as we were getting ready for church. Once the bombs started falling, there was no time for anything, except to grab a few clothes. We only just got out. We had nothing to eat except what we could get from the Black Market or by walking out to the surrounding farms—nothing nice like aftershave. And then *you* parachute in smelling like bath salts.'

He inclined his head towards her.

'Is that what I smell like, Mara?'

Mara blushed.

'Um...'

'No parachute, though. Actually, I came by submarine.'

'Oh, how exciting!'

'Not at all. Nasty, smelly things, submarines.'

'Though you seem to have cleaned yourself up.'

160

He turned towards her again, restraining a smile, and she realized she had put her foot in it a second time. Examining his fingernails, which she noticed were manicured, he remarked, 'Užice looks civilized to me. Tito seems to have set himself up very nicely here. Shops, schools and railways. Political propaganda. One would think there was an election coming up.'

'Yes, we hardly know there's a war on.'

'When I have to strike out of here, I shall miss it, I'm sure.'

'You're leaving!' Mara gasped. 'When?'

'Unfortunately, Britain didn't send me here for a holiday.' He looked almost sad and Mara experienced a flash of pity. She decided she would ignore her forebodings, and he picked up her weakness like a flash.

'Well, you know,' he said, adding a trace of pathos to his voice, 'it could be any day.'

I was right, thought Mara, he is experienced with women.

'Oh, goodness!' She held out a hand. 'I ought to at least thank you for helping me.'

He shook it, as they stood in the small room that had abruptly developed an intimacy that she decided would be cruel to deny him. Poor fellow, he was leaving.

'Perhaps you would like to have dinner with me, Mara?'

'Dinner?'

'Standard operating procedure.'

'But, of course!' declared Mara stoutly. 'When?'

'Tonight? That local restaurant on the corner near the park?'

'Yes, they serve a wonderful rolled schnitzel.'

'For two?'

'I should think so.'

'Dessert?'

'Something sweet to finish off the evening, Mr Hudson.'

'And what shall we have afterwards?'

'Coffee?' suggested Mara. Just one dinner wouldn't hurt. He was so nice.

CHAPTER SIXTEEN

'So the British are here, are they?' thought Miroslav. 'How very interesting.'

Listening from behind the corner of the warehouse, he hadn't heard clearly the conversation between Mara and the tall British officer. Miroslav's German was quite good. He had studied it at school and in any case, German was frequently spoken in Croatia. He couldn't speak English very well (although he could read the newspaper), but he recognised the language the instant he heard it. Following Mara, it seemed, had brought some unexpected benefits.

It was apparent to him that the suave manners of the officer hinted at far more experience, and very possibly in unusual areas, than your average soldier off the street, but he hadn't seemed like a military man. Too self-aware. Miroslav wondered what he was. There were always foreigners in cities. Engineers, businessmen, diplomats, tourists. But for the British to be in a rural area recently liberated by the communists didn't sound like business interests to him. The man had been dressed as an officer but more on the casual side, rather like a field man. *He's jumped from an aeroplane, or landed from a submarine, although his manners indicate he's more accustomed to the office.*

Through Forests and Mountains

Watching the assured stance that suggested he was a lady's man, Miroslav wondered if Mara knew what she had got herself into. He wouldn't call the man a womaniser—a bit too sophisticated for that. Admired himself, obviously. (Being of that nature himself, Miroslav recognised the type.) Confident, cuff linked and upholstered, not easily thrown off balance, not even by the bucket of tears Mara had just showered all over him.

He watched them disappear together and knew it was a little early in the day for love, even by his own standards. *Where are they going?* The officer's manner was solicitous, almost kindly, but Miroslav wondered what expectations lingered beneath his façade. Briefly, he waged war between jealousy and the genuine interest of the investigative journalist before his professional side won, and he began to speculate what interest the British might have in this backwater. If they wanted to spy on the Germans, they ought to be in the cities.

It stood to reason that the conservative British government was diametrically opposed to communism in any form. Miroslav doubted, as well, that they had positive proof of partisan activities in a war that, for Yugoslavia, was only seven months old. So the communists had liberated one small area of Yugoslavia the minute the Germans turned their backs to invade Russia? Big deal. The Partisans may have captured Užice and its surrounding territory, but they had no big canons, no tanks, no air force, no navy and little experience as an organized army. It was early days yet and their headquarters must surely know this. What threat could they conceivably be to the Germans, and, therefore, of what interest to the British? Might it have something to do with Russia? Miroslav knew that the communist partisan leadership would expect aid from Moscow, although, with the Nazis in their backyard at the moment, he couldn't see it arriving in any hurry.

For two weeks now he had been lurking around the outskirts of Užice, clad in his oldest clothes to ensure he didn't draw undue attention to himself. He was masking his Zagreb accent by speaking as little as possible, carefully imitating the speech of the locals when he did. An educated man with a Zagreb accent was a dead giveaway in rural Serbia.

He had finally come across the leader, the one they called Tito. A common enough nickname in North Western Croatia but, in Užice at the present time, it was coated with something like allure. Miroslav heard it whispered in awed tones everywhere he went and it hadn't been too hard to piece together the puzzle, to determine who the man was. Now that the days were chilling with the approach of winter, he had seen the one people said was him, parading around the streets with his head in his great coat, like some latter day Napoleon. By his side was an Alsatian and, as he progressed, people would walk over and pat the animal, saying 'good dog, Tiger!', and pass the time of day with its master, who seemed cordial enough. Sometimes he tossed the dog a ball, sometimes he would hand it to one of his callers. But how to get a photo for the general back in Belgrade, so that his men knew who to capture?

Miroslav didn't care to put himself in any danger, so he could lie, of course, and say he hadn't found him. But he had eventually seen a picture in the free partisan newspaper, *Borba*, *The Struggle*, that came out every two days, with Tito's name in the caption. Miroslav immediately purchased a copy and took it home, where he sat upon his bed and stared at it intensely, as if it were a religious icon and he a zealous convert. The greatcoat was not in the image. Instead, Tito was portrayed as part of a group of men, war leaders clearly by their far-sighted gazes. The immediate impression of this mysterious communist was one of neatness and authority, as if he was on his way to an international conference instead of leading a motley group of farmers and peasants—who knew where. He was said to be charming. *Well, I can't speak from personal experience,* mused Miroslav, gloating at the image, *but he certainly takes himself seriously. I don't know that I would, if I were in his position. I think the whole thing's a bit of a joke, really—fancying oneself the leader of untrained men against the German army. The man has an attitude problem.* Did he have any idea what Užice was in for, once General Bőhme had his way with it? They'd blast it with everything they had, their heaviest equipment, the might of the Luftwaffe, the anger of the Führer, and they would slaughter to the last man. The Führer despised communists and anyone who opposed him, and the Partisans ticked both boxes.

The only foolproof way of getting the picture to the general would be to hand it to him personally, but now that Miroslav had found Mara, he had no intention of doing that. His wireless telegraphy officer was trapped at a small hotel on the outskirts of town, fearful of poking his nose outside the door, terrified of being labelled a spy and knowing full well what the communists would do to him if they found out. Miroslav kept forgetting to feed him, which didn't improve his mood. The man had been waiting impatiently for food all day and any titbits to relay back to the general's headquarters in Belgrade. He was a Serb, employed by the quisling Nedić government to send messages in German. Miroslav, whose first priority was to the Ustasha and its hatred of Serbs, could scarcely look him straight in the face, and was quite happy to let him suffer from hunger. He brought him back the bare minimum to eat and spent much of his time, otherwise, observing the technique of sending messages in Morse Code and learning how the machine operated. By this means, he had discovered that the Germans changed the cipher in which they sent their codes once a day, by the use of an intriguing machine, like a small typewriter, called an Enigma Machine. What a name! How Wagnerian. Why not just give it a number, like their submarines? That would conceal its purpose more effectively. Even he had been attracted to the gadget, merely because of its name. The British would have a field day with it, and he had just been in the process of learning how to use the machine, quicker than they could, when he had gone for a walk to stretch his legs and had the extraordinary luck of running into Mara.

He had run up the street, jumping on and off gutters for the sheer pleasure of exercise, stopping in at the baker's to satisfy his hunger, before deciding to investigate the German arms factory the Partisans had exploited since they'd liberated the city. It was here that he had come upon Mara in the arms of the British officer. She had laid her head on his shoulder and Miroslav could have killed her straight away, he was so angry at seeing her with another man. Had she been a village Serb in the Krajina region of Croatia where the Ustashas had done the most harm, he probably would have. But, no, he thought. He would allow her to enjoy her time with the competition and he would watch and wait until his jealousy built up to its bursting point, and see what he could learn in the meantime. It suited his vanity to allow this crescendo of emotions, for then he felt justified in doing anything, including some quite creatively violent acts towards her. Like an animal, he had blood lust in his scent. Wolves stalk patiently, thought Miroslav, and so do I.

He accosted her the minute she left Hudson's temporary office and crossed the street, a light smile turning the corners of her lips, and expressing feelings on her face far from hostile towards the English. Miroslav leapt out in front of her, seized one arm and dragged her back into the lane from where he had stood watch. The bag she had been carrying fell to the ground and he heard the smash of a bottle against the stone gutter. Gratifyingly, she didn't utter a sound as he rammed her up against a wall and pinioned her there with one hand clutched around her throat. Sheer anger at her actions warped his handsome features and made his eyes protrude until their whites bulged at her like twin moons.

'Been disobeying me again, I see!' he hissed.

Beneath his fingers, Mara could only gasp, 'What... what...?'

'Communists, Mara, communists.' Miroslav wagged a finger from his free hand in her face. 'You've been working with the enemy. I'm disappointed in you.' He tightened his grip, 'Very disappointed—as I informed your father.'

'My father, my father,' Mara choked, too terrified to struggle. 'Don't understand... Please, Miroslav... What are you doing here?'

'Looking for you.' He shoved a hand up her skirt. 'Why are the British here?'

'D-don't know.'

'Don't lie to me.'

The force of his hand quickly broke the two small buttons at the top of her knickers and he shoved his fingers down into the soft flesh between her thighs. How many times had she allowed him this intimacy but never any further? Never, never, never, letting him get what he wanted. His breathing built up with anger, and her eyes closed in the hope, he supposed, that soon it would be over. Had he had a free hand, he would have forced them open.

'Not... not lying. Wants to see what we're doing. That's all, Miroslav. I swear. Ow... ow! You're hurting me. Stop, please, stop.'

'Bitch,' he said.

Then he was pushing hard against her until his breathing came fast and urgent and he had pushed her spine into the cold wall.

'...Marko.'

Then suddenly he let her go.

'Did you enjoy that?' he panted, swiping perspiration from his forehead despite the cold afternoon. 'Marko. That his name? Well, touch Marko again and I'll kill you.'

Then he let her go and waited, feeling exhilarated and released, watching her stagger away from him and disappear around the corner.

*****

Bill Hudson could tell at a glance that dinner was going to end with coffee. Mara's breath came in short gasps, as if she had run all the way to the restaurant, though she could not run. She was walking oddly, had he known it, because Miroslav's fingernails had scraped the sensitive skin within her vulva. Looking back over her shoulder, her eyes were wide open and frightened but, most disturbing of all, Hudson saw a livid red mark around her throat.

'Mara, whatever is the matter?'

He extended a supportive hand beneath her elbow and lightly brushed a strand of hair from her face.

'He's here,' gasped Mara clutching the mark, as if she still remembered how it had choked her. 'I just don't know how he's found me.'

In the two hours since he'd last seen her, she had changed her clothes, made some attempt to cover her distress with powder and lipstick. But the sight of him, like a beacon in her distress, brought rushing back the details of an incident that had occurred since they had last met. She dived towards him with undisguised relief and began slowly to calm down, now that the run was over and she no longer had to face her fear alone.

'Come inside.' Hudson opened the heavy glass door. 'Come in and sit down.'

He stepped aside to allow her into the small restaurant of two white-clothed rows of tables and a bar at one end with a colourful array of herbal spirits, and snapped his fingers at a waiter who hurried down the single aisle, then spoke to the man in rapid Serbo-Croat. The waiter seated them at a table away from the window and very shortly brought three glasses, two shots of a local pear rakija and a glass of sweet dessert wine. Then he addressed Mara in English, as if he knew that in these circumstances the language would reassure her that she was safe.

'Now, if you drink the rakija,' he said. 'You will be following local custom, but I have it on good British authority that alcohol and sugar are effective remedies for shock.'

'Whose good British authority?' whispered Mara watching him through her lashes.

'Oh, my grandmother's,' he quipped airily and, despite her pain, Mara laughed.

'So you must be the best judge of these two opinions, Mara, by drinking at least one of them.'

'I'll have both,' she said. 'But this third one is for you.'

There was genuine concern in his tone, and she had been to many dinners with Miroslav, who had not half the consideration of this Englishman. He was very nice to gaze at across a white cloth—not white exactly but a light-ish beige, robust and obviously spun and woven locally, embroidered at one corner with the name of the establishment. They had laid a single rose in a vase between the two places set for dinner. Hudson didn't smoke; whether it was because he thought that Mara was half choked already and one cigarette might undo her ability to breathe at all, or whether it was because he was a non-smoker, she never found out. Too quickly, she consumed both drinks and now sat gazing cross-eyed at Hudson as if he was there and yet as if he wasn't.

'He was so lovely in the beginning,' she told him, musingly. 'He was charming and generous. I felt that I was blossoming in the relationship, that we were growing together. I see now that that was what he wanted me to believe, and that it flattered his ego.'

'Why did you stay?'

She sighed.

'Emotionally confused, I guess. Miroslav's really nice looking. I'd have this gorgeous guy telling me I was mistaken, even in things that didn't matter, like feeding the cat. You know, he once told me that I shouldn't iron my silk blouses when they were damp. I mean, who cares? He had to be on top all the time. I ended up doubting myself.'

They ate and she could see, from the slight distraction of his brows and an occasional flicker out of the window, that he had something on his mind. She asked him and his face grew serious.

'Mara,' he said. 'I predict that very soon the Germans will have reoccupied this town. They're not going to let a communist community go about its business under their noses. Every day they are getting closer. The only reason you're still here is that the Germans haven't had enough divisions in the country to commence an offensive. We've had warnings from London about the massive military build-up planned in Belgrade. The Luftwaffe, as well as the infantry and tanks divisions, will commence the final phase of their offensive and you are going to have to leave. Soon.'

'You don't think we can win?'

'No, I don't. And Tito is no fool. He will know that he can't win either. The skirmishes in the vicinity of the town in recent weeks have been small fry. Guerrilla fighters from

171

small villages can't defeat a determined German army. The Germans will burn anything that stands in their way and kill everyone. And so will the Italians and so will the Ustashas. And don't think that Tito, inspirational as he is, can control inexperienced peasants by telling them that he is creating a new world order. Your villagers will just go home, if they have homes left to go to. Tito will be lucky if his whole communist experiment doesn't fall apart.'

*****

The minute he watched the English officer leave his barracks and stroll away in the direction of the park, Miroslav hurried across and tried the door, still warm from his fingers. It was locked, of course. The building was a solid stone structure, its windows crisscrossed with iron bars of formidable strength, but he wandered around the back, where a driveway disappeared into a yard and his shoes scuffed on loose rocks, gravel and tufts of overgrown grass, and discovered a back entrance, also locked, but beside it a small glass window, this time bar-less. There was no one around, so Miroslav simply picked up a rock from the lane and threw it against the glass. It shattered, partly inwards and partly sending shards onto the ground. He cleared out the sharp glass that remained and climbed through.

A cold late autumn evening pulled the city into night. The day's bustle was ending. The streets darkened. People went home. In the pitch blackness, Miroslav wandered around for ten minutes, lighting one match after another to see his way, and finally came across a series of rooms that were given over to communication. He investigated three, then a fourth, which looked more hopeful due to a pile of code books in German and the Serbian Cyrillic text and a very old wireless telegraphy set that had clearly been stolen, for it was labelled in German. There were also two beds in the room, which, although neatly made, gave the appearance of having been slept in.

Fine, fine, thought Miroslav. *It looks like I'm getting somewhere.*

A similar set up existed in the fifth room but the books, in the yellow light from the match, were in English.

Ha! Got you!

The match burned down to his fingers and he dropped it. He lit another and had the good fortune to behold on the table in front of him a similar radio set, but much newer than the one stolen by the communists. Resplendent in a box of polished leather sat a head set, a Morse code key, a microphone, connecting cables and various dials and wires. Miroslav wasn't entirely sure which dials and cables operated what, but he was fairly confident he could work it out. *Very neat and tidy,* thought Miroslav surveying the set with interest. *Very British, in fact.*

One couldn't parachute in, carrying a set like these. The officer had arrived some other way. Submarine, probably. He closed the box and secured it, then, picking it up by its leather handle, stuffed as many code books as he could carry under his arm and strolled back down the corridor. Then he careful leaned out the window, laid the set on the ground, the books beside it, and climbed out, picked up his booty and returned to his own W/T operator.

Within the dim flat smelling of lard, sweat and cigarettes, his operator was tapping out the day's message to Belgrade enveloped in a pungent cloud of smoke. He turned his head as Miroslav came in but said nothing. Miroslav threw him a rind of ham and a loaf of bread, which the poor man pounced upon hungrily, then sat and watched him scoff it and return to his work. He had watched him many times, first getting the day's codes from his code book then operating his little Enigma cipher machine and finally adjusting his frequency and tapping out an entire message. Without clues of a cat-astrophic nature from Miroslav, all he sent day in, day out, were weather reports and, in the previous two days, phases of the moon and times when it rose and set. Why he did this was beyond Miroslav, who was certain the weather couldn't be much different here than in Belgrade, only 150 km away. He put it down to fanatical Germans having to be so exact about everything that they gave themselves ulcers.

He handed the operator the British code book and watched as the man flipped through its pages.

'This is a codebook,' said the operator rather obviously. 'The Germans can read these codes, I think.'

'Is that all the British have?' Miroslav asked him.

'No. I have heard that they also use a machine, like ours,' he tapped the Enigma machine. 'But I have never seen one.'

'Can you send a message to Britain on this?'

'You can send a message anywhere, if you know the fre-quencies they use. You don't even need to use the code. Just send it in plain language. I can do it for you.'

Miroslav handed across the leather box.

'I can do it myself now,' he said, opening it before him.

The man eyed the box with interest.

'The Germans will want to know why the British are here,' he said.

'Why one British officer is here,' corrected Miroslav with a wave of his hand. 'And he won't be sending them anything anymore, will he, because I've got it.'

'He'll want it back.'

'How? What is he, a fly on the wall? They've stolen a German one themselves.' He fingered the Morse key. 'What happens if I don't use a code?'

The operator was guarded.

'You can use plain language,' he repeated. 'I've known it done in emergencies. Just don't make a habit of it, if you want to be taken seriously.'

'I am serious,' snapped Miroslav. 'Show me how to use it.'

*****

Hudson walked Mara home after dinner and, when she saw him again the next afternoon, he was friendly but terse.

'What is it?' she asked.

He put a hand to his temple, as if to help him think.

'Nothing at the moment.'

'Mr Hudson, please…'

'Do you recall anyone following us yesterday or last night?'

Mara hesitated.

'Mara?'

'No,' she replied. She paused. 'Unless it was Miroslav? He saw us together.'

'We have had a burglary,' he explained quietly, shielding his voice by putting his face close to hers. No intimacy this time, only the hint of trouble. 'The wireless set and the code books that went with it.'

They stood at the street corner and Mara realized at once that she was horribly obvious to Miroslav.

'I can't stand here.' She stepped back.

Hudson shook himself. His mind had been on other things.

'Of course not.'

He drew her into a shop selling newspapers and tobacco yet, even here, he seemed reluctant to give exact explanations. This was war. This was spying.

'You don't have to tell me any more,' she whispered. 'It's all right.'

'Do you know where your boyfriend was staying?'

'No.'

'He gave no hint?'

'No, Mr Hudson.'

He stood reflectively, still polite and elegant, well-dressed but more evidently now a member of the British Secret Service. Its twin faces. Across the road a group of school children walked in lines, holding hands, like two rows of ducks. Their teacher glanced momentarily at the tobacconist's and walked on.

A yellowy haze hung over the town, reminding Mara that winter was nearly upon them. The trees in the park were bare; from a branch hovered a single lonely leaf, the remnant of summer. From above the solid building across the street appeared a white cloud, dirty at the base like a brush fire, white and puffy as it ascended. Traces of ash in the air. Once, she would have thought the fire very close, but she had learned by now that a skirmish could leave visible traces, even from a long way away.

'I wonder what that is?' she asked, for the scene stirred nerves in her chest. Like fluttering beetles, they would not be still.

'It's two things,' Hudson replied. 'Gun fire and a burning building.'

'Is it the Germans?'

'Can't be anything else at this stage. You and Aleksandra need to think about leaving, Mara.'

She stood by him, feeling his reassuring warmth, feeling dead in the pit of her stomach.

'Poor Aleksandra has already lost her home once. Couldn't you tell me about the burglary?'

He shook his head.

'It's not life and death. And I don't want to put you in any danger.'

176

No more to be said. He was silent on the issue and she thought that, though she had her teaching to keep her busy, how pleasant he had been in the midst of it all. She felt a fleeting sadness. *He has a life other than me. And I am the centre of my world. I had better remember that I am the ambassador's daughter.*

She held out her hand and he took it.

'Thank you, Mr Hudson, for dinner... and for everything. I guess I'd better be getting back. I have a class tonight.'

'Mara,' he said earnestly. He still held her hand. 'If it comes to the worst, stay with the main group. Keep close to Tito and his commanders. That way, we might have some chance of finding you. Good bye, for now.'

'Goodbye, Mr Hudson.'

Mara walked sadly back to the room she shared with Aleksandra. They ate and she took her class, with the girl in the front row learning fast. Before they went to bed, Mara began to pack for the exit that they must surely make soon. And, in that cold and bitter night, Aleksandra asked Mara why she was packing. Mara thought at first it was a bird. One of those that sing in the velvet night. On perceiving the little voice, so seldom heard, Mara felt a love in her heart for the orphan that she had not known fully until now.

'We have to leave, darling,' she said. 'The Germans are coming to take over the town. Now don't cry. Mr Hudson told me what to do.'

But it was Mara who cried. Losing her home yet again. She pulled her small pile of clothes from their shelf, ensured that they were packed in her rucksack without undue creasing and began to fold what little Aleksandra had, another blouse, a comb, two pairs of socks, a jumper they had given her in Drvar. Behind the door, two coats hung from pegs ready to be grabbed when the desperate haste arose. Then, in the deep misted night of that small room, they drifted together into such a despairing slumber that they no longer perceived the distant rumblings of the army coming towards them, nor had the clairvoyance to see the aeroplanes in far-away Belgrade preparing to bomb the rural location with the savagery it might have reserved for London.

Others, though, had had news of the approach, and in the morning the mood in Užice was tense. Mara, with Aleksandra beside her, methodically combed the outskirts of the town, armed with a pencil and paper, asking the guards and townsfolk who went in and out with their farm produce to the markets whether there had been a sighting of Miroslav. She had prepared a list of characteristics: a stranger, her height, well dressed, good looking, Zagreb accent, attitude of superiority. Her total tally for that tense and unhappy day was zero. No one had seen a thing. She showed them the bruises around her throat. They were sympathetic, but nevertheless returned her the same blank reply. For the first time since she had known the journalist, Mara began to feel superstitious—a nasty crawling feeling that shifted her eyes constantly from side to side. She made sure that she and Aleksandra were never alone, and each day, when the pallid winter sun sank behind the council buildings, she engaged the services of two brawny pig farmers to accompanying them to their lodgings.

By the 28th November, the Germans had freed the lines of communication they relied upon and begun to close in on Užice. Three forces approached from the north, north-west and east, their tanks and motorized infantry divisions scorching the countryside in retribution for the insurgents who had dared to fly their flag in the face of the Swastika. They came, destroying villages and slaughtering men, women and children as they went. Reprisal was in the air and panic-stricken villagers descended on Užice, but, before

Tito could give the order to evacuate, the Luftwaffe arrived in the dim pre-dawn, a repeat of the horror Mara had known in Belgrade. Unwilling to leave immediately, unsure whether the lonely road was a safer alternative to remaining, as she had in Belgrade, Mara huddled with Aleksandra in the cellar of their building while bombs rained down around them. By the time the noise had deafened them, dust and smoke had choked their airways and they had realized the imperative of leaving, escape was almost impossible. The sun had long ago disappeared; the night was well advanced. They staggered out into a twisted wreckage of rubble and iron and shattered tiles. Flames roared up into the sky. Frightened families, like them, had little idea of the safest course to take. Impossible to realize that the ferocity had consumed the day and, like a wreckage, had escaped to find peace beyond the horizon.

A man struggled past, hauling a small handcart of possessions. Behind him, his wife and children wept and tripped and struggled and mourned.

He stopped when he saw the bewildered girls.

'You've got to leave, girls!' he hissed urgently.

'But where?' gasped Mara.

'Follow us,' he said, 'into the mountains.'

'But I don't have anything,' Mara returned desperately. 'I don't have food or water.'

'And you'll have even less once the Germans walk in. You've got to leave *now*. Come with us.'

Aleksandra did not need a second prompting, and Mara hurried after her, out of the city, over the river and into the hills that lapped the town. She did not look back. A trail of families and peasant soldiers accompanied them, but not the number she would have expected.

'Where is everybody?' she asked the father with the cart.

'Either fighting or gone home.'

'Home?'

'They won't leave their homes to fight for Tito and they won't turn communist. It's their homes they want... or they'll be hiding somewhere in the woods.'

Mara and Aleksandra did not walk quickly. In the pitch black, familiar faces melted into the visages of strangers, but the tall girl and her small companion had been a familiar sight, and everybody who had a child at the school, as well as the young mothers who attended Mara's evening classes, knew their silhouettes. They walked so slowly that many refugees passed them. At length, Mara felt a strong hand on her forearm. She jumped from her reverie and turned. It was Ivan, one of the men on patrol at the eastern gate.

He didn't waste words.

'I think I saw that man you were after, Mara, passing out into the countryside a night or so ago. I didn't notice when you asked me at first but, afterwards I wondered, "Was that Mara's man?"'

'Yes?' gasped Mara.

'Well, he was dressed like everyone else, so I forgot about him, but later I got to think, no locals scan the road ahead of them looking for trouble. And that's what he was doing, taking us all in. And he was carrying a wooden box about the size of a small suitcase.'

Mara stopped.

'Oh, what have I done?'

She turned immediately and headed towards the town, followed by Aleksandra.

Ivan gasped.

'Mara, you can't go back!'

'It's all my fault,' she called over her shoulder. 'Ivan, did you see Marko?'

'Well, I know a lot of Markos,' remarked Ivan with peasant resignation. 'Please, Mara, think about what you're doing.'

'I promise I won't do anything stupid,' she gabbled.

'You already have.'

'But I feel so dreadful. I'll just see if I can find Marko then I'll catch you up, Ivan, I promise. Is anyone still there?'

'The commanders haven't left yet.'

'And Tito?'

'He's still there.'

'Then I can go.'

'No, Mara, you can't....'

But already she had gone.

CHAPTER SEVENTEEN

Anton drew back into the trees. 'I don't like the look of that.'

At first the distant orange glow had seemed like a summer scrub fire, except that it was winter. It was, perhaps, five kilometres away and, in the prescient darkness before first light, they were only able to see the trunk of the flames that reached upwards, like an umbrella pine the colour of smoked cod. As he studied the scene further, he detected an amber radiance in the sky that was fire, reflected upon a cloud of its own making.

'That's Užice, Nikola. I'm sure of it. And it's been burning for some time.' One usually came down the hill and over the river, past the ruins of the Old Town and into the new. 'But we won't be doing that now.'

Weary from a night's walking, Nikola sat down with a heavy thud upon a bush that would not hold his weight.

'That wasn't the rock I thought it was,' he said as it collapsed beneath him.

'What did Erik say?'

'That that was the Partisan republic.' Nikola scanned the sky dismally. 'Germans! Can't leave well enough alone. So much for our safe haven.'

'I might be wrong,' said Anton.

'But...'

'But I don't think so.' He stretched and sat down beside Nikola. Behind them Slobodan and Boško sent them hungry looks. 'Dawn's coming.'

'How do you know?'

'Because I'm a sailor.'

'I'd like to challenge that but I can't see my watch.'

They prized themselves up and trod cautiously down towards a broad tree trunk by the road. From time to time, a thin trail of people passed by, fixed faces, one step after the other, not daring to look behind, only wanting to put as much distance as possible between them and the inferno before daylight. Eventually, Nikola squeezed out from behind his tree and laid one kindly hand on the shoulder of a traveller, who seemed barely able to speak from fear and shock.

Brushing Nikola aside, the man cried, 'It's a catastrophe! Fucking communists! Look what they've done! Look what they've done!'

He burst into tears and commenced running up the road as it wound into the trees, glancing back once towards the burning town and then hurrying on.

Anton, Slobodan and Boško came to stand beside Nikola. For some time, they remained watching as face after tortured face struggled past them up the hill. Even now, some turned aside into the forest, as if the day might come early and rob them of the night's friendly shelter. As dawn approached and the eastern sky lightened, they heard the low drone of aircraft. With a note of urgency, the crowd surged along afresh, and they went with it, increasing their pace with the flow until, along the fleeing path of refugees, they noticed two young women, one tall and one shorter, struggling against the tide, apparently in an effort to return to the beleaguered city. Nikola shook his head.

'Some people!' he said, and pushed across the flow.

*****

When the large, homespun farmer bowled her over, Mara was too intent on her task to see him coming. She lost her footing in the collision and would have overbalanced into the mud, had he not placed two meaty hands on her shoulders and straightened her up. By her side, Aleksandra stopped.

'Other way,' instructed Nikola.

'No, no!' Mara struggled against him. 'I have to get back. He's lost his radio.'

'It'll turn up,' said Nikola, swiveling her around and pointing her in the opposite direction.

Boško nodded to Mara, doing her best to wriggle out of Nikola's grip.

'Tata is known for his optimism,' he commented.

'There's no use struggling, honey,' pursued Nikola. 'You're not returning to Užice and I shouldn't have to explain why. Whoever he is, he will have to do without his radio.'

'Tell your father not to call me honey!' Mara snapped angrily at Boško.

'Then, do you have a name, miss?' he replied.

'My name's Mara,' she told him. She didn't want to defer to Nikola. He was not nearly as exciting as the dashing Captain Hudson, and his efforts to forestall her advance into enemy territory rather spoiled her memories of being embraced by a man. 'And this is Aleksandra.'

'Well, good day to you, Mara.' Despite her annoyance, Nikola continued to push her along with the hustling crowd. 'And to you, Aleksandra. I'm Nikola Mugoša. These are my sons, Boško and Slobodan, and that dark monstrosity over there is Anton Marković.'

Mara glared across from beneath Nikola's hand and saw two tall, lean boys and another man who walked rapidly be-

184

side them holding his right arm at an awkward angle, as if he wasn't sure what to do with it.

'The radio is British,' she insisted. 'It's very important.'

'If it's that important, someone else will have it by now,' said Nikola, striding onwards.

'That's exactly why I have to get back!'

Immediately, the man with the funny arm confronted her.

'Why are the British here?' he demanded.

Mara shook her head.

'I can't tell you because he said he was a spy.'

Nikola burst into a great roar of laughter and laughed so much that he let Mara go, although his warmth on her arm remained.

'How many other people have you told?' he chuckled.

'Well, I don't see what's so funny,' said Mara with offended dignity. 'Poor Captain Hudson, and now his radio's been stolen, all because of me!'

Nikola wiped his eyes.

'His name's Hudson?'

'Marko,' subsided Mara. 'He said to call him Marko, except in private.'

Nikola exchanged glances with Anton.

'Then perhaps that's how you'd better refer to him from now on.'

*****

The rivers of Serbia wind through forested gorges like lazy aqua snakes. They're not self-conscious about their beauty and, though the mountains they pass seem desolate, yet they are replete with millennia of human witness, of copper and bauxite and human symbols older than the Fertile Crescent. Though a stranger might succumb to the insanity of isolation, the mountains divided by these waterways are not a mystery to the people of Serbia. They merely separate one village from another. To evade capture by the Germans, the great arc of refugees walked by night, through this ancient landscape, up and over the mountains into Bosnia. Two tortuous nights and, at the end, a slow drift down the other side.

As the twilight deepened on the second night, the common sense that had served Mara so well until now faltered in this primitive place and fear had come to keep her company amongst the black boughs. *What's out there, now that the sun has set?* A snap in the forest was a threat, for the day gave warmth and a cheerful heart, and the night was sinister without it. Mara pulled herself together. The night is an absence of light, that's all. But men hate the light because their deeds are evil. *Now what had Christ meant by that? What did he mean by evil?* For it was not manmade evil she feared here, nor the fiend of her imagination that whispered in her ear: 'Shut out the night. Draw your curtains and pray that God will lighten your darkness.' *Then what is it I fear? I fear wild animals. I fear the dogs that tear and kill. Yes, but I fear, too, the ill-defined and the unknown. I can't help it. These people with whom I walk don't fear the spirits of this land because they belong to the earth. Perhaps there is something in the old stories after all.*

The wind was rising. The coat of wool, stiffened with buckram and lined with silk that Mara's father had bought her from Belgrade and that had formerly kept her cosy, seemed like the thinnest muslin and offered no protection from the wind, the sleet and the biting cold. She was so cold that she was sure her arms and legs were bathed in ice and that a motor had been switched on inside her. Rather than drive her forward, its valves and gears established a violent shivering deep within her body that would not ease. She rubbed her arms so that the friction on her skin might suggest warmth where there was none. Onwards and upwards.

186

Margaret Walker

Fir trees began to replace the oak and beech, whose leaf-less branches had provided no shelter. Mara imagined her-self sleeping forever on their generous branches, a warm sleep upon a mattress of needles and the scent of pine sooth-ing her rest, but the clouds above them sank like portentous cocoons and, sure enough, the sleet soon changed to eddies of snow. White in the grey air, they looked like ash from a forest fire. But the forest was not burning. Instead, the lonely mountain passes loomed in a great, omnipresent blackness above her, bathing her in such loneliness that, for all the companionship, Mara experienced a detachment from her-self and was, for the first time, frightened of death, for she felt that she had forsaken the roots that bound her to the earth.

She did not doubt that there was a link between this de-tachment and her fear of wild animals with their keen sense of smell and their sensitivity to the metaphysical. Her fear was drawing them in. Hungry eyes watched the slow train of refugees and singled her out for consumption. She made a renewed effort to keep up and to stand strong beside the men. Wolves never attack the leaders, she reasoned, it's mostly children and weak women like me. *It had been a hungry winter, and at twilight the wolves came stalking through the village. Poor Mara had just stepped out to re-lieve herself...* She imagined she heard a howl, and dragged Aleksandra closer beside her, until they were walking be-tween Nikola and Slobodan, who didn't seem in the least concerned.

Visibility was dropping fast. It was nearly impossible to see, except for the snow reflecting the light from its own clouds. Mara took Aleksandra's hand and, with her free hand, grabbed Nikola's coat so that when his silhouette was lost in the night, she would still know that he was there. From being an irritation, he had swiftly become a stalwart

187

comfort, and she half admired him and his sons, for they were clearly much tougher than she was and accepted the discomforts as something to be endured without complaining.

But I'm so cold. I'm so cold.

They had reached the top of the present incline when Mara, pushed to her limits to keep up with the men, vomited by the side of the track. As she had eaten nothing for twenty-four hours, she brought up only bile and bubbles of phlegm, and the entire unpleasant mixture cooled from the heat of her body and began to solidify on the rocks.

'You need food,' said Nikola.

Mara swiped her hand across her mouth where traces of bitter vomit still lingered.

'I'm cold.'

From this height, the light dusting of snow faintly illuminated the outline of the hill crest on which they waited, and the dismembered line of men and women who trailed along it seemed like black ants who had lost their way to the nest. Some trudged in larger groups, others singly, hurrying to catch up lest they lag behind and lose the main body.

Nikola stood watching them reflectively.

'They'll have to rest sometime.'

He took off his coat and laid it on Mara's shoulders.

'Oh, no, Nikola, no!' she protested, handing it back to him. 'I can keep going. I can. I can.'

Nikola nodded and looked far ahead to where a group appeared to slow. Raised hands gave the impression of seeking a temporary shelter.

'All right,' he said. 'When they stop, we'll light a fire.' He prodded the track with his rifle. 'Have you noticed the animal droppings? There's hares around and they're night feeders. I'll get you something to eat.'

Margaret Walker

They trudged on until they met the main group, already moving off the road, and sat in the new snow under the specious protection of a spindly spruce, for the wind agitated its branches and there were vast holes in its canopy. Nikola made a fire—no one had matches, but he kindled one anyway—and some more from the long arc neglected their march to rest with them around the blaze. It was no rest, really. With only leafless trees to cover them that first day, they had still been bombed.

Fear, cold, hunger. The people groaned and bemoaned their fate. They were not tortured—they were the lucky ones who had escaped—but they saw in their imaginations the intentions of the torturers. Around the fire, they sat in a tight circle so that when its blaze was reflected in their eyes they seemed to each other like ghouls with burning pupils. One woman had pulled her beautiful hair from beneath its headscarf. It fell upon her face and she writhed it through her fingers as though she would tear it out. Farther around the circle, an old woman with hands raised upwards beseeched heaven to save them. Mara was too cold to pray, but she must trust that God could hear thoughts as well as words. Children were crying from hunger and thirst. 'Water! Just give me a drop of water!' The babies bit their own arms. Soon they would cry themselves to sleep. For distraction from the horror, Mara stared at the fire and saw only the flames sucking in oxygen, burning anything it could lay its hands on. Fire was the best and the worst. It warmed and yet it consumed and, as Mara thawed her hands, she was aware of its duplicitous nature. Grey smoke in coils rose up and melted the snow, for the fire, like the wolves, was a hungry predator. The great forest stretched out from their sanctuary in all directions and she could see no end to it.

Nikola disappeared into the trees and Mara didn't even notice, nor did she wonder how he could hunt in the dark.

She had some memory of the stories her mother had told her about her grandfather, how the cook had prepared food for him so that he could go hunting at night, but she'd never asked how he could see to shoot. His dog could see, perhaps, and her grandfather would just aim the rifle. When Nikola returned holding two dead hares by their ears, the night had progressed, strengthening its hold over her, weaving in and out of the canopy of cloud, moving onwards towards the dawn. No sound, only mountain silence and the crackle of the blaze; no feelings save for the intense cold. Mara shivered until her eyes no longer focussed. The lowering clouds were white and full of snow, spreading their authority over the whole sky. The single star over a southern peak was chased away, and it vanished.

Nikola skinned the hares and impaled them on sticks, twisting them over the flames. Even he was shivering now.

'It's a two dog night,' he said. 'And I left the two dogs at home. Here, Boško, Slobodan! Snuggle up to the girls and no molesting.'

Nikola's sons shot him a look that indicated that they didn't know how to molest a woman. It was his fault, he hadn't taught them. They shuffled along the line, and where they had sat, they left a light imprint of their bodies in the snow. Mara was glad at the warmth of their flesh, but she saw the empty sky and watched the wounds of their companions reflected in the flames—dried blood, bruised faces—and she tried not to give way to despair. She sat only, clutching Aleksandra to her left side next to Boško, rubbing into the rough jacket of Slobodan, nestling into his shoulder on her right, staring at his boot laces, at his muscular young hands held towards the flames and, despite herself, inched closer, to remind herself that life sat beside her, tall and warm and vigorous. She felt his thigh, this generous stranger, and without reflection, threw off her scruples about young males and just wanted to be near him. Death, trying to get in, failed this one time, and went off to its own place until a time, a time and half a time. Sensing its rage at the biblical span, Mara shivered from fear and cold and resolutely closed her eyes.

The hares proved tough old mini-beasts and, when finally the flesh began to fall from their bones, Nikola handed them each a small leg, dividing the flesh of the bodies among their companions. The fat ran down the meat and dripped onto her coat but, when she had finished eating, the urge to vomit repeatedly had passed.

The fire was getting smaller now. Its glowing husks of charcoal burst from the logs like bright flowers, sizzled in the falling snow and died.

'We'll be snowed in if it gets any heavier,' said Nikola, rising. 'Time to get going.'

Mara struggled to her feet, regretting Slobodan's lost shoulder, for the cold rushed in to take its place. But there must have been an angel in their world that night and the snow, heeding the ministering spirit, held off until the sky greyed, the long night hours were over, and shortly after sunrise, they entered a town called Rudo, clustered within the descent from the high mountains. By that time Mara had ceased to function. In her head, she heard the purr of a tide that ebbed and flowed. Surely, it was her heartbeat made sluggish by weariness and cold, the herald of her collapse or the flapping of wings?

The angel, who had been poised for fight, perceiving that Mara had heard but not seen him, flew off, and Mara might have been able to watch the curve of his wing gain height above the first sunbeams, had not her eyes become repositories of exhaustion. She drew some out; a saleable commodity?

'Look, here in my hand is a kilo of collapse. How much can I expect for this?'

Lost in exhaustion, everyone ignored her.

'But that tree...' She had stumbled past it and, turning a head she no longer recognized as her own, observed a brown trunk, lichen like oxidised silver, a lone leaf threaded precipitously from a branch. The tree moved towards her, stopped while she regarded it and then moved back to its accustomed place. 'That tree.'

'Yes, miss?' replied Slobodan.

Mara waved a confused hand in his face.

'It moved.'

'Which tree?'

'The one we just passed.'

She didn't think Slobodan understood what she was trying to say. In any case, they had passed a lot of trees.

'Once when I was very tired,' she explained to him, 'I saw the word "elbow", and I thought, that's not how you spell "elbow".'

'Yes, miss.'

She could tell he was trying to be polite.

'Well, that's what I mean about the tree.' She turned to him crazily. 'Slobodan, can you read?'

'Yes, miss, I can read, and I can spell "elbow".'

*****

Mara slept, squashed into the straw on the beaten earth floor of a half-timbered barn by a river. Aleksandra's nose pressed into her shoulder and Boško's gentle snoring brushing the hair on her forehead.

A foot hit her in the head and she woke up. In a half dream, she lay there, listening to Boško breathe in and out and the bitter wind moan down the mountain. Not far away she heard water lapping and imagined ships of cloud racing across the sky, wondering if they were setting sail to transport them all to a safe haven. Around her, the refugees slept on, an ocean of unfamiliar faces, seared with struggle, exhausted by the distances they had trekked and the constant presence of danger while, through a crack in the door, the stars shone and she looked up to their calm reassurance, believing that, as they were always there, then so would she be, somewhere in some time.

The German assault against Užice had brought back the horrors of the Belgrade bombing and what it meant to be at war. Yes, life had gone on in the capital afterwards because life had to, and in Užice she had felt a measure of safety, but, as the harsh winter of those regions approached, Mara pondered the realities of being once more a homeless refugee. The knowledge that such ruthlessness as she had seen existed shocked her and galvanised a strength for revenge that she didn't know she had. The sheer brutality of the Axis advance and the pagan values it had brought with it had changed her.

The urge to fight back... now, that was the crux of the matter. Revenge, once a theoretical concept she had only heard about from the pulpit, was talked about amongst these people without confession or forgiveness. What about Aleksandra? Would she kill to avenge her family? Could one forgive the Ustasha? Could one ever understand a German? Would the Allies convict the Italians for their war crimes? The Hungarians? The Bulgarians? Did one organise an offensive or did one cower? Did one put off the decision until one had shelter and warmth and arms, then simply wait for matters to unfold? What, in fact, was the correct route forward for her? You fight this evil or you have no future, they told her. Now, given the chance, she knew that she could, without a qualm of conscience, and she longed to be allowed the opportunity. But not yet. Mara whispered to the night that she would be ready when the time came, and the river replied in murmurs.

Through Forests and Mountains

Pushed by the point of a weapon, the shambling barn door creaked slowly open and Nikola's terse friend stepped into the crush of bodies. He laid a rifle against a cross post, removed a blanket he had wrapped around his shoulders, refolded it into a double triangle and tied the two points in a knot across his chest. He'd taken it upon himself to stand on sentry duty outside and she had seen him patrolling the peripheries with one of Nikola's weapons slung over his left shoulder, his face set and his eyes looking from right to left, peering into the distance. His black hair mixed into the darkness so that his broad face stood out like bone china below it.

The former arrangement of the blanket, Mara imagined, had not adequately kept out the bitter mountain cold. *He's had a better idea, so now he's stepped inside, where the sleeping bodies have marginally raised the temperature, to reposition it more effectively.* His body was silhouetted in the crack of the door and the faint starlight, and she saw that, though not the tallest of the Serbian men, he appeared so from a distance, resembling rather a pillar than a trained soldier from a military background. (She had decided upon a military history for him because he seemed to know what he was doing.) His clothes hung loosely on him and his trousers were bound in by his belt, so that he had acquired a concavity between his shoulders and his hips, but there was a fragility about him, in addition, that didn't suit such a big man, and she thought that he must be recovering from some illness. That would explain it, she decided. She could define the ridge of his scapular, even through the back of his jacket, as he repositioned the blanket. His shoulders were far too broad for his slender body, the right one lacking the muscle mass she would have expected. This particular night, he held that right arm in a sling, although he hadn't, back there on the trail. She thought that perhaps it was hurting, and this explained the need for support. In the soft starlight, she watched him remove the sling in order to exercise the limb. In his relief of having it off, he first flexed and un-flexed his arm, rotated the shoulder forward and backward, then in a methodical manner, repeated the exercises in the same order. She saw him retrieve a brick from the floor of the barn and lift it a dozen times, bringing the hand towards his shoulder and back.

It seemed to Mara that the limb may have been mechanically unsound and that the man was developing a new way of using it, peculiar to himself. A couple of times he frowned, then quickly got to work again, and she imagined that he had rebuked himself for a shortage of perseverance. Eventually he put the brick down and started practising with the rifle. When he held the gun in the right arm, the fingers performed adequately, but the strength of the arm itself let him down and she noticed that, once or twice, he moved the apparatus to his left arm and practised that way. Well, a left-handed gunner should confuse the enemy, she thought, and then considered that she didn't really know. She was cold and uncomfortable and flattened, like they all were, packed together in the barn. Even sleeping on straw, the ground was hard and her back hurt whenever she rolled over. The cold rose up from the beaten earth and the odds of getting back to sleep seemed slight, so she spent half an hour creating a suitable history for this military man, introduced to her as Anton Marković, but about whom she knew nothing.

He was a pilot. He had been shot down in the countryside north of the Danube, defending Belgrade from the Germans, and some cunning peasant had concealed all six feet three of him in a *baza* lined with truck tyres, and revived him on poppy cakes and rakija. He was a member of the Royal Yugoslav Army, injured in the shoulder after a battle with the sadistic Ustashas, who had first opened fire on his right arm to disable him and then mutilated what remained. He was a member of an anti-tank regiment, an air gunner with the navy, an engineer in a submarine, a decoder of secret information. He was a mountaineer, a member of a heroic Alpine division. He had landed on the shoulder, having miraculously survived an avalanche. He was a priest in disguise, a double agent sent by the bishop to drive the faithless communists back into the arms of the church. He was a Turk. He was a Jew hiding from the Nazis. He was a fortune telling gypsy—a very large Albanian.

And so on.

As she watched, he began to speak with one of the men beside him, who had clearly woken as she had. The man raised himself up on one elbow. A family man, with a wife and a child only, clutched too tightly to him as they slept that cold, quiet night.

'You are too thin, comrade,' the man whispered up to Anton. 'But you have a good heart, standing sentry for us.'

Mara saw Anton stoop down.

'What's your name?' he asked the man softly.

'We are Milošić, I, my wife and my son. We come from a village outside Užice.'

'Then why didn't you go home with the others?'

'The fascists set our house on fire. I was in the fields with the herds and the shepherd dogs when my children were burned, like roast meat. I saved my wife and one child. Blood and gunpowder hang over the mounds where my children lie dreaming, comrade. My land is enslaved, while you and I march on in bleak poverty.' He squeezed his lips from fury. 'My soul, already austere, has become much stronger after this evil, but bitterness has tightened my heart.'

Next to him his wife moaned in her sleep and he stroked her hair.

Margaret Walker

'We are heroes of the new age, a force that will destroy the fascists on their throne and wipe their black blood from our land. We are the bright hope that will lead our people forward and, even if I die fighting for it, I will smile from my grave. *Smrt fasizmu!*'

'Death to fascism,' replied Anton.

'And freedom to the people!'

CHAPTER EIGHTEEN

Bosnia in winter. A thick mantle of snow hid the black land, compressing the fields and hills until whole valleys appeared levelled. Wooden tiles on the steep-roofed farmhouses peeped from beneath piles of snow. As far as Anton could see, the land had been silenced by a great white hush, except for the birds. Flustered little creatures. In the intense cold they shot from house to house, looking for seeds. They perched on the window sills, pecking. Their hard beaks ground and crushed, ground and crushed, until immediately they flew off, looking for more. They stopped, twisted and turned, bent, ground and flew away. Over and over. Like the birds, the refugees and fighters who had chosen to follow Tito had been billeted as far as possible in farms, barns and villages, but there was not enough food to go around, though plenty of wood to burn. The Partisans bought what food they could, and already word was going around that any man caught stealing food would be shot.

Rudo itself was a town on the river Lim, where the deep mountain gorges dived into the water and the sheer white cliffs rose above. The main stream had not frozen over but the village was as white as everywhere else, and here, a handful of days before Christmas 1941, Tito and his staff had handpicked the very first brigade of proletarian troops from the best of the Serbian and Montenegrin fighters who had remained loyal to them. The brigade held over one thousand people, male fighters and several score of women who would form the rear support of nursing, cooking and attending to their needs. Though still reliant on the guerrilla tactics of harassment and surprise, it represented a break from the Yugoslav tradition of local fighting. Now the Partisans had an organized and mobile force that could travel and fight anywhere it was needed.

The day following its formation, the First Proletarian Brigade fought their initial battle against the Italians. Watching them march out of Rudo in the company of their commander, Spanish civil war veteran, Koča Popović, Anton was torn between interest in the creation of something new and his sense of detachment, which was largely concerned with the feeling that he had reached this point by accident. Popović was roughly his own age, but there was nothing accidental about the respect he commanded in the eyes of his troops. Though a cynical observer might comment that they were nothing more than rows of recruits with scarcely more experience than village skirmishes, yet their gaze upon their leader made Anton pause and reflect for, as their eyes were focussed, so was their line straight and their discipline earnest. Aside from an army side cap, the men were dressed in anything they could find to keep the cold at bay. Some wore overcoats; others did not. Some had boots while their neighbours wore only shoes and bound their calves with rags. In fact, none of the uniform was uniform and this was their most distinguishing feature. In their midst was the flag with the Partisan Star, the symbol of the struggle of the National Liberation Movement of Yugoslavia.

This patchwork army was invigorated by Tito's stride as he had completed his inspection. Anton supposed it was a stride of belief, and he thought, well, if Tito believed enough in this experiment he was creating and had the ability to pass on that belief to others, then surely, that was half the battle won. He had been told, 'Tito is father, mother, affection, everything. The son of our people.' That was obviously hero worship and Anton decided he would reserve his judgement until he could tell whether the communism that had faltered after Užice could indeed lead to the death of fascism and bring freedom to Yugoslavia because of their belief in this man.

'The typical German tactic is encirclement,' Koča Popović reminded his men. 'They will try to surround you and kill everyone within that circle. But Germans don't like surprises, and it is to your advantage to remember that. They make their rules and they stick to them. They have superior numbers and, in this offensive, they also have Italian and Ustasha support. Because they are large and have cumbersome tanks and equipment, it will slow them down if you destroy bridges and block roads. Don't allow yourself to be a target for this enemy. Don't stand and fight to the last man. Concede ground. Get out of the circle. Capture whatever you can: weapons, ammunition, food, clothes, prisoners. We will be back and in the meantime, we will spread the revolt and the message of the People's Liberation Army to new areas. Through our forests and mountains, we live in an ideal country for guerrilla warfare. This, above all, remember.'

Anton was aware that the drive to ground the Partisans in communism had not been successful. After the fall of Užice, Tito and the rear guard had been chased across Zlatibor Mountain from Serbia into Bosnia by the 342nd Infantry Division of the German Wehrmacht, which was notorious for its brutally. Savage burnings and shootings in retribution followed. Nine thousand hostages were shot and seventeen villages burned, and the communists were held partly responsible for the slaughter. The rhetoric of Moscow meant little or nothing to the battered mass of refugees whose villages had been burned, whose loved ones had been blinded, beheaded, raped and slaughtered by the Ustashas or taken out and shot by the Germans and the Italians. They could never agree that communism had benefited workers. In order to liberate the country militarily, the Partisan staff was forced to follow a new route, to gain the confidence of the peasants. Now Tito strove to recruit them to the resistance by empathising the pan-national movement that was replacing the old regional boundaries, and was inclusive of all faiths, drawing for its inspiration on the tradition of epic Yugoslav sagas. It recreated Yugoslavia in a way that the previous Serbian monarchy had been unable to do.

However, a convicted communist proved hard to keep down. Anton could not help overhearing the young communist women arguing unwisely with the peasants. In a community of subsistence farmers, the debate made little headway past work roles but, just because peasants toiled hard all their lives, it didn't mean that they didn't enjoy a spirited argument.

'Lenin? Who's he?'

'Lenin was the man who wanted men and women to be equal,' explained the communists.

'In rural Yugoslavia,' the peasant women replied. 'There are very few jobs that women aren't expected to do, so we think equality between the sexes has been around for a while. There are, in addition, specific female jobs that a man can't do because he can't do them well enough: cook, clean, sew, knit, spin and weave, for starters. In fact, what good are men anyway? Once the gloss of marriage wears off, they do nothing but saddle women with more mouths to feed. Watch that light in his eyes—baby on the way. Now take, as an example, Mrs Tito senior. It is said that Tito had a lot of respect for his mother. What was her name? Marija, that's it. Fifteen babies, lost eight; seven survived. Proud, strong, religious. Husband? Subsistence farming was too hard for him, evidently. Took to the bottle when the cabbage ran out. Who did all the work? She did. Dead at fifty-four. Typical.'

'You talk a lot,' declared the communists.

'Yes, we like to talk. Now what else do you have for us?'

'Education! The old empires of Russia, Austria and Turkey have fallen and a new communist order of proletarians has replaced them that will make our world a place that benefits all, not just the privileged few. However, awareness that their world has changed is slow in coming to the wealthy. The evil landlord who lives across the valley says that "educated peasants make poor workers". From birth to death, your life is work, in order not to starve, and that's the way he likes it. When you are hungry, from his fat table, he calls, "let them eat books!".'

The peasants agreed.

'We want our children to be educated, but who will pay for the school? The state? The landlord? In Tito's village, the people had to pay for it themselves, even when they were starving. That was fifty years ago and Yugoslav women are still illiterate, yet well-off visitors are in raptures. How charming is your village!'

The communists agreed.

'To the bourgeois artist, there is nothing lovelier than spring in a village. As the harshness of the winter passes into recent memory, as the snow melts and engorges the mountain streams, as the orchards of white blossoms bear fruit that rounds into the small, deep blue plums to be turned into slivovitz, the apple orchards captivate their minds with flowers. The sheep bear spring lambs, the pregnant cow finally gives birth, and the white washed houses of wood and mud nestle in a countryside of quite extraordinary beauty.'

Margaret Walker

The peasants crossed their arms to express what they felt about all this.

'Yes, it is easy for an artist to be nostalgic in spring,' they pointed out. 'But it is a difficult time to feed a family, because everything is waiting. The fruit is waiting to form, the wheat is waiting to be harvested. What you have left to eat is the produce from last season that remains after the winter. If last year was a bad harvest, you'll starve, and so will your family. It's all very well to rely on education to liberate the lower classes, but our men rely on the women to keep them alive. They say that education for women is not important. These goals, which your communist party claims are yours, have been self-evident to us for many generations. We care little for communism or empire. Men and women can never be truly equal in a village, therefore communism has failed. Let us argue the existence of God, at least that's something we're sure of.'

CHAPTER NINETEEN

Once the Germans had received word, in January 1942, that the Partisans and Bosnian Chetniks were reforming in Eastern Bosnia with local divisions, they began a further offensive, designed to eliminate the resistance movement they believed would not happen. At this time, Nikola was sixty, Tito nearly fifty, Anton thirty-two and Mara twenty-four. Slobodan and Boško were twenty and eighteen respectively and Aleksandra had turned seventeen during the last week. Nikola dearly wanted to return home to Montenegro, from where he had heard gratifying rumours that his experience as a traditional war leader was required. However, the second German offensive presently in progress made the journey a risky proposition, and he contented himself with his role as self-proclaimed advisor on Montenegrin guerrilla tactics. As it was likely that he and his sons were soon to be organised out of any tradition by the progressive communist party, it appeared to him that his primary objective now consisted of being true to himself, and this he immediately commenced upon, with all the resolution at his command.

Mara became increasingly annoyed at seeing only males with guns. Unlike Nikola, she did not value tradition, and was all in favour of anything innovative for women, even if it came from a communist source. Moscow had not yet descended upon Bosnia in all its red glory, although Mara imagined its abuses, over her shoulder, from time to time. Therefore, as the other women trained as nurses and local ladies cooked what little food there was, spun and knitted to help the Partisans, Mara was given a typewriter and a retinue of communist propaganda to type out. She was then instructed on how to set the moveable-type in the printing press, which had been brought by oxen cart over the mountain from Užice. When she complained that she wanted to fight the enemy, she was threatened with a new role—that of interpreting for any captured Germans needing interrogation, prior to being shot. Faced with hearing the last *Heil Hitlers* of half a dozen staunch fascists without the opportunity of shooting them herself, Mara returned to her typing and printing without further protest.

From Rudo, the Partisans from Užice walked north-west to join their Bosnian comrades in Rogatica, a town considered important in establishing an insurgent base in Eastern Bosnia. Then, with the resurgence of the German intention to purge the area of all guerrillas, they were forced in February 1942, to move south-west to the town of Foča, recently liberated from the Italians. The German offensive divided the First Proletarian Brigade of lightly armed partisan fighters. With one half of his command, Tito broke through their ring and reached the Jarohina mountains south of Sarajevo, where he regrouped with the remainder who, with Koča Popović, had walked into a blizzard at twenty degrees below zero, yet still crossed the western mountain plateau. From there, they had proceeded to Foča, where they established their headquarters. None of these towns were more than a two day walk from each other. Sometimes the opposing parties were only a few kilometres apart.

Through Forests and Mountains

As the Germans advanced and the escape from Rogatica became urgent, the remaining communists loaded Mara onto the cart with the printer and hitched up the oxen to the front. A huge Montenegrin picked up Aleksandra and plonked her onto Mara's lap and, with the men walking beside them, they proceeded to Foča by night. As Aleksandra lay across her legs, her head pillowed in the sacks covering the printing press, Mara stroked the girl's soft hair and sung her a lullaby until the sweet words froze into snowflakes and whirled away. Then to prevent them both from freezing, she kissed her warmly and laid blankets across her and, pulling the end around her own head, composed herself to rest. Impossible. Too cold. Too many mischievous spirits out in that darkness. She peered fearfully through the trees, trusting the oxen to frighten them away. But the men, concerned that the startling moo of the lumbering beasts would bring down around them the wrath of the enemy, did everything in their power to placate them on their bitter night journey, leaving Mara to battle the powers of evil alone. A night into the mountains; a day down. A bleak mid-winter landscape, snowclad hills as far as the eye could see. Plunging cliffs, rivers of emerald, forests of pine, bare beech and fir. Now and again, within those formidable mountains was a surprising upland plateau exploited by fields and a farmhouse that seemed to have been deposited there from the plains. When, at last, they rode into Foča she saw that the river was full of Muslim corpses and realized that this evil was from the hand of man.

*****

Foča was clutched tightly between its river, its churches and its mosques. It had a large Muslim population whom the Ustasha, who controlled the area, had recruited to their ranks, in order to rid the area of the hated Serbs. Because she was Serbian, Mara knew that the Serbian Chetniks waged an ideological battle between memories of Turkish atrocities in Serbia and the principles of Serb ultra-nationalism but, in retribution, they had massacred many of the town's Muslim civilians. As the Partisans marched into Foča, they found the inhabitants so traumatized that surely their souls were already halfway out of their bodies, for, from every house, she saw disembodied faces.

Yet, Mara had never known anyone like Tito to maintain such a positive front under such terrible circumstances. He had even brought *A Short History of the Communist Party* in pamphlets to distribute amongst his fighters. (Mara knew this because she had helped print them.) But that was nothing compared with his attitude to the relationship between Muslims and Serbs.

He and his staff set themselves up in a small modern hotel, the Hotel Gerstl, where they received messages and signals from couriers on foot and horseback, and via a growing wireless network. As they had in Drvar, the Partisan women immediately began to explain to the local peasants the importance of the fight against fascism and how their daily tasks could be used to help.

'In Foča, the Antifascist Front of Women for Bosnia and Herzegovina has been created,' Tito told the fighters. 'We have managed to get Serb and Muslim women to work together. It is interesting that, in these most backward Bosnian villages, there is mass enthusiasm among female peasants for our national liberation struggle. Our female comrades from the detachments not only work with women in Foča, but also visit distant villages, where they successfully gather women.

'Here in Foča we will have five brigades from almost every part of Yugoslavia. Among them, there must be brotherhood and companionship in battle and at work. May you be united by unbreakable bonds of brotherhood and love, for you are the army of the Nation. In this, our war of liberation, we are, for the first time in the history of Yugoslavia, uniting all her peoples under arms. Fifth columnists have sought to sew discord among them; we will join them together in brotherhood.'

Mara, who was too talkative to stand aside and listen to Tito's speech with any detachment, wondered about the lives of the women of Foča up to this point. In the opinion of the High Command, the Partisans had achieved a multicultural miracle, for nearly one thousand Serb and Muslim women had attended some of their meetings. But what about their past existence? What had caused them to rally with such enthusiasm now? What could they know of wider events beyond their villages? Was their motivation the racial violence that they had so recently experienced, or could it rather have been something much easier to understand: the recognition of themselves, and the tradition of women fighters, which they had grown up with? Mara had been a witness to the same phenomenon in Drvar and had observed the same astonishment among the Partisan women, that the response to their message had been so overwhelming. However, Drvar had not been the scene of such recent racial violence as Foča.

You know, thought Mara, women can share things with other women. *You are a woman like me? Fine, that's all I need to know; not race, not religion.* Put in this light, the glorious response from Drvar in western Bosnia and Foča in the east did not seem so surprising. Like, no one's ever asked them before? Like, women know nothing about anything because they're just women? If men had to have babies, thought Mara rebelliously, they'd be passing acts of parliament. (This was not an original idea. She'd read it in some British publication.) *Everything about having a baby hurts,* her mother had told her. *Periods hurt, sex hurts, labour hurts and breastfeeding hurts. And men have the temerity*

208

Margaret Walker

to think they can rule the world! We have to feed their precious little egos.

Still, given the history of Serbia's anti-Muslim policies, perhaps, by getting Muslim and Serbian women to work together, Tito *had* created a miracle. The positive response of the Bosnian women should have come as no surprise to anyone but the men.

But I'm sorry I remembered Mum saying that. Mum was not given to sarcasm. Perhaps Dad was grumbling at her because he'd lost his tobacco pouch. No, he had gout....

The outburst from her mother had come after she'd lined up all the dining room chairs, from the bathroom to the lounge room, for her husband to use as crutches, and he'd stubbed the very toe that was aching with uric acid crystals on the skirting board. That burst of exquisite pain resulted in a whole symphony of expletives: *Misjudged the angle of elevation! These blasted British chairs! Nothing English is tall enough for Serbians!*

Dad, that's what I've been trying to tell you.

At the thought of her father, her eyes became moist. Poor Dad. He'd lost everything except the gout.

Speaking of men, wasn't that her group right now, wandering from the meeting to the verge where she stood, just as a heard of cows looks for distraction? Yes, they sauntered across in one mind, four tall, broad, bored males.

But had not Tito just proclaimed nationhood and the importance of women? It stood to reason that the men must listen to *him*. She waited until the four blocked out her sun with a wall of shoulders before asking, with tremulous anticipation, 'Well? What did you think of his speech?'

'Yep, yep,' they said, nodding. 'Yep.'

'But wasn't he great?'

'Yep,' repeated Nikola. His forehead creased in perplexity. 'Don't know how they'll have the time to do it, though.'

209

Anton, the one the girls were calling Captain, stretched a smile across his face. It cost him an effort, Mara thought.

'Do it?' she asked.

'Look after us,' continued Nikola, 'at war, as well.'

'As well?'

'As well as at home.'

'And we'll be fighting!' Mara cried. 'I want a gun, like you!'

Nikola scratched an ear. He raised an eyebrow.

'A woman with a gun?' Amusement rippled in a barely suppressed wave, starting with Boško, the youngest, moving to Slobodan and Anton, and then all the way back to Nikola. 'Can you shoot straight?'

'What's so funny?' demanded Mara. 'There have been women fighters in our history!'

'That was before firearms, Mara.'

His male condescension reminded her of her father, and she was not going to fall meekly into line. No way. Nor were the women who had allied themselves with the Partisans from Užice to Foča anxious to resume their traditional roles.

'Tito is an independent thinker!' she declared. 'I bet if the girls asked him, he'd agree. It's not only the wish of those of us here. He gets letters from women all over the country.'

Anton was the only one educated enough to tackle a spirited debate about the issue, she decided. Captain Anton Marković—she liked the sound of that—but she watched him glance sideways at Nikola and then wander off on his own. *He's thinking it over,* she suspected, although she had no real hope of an imminent breakthrough. She didn't know him very well, and she had been wrong about men before. Right now, it looked like he had shut himself off; needed some space, perhaps, and what could she do to get him talking? She decided she might start with politics.

CHAPTER TWENTY

The British Prime Minster, Mr Winston Churchill, was a conservative, both by nature and by politics, and was averse to the far left, meaning communism. But Britain was at war now, an ally of the communist Soviet Union and, in the cause of victory, one might break one's rules, even at the expense of upsetting one's colleagues in the war office and dismantling their mantra: The British face their enemies head on, The British are neither devious nor unscrupulous, The British play by the rules of war, as they have always done for the British Empire on which the sun never sets.

Think again, Ministers.

The War to End All Wars had not ended any and, finding themselves, only two decades later, faced again with a continental enemy when they were far from ready, the Prime Minister gave *carte blanche* to all ideas large, small and preposterous. So un-British were some of them that they bordered (in the opinion of many) on the criminally insane. In fact, the tactics of one group of desperadoes with a decidedly shady past had shocked Mr Churchill's staff, although Mr Churchill himself had been delighted. It was whispered that some recruits might even have had criminal records. *Why are we resorting to these low tactics?* the ministers demanded to know. *What would King George say? If only America would enter the war!* When, two months previously, the Japanese had bombed Pearl Harbour, they'd breathed a mighty sigh of relief. With America's vast resources available to them, perhaps now they could behave like gentlemen. Naturally, Mr Churchill was overjoyed that Japan had bombed America, but it didn't alter his attitude to underhanded tactics.

It was commonly believed amongst the Americans that the British were a pushover; that they had bumbled their way this far and needed a sparkling industrial nation like the United States, with its huge reserves of manpower, to cross the pond and support them. That without America's help, they would undoubtedly be speaking German, *schnell*. The truth was, when confronted by such an enemy as Hitler, Mr Churchill knew that ruthlessness could only be fought by ruthlessness, although he did not believe he should proclaim this part of his nature too loudly, lest he lose United States money and the young American men who would provide his cannon fodder. He was short and fat and the Americans, to a man, were all as grand and glorious as the wheat on their sweeping plains. Mr Churchill could not command legions, as they could. The best he could do was to be devious.

In early February 1942, he paid a visit to Bletchley Park in Buckinghamshire, that great gathering of English nerds whose eccentricities, he was certain, the wholesome Americans would never comprehend. Higher mathematicians, bridge and chess players, linguists, logicians, engineers, scientists, researchers, riddlers. The more elastic the brains for code breaking the better, and all of them young and brilliant. Bletchley Park was how he would sneak his way into Hitler's inner sanctum. It might have been a leg up into the kitchen window, but the jewels he would steal were identical to the householder who had the key. He was justifiably proud of this great British first, built on the work of the Poles, and the success it had achieved in breaking coded messages, sent between enemy garrisons and enemy-held towns, picked up by listening stations all along the east coast of Britain. At last, with its aid, they were turning around the catastrophic loss of British shipping in the North Atlantic.

The two hour drive from London completed, his chauffeur turned the Daimler from the road, onto the driveway of the mansion, idling the car briefly while Mr Churchill tipped his cigar to the armed sentries in their brick boxes before driving onwards towards the series of creative frontispieces that marked the front of the house, built higgledy piggledy across the lawn and always reminding him of a more chivalrous era. Mr Churchill did not have time for generalized chats. He customarily issued brief instructions, based on the hunches of the old war dog he was, and expected that they be done. This day, however, he had come to pick the brains of one young man, working on the decoded German messages that had recently begun to arrive from occupied Yugoslavia where Britain was interested in all forms of guerrilla warfare, including its own. Britain had been interfering in Balkan affairs for years and, as that year plodded through its chilly winter, Mr Churchill's attention had been diverted from his chilblains to enemy-occupied Serbia in Yugoslavia, where he knew they had agents.

Already he was wondering what part that interesting country, so near to Italy, could play in an allied invasion of Europe. There were several possibilities: an allied landing, an invasion of Italy, the rupture of German supply and communication lines to North Africa through the railway from German-held Belgrade and thence to Athens. It had also occurred to him that any German withdrawal or movement of troops from Greece would have to proceed through Yugoslavia, and this provided possibilities as well. *Keep as*

*many German troops as possible engaged in Yugoslavia
and away from our proposed invasion of Sicily.*

The branch of military intelligence known as MI3 had
alerted Mr Churchill to the presence of a possible double
agent reporting back to German Headquarters in Belgrade
who appeared to be researching both British intentions in
Yugoslavia and activities against German lines of communication by a shadowy band of guerrillas whose leader had not
yet been clearly identified. The guerrillas had not been referred to as Chetniks, the reorganized remains of the Royal
Yugoslav Army that Mr Churchill knew well, and his Joint
Intelligence Committee was not, at this early stage, certain of
their provenance. Although the German of this Morse operator seemed adequate, whoever he might be, he made mistakes in his encryption technique and the formatting of the
messages he sent. Mr Churchill expected the occasional error. It was the consistency of the errors that had aroused
suspicion—that, and the random nature of the messages. The
explanation seemed as simple as inexperience, but in these
desperate days, one should look on all underhand activities,
including one's own, as a threat to national security. Sometimes the operator even sent his messages in English, apparently as he fancied. Curiously, when he did so, he employed
the correct British codes in use for that day. When he wrote
in German, he used the correct German Enigma codes. It was
just the sort of puzzle Mr Churchill relished.

Once inside the mansion, Mr Churchill met the retired
colonel who was to be his host, and together they strolled
across the grounds to Hut 3, where he was introduced to the
first-year university student named Nigel, who had isolated
the peculiar messages from amongst the five thousand or so
they were receiving each day from all over occupied Europe.

Margaret Walker

'If I didn't know better, Mr Churchill,' the young genius informed him. 'I would say that this man has been practising.'

It gave the Prime Minister a queasy feeling to be so completely surrounded by gifted youths, and he was grateful that the stodgy old colonel provided a buffer zone.

'And do you know better?' he enquired with a hand to his watch chain.

'No, sir, I don't.'

Mr Churchill was just about to issue one of his famously fleeting directives when he paused to consider the Fair Isle pattern on the boy's vest, and was struck by an idea. It related to traditional designs and an excess of brains, and the feeling that one must be proportional to the other. He immediately rejected it, as of no consequence.

'Tell me more,' he said.

'They began as weather reports to the German High Command in Belgrade, sir,' answered Nigel. 'But, you see, the dates are wrong. He's written several with the same date, but on different days. It's as if he's copying what someone else has written without setting up the Enigma wheels correctly, because he has neglected the repetition at the beginning, which is what the Germans always do. Then he seems to improve. Now the dates are correct, although the formatting is still wrong. Eventually he gets it. And now, you see, he seems to have moved—I only say 'seems'—I'm not entirely sure. He was writing about Serbia from Serbia, now he's writing about Bosnia, though it seems likely he's still in Serbia. I say that, because he's only made this one mistake and included the location in an incorrect format. These later ones are all about that single railway track near the bauxite mines south of Sarajevo. Here's one shipment of ore being trucked to the coast at Dubrovnik. It's off to Trieste by sea, but they're worried about British bombing. Someone's blown up

215

the line and they haven't fixed it yet. Looks like the Germans are desperate for the ore.'

'Bauxite...' mused the colonel, who knew something about the construction of aeroplanes.

'Which codes is he using?' enquired Mr Churchill.

'German at the moment, sir, though he's transmitting on British frequencies. Well, actually, he's used both, if we can assume that it's the same man. Maybe two strange men, not one. The earlier messages used German frequencies, these later ones British. He's rather gung-ho, for a trained operator.'

'How can we know if it's the same man?'

'Um...we can't, sir. It's just a hunch I have. It's these weather reports that have got me thinking. If he sends any more of this nature, I might be able to establish a pattern.'

'I wonder where he got the technical specifics,' mused Mr Churchill.

'The dispatch rider told you what they were, Nigel?' broke in the colonel.

'Yes, sir. Someone at this wireless telegraphy station has made a note of the frequencies they were picked up on.'

'Who do we have in Serbia?' enquired Mr Churchill of the colonel.

'Captain Hudson, Prime Minister. Our man from Special Forces who's gone missing.'

'Ah, yes. And what were the circumstances?'

'He was sent to investigate the existence of any and all resistance movements in Yugoslavia and we haven't heard anything of him since the beginning of December, when we received a message from the headquarters of General Mihailović in Ravna Gora in Serbia, to inform us that they didn't know where he was. Hudson was the one who sent that message we received from the daughter of the Yugoslav ambassador a week before. It came from Užice, about thirty miles from Ravna Gora. Same general area as our mystery man. But neither of them are there now, or so these messages seem to be telling us.'

Nigel put up his hand. (He had only left high school the year before, and old habits die hard.)

'Yes, Nigel?' said the colonel.

'Well, sir, it's these ones in English with the odd grammatical error that have caught my attention. I'm sure he isn't a native speaker but, even so, I can't understand the reason for sending them. Either the practice, as I said, or he just wants to get our attention, or both. This one here, for instance, regarding bauxite from Mostar in Bosnia reaching the port of Dubrovnik: *20 February 1942, Gruž, 5000 tonnes ore to Trieste. Winds NE 15km/hr. Send notice of partisan offensive.* You see, he's sent the same message in German and English. But here is a possible reply we picked up from Belgrade just yesterday: *Rogatica offensive delayed.* It was written in German, of course.'

'That's all?'

'No, sir. There's also this from 28 January: *Tell Marko to watch his back.* Except he's written 'bark' not 'back' but I think he meant 'back'. Aside from a single dash, R and C are the same in Morse code.'

In the small room there was a sudden silence.

'Marko,' whispered the colonel. 'That's Hudson's code name.'

He shifted his feet while Mr Churchill searched for his cigar. That was the worst part about this job, the waiting. After careful preparation, the months of training, the secret service officers set adrift to a frenzied adventure in a foreign land, and then nothing. Never knowing which man had been sent to his death and never heard from again, or possibly, just possibly, to emerge with information that would prove vital to the war effort. It could be worse than Bosnia, it could be the blizzards of Norway or the deserts of North Africa.

The silence began to last too long. Waiting forlornly for someone else to break it, Nigel raised his hand a second time and launched forth on his own.

'The unknown operator is using the correct British codes for the dates given, which tells us that he has a British code book. Could he also have a British radio set, is the question. If that is the case, could we be receiving messages from Hudson's set?'

'Nigel, my boy, you are a genius!' breathed the colonel. He turned to Mr Churchill. 'It would seem a possibility, Prime Minister. We might commence asking ourselves, for instance, what light these dispatches can shed on Hudson's disappearance.'

'We stumble over the truth,' pondered Mr Churchill to himself. Aloud he said, 'If we can put pressure on the Germans on the eastern side of the Adriatic and find Captain Hudson as well, so much the better.'

He left.

The colonel and Nigel remained alone in the room, one standing, one sitting as they had been.

'Good boy, Nigel!' declared the colonel once more, raising a hand to pat him affectionately on the head. He checked himself. It did not do to patronize the achievements of the young. Ah... good work, indeed. Keep us informed.'

Nigel had red hair and freckles. Both blushed.

CHAPTER TWENTY-ONE

Miroslav was practising several times a day on the radio set he had stolen from the suave British officer and was very pleased with what he had accomplished. As well, he had his German Enigma machine and the British code book, but discovered very quickly that the three items were too heavy to carry. What he needed was a horse.

The villagers who had fled their homes before the German advance on Užice were hiding in the forests until they deemed it safe to return to what remained. Miroslav moped around the deserted ruins that smelled of charcoal and death, finding several oxen, a donkey and a mule, but no horse. Finally, by dint of a coil of rope and a partially-burned saddle bag he had found in an outhouse, he constructed a type of double-satchel, which he slung over the donkey.

The trouble with these villagers, or perhaps the blessing, was that there was always a sizeable number among the population who just wanted to get on with their lives and were happy to change allegiance in order to do so, depending on the occupying force. Sometimes they changed allegiance more than once: German, Italian, Partisan, Chetnik, whatever, as long as they were left in peace. On one occasion, in a hamlet so tiny it looked like it would blow away in the wind, he found a fat, militant widow who proudly declared that she had never fed a partisan, but fed Miroslav until he was bursting, merely because he had told her he was a monarchist, which was a lie. On her wall hung a portrait of King Alexander of Yugoslavia, assassinated in 1934 by an Ustasha sympathizer and, had he required morals these days, he might have manufactured a by-road, via that nefarious connection, to the exiled monarchy in order to satisfy his hunger. He had knocked on several doors looking for meals and, on the whole, he had been successful. He exploited his looks; he manipulated each situation with the skill of a confidence trickster: he defended the dead, he praised the living, he hailed Hitler. Anything for food. He was truly thankful to the British for their devotion to Queen Victoria, who had spread her arms far and wide. He knew that the British would flatter anything royal and do their best to reinstate the eighteen-year-old King Peter, great, great grandson of Queen Victoria, because of their devotion to an idea.

Sycophant? It tastes good to me, said Miroslav.

With the fall of the Užice Republic, his own Serb operator had returned to Belgrade. Miroslav had extracted the Enigma Machine from the man at gunpoint and remained with the German troops, who had been clearing the last of the insurgents from what was once again German occupied territory. He had contemplated moving further west into Bosnia, held partly by the Italians and partly by his own Ustasha forces, where he would have got the support he sometimes needed, but would never have made it over the mountains with the radio set and its accoutrements, which were quickly coming to dominate his life.

If it wasn't for his declared task of stalking Mara, he would have gone home, first to Belgrade and then to Zagreb. He had more than a trait of obsessiveness in his personality and at the present, he was obsessed with his radio and the possible ways he could use it to find her. One, radio, two, Mara, in that order. Through its use, he hoped to reverse the order of his obsessions. There's always a way, his obsessive father used to chant—that father who was too perfect at everything to show him how to use anything. Of necessity, Miroslav had grown up accustomed to figuring things out for himself and hated to admit that he had inherited something from that frustrating parent. But it was true that he was obsessive himself, and the notion that this interesting piece of modern technology could be used as a detective had him by the horns. There's got to be a way. And how much more sensible to stay in one place and figure it out than to attempt to follow her over a mountain range in winter, donkey or no donkey.

He did not stop to evaluate his actions towards her. Was it not true that communication had forged modern warfare? Gone were the days of Pheidippides. No more marathon running for Miroslav. He would use this communication device as his legs. They were all at it, the Brits, the Nazis, the Americans, the Japanese, and undoubtedly the Partisans and Chetniks as well. Sending off coded messages and decoding the commands of the enemy as they were able. Confusing them by writing messages that were untrue. Waving them away in the opposite direction. This spy stuff had really grabbed him. Its possibilities seemed endless, rather like himself, because he was quite clued up on his own possibilities.

He had heard from the commander of the German division that the Partisans were moving south west into Italian-held territory. So, he wondered, where might Mara be now? Snowed in, naturally, and he couldn't see her trekking through snow drifts to escape the Germans, although there were plenty of locals who would walk barefoot in the snow if they had to. (The trick, he had heard, was to raise your feet quickly so that your toes didn't freeze.) He considered how Mara was faring without him. Well, she wouldn't have that top-tailored British officer any more. He'd be off on his travels, looking for his radio. Once he'd realized that he'd never find it—about twenty-four hours, Miroslav estimated—he would need to make some decision about completing whatever mission had sent him here, then use somebody else's. No time for love, as they said.

So Mara would be somewhere very cold, and she wasn't a peasant like the rest of them. With her generalized education, her posh accent and her impracticalities, she'd light up her location like a flare. He'd find her.

What a shame he couldn't get a message to her—or, wait a minute, maybe he could? The Partisans would have to have a radio. *I wonder what codes they use? I know all about codes now.*

He had sent the newspaper clipping of Tito from *Borba* to General Böhme and, that duty done, was spending most of his time practising Morse code and familiarising himself with the frequencies used by both the Germans and the British. The Enigma really was a dear little machine, he mused, stroking its ironwork fondly, a cross between a cutlery box and a typewriter. Whoever put these things together had coaxed the best out of him, of which, with Miroslav, there was always an endless supply. As long as you didn't open it up and try to make sense of the rotary pieces, the outside of the machine made perfect sense. He was delighted that he could increase his self-respect through such a device created by those lumbering Germans for, up until now, he'd believed that they had no finesse. He wrote his first messages in German, as thanks, believing (correctly) that the British code-breakers would be well supplied with translators of that language. He used the Enigma codes specified for the month and the day. Occasionally, he even composed messages in

Margaret Walker

English, although he wasn't as confident in that language, but, when he did, he used the British code book. He wished he had access to one of their Typex machines so he could show the world how awfully clever Miroslav Novak was and how he knew more than anybody else.

He continued to play the field for his needs and, by such devious means, had acquired volunteers to crank the generator and hold up the poles for its antenna when it threatened to collapse in the wind. Establishing reception had caused him a great deal of trouble. Initially he'd raised the antenna two metres above him by manipulating two sticks and securing it to a tree trunk. That didn't work. Clearly, he was attempting to send and receive messages in what must be a poor reception zone. Once, he thought he picked up a faint signal, only to have the antenna fall onto the ground because the stupid peasant had dropped it. After that, he climbed to the top of a hill and, with a quick glance around him for any signs of any enemy, got the farm labourer assisting him to hold it up as high as he could and wave it around. Height clearly was an advantage, for now he could definitely hear something. Excitement took hold of him. Ignoring the biting wind at this altitude and the rain that was turning to sleet, he sang so many glorious songs about his new technology that the labourer believed him to be one of the bards resurrected, and actually waited in the horrible weather until Miroslav himself had turned blue. The peasant was reasonably comfortable despite everything, and went home to his wife with the news that the strange young man was not from around here, because he sang songs in an unfamiliar accent and became cold in only mild weather. Could he have been American, a country the man had only vaguely heard about?

Miroslav, indeed, went home suffering from hypothermia, but nevertheless wondering if he could send an actual message better from the hill than down in the valley, as well as receive one. It made sense but, as he had no notion of whether his previous practice attempts had worked, he couldn't be certain. No one had replied, and, when it came to that, he wasn't sure what a reply would be like. Was there something magical about wireless transmission that would signify to the receiver from whom it had been sent? The thought that the whole thing might be entirely random was unnerving. City born and bred, and most comfortable well-dressed in bars and cafes, while stuck out here in this endless natural landscape, Miroslav had even begun to think of himself in random terms. His wasn't used to his hair being windswept, for instance, nor the collar of his jacket beating around his neck, nor having his boots covered with mud. Generally, he wore shoes. Boots were his grudging concession to bushwalking.

At some point in his grand adventure, he realized he was getting a solid feel for this Morse code stuff. *'Übung macht den Meister,'* he chortled as he tapped away. 'Practice makes perfect.'

Having established the antenna and his fluency in Morse code itself, he thought he was home and housed, only to discover that tuning into the airways was like listening to the universe on a rolling boil. The seething concoction defied any attempt at translation and was constantly changing. Once he thought he had a pattern established and he made a rough attempt at decipherment, using first the German Enigma machine and then the British code books. It looked like Hungarian, which he couldn't read, and yet it was on a frequency used by the British. In other words, it made no sense at all. Morse code had looked so easy in the instruction book, but cracking any message at all that he received became his new obsession. He listened to the radio for so many hours on end that he heard the repeated messages even when he had switched his set off. He began to believe that it had altered the way his brain worked, so that he had, indeed, cursed himself. He could never switch that fug off, nor quiet its interminable tapping, and he would continue to receive messages, as if he himself were a wireless, until the end of his days.

However, eventually his persistence bore fruit and he began to recognise whole letters instead of merely listening for dots and dashes and, when he did so, he realized, for the first time, that a person was sending a message instead of a factory monotonously churning out symbols. That was a liberating discovery. It made all the difference, knowing that he was connecting with a flesh and blood man who got hungry like he did and thought about sex all the time like he did and might even have enjoyed proving his own superiority to himself and everyone else every hour of the day, like he did. On a piece of paper beside him he carefully recorded what he had heard, consulted his code book for the day and translated the dots and dashes, first into letters, and then translated them, as well as he could, into words.

Miroslav was well aware of how upset the Germans were when Churchill, the war leader, had succeeded Chamberlain, the peacemaker, and that they held him solely responsible for denying them the pleasure of victory on British soil. So, at first, the sense of the power he had over this nation, which could actually be a threat to Germany, overwhelmed him. He sent messages to Winston Churchill and George VI, he wrote a brief obituary for Neville Chamberlain; he left veiled threats at the war office. He even wrote letters of eternal love to Mara that he knew she'd never get, but he imagined her reading them anyway, all about his bleeding heart and how his ego was awaiting her return.

'I'm watching you,' he wrote. 'Keep those hands where they belong.' Then one day he wrote, 'Love you, darling.'

Then on another occasion he was so angry he wrote, 'I know where you are.'

That'll get her, he thought.

CHAPTER TWENTY-TWO

'You're a trained military leader, Captain Marković, of which we have very few,' said the political commissar.

'I'm navy,' answered Anton.

'Doesn't matter. You're fortunate to be living in an innovative time and we need you. Unlike the armies of Germany, we are organized into independent units that can operate without awaiting orders from any Supreme Command.'

'There are lots of local units.'

'Yes, I know.'

'I've come from one in Montenegro.'

'These are different. The traditional *odreds* you're talking about defend their homes and go back to those homes after the fight. Our new units are mobile. They go anywhere. They are shock brigades. Now, this company I'm thinking of for you, while you're still rehabilitating, holds some of the younger women.'

'Women?' Anton started fiddling with his arm, and the man noticed immediately. Someone has told him, thought Anton, stopping the action. *See, he's doing it again. It's a nervous habit he has.* 'Very well, commissar. Women. What do they do?'

'Oh, the usual: nurses, typists, food; but some are training for combat roles.'

'Combat?'

'Soon. Not yet.'

'And they are... how old?'

'Upwards of seventeen.'

'A young woman with a gun in a combat situation?' asked Anton. 'Is that appropriate?'

He felt that the man didn't quite understand his implied misgivings, for he stood squarely before him exhibiting the blank face of a teacher when queried by a junior student about the purpose of trigonometry. *Yes, I heard your question, but the function should not have to be explained.* Here might follow a chapter reference.

'Some of them are replacing lost brothers and fathers,' the commissar responded, still with that mask that brooked no dissension. 'They want to continue the struggle in their place. They've lost their homes, been the victims of enemy reprisals or been raped. They're very keen to vanquish these fascists.'

Following the departure of the First Proletarian Brigade, the men and women remaining were organized into military companies to serve the Army of National Liberation. Better known as a *politkomesar*, a commissar was appointed to each. Despite promoting the communist ideology to their troops, they were not all atheists—some were even priests, who ministered as well to the spiritual necessities of the Partisans. Others, like Josip Cazi, were as romantic as the beauty of the countryside. He was an expressive man with a self-regarding slant over his right eyebrow. He wrote poetry to warm and cheer him in those days of cold, deprivation and persistent danger.

'We are the new wave that will liberate this country,' he told Anton. 'These women want to fight and Tito supports that desire. His directive on the matter acknowledges their petitions to him.'

'But a seventeen-year-old girl with a rifle?'

'Yes, Captain Marković. I believe Tito used the word "rifle".'

Something about this parting shot must have amused Cazi, for he went off with a spring in his step and Anton watched him leave apprehensively.

Anton had always thought of himself as a practical man, but what did one say to a proposition of this nature? Girls with rifles! Within the range of his disability, he was aware that the commissar had given him what he thought would best aid their cause and, in theory, he acknowledged the correctness of that decision. In the present instance, he had been instructed to train inexperienced young people, some of whom were female, in the mechanics of warfare. Well, he would do what he was told and try not to let slip his belief that a woman in a combat role was against the natural order. He knew that being chained to the home did not appeal to the modern girl, but the image was firmly entrench in the memories of his childhood—his own mother rarely left the kitchen—and he had romantic associations with it, connected largely with pleasant memories of being loved and well-fed.

As for the self-knowledge required in a relationship these days, he knew that he didn't possess bottomless wells of charm, but at the same time he would not have described himself as a difficult man. He just knew the way he liked things done, that's all. Once people realized that his way was the right way, they would all be much happier, yet he was not spring-loaded to explode when he didn't get his own way, and he felt that men who behaved like that were being self-indulgent. It was no one's God-given right to be a terror to his family. On the other hand, he saw no reason to deny himself emotional expression, if he was frustrated, because it was not truthful to pretend to be something you weren't. That sort of behaviour slotted into his notion of deception. Honesty served him better, though it could sometimes be isolating. Women, he had found, didn't want a man to express all he felt, all the time. They worked better with a bit of subterfuge: charisma, allure, romance, the long, slow burn, and all those things that he wasn't good at.

It wasn't as if he didn't like women. He did like women. He'd had his share of girlfriends over the years, for he was a sailor, and he understood that 'a girl in every port' applied to him. Lana, the scholar from Split, Ivana, that buxom sales girl he'd met over a counter in Dubrovnik, clingy Clementina from Trieste, too refined for him really but he liked the way she seemed to need him, even after he discovered that fragile women were vixens beneath the gossamer. She had cloaked her requests in such plaintive rhetoric that he couldn't say no, and it wasn't until after the event that he realized he was being controlled. On the principle of transparency, he had decided, after her, to experiment with more assertive women, but that didn't last long because he didn't appreciate being spoken back to. Then there was Adriana from Bari, who pretended to feign indifference, but then would catch the ferry all the way across the Adriatic to tease him. He'd be casting around him, wondering why his hormones were up, and there she'd be, pouting along the docks in stilettos. If the whole truth were to come out, he had inherited a tendency to pick women like this from his father, and his domesticated mother had, nevertheless, been a living example of a cat in the dog kennel. (It never occurred to Anton that she might have been frustrated.) After Adriana had come Marina, who never said no and was the nearest thing to a perfect mother he could imagine. He was bored after three months. His longest relationship, that girl in Kotor he'd really liked, who was neither intellectual, nor stupid, nor sophisticated, nor authoritative, nor feline, nor maternal, had refused to marry him because she had tuberculosis. She'd then married someone else while he was away at sea, and survived to have two children.

That had been the last straw with women, really. He acknowledged that he was a victim of himself, but he had no idea what to do anymore. So here he was, still a bachelor and, as he became more gruff and grumpy with the years, was likely to remain one.

The good news was that the girls he was training to fire a deadly weapon were farmers' daughters, dedicated with rural pragmatism to learning quickly and efficiently, and had no inclination to judge him. The exception was Mara, the ambassador's daughter from Belgrade, fluent in English, French and German, who very quickly drew attention to herself by asking questions that only served to illustrate her grasp of the theoretical. Anton noticed that she spoke well and gave thought to her words when conversing in public, suggesting that she had been coached in the art of self-expression. In a village house so cold that there were icicles hanging from the eaves, she dominated the conversation, using her drawing room conventions, and the implications of her control were that she had to get all her thoughts out in front of him before she forget them and had to wait in the queue like everyone else. It made it hard for him to relax when she was butting in all the time.

Her questions as to the complicated nature of Yugoslav politics drew little interest from the other girls and only served to waste time better spent on practical matters. If she wished to discuss politics, he tactfully suggested, might she not query the commissar in the evenings rather than divert his attention from these young women who genuinely wanted to learn how to clean and load a gun and know what to do if it jammed? She seemed disappointed, as if she saw in him an officer who had worked his way up through the education system, rather like herself, and was therefore a kindred spirit. What he found really irritating was her insistence on calling him Captain whilst she referred to Nikola as Nikola. Playing at wargames, but being selective! Just like a schoolgirl. If she started calling him 'sir' he would really have to talk to her about it.

As well as learning practical warfare, most of the young women were eager to acquire literacy or to improve the meagre schooling thought necessary for a village girl. Had war not disrupted the masculine hegemony they had come to expect, they would, by now, be married and pregnant. So, in the evenings when she was not washing, he knew that Mara taught, first those women who were unable to read at all and afterwards, listened to other girls read and corrected their letter writing and basic maths. Anton wished she would teach during the day, as well. He might be able to finish his lessons without her interrupting him with her current debate about the probable form of the post war Yugoslav government.

This morning he had to be brisk with her because the girls in front of him were loading a rifle. 'As Yugoslavia doesn't exist at the moment, Mara,' he informed her tersely. 'The government's going to be completely new, obviously.'

'That's only your opinion,' she shot back. 'The king is in London with my father. What's going to happen to him?'

'What king?' Anton scoffed, and she was too animated by her polemic to pick up what he thought about monarchs.

'King Peter, Captain!'

Anton winced. 'How is a king good for Yugoslavia?' To a girl beside him he said, 'Point the weapon nearly up. That's it.'

She did exactly as she was told, as if he were her father, which he was almost old enough to be.

'You don't need to sound like that,' Mara insisted. 'After all, the British supported the *coup d'état* that made him king,'

'That's because it got Hitler off Allied backs. That's the magazine there. Keep loading until it's full.'

'What do you mean?'

'I mean that he bombed Belgrade instead of sending troops to Russia.'

Mara was miffed; her argument had sprung a leak.

'And the British have a king themselves.' Anton drove home remorselessly. Touché.

'But King Peter is only eighteen,' Mara argued back as vigorously as she was able. 'This is not his fault.'

'His father was a dictator. Is it tight? Good. Now remove the ammunition.' He watched as the girl carefully rolled the bullets into her hand, then added, with his eyes averted, 'In fact, an assassinated dictator.'

'That was the fascists!' stormed Mara, displeased because his full attention would have justified her position and she knew he had deliberately withheld it.

'I know. All right. Check it again. Now it's safe.'

Mara tapped him on the shoulder. Not the wonky one— she was superstitious of disabilities—the left one.

'But don't you think Peter would be a lovely king for Yugoslavia?' she persisted. 'I'm sure he has the best interests of the country at heart and he's so nice looking.'

'And who did his grandfather disembowel to grab the throne?'

'That's not fair! The army did that.'

She had finally succeeded in provoking him. He turned around and the village girls sniggered behind his back.

'You like him, do you?' he asked Mara bluntly.

'Not in that way, I don't.'

'How old are you, Mara?'

'I'm twenty-four.'

'Then he's too young for you.'

'I said not in that way. You're jealous.'

'I am not jealous. I'm giving a lesson.'

'But he was very popular, Captain. He had the support of General Simović.'

'You want to be in the Royal Army, do you?' he demanded. 'Armchair generals, clean my boots, don't answer back, peasant! You don't like this one?'

'I love this one,' she replied.

'Then why are you arguing?'

'I'm not arguing! I only said that I thought the King would support the old army in the fight against the Germans and the Italians. If he did, then it would mean that we were all fighting together, and we could get British support through the embassy, where my father is.'

'We would like nothing better than British support, but it's a shame your army didn't last longer than eleven days.'

'Kren betrayed us!' she protested passionately. 'He defected to the Germans! He gave them all the information their bombers needed to defeat us.'

'Point taken.'

'And what remains of the Royal Army, the Chetniks and General Mihailović who leads them, are fighting with us again.'

'I have heard that some of the Bosnian Chetniks are fighting with us,' stated Anton flatly. 'That's all. The other Chetniks would have to agree with Tito's communism, and they don't.'

'But we're not even half communist!'

'I know, but Mihailović hates communists and he won't have women.'

'Yes,' agreed Mara. 'Women are better off with Tito. Was Tito ever in the army, Captain?'

'In the last war he was a non-commissioned officer.'

'A what?'

'Poor—and unconnected. But he came to someone's attention, hence the promotion.'

This gave Mara pause for reflection.

'And a communist?' she said. 'That's a slap in the face for the old order.'

'Yes, I can't imagine Mihailović welcoming Tito into the Old Boys' Network.'

'All right! Tito and King Peter as the government of post war Yugoslavia? What do you think?'

'Not sure about your logic there, Mara.'

Anton sighed. He was tired and his shoulder ached from the endless demonstrations with rifles. He was irritated. Unwittingly, he had allowed Mara to stimulate his views, and now he was in a debate he felt he had to win. Honestly, he should have let it go.

'You're too political,' he pointed out, while she listened with rapt attention. She had got what she wanted. She knew it, he knew it, and so did their audience. 'You've missed the point. For this army, these people, it's not about politics, communists, or kings. It's a moral war, good and evil. They want to rid their land of fascists.'

'But...'

'The end.'

He really mustn't get so involved in future he determined, although a diet of nuts, bolts and male jokes could only sustain him for so long. And it was true that he occasionally felt lonely and didn't mind some intellectual stimulation. So he saw no reason to shun her advances, although he knew he was contradicting himself. He would make sure he kept her at arm's length. Next time.

*****

Through Forests and Mountains

The theoretical idea of a female with a gun was taking shape, and the young women were pleased. No amount of insistence from their superiors that their most important role was to support the male fighters could eclipse their desire to fight, too. Even Anton admitted that getting a group of girls to lie flat on their stomachs behind a row of mounted machine guns helped them forget the anguish of their lives and the trauma that the war had brought. Whenever standing, they kept their rifles strapped to their backs, one or two grenades hanging from their belts—mostly one—and they were not frivolous about their intentions.

'You can't reason with a fascist,' Jana assured Mara. 'They are degraded beyond redemption. All you can do is shoot them. Hitler called the Poles animals. That's what he thinks of Slavs.'

Jana was a girl caught between the two worlds of the village and the Partisans. At sixteen she had rejected a proposal of marriage, yet men were often attracted to her. Like a magnetic earth mother, she seemed to have positive and negative ends, between which she fluctuated, because fraternizing between the sexes was strictly forbidden. She had come from a village near Užice and, at the German offensive, had fled with the others. Broad, strong and as lively as the birds in the trees, it was unlikely that her raw sexual energy would remain unappreciated for long, and the joke about Jana was that she was the only Partisan the Nazis wanted alive. Nevertheless, she was the first woman to kill one.

February was almost over. In an effort to clear Eastern Bosnia of both Partisans and Chetniks and thereby safeguard their supply lines, the Germans invaded the mountains in the depths of winter to encircle their enemy. This standard technique was not effective in the deep snow, and for the Partisans, as well, winter was a poor time to wage guerrilla warfare. Too early even for the first buds, the taller trees were bare and provided little cover.

Jana and Mara marched out as part of a small platoon that Anton had chosen and, with the other men and women, had taken up positions well back in the forest behind boughs and undergrowth. The road blocks they had set up, made from stones and girders remaining from a dynamited bridge, delayed the German columns but didn't stop them. Too soon through the utter hush, they caught the steady tramp of thousands of feet approaching their sanctuary. Behind came the tanks and heavy artillery, sweeping aside the dirty snow that clung like brown slush to the road. Further back again would be the field canteens and the other necessities of an army division; nothing left to the vagaries of chance, everything in its proper place. Despite the weather, the Germans had polished their brass; they had perfected their dress. To see their relentless war machine, made up not of men but of brainwashed robots marching on without reflection, was as much a performance as a rally at Nuremburg.

As she watched the confident rulers of Europe, Mara fought against the intimidation they inspired. They could *not* march on, day after day, feeding only on the fear they provoked, sleeping on their feet like horses. Their superiority *could* be annihilated. One could destroy them. Yet, that first step eluded her. To the men and women of Yugoslavia whom they had driven from their villages, whose land they had taken, she knew that they were no longer men but devils, fit only to be exorcised. Thus 'death to fascism' was a common greeting amongst the Partisans. Indeed, nothing else was left for them but to fight. They would fight and they would die, and eventually, when enough had perished, the recognition that they had died for freedom would enable those who were left to complete the battle. *This is our land, we will never surrender it.*

Through Forests and Mountains

The day passed, the sun set. Throughout the daylight hours, they had engaged in a few skirmishes, and were retreating back into the long shadows of the woods when Mara saw Josip Cazi touch Anton on the shoulder. A German soldier was stalking silently towards the platoon, thrusting his bayonet into the frozen earth. The ground was too solid for the *bazas,* the holes the Partisans were known to dig as hiding places, yet here and there, the soldier paused and knelt down, as if he could smell the Partisans hiding in the understorey of the forest. Anton motioned to his company to retreat, pointing out silently the German in front of them, and Jana squeezed herself behind the bare trunk of an elm, dragging Mara behind her, with the result that the girls became separated from the main group.

When Jana cocked her rifle, waiting calmly for the soldier to come within range, Mara's heart began to pound, as if it would leap from her chest. The man turned. Yes, he had detected the recalcitrant organ. No, he could not have! His turn was too slow and her heart—she quickly checked—was still in her chest. The soldier, she saw, was a youth of a reasonable height and broad shoulders, but lacking the rough cheeks older men had usually acquired this late in the working day. Not a lot to shave and the battle helmet he was wearing only emphasized the contrast between his innocent skin and his murderous intentions. A genuine Hitler Youth? Perhaps, after all, her frantic heart was luring him on, as surely as Jan's rifle was at the ready, barely concealed by the tree trunk.

She willed herself to remain calm, yet wild thoughts roused her. A rifle weighed three or four kilograms, did it not, and, at that weight, wouldn't Jana require a certain amount of visibility to aim straight? How was she expected to do so when her visibility was blocked by a tree? Leap around the trunk, point and fire, or point first and remain seated? Lure the soldier towards them by devious means?

Request the tree to politely move out of the way? Anton had not adequately prepared them for this situation—that much was clear. Mara searched behind her but he had gone, evidently unaware of their predicament. The forest was still, with that utter absorption nature seems to acquire between sunset and nightfall, so that it is at once both lurking and desolate. The soldier was less than twenty metres away now and Mara was not sure which menace was the worst.

'Jana,' she whispered. 'Are we doing this right?'

Jana put a finger to her lips. The hairs on the back of her neck rose and her breathing halted. Silently she brought the rifle up to her shoulder, balanced one finger on the trigger and brought her other hand beneath the barrel.

Like a hunted animal, the young German bristled, and his awareness was Jana's signal. She leaped out and fired, hitting him in the lower left hand side of his chest. The rifle recoiled sharply, spraying Jana's elbow behind her and knocking Mara to the ground. A shot of bright blood emerged from the soldier's chest and he collapsed onto his right side. Upon the bushes that formed the straggles of undergrowth, Mara watched transfixed as the red stream cooled and hardened upon the frozen soil.

She got to her feet, trembling and speechless, but Jana herself was pragmatic.

'One down,' she said.

'Ah...' replied Mara.

'I was aiming for his head.'

'Oh...'

'Too low!'

'Um, there's a lot of blood in the stomach... perhaps you hit him there.'

They crunched through the frosted undergrowth until they stood over the soldier. And it was terrible really, a young life slain. Mara counted the seconds since the shot. Twenty seconds ago, he was unhurt. He was hungry. He was thinking of dinner. Something about Jana's firm breasts as she fired at him reminded him of his girlfriend back in Berlin. And then this. Clearly, he hadn't expected to be shot. *Even now he is surprised,* she thought. *He thinks that, perhaps, it hasn't happened to him, and his thoughts are still on what he will do tomorrow.*

The soldier's fingers clutched once or twice at the ground. Long and slender, they were almost like a woman's, and Mara wondered whether he had played the piano or perhaps been a watchmaker and would need such fine fingers for the delicate work.

As the realization of his condition dawned in his face, the young features clouded with sadness. The glory of Berlin slipped away. That girlfriend whose robust love had sustained him in these antipodes was eclipsed by thoughts of his mother. He was surprised, because in all the glory and the propaganda of Nazism, every word of which he had believed, he had forgotten the beauty of new life at her breast.

Jana saw Mara's face.

She said, 'From the forest behind my village, I watched fascists like him rape, burn and kill. Why should I care, now he's dead?'

'He's not dead.'

'Forget it. He'll just bleed to death.'

'Shouldn't we help him?'

'Get his mother to help him. She can feed us at the same time with our food they've stolen. Mara, when are you going to toughen up?' Jana slung the rifle over her shoulder and, after a cursory glance at the dying soldier, said, 'Come on, we've got to get out of here. They'll have heard the shot.'

The girls took off into the thickening twilight, panting hard as the cold breath was squeezed from their lungs and turned their throats into dry ice.

That night, after they had eaten their meal of bread and wild spinach and the remains of a rabbit someone had shot, before they started on the laundry, Mara did a head count and noted a few absences. Heartache wove through the raucous laughter. Who had given their life for liberation that day? That blond girl, the smaller Bosnian whose fair skin she had admired was not amongst them, and another young woman, probably not twenty, who along with her brother, had been orphaned when the Ustashas had burnt their village. She recognised the brother later but could not tell by the taut face whether he was grieving a lost sister or whether she was among the wounded, tended by nurses with scant medicines or bandages. She didn't like to ask and, such could be the mood of epic heroism following a casualty, she felt that whatever she said might be wrong.

*****

Jana's kill was celebrated amongst the women. They were ordinary, decent people, empowered by their struggle and, as a fighting force, experience was teaching them strength, yet Jana did not typify the village women who led their lives in the shadow of men. Andreja Mraz was a better example and, until the war, it was apparent that she would live an average female life of ceaseless work and child bearing, with only an early death from exhaustion as thanks. Mara was teaching her to read and write, because she was unable to do either.

'Well, you know her story, don't you?' Jana told Mara. 'Married at sixteen to a lout who belted her when he was drunk—and when he wasn't. Why? Because his father belted his mother. You see her broken nose? Now she's thirty. She's had five miscarriages and borne two sons, and then one day the Germans come and shoot every male member in her village, including the hideous husband and the sons, who were only twelve and thirteen. Some retaliation for the local *odred* burning the hemp warehouse and killing one or two German watchmen. She loses her father, her sons and two of her three brothers—the youngest was in the woods at the time, looking for the boar. Now suddenly she's free, and she joins the Partisans for revenge.

'You've heard the tales of these abused women. They're always looking backwards. *When we were first married, he was so considerate, he milked the cows for me. He even ploughed the fields for me. He came from the next village and I didn't know him very well, I suppose. My mother told me my father even hit her once, so I thought, perhaps if I cleaned the house better, he wouldn't belt me.* Well, she still loved him. You know the Germans marched the men out of the village and Andreja went looking for the wretch afterwards and found him in a ditch with a bullet in his back. So she cried, just because he was husband. Honestly, some women! But now she's got a satchel on her back and a rifle over her shoulder and a look of determination in her eyes because she finally has the means of fighting back.'

Andreja's eyes, indeed, had a permanent attitude of disdain, which said to Mara, as no words could, what she thought of it all. She wasn't very big and when she pointed the butt of her rifle to the ground, the barrel went up to her shoulder. Mara hesitated to state that she would even have the strength to fire it. One only had to look at her face to put paid to that notion.

'With a rifle in your hand you're no longer a slave to a man!' she said.

'I'm not married,' answered Mara, regarding this woman for whom marriage had been a captive experience and who was now discovering freedom with a gun.

'They know who they are, those who burned my house and killed my sons. Now that I have a gun in my arms, I'll pay them back.' Andreja clenched her fists around her weapon. 'Oh my rifle! You and I will never be parted. You'll be at the end of my wrist until the last day!'

Mara felt quite stirred.

'That's great, Andreja. Did you write it?'

'I? No. My last brother, Franjo, wrote that about me.'

'Nikola Mugoša has written some war songs,' Mara told her. 'But I thought we were an army.'

'We are a people's army, a community. We have a hospital, people to deal with money and supplies, a local court, but not a courthouse. We have everything we need and what is a community without culture? Josip Cazi, the commissar, is a very good poet, and Spiridon takes the choir. We have created a freedom for ourselves amidst blood, songs and colour. As you are teaching us to read and write, Mara, perhaps you can have a poetry class.'

'Of course!' said Mara. 'And I think that gear really suits you, Andreja.'

'Yep!' agreed Andreja. 'See and tremble! Listen to the woman warrior! The woman partisan. This is the best thing that's ever happened to me. I'm never going back to marriage after this.'

CHAPTER TWENTY-THREE

'Of whom are you thinking, partisan poet, while you march along with your feet in the dust and your head in the clouds? Of that nice wife of yours from Slavonia?'

'Yes, Mara, and of my little son. Of how much I love them. I am thinking of how his downy hair catches the sun beams. I am thinking that I will lay my wife's head in my lap and shower it with kisses, my partisan rose, my small hero in the blushing dawn. I have a vision that the sun sent me her fragrant and tremulous hair in greetings of golden ribbons.'

'You are very sentimental for a soldier at war, Commissar.'

'I *am* sentimental, because last night we were in a terrible gunfight. The struggle raged. The brigades assaulted in whistling shots and spattering shells. The thunder pounded and our lightning razed the blood-sucking fascists. But Tito guided the battle carefully and this morning I was lying in a field of flowers. From up the hill, I heard the voices of my comrades singing.'

'Where do you come from, Josip Cazi?'

'I come from Slavonia. From a small town near the Drava river, just before it flows into the mighty Danube.'

'Lots of nice girls in Slavonia?'

Margaret Walker

'The best girls; the daughters of factory workers and fishermen from muddy factory towns beside the Danube.'

'You soft-hearted old thing. Where are these girls now?'

'Some of them are partisans now, comrade. Their mothers have been taken to camps, their houses are devastated and, of their gardens, only rank weeds remain. But I am in love with Slavonia, the land of the partisans, a cradle of rebellion; a region of sweeping fields, forest glades and dewy shrubs. The golden wind sweeps over fields of stalks and my heart is woven into the land, into the fields themselves and the yellow plains. Fireflies dart into the bruised dawn, a rooster crows with the sun and a blackbird plays its silken flute. But since the Germans have come, I mourn the rape of Slavonia and how they have laid waste my beautiful country. The villages were on fire, the bushes choked. My native village that was so lovely now looks like a graveyard of walls, without windows, without doors, roofless. Where once our plains were carpeted with grain and the orchards with fruit, only burnt branches now protrude. Slavonia itself was a blazing sea. Trees, centuries old, were swallowed in a fiery hell. The ancient forest of Papuk, our mountain jewel and the shield of our land, was burned from German planes to expose the Partisans taking shelter in the glades. Deer and wolves ran frightened and moaning from the trees, while Lucifer and his legions danced beside Papuk. All day the demons shrieked.'

'And did the Germans find you?'

'No. The Partisans penetrated the German ring by a stormy impact. With sunburnt faces and black eyes sparkling like flashes of lightning, they blasted the fiery chain in a bloody assault. Blood was in the air, gunpowder and fire, shrouded fields and tired soldiers. Decency and struggle were written on their faces, and their hearts were without trivia, even to the last smile of a dying fighter whose eyes

245

looked to the future, in which they saw our freedom. On the roads our columns sang victory songs in the morning sun, but black peaks of wood smoke rose up to the clouds, the frozen earth was a desolate grey, and we buried our dead in fresh graves by the goat tracks. When, once again, I will see my lovely country, there will be a new law, a new brotherhood. Not today, perhaps, but soon, the whole nation will be walking with us. Those who won't fight are swimming somewhere in a fairy tale, living on illusions and dreams while we go forward in companies, battalions and brigades to wreak revenge on the fascists. Our hope grows stronger every day because of Tito.'

'Captain Marković is not a poet like you.'

'No, Anton is not a poet but I can read his heart nevertheless.'

'He isn't happy to be a Partisan?'

'No, Mara, the sea is his mistress and, wherever he goes, he is thinking of her.'

*****

'It's a cow!' exclaimed Mara.

'Yes.' Anton removed his rifle from his back and rested it against the rickety fence. 'It's a cow.'

Milking was overdue, the farm had been burned and deserted. From far away, he heard the distress of its forsaken family as a sigh on the breeze. What had become of them? To which forest had they fled and what story could be told by the blackened walls they had left behind? He walked into the house to see if he could get a feel for the depressing and increasingly familiar schedule of approach, attack and departure. Although the embers were cold and sludge had formed from a spring shower during the night, he smelled acrid smoke. Wet soot hit him on the forehead and he looked up to see a slow drip from a charred rafter. Out in the yard, the dogs had gone and two dejected chickens dug for worms. A pile of feathers by the fence indicated the fate of the others.

The condition of the cows itself spoke more of their own discomfit: swollen udders, mooing with distress. How long had it been since they were last milked? One day, two days? Some still cropped the grass, but others had lain down in the sun, perhaps to sleep in the late morning, perhaps never to get up again. Hearing a low drone, Anton looked out through a window frame to see a spreading black stain in the paddock beyond the yard and hundreds of blowflies hovering over what must be blood. Some of the animals had been slaughtered, but by whom? The cows, he noticed, avoided the area. They were like ungainly children—the ones that stand out in a classroom because they are the largest—gently roaming around the paddock, sensing something they were unable to express.

Now, look at this poor animal swaying towards the group of Partisans across the grass, the dung and the small lumps of limestone, who mooed and lowed and bent her big brown eyes towards them as if she instinctively knew that they could provide the relief a calf might have given, by relieving her of her milk.

'Golly.' Mara had come to stand beside him and was gawping at the lumbering animal. 'You don't realize how big these things are until you're up close, do you? He's terribly big and he's terribly wide, but he's not an elephant.'

Anton walked over and patted the cow on the head, and she mooed louder. That upset him. He felt sorry for her and dimly realized that he had never felt sorry for a cow before. Her plaintive request to be milked subtracted from the peaceful image of rural tranquillity which, save for the ruined farm, could have been an idyll. Ah, I'm getting soft, he worried. Still, what sort of a world was it if he couldn't help a cow? They had no means of keeping all the milk, but they could relieve the animals and drink what they wanted. Much of it would end up in the grass anyway, but they could lead several away to be slaughtered afterwards.

Most of his company got onto the task without a word. They all came from farms. After a brief search in an outhouse, they discovered the remains of a several wooden buckets, but most of the men and women simply drank as they went. Anton stood watching them before squatting down and preparing to milk the animal before him, which was exhibiting the first traces of apprehension that her plea might have fallen on deaf ears.

'Can I have a turn?'

He looked up. Mara had not left him after her first pronouncement, but was waiting about a metre away, eagerly observing his actions. He sighed, looking around for an animal that seemed more docile and mightn't mind having an amateur holding the reins. However, each had a willing participant at their teats and several more waiting behind, who wanted a drink.

'Okay,' he said finally. 'I'll just settle this one down first.'

He caressed the teats gently until he felt the animal become calm and allow her milk to be squeezed freely.

'You can milk a cow!' Mara exclaimed, as if she had never seen a cow milked before, which she hadn't.

Anton heaved himself halfway up, only a little smug.

'What made you think I couldn't milk a cow?'

His forehead was clean. He had wiped off the soot from the rafters but, had Mara looked, she might have seen it smudged against the curve of his palm. But she hadn't. She'd barely noticed him, too concerned about her chances of success and how to handle a possible failure. Had she been at school, some tweedy teacher would have been marking her right now, clipboard balanced upon a stockinged knee, fountain pen in hand. Anton stood up, roughly eight centimetres taller than she was, and she barely registered her pleasure at waiting beside a man with that much height, because she was bracing herself to succeed. She was going to milk a cow.

'What do I do first, Captain?'

'Anton, if you please, Mara.'

'I don't know whether I can.'

'Can what?'

'Refer to you informally.'

'Just try, would you? I feel like a bureaucrat.'

She needed a little more instruction, this green city girl who was being marked by a teacher ambitious for her future. But she would show these communists a thing or two. She touched the teat hesitantly. It was hot, red and hard.

'It's quite, um,' she smiled back at him encouragingly '– now let me find the right word—engorged, is that it?'

'It needs milking, that's all.'

With a quick glance at the other men and women working with ease, Mara positioned herself as far from the cow's back legs as she could and put her hands where Anton's had been. Then she clasped one teat quickly and released it.

'Easy,' he cautioned. 'You'll scare the cow.'

The animal shuffled its feet. Mara jumped up.

'He's going to kick me!'

'She's not going to kick you. Just relax.'

'Good idea. Yes, thanks for that. You see, I would like to tell them at home that I've done it.'

The cow looked back reproachfully, so Anton got down again, squeezing first one teat then the other, getting into a rhythm. She watched him work.

'Did you grow up on a farm or something?' she asked.

'No,' he said.

'Did somebody teach you how to do it?'

'Yes.'

'Then one can learn these activities of daily living without being a farmer's daughter! I would like to be taught like you. I would like to do it properly.'

'No one's marking you.'

'Hey... why did you think...? You know, you're a mystery man. Wait! Do you think you can leave some milk in it for me?'

It was still easier for him to be the teacher. He stood up.

'Off you go, then,' he said, indicating the cow, waiting expectantly for him to finish the job.

Mara looked at it hesitantly before descending to her knees and again placing her hands gingerly on the teats. The invisible examiner vanished, though she still looked for her because a good school report would please her father.

'Nice cow. There's a good cow. Hey, I think I'm getting it! Milk's squirting out the end. That's a good sign, isn't it?'

'Do you want a drink?'

'What? Straight from the...um...'

'Teat.'

Mara stopped.

'I'm not that desperate, thank you.'

The cow, sensing Mara's rejection and tiring of the fuss over what ought to have been a straightforward twice-daily ritual, expressed her discontent by kicking Anton in the shin.

'Shit!!!'

'Oh, Captain! Oh, my goodness!'

Mara put a hand to her mouth. Here followed an exhibition of coping in a crisis that she had learned at school, upon observing that English girls cover up their ignorance by flustering, in order to present an appearance of action. Even when she had thrown all other peelings from England onto the compost heap, this alone remained.

She knelt beside him, flapping her hands.

'Are you all right? I'll get nursie to put some comfrey on it.'

'I'm fine,' Anton muttered though it was obvious he wasn't.

'Nursie won't mind, honestly.'

Anton gritted his teeth, but it was an inadequate bulwark against an upper-class English education.

'Speak like an adult, Mara!' he thundered.

He tentatively prodded the impact point that was swelling to resemble the size and consistency of a soft-boiled egg while the pain assaulted him with the cruelty of casual violence. The usual frustrating realization that he been misplaced in his own situation by a woman, wormed its way to his surface and he didn't know what to do about it. She was hovering around him now, spewing the usual sympathetic drivel, drawing all eyes to the circus he'd got himself into.

'I had no idea the cow would do that.'

That was not true and it wasn't helping. Mara extended a helpless hand like he was in childbirth and she the blundering midwife, while he attempted to weight bear on a leg that was wallowing in self-pity and refused to support him.

'Aghh...fuck!'

'Yes, yes, sorry, sorry,' tweeted Mara distractedly. 'I'll get...'

'I don't need a nurse.'

'Right-oh! I'll just shoot off and get one.'

The two nurses, aged about eighteen, were well aware of what had occurred, as they had been observing the situation with quiet interest ever since Mara had requested a lesson in milking. From time to time, they had raised their heads from behind a teat and had witnessed the unfolding drama from across the paddock. As Mara came rocketing towards them, squawking like a parrot, they rose from their own milking, waded through the long grass and upbraided the cow loudly.

'Shame on you!' yelled the first. 'Kicking Captain Marković! Who do you think you are, the boss?'

'You keep those hooves to yourself,' shrieked the second, 'He'd love to eat a cranky cow like you. Look how thin he is! You watch yourself or you'll be dinner.'

The cow looked up resentfully but submitted to the authority of the country girls. Her brown eyes subsided into bovine tranquillity and she wandered off to graze.

The nurses were delighted to help, and expressed confidence that Anton would survive his injury. To his protests, they paid little attention and carried on in the same vein as they had with the cow.

'Now do as you're told, Captain. We'll look after you.'

In ten seconds they had him seated on the grass in a position of submission and were inspecting his leg diligently. The procedure was completed without him being able to utter a syllable and represented a superb example of strident organization that refused to be challenged.

CHAPTER TWENTY-FOUR

'*Dear Winston, How are you? I am very well. Thank you for the radio set. My best greetings to King George.*'

Because Nigel was an elite athlete at cryptic crosswords, decoded messages that didn't suit anybody else at Bletchley Park arrived upon his desk from the Cipher Section, where he gave creative thought to their significance. From the day he'd arrived, fresh-faced and humbled by military security, bearing a letter requesting his immediate presence, he had evolved his own job description piece by piece. The older staff were not initially sure what he was there for and the summons to help his country that had so excited his parents, at first disappointed even him. Most of his days were spent reading random messages sent from one spy with a grudge against another, a love sick radio operator, an intelligence officer from Cairo succumbing to depression in the windswept ravines of Northern Greece, a sexually frustrated English captain wallowing in an Egyptian brothel. Just once in a while might come something that might help somebody somewhere. Or might not.

The message to the Prime Minister in front of him this morning scarcely required his talents.

'Same sender?' asked the colonel.

'Possibly,' Nigel replied. 'It was sent on an identical frequency to the others, but this one's in English, using British
codes; and again they are the correct codes for that day.'

'Where's it from?'

'Serbia again.'

The colonel scratched his head.

'"Best Greetings", he read. 'That's an odd valediction.
He's got a British radio set, but he's clearly not British.'

'And he's not German,' suggested Nigel. 'Even though he
uses German codes.'

'Why do you say that?'

'Because he practised first. Therefore, he wasn't a trained
operator.'

'Good point... um, inefficient... not the Germans' usual
style. Well done, Nigel.' He cleared his throat as pompously
as he was able. 'How did you know that Hudson had lost his
radio?'

'I didn't. I only assumed that it went missing at the end of
November after we received that message from him to the
ambassador, and while Captain Hudson was still with the
guerrillas. He was transmitting then on *his* radio, using our
codes and frequencies. The next time we got a message using
those settings it was from this mystery man. Nothing further
from Captain Hudson.'

'We knew it had been Hudson's intention to proceed
northeast to the headquarters of the Chetniks in the first
week in December,' mused the colonel, 'to reconnect with
General Mihailović. I wonder, do we reply to this chap in the
hope that he knows something of Hudson's whereabouts? I'll
have to speak with the Prime Minister. Hudson was only sent
to Yugoslavia to research resistance activities. It's his information the Prime Minister needs: How many Germans are
being killed and who's killing them.'

'Sir?'

Margaret Walker

'Where are we now... March?'

'Excuse me, sir....'

The colonel checked himself. He was talking to himself again, just as his wife complained that he always did. Coming home late, or not at all, talking like some fool. *Loose lips sink ships,* she told him. *I was not babbling anything confidential,* declared the colonel. War put such a strain on marriages. He yawned and straightened his tie.

'Yes, Nigel.'

'I've got an idea, sir. Let's see if we can get this guy to reply to us. Send out the same message, on the same frequency, at the same time and using the same code. Make it really simple. See if he can recognize it from amongst the other traffic on the airwaves. If he's interested enough to practise, there's just the possibility that he will be on air enough hours to pick up a repetitive signal. You could even send it out in plain language rather than code to make it easier for him.'

'Could that be a security risk?'

'Just don't say anything in particular,' suggested Nigel affably. 'And make it as simple as possible if you want to communicate with him, given, sir, that it appears he is an amateur.'

'He certainly has not received British training. These whimsical messages, even outbursts of emotion... no British officer would do that...

'Well, once or twice, sir...,' stammered Nigel. 'Just once or twice....'

'No, Nigel! No British officer would behave in an unseemly fashion.'

'Yes, sir.'

'All right, young Nigel.' The colonel was on top again. 'We'll ask him how he came by his radio. See if we can find out what happened to Captain Hudson, but don't mention him by name.'

Through Forests and Mountains

*****

Miroslav was used to being euphoric about his achievements—modesty was for imbeciles—but there came a time when even he tired of never receiving a reply. It was a bit like sending invitations to your own birthday party, knowing you were never to hold one. So he began listening in to the cacophony of transmissions on the general radio waves, just by way of amusement. There was a great deal of noise. Until he had some sense of what he was listening for, it sounded like a dozen orchestras tuning up at once, but never starting the concerto. And then, of course, very little communication was sent in plain language; most of it had been encrypted. On certain frequencies, he'd also interrupted radio broadcasts from Berlin and Moscow—once he even found a church choir from Geneva—until he learned which frequencies to avoid. In addition, there was the problem of decoding the messages. He had the small Enigma Machine and his British code books, and the accompanying calendars that showed him on which days to apply them. The trouble was that, despite all his talents and his obvious good looks (which helped him in most situations but not this one) he was woeful at recognising patterns and always had been. He had a great talent for invention and self-preservation, two things of obvious advantage to a journalist, but he had been bad at maths lessons, where the patterns had been taught. So, aside from a few cursory attempts at code breaking, for the most part, he gave up. He used the books as his operator had showed him, but got no more creative than that. It did appear to him sometimes that he would never be able to recognise anything in the cacophony of sound on the airways, just as he could not distinguish between the sound of a clarinet and a saxophone, and calculus remained the mystery it had been in high school.

Margaret Walker

Finally by blind luck, as he termed it, he realized that one particular transmission was showing signs of repetition that even he could recognise. Dot dot dot dot dash dash dash dot dash dash dot dot dot dash dash dash dot dot dash dot dash dot dot dash dot dot dash dash dot dot dot dot dash dash dash. Over and over again at the same time every day, for a fortnight. He had managed to latch on to the four dots and three dashes at the beginning, though he often got confused after that. But that beginning! It was starting to replicate in his brain like musical frog spawn. During those momentous days, once, just once, he had noticed that the same signal was sent two days in succession, on the same frequency.... On the third day, there it was again! He wrote out the strange letters, checked the enigma specifications for that day and discovered that it had not been encrypted at all, but sent out simply in ordinary German.

Miroslav was not suspicious and this was unlike him. The slip, he was sure, was caused by the stress of sitting on a desolate mountain top in a cold wind entertained by punctuation. Normally he was suspicious of everything, every human action, every military action, every plan, every failed attempt. He was, in particular, deeply suspicious of human nature and had come to believe that life was, to most men, about sex, power and money, in that order. But now, what had commenced as a whimsical exercise, born out of his own achievements and cleverness, suddenly caught his interest in a very tangible way.

The message didn't say very much.

How's our radio?

But those fourteen repetitions! The lure was so simple, yet so clever.

Miroslav licked his lips. *Now here is an adversary worthy of me*, he thought. *Who, having defined the dimensions of a square to his satisfaction, takes the obvious step and*

257

moves into the eerie silence beyond it, not for reasons of enterprise but simply because he is interested enough to wonder What Might Be Out There. The company he keeps bores him. When you have to instruct your colleagues in the right way of doing things all the time, how weary life becomes!

The question is, How shall I reply?

He thought long and hard about this, then adjusted his antenna and cranked up the transmitter, wishing he had an ignorant peasant to do it for him. Then he commenced typing. Click, click, click went the key.

'It's my radio now.'

*****

The elderly colonel had had to get used to a few deviations from strict military behaviour whilst working at Bletchley Park. Dealing with the eccentric nerds and boffins he found there was one thing; interpreting the language of the young was a second. At Nigel's whoop of joy, shortly after the courier's arrival that morning, he had adjusted his tie and hurried into the main room of the hut, hoping that the sound was not an unknown illness, to find Nigel at his desk quite well, surrounded by piles of the day's transcripts.

Like the teenager he was, Nigel couldn't stop grinning.

'Gotcha!' he said, waving Miroslav's message in the colonel's direction.

Here we go, thought the colonel. He put on his glasses and scanned the brief words.

'Is this the man who has Hudson's radio?' he asked.

'Yep!' Nigel had yet to calm down.

'But how do you know, Nigel? Are you quite sure?'

'No, sir, but if I proceed on that probability, then certain things become evident. He has transmitted from the area where Hudson went missing. Although each message is coming from exactly the same place, he is writing to someone. He

258

has said, 'I'm watching you,' 'I know where you are'. Though how could he know, if he himself hasn't moved? He is interested in someone who *has* moved, clearly, although he couldn't be watching them physically. But he wants them to think that he is.' Nigel paused. 'I wonder where they have moved to. It may suggest that he is interested in the same things we are, though not necessarily for the same purpose. We are also interested in someone who has moved. He uses British codes, which he evidently acquired with the radio, but he also has an Enigma Machine and the book which tells him which German codes to use and when. This suggests he is either German...'

'...or, in that part of the world, Italian or Yugoslav.'

'Let's keep it simple and say that he is working for the Germans, whatever his nationality.'

'But we don't know any of this, Nigel.'

'No, sir, we don't. However, one can work on the probability of something being correct, and thus arrive at a supposition of what might be going on.'

'Where do you get this idea from?'

'From school, sir. Mathematics, sir.'

'Indeed. Then if you are so certain about this probability, Nigel, inform our friend that he has Marko's radio—take care not to call him Hudson—and that Marko needs it.'

'I don't think that will help if he doesn't know where Captain Hudson is, but we could factor it in to the equation.'

'Yet, locating Captain Hudson must be our highest priority. It is true that there are only one or two Englishman around Eastern Bosnia and Western Serbia, his last known whereabouts. That must narrow it down.'

'I hope he survived the severe winter there, sir.'

The colonel's face firmed quite severely at this slight.

'Be British, Nigel!' he commanded. 'Let us not indulge in melancholy speculation. Captain Hudson is a resourceful chap.'

'Yes, he is, sir, but he has lost contact with his radio operator and he has only basic knowledge of how to send a message to us in Morse code, even when he locates a radio that he can use. Now, I could put together a likely scenario, based on what we know. There is no problem that can't be solved.'

The colonel could picture Nigel in ten years' time leaning over a gargoyled balustrade in some college of Cambridge or Oxford, coffee in hand, chatting amicably and unintelligibly to students similar to a youthful version of the colonel. A young professor, perhaps, still wearing his trademark Fair Isle vest and broad trousers, whose pleasant response to the confounded puzzlement of his students would be simplicity in itself. The colonel, stuck in the nineteenth century, could only admire someone for whom the world made so much sense. War made sense to him only on the field of battle, though it was clear to the legion of workers within Bletchley Park that the real war was being won behind the scenes by the intelligence service, through the thousands of encrypted military orders it received daily. It was fortunate that Hitler did not take codes, nerds and spies seriously, and was unable to appreciate the profound logic necessary to break a code and read the enemy's intentions, almost before they reached its own forces. Aside from being a talented mathematician and a student of the philosophy of science, Nigel also held his school's record for breaking the cryptic crossword in *the Daily Telegraph*, six minutes and twenty-nine seconds.

The colonel sighed.

'Thank you, Nigel. Do that, if you would be so kind; and when you've finished, I will put it to the Prime Minister.'

Margaret Walker

'I bet this guy's stalking his girlfriend,' said Nigel, almost to himself. 'Why else would he stay stuff like, "I love you, darling" and "I know where you are?"'

'Aren't you too young to know about such things, Nigel?'

Nigel shook his head.

'One of the masters at school did that to a pupil.'

The colonel was too shocked to reply.

CHAPTER TWENTY-FIVE

In March 1942, as the spring snows trembled and winter loosened its grip on the landscape, Tito formed the Second Proletarian Brigade in Foča and this time, Mara was one of the hundred women amongst the thousand, proudly holding her rifle from the German factory in Foča, with an Italian grenade dangling from her belt. As a lieutenant commander, Anton was placed in charge of one of the companies, although he felt Nikola would have been a more obvious choice, and so did Nikola. At Nikola's grim face, the Montenegrin was placed in charge of a smaller company, until he discovered that they had been planning to put him there anyway, when his mood lightened somewhat. In the line-up before the supreme staff, Slobodan, Boško and Aleksandra stood at a distance from the leaders, although Mara still made sure that she and Aleksandra remained together, and secretly shuffled up a row to ensure it. Then, as if to welcome the new force, in the second last week of April, the Germans launched Operation Trio against all Partisans and Chetnik forces between Sarajevo and the Drina River, upon which Foča was built. Couriers sneaking like wraiths across enemy lines brought news daily of their advance and conveyed the activities of guerrillas in their areas to the Partisans' command. Giving the clenched fisted communist salute, they relayed with grimy faces and taut nerves the movements from other areas.

An enemy army can be slowed down considerably by destroying bridges and railway lines, and the large, lumbering armies typical of standard German procedure were considerably frustrated by these and other partisan tactics. In their opinion, the inexperienced fighters of these early days had been swiftly dispatched and overrun by a well trained and equipped force. In a sense, this was true. Partisan casualties in 1942 were much higher than German, Italian and Ustasha. Lose the battle they might, but disappear they did not. And they were learning. Once they had been driven from an area, they always returned, to sow the seeds of revolt and partisan warfare among those displaced villagers who had taken to the woods. So, the enemy could never truly get rid of them. In an attempt to prevent their revival in the reconquered areas, mopping-up activities included deportation of locals and destruction of villages over a wide area.

Anton had explained the information from the Supreme Command and Mara had pieced together what she understood of it, in a manner similar to her university days in London, when she had been trying to make sense of the syllabus. She would never forget the cold, the fear and the hunger of that winter in the mountains of Bosnia, but she was learning to live with the pattern of warfare and developing resilience. As she was never alone, she was learning comradeship. The terrible casualties could not stop the flow of new recruits, and monthly their numbers swelled. For a people who had lost everything, there was no other alternative to occupation but fighting and dying. Partisan warfare was not merely the matter of defeat and surrender that the Nazis had come to expect.

Through Forests and Mountains

*****

'Those God forsaken Germans!' bawled Nikola to his sons. 'They never learn. They have to prove their superiority the German way every hour of every day, and they can't un-learn their German-ness because some inferior Slav might actually teach them something!'

'They don't like us, Tata. If they kill us, it is because we are the enemy but, if we kill them, they call it murder.'

'Good.'

'And they are calling us Bolshevik Bandits.'

'I'm not a Bolshevik, Boško.'

'But we are bandits.'

'We are mountain guerrillas.'

'Which are bandits. You talk too much, Tata.'

'I have not heard you stop talking this evening, Boško, not once. You answer your own questions before you ask them. Now sit and listen while I tell you something about Germans and Italians that you don't know.'

'How did you find this out?'

'Because I listen and you talk. At this moment the Germans are protecting their transport routes through eastern Bosnia. You think they take our land and sit on it, but that's where you're wrong. They need food, they need clothes, they need ammunition, they need petrol, and that's where we come in. We disrupt those transport routes and, when we do, the Germans have unwittingly donated to us their supplies and their uniforms. Basking in their German superiority, they know nothing about mountain warfare in Bosnia and don't care to learn, because they think they know everything already. Their generals will insist on surrounding the enemy, but this will only work in suitable terrain.'

'Which is not Bosnia in winter.'

'Well done, Slobodan. You've been listening. But it's spring and the snow is melting now and here come the clumsy Germans with their troops and their tanks and their heavy artillery. To leave nothing to chance, they follow this up with a field canteen and a hospital and everything else that is cumbersome. Then, they attempt to exterminate us by using their classic encirclement technique. But we sense the weak point in the ring and escape, because we are lightly armed, moveable guerrillas. Why can't the Germans get this through their thick heads? Because Germans hate surprizes and they are too well-trained to change.

'Now I'll tell you something about Italy. Italy should stick to food and culture because it is no good at warfare. They say that Italians are superior and inferior Slavs should be happy if they kill us, because under Yugoslavia we will only degenerate further. They are putting us out of our misery. You have noticed, boys, how miserable we are. As we speak, the Italians are driving the Germans to fits of frustration because they are emotional, instinctive and operatic, as opposed to tactical, logical and methodical.'

'The Germans?'

'Well done. Italians are too pre-emptive for the Nazis in warfare, because they allow their hearts to rule their heads. This weakens the precise Germans strategy, which, we have already established, is unsuitable for Bosnia. Like a rubber boat, it begins to leak and must be continually reinflated. Therefore, I predict that Italy will change sides in this war, like they did in the last, and that Germany will invade them as it has invaded everything else. Now look at this Italian mess in North Africa. If Mussolini hadn't insisted upon invading Egypt from its colony in Libya, Rommel would never have become famous by coming to the Italians' rescue. But in the end, the Allies will kick them all out.'

'How do you know?'

Through Forests and Mountains

'For the same reason I know that we are going to beat Germany, Boško. Because they are wrong and we are right.'

'But what about our tactics? We're not a real army.'

'Yes, we are. We are the People's Liberation Army of Yugoslavia, and we know our own country. The Balkans are not called the haunt of brigands and witches for nothing, and our countrymen know who we are now so, when we return, they will be ready to support us.'

*****

Slobodan was shot through the abdomen, with a bullet he hadn't seen coming, fired by a Ustasha corporal. The bullet passed right through his young body just below his rib cage, narrowly grazing part of the large intestine, and it was some days before the nurses on duty following the battle could determine that the intestines had not been punctured, largely by the absence of rampant infection. In that case Slobodan would almost certainly have perished. Happily for Slobodan, who had inherited his father's positive nature, the bullet had passed through in the right direction, from the front to the back. Dire threats of cowardice would have been ensued, had it gone in the opposite direction. For some time, he lay in an icy puddle, passing in and out of conscious, while bullets whizzed about him like pot shots from a gumball machine, until two nurses were able to brave the inferno and assist him to stumble from the field and into the safety of the woods. It had not been apparent to them in the darkness whether Slobodan was still alive, until he managed to wave a hand into the air during one of his intermittent periods of consciousness. His sleeve glowed in the sun, which was hovering barely beyond the horizon, threatening to flood the scene with daylight. Those Partisans who were more obviously dead, they left to its harsh ravishes. Wobbling along and clutching his side, making jokes about the direction of the bullet, the nurses figured that he could not be that much hurt, until they peeled off his coat and shirt and saw the wound.

The entry wound itself was a classic study in gunshot wounds, small and dark with red around the outside and a continuing trail of blood down the abdomen that took the nurses some application of pressure to staunch, but the exit wound was substantially larger, so that they were at a loss to explain it. Somebody found a bandage, but there was little to be done about the risk of infection until Slobodan could be transported by horse and cart behind the main arc of the travelling brigade and taken to the Central Partisan Hospital in Foča. Here, there would be whatever antiseptics had been stolen from the enemy and scraps smuggled out to them from pharmacies in occupied towns. It was absolutely essential that Slobodan not be left behind as the company moved on—even with a nurse to look after him—or the Germans, the Ustashas or the Italians would shoot him, through the head or the heart this time and not just the abdomen. Slobodan continued to make light of his injury until he passed out from the pain and blood loss. In the evening Nikola was found and told about his son.

At the hospital, distributed across a riot of village houses and recently-built shacks, Slobodan was seen by a properly qualified doctor from Zagreb, of a communist persuasion, and attended to by nurses that the doctor had trained. He lay on the ubiquitous straw bed while a young nurse provided pain relief by distraction, since the morphine donated by a large pharmacy in Sarajevo had run out. As she chatted away about her fiancé on the other side of the river, and how well the poddy calf got on with her three-legged puppy (although they both chased the chickens) Slobodan fell asleep and, when he woke up, his father was sitting by his bed with his head in his hands, having competed his prayers for his son.

Through Forests and Mountains

As Nikola entered, the nurse rose. She wore the same clothes they all did, half peasant costume, half stolen German and Italian uniforms. By her feet lay a small collection of pharmaceuticals and bandages, but not very much. Earlier, they had been able to buy medicine from the pharmacy in Foča, but now supplies had dwindled, and what they had captured from the enemy needed replenishing. The shack smelled of new wood, but already spiders had taken up abode in the angles where the roof sloped up to its peak, and the lack of a ceiling, plus the unwanted arachnids, lent the building an air of antiquity that reminded Nikola of an old church. Around Slobodan lay a dozen other patients, as serene as a political prisoner he had once ministered to under the Austrians, who had gone on a hunger strike to protest the rigours of empire. They lay silently and watched him, composed by the air of righteous suffering for a cause greater than themselves. In fact, the hospital, such as it was, was very calm, as if it were holy, for the wounded, body and soul, were members of the entire company. The success of the Partisans depended on this intimate relationship. Care of the wounded was as important to Partisan philosophy as fighting. Exterminate the wounded and you weaken the main force. Hence, the enemy killed any of them they found.

Whilst the Supreme Command was stationed in the town, the hospital openly went about its business, but across the nation, field hospitals sprung up, positioned with the utmost secrecy, in the wild mountains, through caves and waterfalls, with bears and wolves as silent witnesses. Secret passes, deleted footprints and hidden trails alike led to Partisan hospitals and, when forced to flee, the wounded made up an extensive train in the rear of the marches, dragged through the mountains and across rivers and ravines in their thousands, and never abandoned.

CHAPTER TWENTY-SIX

Mara's heart began to harden as she watched Slobodan carried into the Central Hospital in Foča. Here was a young man she had known, reduced from vibrant health to morbidity, and all because her country had been invaded by an army of well-fed, arrogantly self-righteous fascists. She had seen others taken away, too. They got better, they died, or they joined the long trail of wounded whose care was paramount, but which was beyond her skill. She felt helpless, she felt angry, and Anton noticed the change in her.

Cows excluded, his directive to himself, regarding keeping Mara at a professional distance, had so far held up, but he had not forsaken his misgivings of women as fighters. The Second Proletarian Brigade contained ten percent women. Presently, they were besieging the town of Rogatica, a twelve hour walk north of Foča, from which they had been evicted by the Germans only two months previously. Rogatica was now held by Germany's allies, the Ustasha. The Brigade was wearing the enemy down, but had not yet taken the town. To besiege it involved the most risk because there had, at some point, to be a charge. Watching women assault a town, often with an enthusiasm that put the men to shame, and with a higher casualty rate, was a sight Anton thought he would never come to terms with. Not women, not dead, not on a field of battle. Since his mother had died, he had never seen a woman dead, and he could not look with anything but horror on the body of a girl. It seemed to him that a girl slain in battle was like a four-legged spider: limbs at unnatural angles, dark hair, young skin, and a heart that the enemy could not conquer. If not, then why run towards death with such courage? Why keep demanding to fight? He could not understand it. Wherever possible, the girls were buried afterwards, but sometimes they had to stay where they had fallen, to decay into the earth and be found, perhaps, in a year's time as a gentle skeleton covered modestly by the remains of their clothes.

That they were a small force and had the support of the town's community was in their favour, but they had lost a few of the girls in earlier assaults and, during the last one that afternoon, Anton had deliberately held the women back until the main attack had taken the steam out of the Ustasha's defence. He was running up the hill with his men, his rifle cocked and his eyes on the enemy when, without warning, Mara uncovered herself briskly from her hiding place further down and charged towards two Ustasha soldiers like a wild animal. Her height initially camouflaged her gender, so that he wondered how their numbers seemed to have suddenly increased. It was only when he had a better look that he registered alarm at the sight of her, and the same could be said of the soldiers towards whom she ran. It was hard to tell their ages beneath the uniforms and heavy helmets, but Anton guessed that they were barely older than Mara, and a woman's sudden appearance in a company of men took them completely by surprise. He registered their confusion when the mad harpy ran at them, all emotions and no regard for her own safety, and noted the shortest pause before they aimed their rifles, during which they fought with the upbringing that insisted they should never harm a female. That hesitation gave her the advantage. In three seconds, she was so close that she could have hit at least one of them with her eyes shut. She pointed her rifle at the closest and fired. The man flailed his arms and dropped directly forward, while Anton watched the man's companion rally himself and aim his weapon at her. But in that half second, Anton had fired himself, and the second soldier dropped to the ground beside the first. The blood of the young men welled out upon the grass.

Anton paused, his chest heaving and his mind a torrent of shock.

Mara. Where was she? Was she all right? He searched around him, panicked when he couldn't find her immediately. A disabling fear. For her. No one else.

Until there she was, right beside him.

Overwhelmed with relief, he seized her arm and steered her forcefully back down the hill and well into the forest. A bullet whizzed past his head and he worried that she had been hit until a warm stream began to course down one side of his forehead and he felt a blunt burning throb above his hairline. And he was suddenly unreasonably upset, because he had read that wounds never hurt in the heat of battle, so why was the fucking thing tormenting him now?

He slammed his rifle into the ground. Ah, what was he doing here anyway, marooned in this shithole supervising hysterical women? This whole Partisan experiment was ridiculous. He should have stuck to the ships he knew and not be in a forest in Bosnia with a rifle in his hands and a bullet in his head, and a woman by his side cackling like a throttled fowl in some dazzling display of hormonal triumph. He was so upset that he wanted to shake her, and only barely restrained himself. Nevertheless, he pinioned her shoulders in such a firm grip that the knuckles of his fingers stood out like marbles. Then he heaved a shuddering sigh and lost his temper.

'You fucking threw yourself at them!' he roared, briefly releasing a hand to wipe blood from his eye. 'What the hell were you thinking? You could have been killed! You didn't think, did you? You'll be dead and I'll be dead trying to save you.'

But his outburst only animated her.

'Let me go, you big bully!' she cried, wriggling to get out of his grasp. 'I've got to get back!'

'You're not going anywhere, young lady.'

'Yes, I am! I killed a fascist and I'm going to kill another one.'

'You were ordered to stay behind the men.'

'I'll do what I like!'

'You can't do what you like in the army.'

She'd lost her head besieging Rogatica—he understood it clearly—and she was nothing but a headstrong woman, the product of a privileged upbringing. Her face below him was exuberant, breathless and beautiful and her eyes, as she struggled with him, were so close that he was astounded by their depths. She threw back her head and he saw the sunset brighten the tips of her hair. Already the light was fading and soon night would fall. Anton was sad, as one is at twilight, though he didn't know why. Before him, her eyes paled, her hair darkened, and she was too exhilarated to perceive his bewilderment.

'I want to fight!'

He took a breath. He forced himself to reply reasonably.

'I'm not happy with you fighting.' He released her and placed a hand flat down in front of him as a conciliatory gesture. 'Now, I know that you type. Please stay in the typing pool where you'll be safer.'

Margaret Walker

'But I shot a fascist!' She clasped her hands together over and over, in an effort to express what she had achieved and gabbled on, regardless of his distress. 'In his chest where you showed me. He went like this.' She threw the hands over her head, stuck her tongue out and blurted from its soft circlet of lips that he suddenly wanted to kiss. 'I did just what you told me and you are being illogical to show me one thing then tell me another. I'll tell everyone that Captain Marković has failed the first principles of consistency in command and should be demoted to fetching water! So there! And while you're down at the river, the women will triumph on the battlefield!'

She wiped her palms down her trousers but he saw not the blood he dreaded, but perspiration. He found himself wishing to protect her; absurd, given that he'd been shot and not her.

'Calm down, Mara.'

'That's rich, coming from you.'

'Look,' he persisted. 'I never taught you to deliberately put your life at risk. The women in this company have a consistently higher casualty rate than the men, and it's because they're not considering their approach. If you'd been a man, that soldier would have shot you without hesitation.'

'He was a disgusting fascist!' she spat back. Either she hadn't listened to a word he'd said or she treated him with disdain. 'Do you realize what these monsters have done to us?'

'Of course.'

'Then, if I'd only wounded him, I would have finished him off with my bayonet, *Captain*.' She finished with an emphasis that indicated her estimation of his attempts to suppress her.

He saw her determination and, despite himself, wished to level them so that he might understand her better, this young

273

woman who had just killed her first human being without remorse and whose safety it seemed he was unable to neglect.

'I really wish you would call me Anton,' he said, 'not Captain. I was never an army captain. I was the captain of a submarine, from Belgrade, like you. You have to understand that in the navy, rank and captain are two different things.'

But the other fighters were returning now, traipsing back into the forest and dissolving away. Mara waltzed off to join them without another word, leaving Anton in a fulminating stew of rage, vulnerability and frustration. *I might have well not opened my mouth. She's not listening to me and I need her to listen.* He was upset because he didn't know why this should have upset him. Why him? Why her? Why now?

One of the older nurses waylaid him, stalking back to their temporary camp with his teeth set and blood running down his face, and dressed the wound on his scalp despite his protests. He tried grumbling at her, and then he pleaded a heavy workload to get away from the fuss she was clearly enjoying, but she shut him up with brisk female authority.

'You are in no position to argue, Captain.'

'Call me Anton,' he said wearily.

This cultivation of intimacy was not his style. These days, he just didn't know what was happening to him and he thought Mara had forgotten the request about his name as well, until he saw her that evening, washing the men's shorts with the other girls and making jokes about whether "the big ones were Anton's".

Later, in the quiet of that night, Josip Cazi paid him a visit. Calmly he sat down beside him and they remained staring at the thin line of silver beyond the trees that marked the river, in the soft air of the mountains, in silent comradeship.

Eventually the commissar began, 'I noticed you were angry today.'

Margaret Walker

Anton scratched his wound and wondered why now. Because she was alive and he had saved her? But he had spent his emotions and had none left, and that was a relief. In fact, he couldn't discern why he was now calm, nor why he had been so distressed.

'Mara is headstrong, commissar. She was doing her best to get herself killed.'

'We're at war, Anton,' the commissar replied soberly.

And it wasn't as if Anton didn't know that. He had had a career in the military, had he not? He desired to liberate his country. The peasant girls wanted to fight, and the traditional philosophy did not shirk at the sacrifice of the individual for the sake of their country. They put their heads to the block and sang joyfully, even as the axe descended. What had Tito said about not fighting close to home, so that their families didn't see them fall? Take Aleksandra, for instance, that little friend of Mara's, who still wore the tattered skirt and blouse in which they had found her, with a jumper hauled over the top. Someone had got her a greatcoat taken from a dead German, as guard against the Bosnian snows, and now she wandered around looking like a lost deer in the skin of a wolf, but with the eyes of a hunter. He didn't want to say anything prematurely, but he could predict that very soon Mara would lose her. She watched his lessons with intensity, as if she could already see a way of reunion with her slain family and be revenged upon the brutal occupiers, Ustashas, Germans, Italians, Bulgarian, Hungarian, whoever they might be. And by dying with a smile on her face, her blood would greet the friendly soil. He was amazed that Mara couldn't see it. 'I just want Mara to think about what she's doing,' he persisted, determined to justify himself to the commissar.

'Her problem,' Cazi told him. 'Is that she thinks too much. She's all out on her political crusade to defeat the philosophy of the fascists. Apparently her ex-boyfriend was in that category.'

'I didn't know that. A German?'

'Ustasha. And Mara lacks the canniness of the village women. It might help her, if she could acquire some.' He paused. 'I'll tell you a story about Tito. You should pass it on to Mara. It could have applied to her. After Belgrade was bombed, several politically minded youths arranged to meet Tito, armed with a lengthy dissertation about the enemy's political ideology and their particular plans for righting its wrongs. Tito's response was a thirty minute talk on how to derail a train.'

Anton flexed his right arm.

'I think Mara would like to derail a train,' he replied.

'Then perhaps she's on the right track after all, excuse the pun.'

They remained in silence until the commissar asked, 'What has the enemy given us today?'

'Rifles, ammunition.'

'Any boots?'

'Yes, a lot of smaller pairs.'

'I thought Germans had big feet.'

'Not these Germans.'

'Then give them to the women. They're most in need.'

'I'll give a pair to Aleksandra. Also there are jackets, trousers and grenades.'

'Food?'

'A little.'

'Medicine? That's what we need most. Food, medicine and ammunition. Tito is hoping for help from Russia.'

'And?'

'As we speak, none is forthcoming.'

CHAPTER TWENTY-SEVEN

Nigel composed his message to the Prime Minister.
To investigate the probability of locating Captain D.T. Bill "Marko" Hudson.
On 25 November 1941 a message was received, care of Captain Hudson, from Užice in Serbia, allegedly for the daughter of the Yugoslav ambassador to her father in London. On 1 December General Mihailović sent us word that Captain Hudson had not returned to Ravna Gora as was expected. Cairo has received no further communication from, or about, Captain Hudson.
On 19 December, we began receiving messages from an unidentified source, written in German and occasionally English, using both Enigma and British codes and the correct radio frequencies. From the errors in language and format it was apparent that the operator had not been trained either by the Germans or the British. With time, these errors decreased; it is therefore assumed that he was practising in some capacity. The messages did not have a military content.
It is doubtful, given the difficulties our own forces experienced before the Royal Navy captured U110 with its Enigma Machine and cipher documents, that the op-

erator would have been able to steal both British and German material. At this time, Captain Hudson was the only member of British Special Forces in the area. It is therefore more than probable that the British code books belonged to Captain Hudson and that the Enigma Machine and German documents indicate that the sender was working for the Germans. The nationality of the operator remains unclear. We have already concluded that he is not military trained, so what is he? A spy? A field journalist? What we don't know are his motives.

How can we assume that the unidentified operator is sending these messages on the set belonging to Captain Hudson? The dates between Captain Hudson's last message and the first unidentified messages are correct.

Once the sender commenced using British codes, a successful attempt to identify him was made, in order to locate Captain Hudson, by sending repeated messages using consistent settings.

We can assume that Captain Hudson's main aim is to resume contact with us. What is the probability of him doing so? When he disappeared he was in regular contact with the leaders of both the guerrillas and the Chetniks, therefore it is quite high.

*****

'Do you think the Prime Minister will read all that, colonel?' asked Nigel.
'Probably just the first line,' the colonel returned.

*****

A day later, the colonel paid Nigel another visit. Nigel had just completed the cryptic crossword in the Telegraph. As the familiar plodding tread approached the room, he hastily put it away, thrust his stopwatch into his pocket, and tried to look as if he had been saving the nation since eight o'clock that morning. Being under age, he was not allowed to relax at the bar like the other staff, and he reasoned that he was owed a little relaxation of his own.

'I asked around the tea room in Hut 4, Nigel,' remarked the colonel, as nonchalant as Nigel was guilty. 'Their best time on today's crossword was eight minutes.'

'Seven minutes, ten,' stammered Nigel.

'Then, as you have so much time on your hands, you may like to get those exceptional neurones of your working a bit harder. The Prime Minister allows you enquire after Marko only. It is his health and well-being we are concerned about. There, now you can decide what message this mysterious man might respond to and run it past me. After that we will send it out.'

'Thank you, sir,' replied Nigel, and put his thinking cap on.

This time he quickly came to the conclusion that a simple, repeated message would get the best response.

'Where is Marko?'

The colonel agreed at once and in less than a week a reply landed on Nigel's desk.

'Haven't seen Marko recently. Ask Mara.'

CHAPTER TWENTY-EIGHT

Captain D.T. Bill Hudson, alias Marko, was indeed a resourceful chap for, as the colonel predicted, he was alive enough to send a message to England by the end of April 1942. He had survived the bitter mountain winter, not in Bosnia but east, in Serbia. The colonel received the news at morning tea and was so delighted that he dropped his ginger-nut into his tea cup, where it landed with a soft plop.

'Message from Captain Hudson sir,' Nigel had announced breathlessly as he scooted into the doorway. 'He's nowhere near them.'

'Ah, yes, well done, Nigel! There we are, you see! Jolly good show! Absolutely first class!' He dug around in his cup for the tea-laden biscuit. 'Where did you say he was?'

'Well into Serbia, Colonel. He's radioed from Chetnik HQ.'

'And where has he been all this time?

'He was lost.'

'Yes, I gathered that.'

'Captain Hudson returned to General Mihailović's headquarters in Ravna Gora in Serbia just as the general was departing. He spent the winter in a Serbian village, being looked after by peasants. All he's eaten is potatoes.'

Nigel thumbed through a stack of messages he had seized from his desk, commencing with, *Haven't seen Marko recently. Ask Mara.* He handed it to the colonel to read.

'Remind me who Mara is,' said the colonel, glancing up.

'It doesn't say here. But what about these?'

'*Dear Ambassador,*' read the colonel to himself. '*Do you still want me to find Mara for you?*' And the next one from Captain Hudson. '*Advise ambassador, contact dangerous.*'

That wiped the shine off his face. He swallowed hard.

'I expect, as he is in Yugoslavia, he must be referring to the Yugoslav ambassador here in England, and Mara—yes, I remember now—was the ambassador's daughter on that message to him. From whom were they sent?'

'The second from Captain Hudson, the first from our unknown man. Here's his motive coming out, our unknown contact. I did feel all along, Colonel, that he was stalking someone. Now it appears that Captain Hudson crossed from Užice to Bosnia with the guerrillas the first week in December, then he returned east towards Chetnik HQ. Can he be contacted?'

'Yes, Nigel, as long as he remains where he is. I will have him asked if he has any knowledge as to the whereabouts of this daughter.'

*****

Captain Hudson surely had his ear glued to the airwaves, for two days later he sent the following reply:

Advised Mara to remain with Tito.

'Who?' asked the colonel.

'The leader of the guerrillas?' Nigel suggested.

'Then don't tell anyone about Captain Hudson's reply, Nigel. Anyone at all.'

CHAPTER TWENTY-NINE

Miroslav arrived back in Belgrade just as Operation Trio was beginning in Eastern Bosnia and in time to hear that, in his absence, General Böhme had been transferred to the Second Panzer Army, to continue his history of war crimes against Slavs. The new Military Commander, Lieutenant General Bader, was an altogether different man, no less imbued with the correctness of German nationalism than his predecessor, but having the ability to distinguish between the fruits of brutality versus efficient management.

After his rural sojourn, Miroslav had returned to the city with relief, brushed the squalor from his clothes and collapsed upon his bed in a sweet-smelling room of the Hotel Moskva, just along the corridor from his first. He lit a cigarette and impatiently awaited the porter as he staggered out of the lift with his boxes (it had been hard enough for the donkey) then arranged the radio and his Enigma Machine like prizes upon the room's writing desk. He blew smoke rings into the air over the little encoder until it looked like a typewriter in the seventh heaven. The remarkable device elicited his highest respect. There it sat, as impregnable as the Germans who had designed it and declared its codes unbreakable. That was what attracted him to his theoretical German, the confidence that once Nazi rules were put into place everything else would follow. You'd soon as meet an eccentric German as you would a boring Englishman. It was true that Germans didn't like surprises, but then, neither did Miroslav. He liked to be on top. He had followed Hitler's rise to become the German chancellor—he was nineteen at the time and a cadet journalist—and strangely, Hitler was the only Nazi he really didn't admire. Though practised in duplicity and propaganda himself, the man's lust for power worried Miroslav, because it was subservient to the reverence for his own intelligence, which was the thing that he most admired.

The hotel had considerately moved his clothes to the new wardrobe, and all that was left for him to do was bathe, shave and present himself, as obsequiously as he was able, to the new authorities. Having done so and coming across the door to General Bader's office open, Miroslav paused at the threshold to observe him at his desk methodically studying a topographical chart of Eastern Bosnia.

Miroslav was calculating his approach when, without warning, the General looked up.

'Bosnia is a mountainous region,' he said.

'Yes, General,' Miroslav replied, watching as the man again surveyed the chart. Eventually he raised his eyes a second time.

'You are?' Bader asked.

'Miroslav Novak, General.'

'And what are you doing for us, Herr Novak?'

Not, *'What can I do for you?'*

Miroslav frowned. 'General Böhme didn't tell you?' And when Bader responded with neither curiosity nor words, he continued, 'I'm an investigative journalist from Zagreb. I belong to the Ustasha, but we were asked to give you full support. Your predecessor wanted information on the leader of the communist rebels—known as the Partisans. The leader called Tito?'

Through Forests and Mountains

Bader went back to studying his map. It appeared to Miroslav that he had been interrupted at a pivotal point in his thoughts and did not appreciate it. Miroslav experienced a piercing resentment at having his work ignored by a man past his prime. He felt like he was at school, waiting for the grace and favour of a teacher to turn a forty-nine at maths into a Pass Conceded, merely because he had turned up to every lesson. *The guy must be retirement age!* he blustered to himself. *Won't give young people the credit they deserve. Won't talk to me. Treats me with the disinterest he might show to a child.*

He leaned forward and his words tumbled out. 'I suggested to him that I commence investigating the stronghold of the insurgents at Užice. That's where I've returned from—following, eh, your recent reoccupation.'

He neglected to inform Bader that he had spent most of his time tracing Mara and learning how to use a wireless transmitter.

Bader struck an instructive finger into the village of Rogatica.

'Our divisions are pinned down here by the incompetent Italians and your Tito, when they are needed to be deployed...' He paused, as if in thought, but merely concluded, '... elsewhere.'

'He's not "my Tito".'

'I wasn't asking your opinion, Herr Novak.'

'But I heard that you won your last offensive against the Partisans,' insisted Miroslav.

'Won, do you call it? That's an arbitrary term in this country. No, we have not succeeded in exterminating the insurgents, as I said. Like the poor, they are always with us. We might have won comprehensively, had we been allowed to act alone, but we had to negotiate with the Italians and the Ustasha before our most recent operation even started. The Italians are accident prone, it seems. They expect German help with monotonous

284

regularity and cry foul more often than an infant. There is always a reason to justify their latest inactivity: the bridge is destroyed, the road is unnavigable, the Ustashas have crossed
their demarcation line. Italians are always the same, they demand more territory on the basis of the number of men they
have in the field, but do nothing to improve their reputation as
poor soldiers. Your Ustasha, meanwhile...'

'Yes?' said Miroslav.

'Your Ustasha are arguing and fighting before we even start,
owing to the mutual suspicion between anyone and everyone in
this country. It is wasteful to commit German troops so often
and in such large numbers to subjugate a country that has already been conquered. It is unpardonable that we are forced to
negotiate with bungling allies.'

'The Ustasha are very grateful to the Nazis for supporting
Croatian nationalism.'

'Yes, I'll bet they are.'

Bader rose from his chair, folded up his chart and returned
it to a bookshelf along the dark side of the room. The shelf
bulged with maps, all well-thumbed, and shadows folded in
amongst them like a glade. Miroslav imagined what the dog-
eared pages represented: Europe, Northern Africa, the Balkans,
and what the Third Reich would like them to represent: America, Britain, the world. Peace was an anathema to a military nation; something of which to be ashamed. People asked, where
did this predisposition to dominate come from—from Prussia,
from Austria, from history? The First Reich, as they said, the
Holy Roman Empire, neither holy, nor Roman, nor an empire;
The Second Reich, Imperial Germany until the disaster of
World War One, and the now the Third Reich, the last and
most brutal of the three. Glory in triplicate.

Bader returned.

'We heard, allegedly,' he said, still with his thoughts anywhere other than Miroslav, 'that the Serbian partisans we
285

had categorically defeated at Užice have regrouped with sim-ilar-minded members in Bosnia and that this is the cause of the latest outbreak against German lines of supply. Perhaps you can offer your interpretation? I can't afford to keep too many divisions occupied in never-ending guerrilla activities.'

'That's what the British want.'

'I know that!' Bader replied curtly.

'There are guerrillas all over this country, General,' insist-ed Miroslav, 'as I informed your predecessor. And the more Tito's fame grows, the more they will communicate with him. The whole thing will snowball.'

A cane lay beside Bader's desk with an engraved gold handle, evidently of some significance to his deportment for he picked it up, inspecting the shine on the handle. Evidently his thoughts were on departure. 'Is there is anything else you can tell me?'

'The British were there,' replied Miroslav.

The eyebrows rose a fraction.

'Where?'

'Užice,' Miroslav replied quickly. 'A British officer, but they call him Marko, so he's undercover. He's a spy. He speaks the language, so I doubt that he's had a career in the military. He'd be someone they've roped in, I expect, a pro-fessional of some nature before the war who worked in Bel-grade or Zagreb for a British company, mining, importing, engineering and so forth. He came ashore from a submarine and he must have had partisan support to reach Užice, in or-der to investigate their resistance activities. At this stage, I think it's most likely he will have had some contact with the Chetniks as well as the Partisans. As I can see no evidence of Britain helping anyone except Britain, I stole his radio and his code books, which I know you can break, but there are at least two of them, so he must have had an operator. He is one hundred and eighty-two centimetres tall, dark hair, educated... do you want me to go on?'

The general sat before him as mute as a schoolboy in an algebra class. His mouth was rigid. Evidently, he didn't appreciate being addressed in this cavalier manner, adapted to give the impression that Miroslav knew more than he did. In fact, the general had met many Miroslavs before him, and knew exactly the type of self-important game the journalist was playing. Anything for attention, as long as he avoided giving his loyalty whole-heartedly to anyone. The general worked with facts, not speculation, and in his mind, the young man before him was a little too confident for the German military machine. He rose from his desk so that buttons on his uniform sparkled in the single bulb and his epaulets stood out briskly across his shoulders. He brushed them down, inspected his cane once again and eyed Miroslav with disdain.

'You're sure about all this, young man, although you saw him only once and you didn't speak to him?'

'I am,' replied Miroslav. 'It's my job.'

'We must see if you are worth it then.'

The general shuffled through a pile of papers to his left and Miroslav recognised the five letter groupings of codes, of which he had seen so much.

'The Germans have deciphered British and Yugoslav encrypted messages from the area south of Užice,' he began. 'You see, we knew he was there. As you claim to have returned from that area, and as you claim to have seen him, you might shed some light on their contents. If the British have plans for Yugoslavia, the German High Command needs to know.'

'Their plans may be connected with an invasion of the continent,' suggested Miroslav.

'You employ too much speculation for German tastes, Herr Novak. Go to my secretary in the next room along this corridor. He keeps the transcripts intercepted by our intelligence services. I have the ones I need. If those that remain make any sense to you, return to me with your interpretation. I expect a report, not guess work, by this time tomorrow.'

When we win this war, thought Mirolsav, *I'm going to kill him, if he hasn't died of old age first.*

*****

Miroslav sat in his room before the open window, Bader's pile of transcripts before him. He saw the view across the square, the odd green blanket of summer trees, people going about their business; he felt the breeze through the frame. He turned his attention to the pages before him, not excited. He felt disappointed before he even started. And the first few messages seemed to confirm this. Two agents he had never heard of abusing each other by Morse code. 'Turn on your receiver, you lazy bastard!' But almost immediately afterwards, he read his own message to Winston Churchill, another to General Ilić, Minister of the Armed Forces of the government in exile, a third to the abdicated King Edward, asking about his relationship with Hitler. Then followed the many he had sent when he was learning to key in Morse code, the weather reports he had copied from his operator, and finally the string of messages between himself and someone called Nigel. It was odd that he hadn't registered who he might be at the time, for the name 'Nigel' implied somebody quintessentially British, mused Miroslav. A man who backed horses at Ascot and drank sherry, who had a wife and a mistress, discretely aware of each other's existence, who rubbed shoulders with minor royalty. He re-read Nigel's messages.

How's our radio?
How's our radio?
How's our radio?
And his own.

It's my radio now.
Tell Marko to watch his bark.
(Damn, I screwed that one up.)
'I'm watching you. Keep your hands where they belong.'
'Love you, darling.'
'I know where you are.'
Then Nigel's again.
Where is Marko?
And his own bantering reply.
Haven't seen Marko recently. Ask Mara.
Now he'd thrown down the gauntlet. But would they take the hint?

Dear Ambassador, Miroslav had continued. *Do you still want me to find Mara for you?*

No, thank you.

Trust the British to be polite.

And then, *'Advise ambassador, contact dangerous.'*

Now, this made him feel wonderful. He was suddenly full of the type of energy he only read about in his own articles.

And finally, the best of the lot.

'Advised Mara to remain with Tito.'

Miroslav Novak re-entered General Bader's life more quickly than the general had wanted. Poring again over a map, he grunted at the young man's rapid reappearance and it was lucky he was distracted and gave so little interest to Miroslav's supplication.

'Where is the Partisan Supreme Command?' asked Miroslav.

'Foča,' replied the General and went back to his map.

CHAPTER THIRTY

Growing numbers of men and women were joining the Partisans because of the German, Ustasha and Italian outrages. They had acquired a reputation as totally egalitarian, nationalistic Yugoslavs, neither Serb, nor Croat, nor Slovene; neither Orthodox nor Catholic. As well, there were Jews and Muslims united under the Partisan star. As Tito had said, freedom and nationalism were closely connected. Victory over the oppressors of Yugoslavia, past and present, was their motivation, while the ancient regimes were swept away.

But, as their numbers grew, their hunger increased in equal measure. After the Partisans had paid for and distributed what little food could be had in the spring, nettle stew, boiled clover and wild spinach, birch bark and roots made up the shortfall.

Anton would have liked to say that the chronic hunger distressed him, but in normal times he ate what he was given, having never in his life been obsessed with food. He was a sailor and what he missed more than food was the sea. This evening, after he had eaten what was largely green vegetables, he had come up to the hillside where the women were gathering herbs for the morning, in order to find solitude in the evening air, because its peace recalled to his mind what he had lost. Dusk had settled upon the hills and, as always, it brought with it that exquisite yearning that comes only at sunset and the knowledge that what fulfilled him lay a long way from here, and was blue and limitless, and glorious and everlasting.

Mara was the first girl he saw, and his initial reaction was to leave. He sighed to himself, remembering his outburst and her reaction, and looked around for a suitable exit, but there was none. He would create a greater fuss by leaving. The sensible option was to assume nonchalance, but the habits of command came too easily to him and he decided to pause to observe what she was doing instead of wandering casually away, which might have sent a clear signal to all observers that nothing out of the ordinary was going on.

She had tied a band of fabric diagonally around her shoulder and under an arm to use as a hold-all, and he could see straight away that she had been filling it with immature nettles.

'Not those nettles!' he called.

She stopped, while he tried not to look too hard at her, lest all his feelings come rollicking back like heartless children. He didn't need more emotions connected with her. He really didn't.

But she wasn't resentful. She waited as he walked over to her. Evidently she had recalled that she was the ambassador's daughter.

'I know what a nettle is,' she replied politely. 'Anton.'

Finally! He smiled. 'Thank you,' he said.

'What for?'

'Well, for...ah, nothing. Never mind.' He inspected her collection of nettles. To maintain his appearance of objectivity (this was very important), he fingered one or two. 'I appreciate that you know what a nettle is, Mara, but what you have in your bag will make you sick. You see those little flowers forming? You can't eat nettles when they're flowering. Pick these younger ones over here, and try to avoid the purple leaves, because they will taste bitter.'

Mara stretched her stiff back and rubbed her ribs, which were more obvious than they used to be. She was accustomed to hunger now, but had given up trying to pass off concavity as a fashion statement.

'Beggars can't be choosers, I expect, but I can't believe I'm eating nettles at all.'

'Nettles are good for you.'

'So are roast beef and chocolate pudding.'

A dozen of the girls were out on the slopes gathering wild herbs to cook: Mara, Jana, Aleksandra, Nada, Ana and others. They were deep in discussion, no doubt all of it more important than gathering food. Some of the men were with them, reclining on the hillside to enjoy the twilight.

Anton saw Mara's look of disgust.

'Didn't you know that men liked the twilight, Mara?' he said.

'Yes, I did, but the women fought, too, and we would like to lie on a bed of flowers after a battle and write poems just as much as they would.'

She untied the hold-all, and placed it and its contents carefully on the ground. When she stood up her hair flopped over her forehead.

'How do you know all these herbal things?' she asked, pushing the fringe back. 'You're not a peasant.'

'I'm older than you.'

'That's not a satisfactory answer.'

'All right. I'm observant. Happy?'

'No,' she said. She addressed him with demanding eyes. 'People who know what you know about mountain herbs and cows and things grow up with them. They're not submarine captains from Belgrade. Did you grow up in an apartment?'

292

'Yes. And you?'

'Until we moved to London, then we had a house. So, are you going to tell me why you know all this, or not?'

And so, they made themselves comfortable on the grass and he explained about his time with the widow, because it was no great secret. She might as well know.

She sat at his feet with her arms around her knees and listened to him, for once without speaking. He decided to take full advantage of the unexpected attention, although he did not over-elaborate his story. He didn't tell her how many ex-girlfriends he'd seen in his delirium, for example, and he deleted the naked nymphs.

It was incredible, she remarked, what had happened to him. How extraordinary to actually live with a peasant while the Germans were invading Yugoslavia!

'You mustn't deride peasants,' he told her.

'Sorry,' she said but she didn't hang her head like he thought she might. She was like a sheltered child, really, the only child of protective parents.

'And it was the Italians in Montenegro, Mara. Had it been the Germans, I'd probably be dead.'

She was intrigued. She looked up at him, this storyteller, this weaver of tales.

'Tell me what else you can do.'

'I can spin,' he said.

'Anything else?'

'I can make cheese.'

Her eyebrows raised.

'And kefir.'

At this she became enthusiastic.

'Can you make strawberry kefir? I like strawberry kefir.'

'No, just plain. The widow didn't have any sugar or strawberries.'

Mara considered this.

'Did she ask you to marry her?

He laughed, and it had been a long time since that had happened. He saw straight away that she approved and that he had sparked her interest. *He's not so inaccessible when he smiles, Jana. He looks much better.* That was all it took. His resolution to remain detached flew out the window. He saw, for the first time, that she was curious about him. He started to enjoy himself.

'No, no wedding bells,' he replied. 'Disappointed?'

'Yes. I wouldn't put it past her. Old people never think they're old. She's probably been husband hunting for years.'

'Her husband had just died, actually.'

'Oh, dear. What did he die of?'

'Old age. No, wait, I think it was pneumonia.'

'That's what my mother died of.'

'I'm sorry to hear that. Recently?'

'Late in 1938.'

"In Belgrade?'

'London. Poor Mum. I would hate to die so far from home.' She lost her gaze for just a second. 'How long were you with your old widow?'

'Four months.'

'Well, I think she's missed a golden opportunity, Anton. I would have asked you to marry me after four months.'

A tiny grey moth flitted in and out of the waving grass and an evening cricket piped unseen from its hiding place, a thousand tiny bursts of sound all joined into one long rolling croak. Mara tried to find it and, while she was searching, she swallowed a fly. She spat it out, coughed, and again Anton smiled at her.

Mara considered. 'What was wrong with you, exactly, that caused you to stay quite so long?'

'Wound infection, blood poisoning, shock. And I had blistered feet from all her garlic.'

Margaret Walker

Mara was intrigued. Without asking, she had put two and two together.

'Can I see the villain that caused all this trouble?' she asked, pointing to his shoulder.

'You know,' he said—and he just wanted to know what it was about female intuition, how they always seemed to sense these things—'I could have been crippled as a child.'

'But you weren't,' she replied. 'Were you?'

One day, he thought, one day he would realize that he had a choice with women. He could have said no... but he didn't. All men like to talk about themselves.

So he undid his buttons while she watched, wondering what he was doing, undressing before this importunate young woman. Largely because he was still switching hands for some tasks, he fumbled the first and second buttons. The slip gave him the impression of being nervous and suddenly he knew, quite certainly, that her interest had turned to compassion, as if he were a small boy and she was teaching him how to dress. *That's a tricky one, isn't it, darling? Naughty button.* Indeed, one delicate hand raised itself a fraction, but no, she had realized her error and his feelings, and regained control. The hand slipped back, but the temptation lingered. *Right now, she's biting her tongue.* He pulled down one sleeve and half his shirt until she could see the neat black hairs down his sternum, the only neat thing about him these days. Aware that they were missing out on a free show, Aleksandra, Jana and several of the others hurried across from gathering herbs to observe the disrobing, until Anton found himself surrounded by a small crowd of girls, hovering with the absorption of mechanics around a motor. No one said a thing. *You're like guinea pigs,* he thought. *You think, if you're quiet, I won't know you're gawking.* Well, yesterday Jana had sneaked down to watch the men bathing naked in the river. Anton, stroking lazily downstream, had

295

seen her through the trees. She'd given him a significant appraisal then, shoulder included. Well, she could put her shoes under his bed all she liked, he wasn't rolling over for her. *You should keep your mind on your job, Jana,* called the guy who cleaned the guns. *I am,* Jana replied.

She had that predatory look in her eyes again, right now, when he found himself most vulnerable, half undressed, and normally in a position that should logically proceed in one direction or the other. The girls were waiting for him to decide, all brown eyes and scarcely a breath amongst them. It wasn't likely that he could remain long in front of them like this, his composure undone by a button. He opened three only and pushed his shirt further down below one nipple while Mara wrinkled her nose in anticipation of that most pungent aroma, male underarms; the smell that always reminded women that men worked hard. Except tonight, when the girls were doing all the work.

He got in first.

'I don't smell,' he informed her, 'because I've been gathering herbs.'

'They've embalmed you,' she replied.

Or maybe it was those three hundred shirts the women had laundered in the evening two days before, including his? Even silent little Aleksandra had been in the woods all day on patrol before she did it. And now the girls were at work again gathering herbs for dinner while the men rested their weary limbs. From far away, he heard the rumble of guns, and he deliberately mistook it for surf crashing against a hull.

Mara examined his shoulder as inquisitively as a child. She had overcome her fear of disabilities now. The shoulder wasn't going to turn her into a frog and, in any case, she didn't intend to kiss it. There was that artery pulsing up into his neck. That had her transfixed, but beyond his collar he was as white as the pages of a story book and, because he hadn't let the shirt slip down any further, she was wondering about the contrast between his deeply tanned neck and everything she couldn't see. *You should have been down by the riverside with Jana*, he thought, *if you wanted a more comprehensive view*. That shirt had given him authority and covered up the defencelessness of his sunless skin. He had lost much muscle mass and, without it, his right shoulder appeared shrunken and elderly. A deep purplish gorge coursed down one side of his upper right arm. The V-shaped scar on the top of the shoulder was distorted where the surgeon's precise stitches had become warped by infection and swelling.

'Wow!' said Mara.

Like shiny highways, broad areas of new skin had formed to fill in the gaps, and the whole thing reminded her of a map that she wanted to follow.

'That's the triceps there, I think.' She prodded it gently. 'Does that hurt?'

'No.'

She ran one soft finger along his skin, hovering over the irregular shapes to try and make sense of the mutilated muscles.

'It used to be the triceps,' he answered. He shrugged the arm back into his shirt, noting that he wasn't besieged by offers of help. 'I'm glad I've impressed you.'

The girls all jumped up and ran away, except Mara.

'Can you use it?' she asked.

'Yes, although sometimes it will decide it's had enough, right in the middle of a job, and collapse. My left arm is the strongest now.'

'What happened?'

He sighed. Exasperation and memory.

Through Forests and Mountains

'Nothing but a typical propeller accident, Mara, in dry dock. I was taking off my jacket when a young crew member flicked a switch and the sleeve got caught. Just poor timing; the way I moved when the propellers started. Dragged the whole shoulder in.'

'That's bizarre,' she commented. 'What was the captain of the boat doing in dry dock?'

'Answering the boys' questions. Showing them I knew everything. Being arrogant and stupid. It wasn't even my boat. It was a torpedo boat.'

'Even more reason to ask what you were doing there.'

'There's not a day goes past, Mara, that I wish I hadn't been at that boat, at that time.'

At the stress he laid upon these words, he saw her wriggle uncomfortably and turn away. Immediately, he wished that he had expressed himself with less feeling. She looked for support towards Jana and Aleksandra, and he was certain she was going to wind up the conversation as quickly as she could, for he had exposed his heart, and now she saw his needs. She could have decided to show empathy, but she didn't. He saw that she felt too uncomfortable to let him get any closer. Her face, which had been absorbed, began to assume a rather point-blank attitude to the accident that had derailed his life, as if she didn't care. It was his problem. She'd done the same sort of girlie thing with her rich friends back in London: made non-committal girl-talk and jokes about men. *Her background is going to come in handy now. To protect herself, she's going to pass on the disapproval of her sheltered world to him.* But he wasn't going to get disappointed with her. The feeling rose up and he said, *no, I won't go down that path.*

'I like engines,' he confessed and spread out his hands to illustrate. 'I was always tinkering with things. And I like to

298

teach the boys. I never really got used to telling people what to do.'

'That's a rare confession of humility.'

The curt remark hurt him, as well as the casual laugh that accompanied it. He asked himself why he had expected any more of her. Back came the answer: because he had decided that he wanted to. 'I have little choice here.'

'They like you. That's what I think.' Mara shrugged. 'Maybe you should have joined the army instead.'

'Why?'

'I don't know. It was just something to say.' She scratched the back of her hand where the grass had brought up a lumpy rash.

This could go one of two ways, he saw. She could decide to open herself up and let him in, because she knew that this was what he wanted, this evening, on this hill, gathering herbs. Or she could reject his overture and go back to her girlfriends, putting him down first in order to justify her actions.

'No, Mara,' he persisted patiently. 'I like boats and I like fiddling with engines.'

'Yes, so does my father.' She threw back her head. 'You men. You're your own worst enemies.'

So, the conversation stumbled along towards a tired old ending, when he knew he shouldn't push it any further. Yet he had enjoyed their chat. It made a break from the last lonely year. He felt that he was getting somewhere with a girl again. From the forest a twig snapped. Anton did up his buttons and smiled at Mara. Last try.

'Coffee and off to work, then?'

Mara froze. She didn't do one-night stands. Up she jumped at once, to leave the atmosphere he had implied and, despite himself, Anton could not help staring at the bounce of her breasts beneath her shirt and the rounded buttocks that filled the male trousers she wore. He noticed how the evening light separated the strands of her hair like streams in an amber waterfall and he was unable to stop himself fantasizing how it would feel, running through his fingers. Beneath the shower, he waited for her to come to him, because it had to be her decision.

Instead she said brusquely, 'I'll see you later.'

'Mara, it was a joke!'

'Whatever.'

This, then, was the manner in which their moment died. Anton was sorry, but not overly surprised. Resigned, really.

*****

From behind a tree, Miroslav watched apprehensively to see if Mara would touch the angular officer with the mutilated shoulder, in which case he would be forced to kill her, as he had warned. He had become much more obsessively rule-conscious in these rural days, without the city to hold his head together. Sometimes he felt like a wild animal closing in for the kill. Sniffing blood on the wind. But that one finger touching the scars. Was one finger worth death, or just a roughing up, like last time?

Miroslav had long ago summed Mara up: playful, only half-serious around men, a school-girl who would rush in with enthusiasm but fear to go all the way. Spooning over any man who interested her, teasing him, falling into his arms, rejecting him. A cascade of methods all bent on control. She was leading this one a merry dance and Miroslav almost felt sorry for the man. Mara had got what she wanted, but had in no way registered the effect she'd had on her quarry, and the officer looked like just the sort of guy who would have trouble with women anyway—absolutely woeful at playing feminine games. Miroslav could bet, watching the way Mara engaged his interest only to lose her own a moment later and dump him, that he'd fallen for a lot of women over the years, who had treated him in exactly the same way. She'd had her little tantrum and stormed off and, even at this distance, the guy couldn't keep the disappointment from his face.

Why hadn't he leaped up and followed her? *Now that's what I would have done; prove to her who's boss.* Well, he was lonely, or in Miroslav's parlance, marooned. He couldn't get off his own island. Miroslav wagged his head at the officer in frustration. He pulled a face and stuck out his tongue. *Run after her, you moron! Slam her up against a tree and ravish her. Tell her you're a prince. Promise her diamonds. Lie to her. Exploit some of that officer's authority. Don't just give up.*

Something has conditioned him to react in his way, Miroslav reasoned, and he would bet it was those half a dozen or so previous and depressingly similar relationships. Mara and her antics would be the last straw; he'd end up completely pissed off with the other half of the human race and announce that he'd given up women for Lent. Go home and have it off with his car. What Mara really needed was for someone to tell her what a prick tease she was.

She simply couldn't keep her hands off men—that much was clear to Miroslav—and the world would be a better place without her. If it wasn't one man, it was another. First that suave British spy, now this wooden petrol-head. She had finally succeeded in making him laugh, and Miroslav was amazed that his face hadn't cracked under the strain. Seriously, what did she see in him? His features, tanned by days out of doors, were a montage of rugged and wary, lined in ways Miroslav would not have expected in a man probably— how old would he be?—early thirties? Nice skin but creased beside his mouth and between his eyes, like someone who couldn't bear something, but had been unable to escape it.

Through Forests and Mountains

The officer's hair was brushed back over his forehead, grey at the temples, black elsewhere. How had Miroslav guessed he was an officer? Well, clearly the guy was used to giving commands without explanation. One sentence finished and the next one started. No more words than were necessary.

Miroslav watched him carefully. How much was he attracted to Mara? All the signs seemed to point that way. But what did he have to offer her? Or, what did he think he had? That was more to the point, particularly if his memories stemmed from when he had last looked in the mirror. Like all the Partisans Miroslav had observed since the German staff car had dropped him off a week ago out of Foča, he had the guarded appearance of the hungry wolf. A sharply defined jawline, narrow wrists and, by comparison, broad hands and bony fingers. Evidently, he had driven extra holes into his belt as he lost weight, for Miroslav could see the end flapping uselessly to one side where once it would have fitted snugly. He seemed clean enough, but his trousers were fraying at the hems, he was wearing the same heavy hand-knitted socks that the peasants wore, and his boots were grey at the toes through constant wear. Miroslav tried to imagine him with an extra twenty kilos. Then he might even exude the type of raw sexuality typical of a man to whom a capable grasp of unfolding events had given reflection to his words. That talent would be something of a mystery to a girl who talked as much as Mara.

Now what about that sexy little nymph who had just bounded off into the hillside, after the officer had done his impromptu striptease? Hmm... she looked like she knew how to handle men. Perhaps she could act as a relationship guru to Mara. Boss her into seeing things Miroslav's way. He must keep his eye on her when next he felt frustrated.

The girls had resumed their foraging. The tall officer, apparently aware that a single glance from one of them would

Margaret Walker

evoke more avid female speculation, had prized himself from the long grass, picked at a couple of the ubiquitous nettles and was wandering away by himself. At a hail from two other men, he left the girls to join them, and the three diminished into the distance, leaving the girls alone. Miroslav counted them. Five—and only one of him. In the long dusk shadows, the three men had assumed the insignificance of figures in an oil painting; but they were still within shouting distance.

Not yet the right time to act. Patience. Patience.

Miroslav had taken the lift from Belgrade to South Eastern Bosnia, to an Italian camp south of the so-called Vienna Line, which divided the part of Bosnia that was controlled by the Italians from that controlled by the Ustasha. He would rather have bunked in with his own countrymen, but Foča was in the Italian-held territory, unfortunately.

From the Italian camp, he had asked his way to Partisan headquarters, querying a series of farmers, children and priests until at last he had seen two columns of armed Partisans marching out of Foča along the road north to Rogatica. He hadn't followed them but instead returned to the Italian camp to bide his time. Extraordinary how close the adversaries could be in this war. One might even set up the flags of the two armies across a field, as in the olden days. Dream of empires and other human fantasies.

Miroslav ate a nice dinner and went to sleep.

CHAPTER THIRTY-ONE

In later years, Mara would remember this time as a series of outdoor photographs, with herself in the middle of every one. Wrapping bandages for the nurses in the snow, sleeping in the bushes, reclining by the trunk of an oak, walking barefoot along a path of pine needles, the light shining from behind her in a thicket while she oiled her typewriter one day to keep it from rusting and her rifle on the next. This is me. Here I am. Together, I did this; abroad, I did that. And accompanying the photographs, charcoal sketches done roughly with a stroke here and a flick there by one of the village artists, a marvel of rustic talent, whose three strokes could bring anything to life on a page—a woman and child, three groiny males waiting for their clothes to dry in the lazy sun, a distraught parent by a grave, and somewhere the ever-present, poignant outline of freedom.

How different life was compared to the very indoor existence she had once lived in Britain. Picnics in the car in the rain. Charades in the lounge room. She preferred to forget the indoor memories these days, for the Bosnian walls were stained with blood and the charred relics of happy families lay on the hearths upon which now-dead children had been nurtured. She heard their ghosts keen on the night wind.

Margaret Walker

By now, she was used to the long marches. If she felt sick, the men loaded her up on a cart with the injured, but, for most of her time she stomped along with the other girls in a pair of German boots, whose split seams she tried to protect by stuffing the holes full of straw and binding the lesions with rags. The long series of deaths and injuries she had observed had carved inroads into her gentle city upbringing and with each week that passed, she saw herself belonging more and more to a land that was hers.

Whenever she saw Anton he was either talking with a group of men or alone, or being fussed over by one or two of the nurses more motherly than Mara. But she had listened to him and discovered that it was true what her mother had said: men like to talk about themselves. He had got too close for comfort that evening amongst the nettles, but what had he done, but act like any other man? Perhaps she had been over sensitive. Since he was forever getting hurt, he was clearly in need of a woman, and she ought to be braver. She was fighting a war, was she not, and clearly on more fronts than she anticipated.

The latest injury had occurred after Anton took a dozen of his men by night to blow up an old Turkish bridge that spanned a river in mountainous Bosnia. Mara knew the bridge to be an important crossing point for any army heading south west to protect the important bauxite mines between Mostar and Sarajevo. That day they had observed the bridge from the woodland surrounds and Mara had heard Anton explaining how to position the dynamite correctly beneath the centre of the three arches, whose destruction would effectively prevent the 718th Infantry Division and its ten thousand men from crossing the river until they had repaired it. The entire structure was composed of marble, worn white and slippery over the centuries, and stabilized for the feet of cattle by raised ruts two centimetres tall and about the same width. As no adjustments had been made for the advent of the motor vehicle, the road from the hill swept across the bridge and bumped over the ruts into town. On a good day, boys would jump from the bridge into the swirling waters below, but today spring had halted its sunny advance and the river was bleak and cheerless, swept by cold winds, and a thin but penetrating rain fell from low lying clouds upon the grey buildings of the town.

Scouts had brought word of the army's advance and the work had to be done. Watching the men leave their temporary camp in the forest, Mara was glad, for once, to stay wrapped in her blanket beneath a tarpaulin, and when they returned an hour before dawn, she saw that Anton was holding his left arm in as tragic a position as his right and was dripping wet and shivering. Not the world's end this time, as might have been supposed. As usual, he had been demonstrating how to do things his way and, upon climbing beneath the span to lay the sticks of dynamite where they might do the most damage, his right shoulder had collapsed and he had hung on grimly with his left until he strained a muscle trying to support his entire weight with one arm, and had dropped silently into the eddies circling around the broad supports of the structure. With two disabled shoulders, he was lucky he didn't drown, a miracle he put down entirely to being a submariner and thus on better terms with the water than most men. Nevertheless, he had got his message across, and the remainder of the work was completed successfully.

The nurses, Mara had noticed, loved to look after Anton. Something about the isolated figure of command he presented and his multiple non-life-threatening injuries yanked pleasantly at their heart strings. Well, Mara's aunt had been right, she was a terrible nurse, but now was as good a time to start as any. Anton passed swiftly by where she stood and his stark and unshaven face was momentarily frightening in the trembling firelight. His hair stuck in streaks to his forehead and the muscles on his chest were etched into the wet fabric of his shirt as he heaved with the effort of hiking back to camp. He shook as if an icy wind were buffeting him from both poles simultaneously.

'How are you feeling?' she asked.

He barely noticed her.

A real nurse, not Mara, threw a blanket over his shoulders and, between the taut smiles shared amongst the men after a successful mission and the bustle to get closer to the fire, she was elbowed out of the way and relocated to a place at the back, where she experienced a redundancy quite as poignant as not being able to knit or milk a cow.

She sat by herself, swatting mosquitos. The night wind had risen out of nowhere. High in the trees she heard its wild roaring and watched black branches rocketing from one cloud to another. *That's me*, she thought. *I have a troubling tendency to use and forget people when something else distracts me.* She regretted her behaviour in this respect—she knew she could be thoughtless—and had commenced dissecting her previous boyfriends (there had only been one before Miroslav) and what about them had sparked the initial attraction. She sorted through a variety of reckless nouns—fun, youth, adventure—before coming to the conclusion that she lacked stability. This depressed her. Though she had never considered, beforehand, the results of her actions on other people, she often regretted them, and her behaviour had not allowed her to develop any coping strategies when things didn't go her way. She wondered miserably whether Anton might prefer to spend time with one of the nurses, who was, at this moment, enthusiastically prodding his most recently injured shoulder. Where did that leave her? Trapped by a possessive ex-boyfriend. Well, she had escaped

Miroslav, or so she had thought, until that episode in Belgrade, and the next one in Užice.

She began to tremble, not wishing to be alone, when suddenly a figure sat down beside her and her arm was brushed by coarse wool, warm from the fire.

'Hello!' he said, wrapped in his blanket.

'Anton! Are you all right?'

'Now I am.' He turned to face her, looking pleased with himself. 'We blew up the bridge.'

'Gosh! Well done!'

'It fell with a mighty roar, boom! Right into the river!'

'Gosh!' she said again.

'I thought you'd like to know.'

'I would like to know. Thank you!'

They sat companionably without further talk until he asked, 'Are you cold?'

'I'm always cold.'

'Would you like to share my blanket?'

'Oh, sure! I mean, um, no. Don't you need it, or something?'

'I don't mind sharing my blanket with you.'

'But the nurses might get angry.'

'Why?'

'Um...'

She was shivering now and he could not fail to notice. He slung a corner of the blanket over her shoulder. Blankets being hard to divide equally, she discovered herself cosied up against one side of him, from his knee to his shoulder. *He's really warm and it's so nice,* she thought, *I could stay here forever.* Except that the awareness of life, separated by only warp and weft, troubled her somewhat. Naturally, he was breathing and she could feel that, too.

'Better?' he asked.

Margaret Walker

How should she answer this? *If I agree, will he take it the wrong way but, if I disagree, will I have hurt his feelings?* (Hurting his feelings hadn't deterred her in the past.) *He is asking me because, from his point of view, the closer he can get to a woman, the nicer for him. Or perhaps he is asking me because he is just being kind. I hadn't thought of that before, but it's funny how you can discover hidden depths when once you had assumed male motivation to be universally shallow. So... he is asking me if I feel better to prove that he's not shallow.* She chewed her lip. *That's endearing, but I am still not reassured that a sympathetic response from me won't be interpreted as the new normal. He'll expect it all the time. 'Where is Mara?' whenever he gets the blues. Oh, men are so plaintive!* She shuffled away from him and experienced, not only the cold, but sadness. Away in the tree tops, a night bird crooned a lonesome song. *Bugger, I'm picking up his vibrations.* Maybe she should surrender herself to his blanket a little longer? *But what if that gives him the wrong impression? I know what I'll do! I'll be politely grateful and then give all the other men equal attention. 'Thanks for the blanket, Anton,' I shall say, 'your fifteen minutes is up.'*

But instead she said, 'Yes.'

He smiled at her, but she kept her head down so that he couldn't see that she was disappointed in herself. The dawn dissolved the night on the eastern horizon and finally, she turned and saw his face. He lacked the crease of perplexity between his eyebrows that made other men appear preoccupied, but he had an attentive gaze and a particularly male mouth, straight and captured at either side by creases that held his smile, as if between parentheses. The dawn advanced and his mouth warmed with the approach of the sun.

She watched it and asked him, 'Are you coming to the dance?'

'I don't dance. When is it?'

'They haven't quite decided, but in a day or so, I think.'

'I don't know. We've got a raid coming up on that Italian camp in the valley. For fuel and ammunition, medicine, food and whatever else we can get.'

'I hope you'll come safely back. You look nice when you're all bristly.'

He stared at her, and then laughed.

'You are a funny girl,' he said.

Mara blushed.

'Funny ha ha or funny peculiar?'

'The first one.'

'Well, what I meant was,' she corrected herself, you're warm and homey, you and your blanket, just sitting there. I haven't lived with a man for ages—well, there's only been Dad—but you can't beat having a man around the house. It gives the four walls a bit more substance, and men are so handy. You know how you said you like fiddling with things? Well, Dad would help me with anything like that, even before he shaved, so to me, a man is bristly, warm and practical.' She cleared her throat. 'Like you.'

'Anything else?'

'Yes. Dad smokes and you don't.'

'How do you know I don't smoke?'

'Because you don't get irritated when you misplace your tobacco pouch.'

'There you are wrong. I do smoke, but I ran out of ciga-rettes when the Germans invaded.' He got up.

'Where are you going?' asked Mara.

'Off to sleep. Keep the blanket. I'll get another one.'

Mara watched Anton head towards the tarpaulin, hunt around for a discarded blanket and wrap himself up with his boots sticking out one end. Suddenly, she felt stupidly vulnerable and stupidly like the girls and their stupid boyfriends she used to criticize back in stupid London.

'Hey, Mara!' Jana sat down beside her with a soft plop, and another blanket warmed from the fire. 'He looked pretty keen to sit next to you! You like him, don't you?'

'Garbage, Jana,' replied Mara miserably. 'A man in a warm blanket beside me is more interesting than a girl in a warm blanket, because I know that, in an emergency, he would look after me.'

'Then list his attributes from A to Z.'

'A is for Anton and Z is for zero interest.'

'No, Mara. Your problem is that you talk first and think later. You know guys are predatory, and anything you tell him is going to translate as interest. You're leading him on. I say, it's because you like him.'

'And I say it's not.'

'Either that, or you're not being honest with yourself. You've got to get to a point where you can say yes or no to him, and you're not there yet.'

Mara rose to her feet. 'I'm going to distract myself. You've upset me. I feel restless and I don't know why.'

'It's because you have all the classic signs,' said Jana.

*****

Before the dancing commenced, Branko the bard sat before the assembled company with his gusle between his knees. He began, in the offhand manner of the experienced musician, to appear to sing to himself, accompanied by the single-stringed instrument. It was only as his voice mellowed and settled into the flow of the story that one realized he was searching his heart to bring an epic story to his audience. Into himself first, then out to his audience, in the way of these bards. Using only a handful of notes, his voice rose and fell rapidly. He seemed to sing to himself, as if the story and the few notes he told it with must first be searched for in his heart. A plaintive voice without vibrato, rising and falling around a note, then up, then a grace note or two, as he fancied, then a long plaintive lament that fell on the ears of those listening along with their eyes, their ears hearing the chant and seeing the epic stories he wove.

He looked far out over their heads, and the colours of the declining day drove deep shadows into his face and made him ageless, like the stories he was singing. He sang first of Serbian battles long past, of mighty warriors, great victories and greater defeats. Then right at the end, he looked into the eyes of the girls watching him rapturously and began to sing the old song of the warrior mothers, who, having given to battle every child of their wombs and seen each one fall, lamented that they had not more sons to give. *If I was able to bear children now, I would give them to the struggle for freedom, even it burst my heart.*

Branko moved to the present.

The grandfather is unable to leave when the fascists tear into his home. He has two holes in his chest where his blood has flowed away, and he can't take to the woods like the others. Now his daughter is weeping over his body. She has placed him within the burned walls of his house, so that he will not remain out in the street for the wolves to devour. Beside him, his wife wails until her sorrow bears her down and she lays herself beside him and cannot rise up again. All the men have been shot, the women raped and the houses burned. Along the river and across the plains, it is the same story. Villages destroyed, wholesale slaughter like cattle from the markets. The fascists are going to weed the insurgents out by the most brutal means and have shut their ears to the moaning and wailing of their victims. They will show no mercy to an inferior race, and an entire country shall lie in ruins for daring to defy them. The towns are razed, the cities are bombed, the farms are laid waste and the people are dead. The catastrophe has ignited all the old ethnic rivalries and now the remains of the nation will consume itself.

The voice of the gusle player rose above his instrument. He sang of anger and grief, of burning cries of suffering. At first, he was only as loud as the bow on his string, but, as he warmed to his theme, he pressed his arm down hard and the bow sank further into the string, even as his voice grew and filled the evening air. And, in the end, he sang of revenge for the suffering, revenge for the dead, revenge for the rape of their country that was so beautiful.

When at last the final plaintive strains had melted away into the whispering evening, Danilo brought out his piano accordion and Ahmed a side drum, and dancing began. Compared to the tunes in the city about love and boyfriends, the melodies that now began were robust, with a steady beat that made you want to rise and rally yourself and throw off your cares. To the beat of the drum, two lines of men and women formed themselves without thinking, linking arms by holding onto to each other's belts. Rapid footwork, wild shouts from the boys. The lines didn't mix, but once or twice two girls linked arms with a youth to make a trio, moving to-gether perfectly, swinging to and fro to the drum and the swelling triplets of the accordion.

You wanted to be wild, you wanted to join in as madly as you could, to throw yourself into absurdity and not care which Englishman thought you had temporarily gone insane. You wanted to stamp your feet and kick your legs high into the air in front of you. You became part of the trees and the wind. You were a *junak*, a hero, a *hajduk*, a guerrilla, a raider at the wild frontier. You wanted to kill the enemy and rise victorious. Music moulded you into itself, and *who you were* ceased to exist. You threw yourself into it, lost your exhaustion of the day, the trepidation and the stealth, the anger and the urge to slaughter the cruel invaders, and did not realize you were exhausted until the music stopped. You could have danced forever, like the old stories, and fallen down dead without realising you were dying.

The evening deepened. In its colours, a drama of lost youth and desperation played out, for who could tell what tomorrow would bring—who would be alive and whose bones would decay into the forest and become part of the earth on which they danced with such ferocity? No thoughts now. Exult in the moment. On the tree trunks were flung monstrous shadows from the dancers.

Anton stood with his arms crossed, leaning against a tree, watching the revellers with the detachment of the non-dancer, his gaze calm, his long body relaxed, for once looking like he really didn't mind to be the loner. In fact, he was considering the wheel alignment of a truck they had stolen during a raid on an Italian camp that morning. In the predawn darkness, amidst operatic Italian panic, he had hot-wired it and driven it back, only discovering the keys in the glovebox afterwards. The vehicle would barely stay on the track, and he put its temperamental behaviour down to the fourteen months since he'd last been behind a wheel and the difficulty he had driving with the lights off, until the guy in the passenger seat had commented on it, too. Fortunately the vehicle had picked up speed after their attack which, given the amount of noise it made, helped them escape. Most of his unit had been sitting in the back, firing willy-nilly at the Italians with sub machine guns, until eventually they had made it out of range. Now he watched the girls and boys like whirling dervishes in front of him, heard their cries of delight, felt their long hemmed-in emotions seek and find an outlet, with his mind still fixed on the truck.

Two boys swept past him like eagles and he thought, *Boris had a couple of wrenches in his collection, I think the bigger one would do it.*

'Hey, Anton! Come and dance!'

He frowned at the interruption, but it was Mara and he smiled at her.

'You know I don't dance, Mara,' he reminded her.

She had been dancing without a pause, he had observed and, rather than wear her out, it had enlivened her. She would dance until the evening stars faded into the dawn. She typified the Slav dancer.

'Don't say that,' she bounced back. 'It will make you feel better.'

'The last time someone said that to me,' he replied. 'They gave me a bottle of slivovitz for the pain.'

She looked disappointed.

'If I promise it won't hurt, will you try?'

'You can promise that dancing won't hurt, can you?'

She looked up at him through her eyelashes and he saw that it was all true what they said about naughty children—they knew when to be charming.

'I am doing this for you,' she insisted.

'Well, then,' he said. 'Thanks for the thought, and I feel much better.'

'Sarcasm doesn't suit you, Anton.'

So, reluctantly, he pushed himself off the tree, and before he knew it, she had grabbed his belt and was steering him towards the lines of dancers weaving in and out of the shadows. He was grateful for their cover because they weren't in a position to notice him. He looked like a marionette, because puppets, of necessity, dance with disconcerted looks on their painted faces and limbs jointed with bolts. Through lack of an ear, they feel no empathy with the music, even when folk dancing is part of their heritage. They can't wish themselves somewhere else, but they would if they could, and their pain comes through nevertheless: varnished eyes aching with the desperation of working out what comes next and wooden feet that refuse to obey their owner's bidding. There is no pleasure in watching a marionette dance. Its knees are as pointed as grasshoppers and its elbows are fixed at ninety degree angles. Piano keys fly up and down with as much sideways variation. The only part of Anton's body that didn't look painful to a casual observer was his injured shoulder, because no one expected it to have any grace. In short, he was dreadful. The one rhythmic thought in his head was how to get out of this, over and over and over.

She still had her hand in his belt, as they all did, but he was stronger. He pulled her off into the trees where they couldn't be seen.

'That's it,' he said, detaching her hand.

'But you were really good!' she protested and stood blankly before him, like a child without understanding.

'Bullshit,' he replied, but not aggressively. 'Listen, I've got a truck to fix before the light fades.'

He was angry with himself again. He was under no obligation to use the truck as an excuse. All he had had to do was say 'no' like he should have in the first place.

Mara put her hands on her hips.

'How are you going to make friends, Anton, if all you ever do is fix trucks?'

'That's unfair,' he replied, and he could see from her face that she knew it was.

'Oh, you're right, you're right, you're always right!' she stormed.

'There is nothing wrong with being logical.'

'Except that logic places no value on spending time with people,' Mara replied tartly.

There she went again. All that female nonsense that didn't achieve anything.

'Please be specific,' he demanded. 'Are you referring to logic or to me?'

'To you,' she replied.

'And why should you care?'

The second the words were out of his mouth, he was disgusted with himself. She'd done it again. She had involved him in a ridiculous argument that did nothing but waste the time he could have spent on better things. It had been almost as if she had deliberately tried to destroy that dawn by the fire that he had found so fulfilling by forcing him to do something he had warned her in advance that he didn't do. He had felt in control of himself (and her) and the world had still turned afterwards. Oh, why couldn't women leave well enough alone? He and his tree had been perfectly at ease this night and now he was upset, and he couldn't pinpoint exactly what had upset him.

Not what—she. She had upset him. She had got under his skin and he couldn't get her out. No! Let him rephrase that. He had let her under his skin and, for once, it was more than sex. But how had he let her do this, because, had it been any other woman, he would have ignored the feminine wiles and strolled away. Now suddenly that emotional control seemed to have abandoned him. He didn't understand why Mara sought him out, what reason she could have for her behaviour and why he overreacted instead of brushing her aside and moving on like the sensible man he used to be. Did she want him or didn't she?

He had allowed himself to be coerced into the dancing, of course. What a thing to do! He made no sense to himself. He was not even in control of his own lurch out of character. Someone else had chosen the music and he was dancing to its tune. If he ever found out where his heart was and not his common sense, it would be a sad day for the Partisan army and Hitler would win the war. They would rejoice in Berlin, and it would all be his fault. What he should do would be to throw his heart away like the tormenting organ it was and give himself some peace. It occurred to him that to hope is to be human; he just didn't know what he was hoping for.

His acerbic thoughts were interrupted by the lusty singing of Nikola, wandering through the trees on his way to the river. It seemed that he, too, had had sufficient dancing for one evening, and would be alone with his thoughts and the songs that best expressed them. This evening, he was singing a lament for a fallen soldier written by Branko Ka-menar, the bard with the gusle, and destined for a solitary evening of reflection. He sung it in the same style as the singer, as if his larynx also had only the single string, and he managed to mimic the style so well that he filled the evening with his own sadness, so that he didn't have to tell anyone how he felt but could entertain, nevertheless, in a style that calmed them. It was no illusion. He knew the style well. They had all grown up with it.

> In a forest far from the world,
> Where sunbeams never penetrate,
> A small mound is found
> Without any ornaments or flowers.
> The only rough thing decorating it, a cross
> And grey moss.
> Dark, rough cross,
> But beneath it Pero, a common man, is dreaming.
>
> Once he was with you,
> We all loved our Pero,
> He was tall like a mountain,
> A son of the Adriatic Sea,

318

With a proletarian symbol.
Yes, tall like a slender fir tree,
Powerful and brave like the wolf of Velebita.
He did not regret his life,
For the people and for Tito.

Since then the summer is over.
Your people, comrade, are as firm as flint.
But that rough cross reminds me of you
And the memory of a timeless world.

Without a word of greeting, Anton stomped away from
Nikola and Mara to adjust his wheel alignment. Nikola
ceased singing and, with a look at Mara that suggested he
had observed her and Anton all too well, he asked, 'What was
all that about, Mara?'

'I asked him to dance,' she replied with eyes downcast.

'So I saw.'

'He was great!' she protested.

'Mara,' said Nikola. He halted his great body and looked
down at her, as reflectively as her father used to. 'Was he really?'

Under his penetrating gaze, Mara was forced to acknowledge the truth.

'No,' she acknowledged then went on in a rush. 'I just...
he... well, you know what he's like, Nikola. I just thought
I'd....'

'Make him look like a fool, sweetheart?' enquired Nikola
gently.

'But I didn't mean to!' wailed Mara. 'I was trying to help.'

Mara loved Nikola. He was so comfortable. He was loving
and truthful.

'Well, I think that's fine, Mara. Maybe next time, don't try
so hard. I can see that you like him.'

Mara stopped.

'Oh, not you, too!'

'Well, well, well.' Nikola smiled to himself and patted her on the shoulder. 'I have just walked back from the Central Hospital. Slobodan is a little better this morning, I think.'

Mara's face flushed.

'Oh, Nikola, I'm so sorry. Always thinking about myself. Is his wound healing?'

'No, not much, though he's been there for so long, but they think the infection is subsiding, so now it might. But he said he was cold.' His words faded off. He stared further into the forest where the trees crackled in the spring grass. 'Last night one of the men took a pot shot at a man in the peripheries. Tell the other girls, would you?'

'Sure, Nikola.' A cold shiver ran up Mara's spine. 'Did they get a good look?'

'Unfortunately, not. They shot at him because he didn't return the hail, and then he took off.'

The light had almost completely faded now. Still wildly gyrating, the dancers, silhouetted only by the flames of the lamps and the thrusted breaths that fuelled them, seemed like the final bursts of an old bellows, dimming because the leather of its squeeze box had thinned and the wooden handles were rutted with borer's holes. Dancing no longer provided the illusion of safety in numbers, and though Nikola still waited by her side and Mara could feel his warmth through his textured vest and the matching cap that he always wore, yet they seemed insubstantial and the night laden with doom. If Miroslav could find her twice without warning, then what was to stop him doing so again? A dance, a lonely night in a vast forest, a friend by her side? Miroslav's instincts were those of the bloodhound. He was good at investigating. He enjoyed it. He had his porcelain ego to consider.

For him, there was always a way, and Mara had never known him to give up.

Beside her, Nikola thought about his home, his wife and his wounded son.

'Stick together, Mara. All right?'

*****

Miroslav watched the dancing apprehensively. The light was fading and he was becoming superstitious of these shadowy bandits, the dark scurrying shapes who attacked without warning from the unearthly silence of the woods and melted back again into the trees. As he watched, they had cast aside their human forms and mutated into fiends. The wild firelight leaped up the tree trunks, almost as far as the rain bearing clouds that had descended from the mountains, and seemed to paint them the same colour and texture of grinning demons, a mocking smile dissolving in blood.

While the torches held out, the whirls and yells of primaeval triumph turned his blood to an icy stream in which snowflakes hardened and bumped along the edges of his arteries to set his nerves on end. Miroslav possessed one artery in particular that troubled him. It began in his brain and descended to his feet, and he had given it a name, because its presence plagued him continually. With a name, he could hurl abuse at it, he could banish it from his presence. He was in control. Without a name, it reigned supreme, anonymous and terrifying; and so he had called it Legion, and on that day when it was exposed before men, he would banish it into a herd of swine, to run screaming into a lake and be drowned.

One of the fiends had shot at him! Blistering with gunpowder, the bullet had surged past his head, very narrowly missing his ear, causing him to dive into a hollow log full of termites and bats devouring the feast. He had seen the little white ants scurrying from the shot that blasted the decaying bark, and the fact that they did not recognize a bullet when they saw one did not cause Miroslav to humiliate the insects. Somewhere he remembered that they were part of an ecosystem, where everything had its role and each supported the other, and this order gave him comfort, for he felt that around him unseen eyes gauged his every movement: invisible, silent, watchful and ruthless, lusting after revenge. Gone in these menacing woods was the regular military formation of the German war machine in which he found such comfort, and which had allowed the Ustasha to flourish. But the vast numbers of Partisans already slaughtered were also like these ants that willingly died so that their fellows could cross the stream on the pile of their bodies. Death, apparently, didn't worry Partisans. Having lost everything already, they had nothing left to lose. They were a terrible enemy.

Just before dawn this morning, the Italian unit he was staying with, only a few hour's walk from this bacchanalia, had been attacked without warning by a group of male and female Partisans. Eight men had been slaughtered over their coffee and ten cases of ammunition carried into the woods. The attack had come from nowhere. The guards on sentry duty, whom he cursed for fools, were killed literally where they stood, the indications of surprise given by the fact that they died only metres from the perimeter and had had no time to alert the base.

As he had stared down at the bodies, Miroslav experienced a horrible sense of his own vulnerability. The usual marks of slit throats and gunshot wounds had mangled the suntanned faces below him and pierced the chests, and the blood bath in which they rested did not give him the customary pleasure he felt after witnessing a battle. There was no obvious indication of the enemy's approach either. Miroslav, hunting in the bushes afterwards, could not easily tell from which direction they had come. Was it possible that they had concealed even their footsteps? He had heard of these things happening, although he couldn't believe it of any army. But later, when a superstitious Italian corporal had claimed to see a devil rising from the lake, Miroslav had collected his gear and announced his intention of quitting the slack Latins who could not discern an attack on their very doorstep, for an Ustasha division closer to home, who didn't believe in ghosts.

He hadn't yet got that far though, and at the moment he was on his own, camped in the woods, living on a large cheese he had stolen from stores, two dozen apples, a ham, a loaf of hard bread and several bottles of Chianti. His blanket was thin but the nights were becoming warmer, and he had his pistol and the small switchblade he liked to carry with him in these dangerous places. He had been really geared up when he saw Mara dancing with that officer. The fact that the man obviously felt uncomfortable didn't detract from Miroslav's certain knowledge that it was she, again, who had initiated the contact. He hated it when he saw her do this. It tightened his groin and his head together, until he got so angry that he needed violent physical exercise of some nature to sooth himself. On the occasion of the strip tease, he had torn the branches of every tree he could find for half an hour afterwards, until he calmed down. This night, not wishing to draw the dancing eyes his way, he had left his tree and hurried as fast as he could to the river, where he hurled stones far out across the stream, over and over, until he gained some measure of control. There was nothing like sex and violence for regaining control over one's self and, the minute he could assuage himself in this manner, he would.

He returned to the dancing.

*****

323

Anton slid his head out from the undercarriage. He was much happier under a truck.

'How much did we get from those Italians?' he asked his companion.

'Only ten cases of ammunition,' replied the man, who also preferred mechanics to music. 'A box of batteries, two jerry cans of petrol and the half tank that was already in it.'

'We need more ammunition.'

'Moscow should send us some.'

'Yeah, well, we keep trying. All Moscow does in response is complain that our communism is upsetting their allies, Britain and America.'

'Communist Moscow said that? You're joking?'

'Nope. Move the torch this way, would you? It's too dark to see what I'm doing.'

The guy shifted his weight from one foot to another.

'That wheel alignment could have waited until morning.'

'You go, then, I'll stay here.'

'Who will hold the torch?'

'All right, I'm nearly finished.'

Are we a real army, wondered Anton, or are we becoming one? Very early this morning, as they were preparing the attack on the Italians, he had seen the low flying planes of the Luftwaffe through the bare spring leaf coverage and knew they had come searching for the Partisans. *The Germans are worried. But are we a threat to mighty Germany or just a passing nuisance?* It was common knowledge that the Partisans trekked during the hours of darkness. Hearing the drone, Anton had looked up at the black bodies of the planes. *They are sufficiently concerned to waste resources hunting us out.* What can they be thinking? *We will exert German might and exterminate the Bolshevik Bandits once and for all? We have trained for this from our youth. We are the mighty German army. We have Teutonic efficiency and Aryan superiority.*

They are brainwashed, thought Anton.

What composes a real army so that it irritates the enemy? Anyone can blow up a railway line. It's not that hard. What is harder is to gain their respect, however begrudgingly, and to have achieved the acknowledgement in the eyes of the enemy that this is who we are—not just bands of local brigands.

He wondered whether Britain had heard of the Yugoslav Partisans and what their response would be. Britain knew the strategic value of Yugoslavia to the Germans. It also knew the value of the Dalmatian coastline in the event that they should choose to launch an Allied invasion from there. However, what about after the war? Would Churchill think that far? Or would he think that a band of farmers and young women was not real, and Yugoslavia merely an exotic holiday destination for rich Englishmen?

What would England think of their struggle for liberation? Would the Partisans remain as they were, fighting blindly, losing thousands, cold, starving, almost naked, with no supplies but what could be captured from the enemy or bought from a local village that would be torched, and the people shot, if it should reach German ears that they were supplying them? Anton had long ago ceased to hope for large dinners, although that didn't stop him dreaming about one occasionally.

Of one thing he was certain, dancing was very bad for him.

CHAPTER THIRTY-TWO

The fight to retain the town of Foča and the area surrounding it was not doomed from the start but hampered by inter-racial fighting, the deficiencies of the German allies already alluded to by General Bader, and the terrain. There was little flat ground in the mountains of Eastern Bosnia and visibility was poor. Often, the enemies ate and slept in caves or beneath dripping forest leaves only two or three kilometres from each other, and the days when Britain might publish the results of a battle based on two lines of soldiers facing each other across a field had been sacrificed to the tragic history of a nation of which they had limited understanding.

The communists effectively employed Yugoslav oral history to promote glorious warriors and dubious defeats. However, that same history worked against fighters from all regions, who were prey to the centuries-old hostilities between the racial groups of which their bards sang. Communism was new and an anathema to many, thus any skirmish for territory invariably involved Croatian Ustashas killing Serbs, Serbs killing Muslims, Chetniks fighting Partisans (and vice versa) and peasant partisan fighters defecting from a communism they distrusted to defend their own villagers, or to Serbian Chetniks, if they were Serbs. Meanwhile, the Ustashas had also begun to target the communists, in order to please their Nazi overlords. The entire thing resulted in a deadly confusion, incomprehensible to foreigners and frustrating to the Germans who had, as well, to put up with demoralized Italian troops, who had little desire to fight ferocious enemies in inaccessible terrain and only wanted to seduce local girls and go home to Italy.

'Divided we fall,' Tito warned them. 'This is what the enemy wants.'

Desperately short of ammunition, a unit from the Second Proletarian Brigade went on a raiding party followed by Miroslav, hot on Mara's trail. Miroslav made it a general rule to avoid anything that might occasion injury to himself, for his thoughts pointed always to the future and the glorious destiny that awaited him in the New World of a Nazi victory, where Yugoslavia would quickly be forgotten by the very Western Allies who had created it. With the failure of the German offensive in Russia, and German trucks coughing up the last dregs of oil in their trek back south, Hitler's anger against Slavs and communism had redoubled. Partisan casualties in any engagement were consistently shocking. *Serves them right*, thought Miroslav. Farmers with machine guns? Women with rifles? How ridiculous! However, he waited anxiously as they surprised a detachment of Ustasha soldiers, camped superstitiously at the border of a forest only three kilometres from the Partisan camp, not in Foča itself, but further north in the German zone.

Miroslav trekked through the forest at a distance behind the party that he calculated to be safe. He did not care to fall into the hands of these desperate people, farmers or not. Heedless of death themselves, they would not hesitate to dispatch him with all haste. However, about halfway through the starlit trees, he trod on a snake and managed to muffle his horror by thrusting a fist into his mouth. Believing him to be an owl from a land of giants, the snake bolted beneath a log, but the flick of its tail and Miroslav's rapid indrawn breath had alerted a young fighter trailing behind the bulk of the party. Despite his shock, Miroslav had hopes that this rear guard might have been Mara, and he kept his excitement rigidly under control until it turned out to be nothing but a slender youth, whose frosted silhouette in the night mists did not match hers. After a glance or two in the snake's direction, the youth had retreated. Miroslav next walked through a spider's web and his fear of detection was almost matched by the temptation to utter a distressed groan. He peeled the sticky streamers from his face and the spider scurried away. It had been quite an assertive arachnid, with muscular and hairy legs, and the possibility existed that, had Miroslav been born with night vision, he might have lost self-control utterly and surrendered to the consequences of a primaeval scream: a sudden rush of terror followed by a bullet in the brain. Mara would undoubtedly have identified his corpse with relief.

The Partisans ahead had acquired two horses, undoubtedly stolen and possibly German, as Miroslav was aware that the German officers had brought quite a few, now that the snows had melted. The horses had been saddled with packs ready to escape with the stolen booty and a blurred figure rode each. *The horses, at least, are happy to eat grass*, mused Miroslav, dodging a pile of steaming manure. With relief, he glimpsed the clearing at the edge of the forest and the tarpaulins slung over branches that marked the start of the Ustasha camp. He felt no guilt at not camping with his fellow countrymen. The dregs of society lived in these outposts. Fighting alongside the Germans and Italians was proving to be universally unpopular. Killing terrified Serbs, Jews and gypsies in imaginative ways close to home was where most Ustasha preferred to be. Only one solitary sentry awaited the silent Partisans and, as Miroslav watched, an arm swung out, and the misted man abruptly sloped against a tree, as if he wished to view a star at an unusual angle in the heavens, then fell to the ground. Behind him, the killer wiped his knife on the bark and beckoned for the others to follow. Miroslav watched them traipse through the camp. There were perhaps fifty tents and, at the far end, several large piles of boxes, towards which the fighters stalked, each silent leg raised above another in the manner of cats on the prowl. Miroslav held his breath. It was not that he didn't want his side to win, but he had allowed himself to be caught up in the drama, and he considered that the likelihood of shouts and shots that would send the blood surging through his heart was highest at this point.

Finally, he came across Mara waiting by the horses, that small girl she always had with her, by her side. As her colleagues waded inaudibly through the mist, the girl became excited and Mara put up a hand to pacify her. They both held rifles and, through the hush, Miroslav just caught the click as the girl cocked her weapon. Presently, about twelve men returned, bearing between them boxes requiring quite a bit of strength to carry; they had reached the ammunition dump without disturbing a soul, quite a remarkable feat, and were presently in the process of loading the boxes onto the horses. At this point, a loud cry was heard from the camp, and Miroslav watched in muted horror as the small girl raised her rifle and fired. He cocked his own pistol and considered how good his aim might be in this obscure location, hemmed in by night and trees. Rapidly, the men with the horses completed their task, slapped the animals and, with most of the party, took off back into the forest. Mara and the girl ran after them.

Miroslav noticed that Mara ran faster than her friend, and it gave him a peculiar pleasure to witness her self-protectiveness in response to the alarm around her. Typical human. A handful of Partisans still remained, shooting into the camp before they, too, turned and fled. Somewhere in the mystery of that night, the paths that had seemed so direct with a group of men, became a maze, when even life and death mistook each other. Aleksandra was soon insulated in her own world, and that appeared not to concern her, Miroslav noticed. He had been following Mara, but lost her in all the running and shooting, and now he watched the odd little girl scurrying around the grey woodland with her eyes focussed, not perplexed, but calm after her achievement, as if she were waiting for something that only she sensed, and speaking to another whom only she could see. Feeling hardly done by that his side had lost even so inconsequential a battle, and resentful of the diminished returns on his prospects, Miroslav casually raised his pistol and shot her experimentally in the back as her isolation from the main body presented an easy target. It interested him how she immediately collapsed without the pause he had anticipated, due to watching too many movies. He felt he could easily become accustomed to this killing business. The idea, so attractive in theory, was more than stimulating in reality. He wondered if his shot had been overheard in the tumult, but fear made one deaf, apparently and, though Miroslav carefully secluded himself in the closest copse, no one returned. So, he left.

Nikola found Aleksandra fallen onto one side, wrapped around a tree as if embracing a lover. He had been hurrying along with the rear guard, back into the forest, when he came across her, lying so still in the silken blackness that he thought at first she was part of the roots themselves. It was only the hem of her white blouse, thrown up as she fell, that glistened in the moonlight and alerted him. Stooping to investigate, he recognised the German greatcoat and the boots that she always wore. Gently, he put a hand beneath her chin and turned towards him the composed little face, the eyes as calmly closed as a sleeping child, the chest quiet, the heart, upon which he laid his ear, without even the slightest pulse to indicate to him when she had departed. Neglectful of his own safety, he slung his rifle around his shoulder and picked her up, carrying her back through the forest to where they were camped.

That night Mara cried as she had not done since her mother died. All the next day she berated herself bitterly for giving way to panic and becoming isolated from her friend when she had most needed her, until Nikola took her aside and told her that it was not her fault. Aleksandra's life was changed, not ended, and that all along, they had known that she could not survive the murder of her family in any real sense. She had only given the impression of continuance.

They had dug pits into the earth, each *baza* held two in close company, and the bodies of several more fighters were found that morning by the Ustashas, as they scouted through the woods looking for the Partisans. But the company had withdrawn behind enemy lines to sleep, and the roots of the trees were closely spaced. If there wasn't a root, there was a rock and if, by some miracle, there was a space with neither, then there was an ants' nest. They were friendly ants, on the whole, but sometime in the early afternoon, Mara was bitten on the leg by a rogue ant while she was asleep. Such intense pain these sudden bites had, like a bullet! Pain right down to the bone and, after five minutes of exquisite agony, there was peace and the whole thing was over.

At sunset, they dug a grave for Aleksandra in the thick of the forest. Mara and her friends stood with Nikola and Boško as they laid the young girl into the friendly earth, like a child at bedtime, and tucked her up with leaves.

Through Forests and Mountains

'Aren't two sparrows sold for a penny?' said Mara. 'And not one of them will fall to the earth without your Father's knowledge. Of how much more value are you than the birds.'

How the words of Christ exhibited an understanding of nature! In the same way, there was not a death, nor a poem, nor a thought that did not link the Partisans to the natural world. It gave Mara a clue to their belief that they belonged to this land for which they were fighting. Imbued, as she was, with literature and learning, well-travelled, city-bred Mara experienced an envy, though not a crisis of belief, for many of these people were deeply devout, yet held a desire to associate with the earth as strongly. 'The forests have become the graves of our fallen comrades,' wrote Anđelka Martić. 'Flower have sprouted on them. We twitch the gentle stems, we roll up the small flowerets and it takes us back to the warm streams of our childhood, where once we ran between the trees gathering red cyclamen. Why, wood in the forest, do you disturb the silence on a peaceful day and the scent of the flowers on the bleak graves? Because the forest is telling the story of a dead partisan. The branches sob, the trees tremble like the lonely mother with tearful eyes, who wails at the grave of her son.'

Mara wondered how a communist could deal with death on such a scale, the proselytes of Lenin who were faithful to his atheism, even as they awaited the hour of their execution? Like that son they had all been talking about recently, who had written to his mother from some stinking prison in Dalmatia: Branko Đipalović. A miracle she'd ever received the letter, poor woman. Some gaoler with a touch of humanity amidst this genocidal madness must have posted it. The reports of what Branko had written had spread from the woman's village like a river in flood, all over eastern Bosnia. 'Be proud, mother, for you bore one of Lenin's students. I am neither the first nor the last to be choked by the thirst for human blood. But what is life without freedom? What is a well without water? What is a river without the ocean, and for what are our tears when they must fall? Goodbye, mother, be strong. And when this poem rises from the earth, let out a mighty roar for freedom and to those who gave the righteous life. Death does not frighten the pupils of Lenin.'

One couldn't just give up and move on, more so now that this land was so richly carpeted with the graves of young Partisans. 'Go cautiously, dear comrade,' they warned Mara, 'because beneath your feet lie fighters who have fallen for the people's salvation. In the country through which we walk, we have stopped to bury many. In the shade of a pine tree, beneath the branches of an ancient oak, along a goat track, at the top of a small village, deep in the forest. For the sake of the partisan's duty and holy principles, rest for a moment by the tranquillity of their graves.'

A creak startled her, a low branch as it brushed a head, and she looked up to see Anton watching them, but when Aleksandra's small funeral service was over and Mara had dried her eyes one more time, he had walked on and she couldn't find him.

Later, she saw him walking in the cool of the evening. Through a thicket, the yellow twilight passed like gold dust around him, as if he were part of the night that was coming and would soon descend with the dusk and, like Aleksandra, end his day forever. 'I'll spoil that,' she thought miserably. 'The minute he sees me.'

She felt a movement in the air beside her and looked up, startled. An owl had flown in beside her, large, soft wings, a big body and wise eyes, perched on a branch of the tree. *Go!* whispered the owl. Mara took a step forward.

'Anton,' she called softly.

Through Forests and Mountains

He turned and she shrunk back, but he had seen her, registered her confusion. He turned and faced her, as directly as ever.

'I'm sorry about your friend,' he said.

Listening to his deep voice breaking the silence, she realized how little she understood him. 'How silly I am,' she thought. 'He doesn't hate me, after all.'

'Aleksandra's with her family,' she replied. 'She's happy now. She died assaulting the men who killed them.'

The barber that shaved the men had trimmed her hair so that it sat below her collar, a bit like the style she had worn in London, a million years ago, it seemed. She wondered why she had ever worried about hair. A strand fell upon her forehead. She pushed it off, poked it into the bangs above it.

'Do you think we should do nothing?' she asked Anton. 'Do you think if we didn't fight back no one would die?'

Well, he had a practical mind, she already knew that and was prepared for his answer. He did not need to give it much thought.

'To do nothing,' he answered immediately, 'would mean allowing the Germans unlimited access to resources, to build German planes from Bosnian bauxite, to run German tanks on Romanian oil, to build German prisoner-of-war camps from Serbian forests, to allow ordinary Germans living ordinary lives to eat, drink and be merry on Greek crops, unaware that starving children were dropping dead in the streets of Athens. And if you don't bomb the railways through Yugoslavia to Greece, you are permitting Rommel's army to defeat the Allies in North Africa and *that* would mean that there would be no chance of any help from them. Does Britain care about Yugoslavia? Not at all. Britain wants to beat the Axis powers and they want Yugoslavia to help them, naturally.'

'You're cynical?'

'No. I understand their attitude. It's a two-edged sword. If you fight, you die, and so does everyone else, but you deprive the enemy of resources and communication. If you're lucky you'll get Britain and America behind you. Then you won't have to steal from the enemy any longer.'

'But people are dying in enemy reprisals. Villages are burnt. Maybe we shouldn't fight, like the Germans warned us.'

'You trust them, do you, after what they did to Belgrade? You were there.'

'No, but....'

'All right, so you sit tight and play it safe. You lose anyway. You lose your country and its resources—and you have a winning side that is arbitrary with their promises. Look how they've ravaged Poland. And don't think things will go back to normal after the war's over. It'll be the old power play just like it was under the King and, before them, the Hapsburgs and, before them, the Turks. Or Stalin will walk into Yugoslavia. Yes,' he concluded. 'Probably that's what will occur.'

He stopped and she wondered what he was thinking, for it seemed to her that his words had a faraway objective. He looked alone, but not lonely. For the first time, watching him, she was able to tell the difference.

'Do you want to go back to sea?'

'Yes,' he said.

'In a submarine?'

'Yes.' Did she hear a sigh as he said it or was that the breeze through the leaves? It was cooling as the night fell, and there was dew on the grass. 'But this is where I am now.' Practical, as ever. No time for poetry.

And now, she thought, she was perhaps finally getting to know him. What would tomorrow bring and would they still be alive?

'Anton,' she asked, turning to him. 'Do you have a family?'

'A small one,' he replied. 'A married sister and her children, south of Belgrade. My parents are dead.'

'No wife, no children yourself?'

'No. And you?'

'Well, I walked out on my father,' she told him with resignation, 'because I was young and selfish. He's in London. But that British officer who lost his radio in Užice sent a message to him from me. I hope he got it.'

'Oh, Britain would have received it,' Anton replied, a little too smartly for Mara. 'As their officer had clearly been sent here.'

And when Mara looked distressed, he softened and asked, 'What did the message read?'

'Mara is well,' she replied as her bottom lip trembled. 'Teaching. Sends love.'

'There, you see,' brightened Anton. 'He didn't repeat himself, so he knows what he's doing.'

'Why?'

'Basic rule in encryption. Never repeat yourself in a coded message. It's a dead giveaway to the code breakers.'

He smiled and Mara smiled back.

'Oh, yes,' she added, 'and I also have a psychotic ex-boyfriend. Unfortunately, he's very clever. He already traced me to Užice.' She adjusted her shirt. It was one of the new ones the girls had been making, of grey army drill, and she wore pants that they had scrounged from a dead German and taken in at the waist.

'What happened?' Anton asked.

'He threatened me. Said if I touched him again, he'd kill me.'

'Touched who?'

'The British officer who sent the message for me. And the worst thing is, because I don't know how Miroslav found me in the first place, I have this fear that he will find me again, even though I don't know how he could.' She flung her arms wide. 'I mean, how could he? We're in the middle of nowhere.'

Anton was thoughtful.

'Could he have been in Užice for another reason and just happened upon you?'

'I don't know, I don't know!' Mara cried. 'His reaction was just like him, possessive, jealous. He hates to lose and I can't help feeling that this will climax in some way. It's ridiculous, I know, but I do.'

'In the middle of a war, it is,' he said reasonably.

She patted the tree stump they were sitting on.

'I wish you were here all the time,' she said. 'Right here, so that I would feel safe.'

Mara knew immediately that that made him feel better than anything; a peace he hadn't known, and perhaps an expectation arising slowly from an unfamiliar source.

She stood up and so did he.

'Perhaps we should better get back before they shoot us for fraternizing,' she said. Anton ran a hand down one leg, acknowledging the need to leave, and Mara grinned in a fractured way. 'Although Jana's pregnant and they haven't shot her yet.'

He burst out laughing, and Mara thought again, how much laughter suited him. It accentuated the creases at the corners of his eyes and the broad folds that captured his mouth when he smiled. When he looked like that, he had the external appearance of a man who was experienced with women, yet something about him still bothered her. You know, if she gave it some thought, she could perhaps guess... yes, was that it? He was attracted by the wrong sort of woman. *Now that's an idea!* He'd go, she bet, for women who could never get further than his surface, and she decided that, in an imperfect world, a man like him would probably put up with second best, merely for the companionship of a relationship. And when they broke up, as those shallow relationships invariably did, he'd never be entirely sure why, but being the self-reliant type, he'd cut his losses and start again.

Then Mara had another really wonderful revelation. If she could fathom his depths, she thought, explore his virgin territory—although perhaps virgin wasn't quite the right word—she might just discover something wonderful. And she was trying to stem her burgeoning excitement when he suddenly said, 'Does Jana still intend to fight?'

'Well, there are two of them fighting now,' answered Mara matter-of-factly. 'So I gave her my lunch.'

Anton smiled.

'I like you because you're funny.'

'Just practical,' answered Mara.

CHAPTER THIRTY-THREE

Oh, those early months of pregnancy! How the baby pressed on one's bladder! Jana went into the woods alone. She began to undo the buttons on her pants, searching for a tree big enough to screen her. It was all very well for men.

'Hey, good looking!'

'Who? Me?' At the engaging summons, Jana whipped her hand up to her mouth, turned around and saw a man she had never laid eyes on before. She took a deep breath and let it out slowly. Whoa! Wasn't he something to write home about? The right side of thirty, agreeable, handsome—and he knew both. He was looking at her with a curious mix of cultured lust and the feeling that he would like to eat her. She stepped back. 'Where did you come from?'

Miroslav tossed his head into the forest behind him. 'Over there. Want something to eat?'

Jana, who had consumed enough herbs lately to give her flatulence for a decade, watched him hungrily.

'And what do you get in return?' she asked.

Miroslav angled his head.

'A romp around the cot?'

Jana hesitated.

'Whose cot?'

Through Forests and Mountains

'I'll tell you what, I'll just go back and get...bread, cheese, ham, whatever you like, and you can take a look and see if the bargain's worthwhile.'

The beautiful face before her hardened with animal expectation and suddenly Jana was very afraid.

'You're a villain!' she exclaimed. 'I can live without food. They'll shoot you, you know that. You've got to leave now.'

That was the trouble in those days of morning sickness and swollen breasts. It was harder to run away than usual. Jana turned to flee, but Miroslav leaped upon her, one hand over her mouth, and dragged her back into the cover of the trees.

CHAPTER THIRTY-FOUR

Nikola had been correct in his rustic assessment of Germans at war. They were slow learners. They were not good at guerrilla warfare. They were unable to mimic Partisan tactics and were constantly to suffer from their lack of knowledge of that land. They were prey to the whims and tempers of the dictator to whom they had entrusted the next thousand years of the Reich, and their allies were a disappointment to them. It was just as well that they were the superior race, because otherwise the constant propping up of Italian and Ustasha forces might have defeated them. However, in the defence of the towns they held in Eastern Bosnia, they had made some improvement, it being obvious by then that Yugoslavia was not the pushover they had imagined.

When Partisans took a town, they initially proceeded along the principle of the Trojan Horse. A small, elite group would infiltrate the town by night and occupy one or two prominent buildings. Once the main force assaulted the town along its peripheries, these elite soldiers would open fire, right, left and centre. The plan for this pandemonium was to ease a breach in the enemy's circle, allowing regular fighters entry. However, the night that Boško was critically injured, the German-held town in Eastern Bosnia was cordoned by brand new concrete bunkers with slits for machine gun fire, and it was clear that these would need to be stormed before the town could be infiltrated. A unit stealthily moved into position during the night hours. They passed the outlying farms, the squat spires of the churches, minarets of a single mosque that rose up in the pre-dawn, feeling the grass wet from the night's dew around their knees. The first cock crowed, a dog barked. Already the mists that clutched the forest were thinning with the approach of the sun. Not a sound. The silence of the hunter among the trees. No place for fear. Eyes focussed.

While Slobodan still lingered in the hospital in Foča, fighting the infection that was slowly claiming his young body, Nikola and Boško had reached the town with the rest. Boško was running up the hill it was built upon with a grenade in his hand, dodging a hail of enemy bullets. Generally, this was a duty for the youngest boys, only thirteen or fourteen, but, due to the dangers of the task, they were in short supply. Boško had volunteered to hurl the grenade into the bunker because he was light on his feet and had a good pitching arm. The distance to the bunker was increased by a row of sand bags and, despite the machine guns all pointed in his direction, Boško successfully scaled the hill, pulled the pin, tossed the grenade swiftly across, then dropped to the ground and rolled back down the hill. The men waiting at the bottom heard a loud bang, saw the expected puff of smoke and registered a brief lull in enemy fire before rushing up towards the town, rifles in their hands.

Safe, as he thought, Boško breathed and stretched, and the last thing he heard was, 'Keep your head down,' before being shot in the side of his forehead.

Death did not come immediately. The bullet had ruptured the large pool of venous blood on the right side of his brain and inexorably, as the blood cascaded into the open air,

Margaret Walker

Boško's blood pressure fell, his kidneys shut down and his heart began to fail. Nikola was not far away and his comrades called to him before he could continue up the slope with the others. Seeing at once that Boško was dying, Nikola did not waste time begging him to remain but commenced the Orthodox prayer at the Departing of the Soul. Beneath the tan from these months outdoors, the young skin paled and the rasping breathing that is associated with the approach of death quieted and stilled. Nikola completed his prayers, hoisted his son's body into his arms, refusing all offers of help and, as bullets whizzed past him, walked back into the woods. Nobody spoke to him, because they could see that his suffering was very great.

That evening, beneath the old oak that spread its branches over Boško's grave, Anton and Mara kept him silent company, and for the rest of that night and all the next day Nikola tramped alone through the woods and farmlands to visit Slobodan in hospital. Being Nikola, he obtained permission from the commissar first, despite his grief. He returned three days later, quiet and gaunt, and in that time, he had aged.

*****

Two nights after her disappearance, Jana was found dead in the woods. No one saw her leave and no one heard her cry out and, when they discovered her body, just as the sun was causing the dew on the spring leaves to glisten with the dawn, it was quite wet, and she had evidently lain there for some time. She was found on her back, and that she had been pregnant when she was killed, was evident by the swelling of her breasts and the slightest small rise of her lower abdomen, where her clothes were in disarray. From the disturbance of the undergrowth she had evidently been dragged from a secluded spot where the incident took place to the clearing, so that she could be found more easily.

343

Through Forests and Mountains

'The murderer wants us to know he's here,' commented the commissar, and he did not see Mara turn away.

A pall was cast over the camp in the woods. Though they had cooked wild spinach and nettles for breakfast and eaten it with the last of the bread bought from the villagers, few had the will to enjoy the scant pickings.

The communist leaders were the skeleton that supported the body. From them derived the discipline that had allowed local fighters to form a national army, so that the Partisans believed the whole nation was walking with them. From the communists came the ruthless determination with which they fought, and that they followed persistently to death. But for Mara, the murder of Jana, the deaths of Boško and Aleksandra, and the steady decline of Slobodan made her think about herself, even though she thought she had long ago surrendered that urge. She did not want to return to either Belgrade or London, even had these been options. She wanted to remain with her comrades and to share their dream of freedom and this had nothing to do with the fear of loneliness, should she do so. They were with her every hour of every day. Though hermits might have lofty ideals, hermits did not win wars, and the companionship of her comrades meant more to Mara than anything else. She conceived of death in ideal terms if she thought about it at all and, of the thousands who had been killed already, as a landscape of sleeping fighters who had not gone to death with bitterness in their hearts like a sour old woman, but who rested tranquilly in their rustic graves by this wayside and by that.

She thought of her father like a distant fairy-tale. He was intertwined with memories of childhood happiness that had retained their innocence because of this distance. She had become, against her will, a witness of atrocities that he could never have understood, not having seen them for himself, but she didn't blame him for that, and in her heart she de-

344

sired him to remain the same concerned, obstreperous parent that she had loved. Though the fairy-tale dream had been muddied by the realities of war, she allowed him to remain forever beside the tranquil waters of childhood.

*****

'Our woods will be free, our mountains will be free. The Partisans have laid aside their guns behind the rocky outcrops and I can caress you, naked cliffs, in my joy that once again you are free.'

Mara paused to reflect.

'I didn't know you were a poet, Anton.'

'I'm not. Josip Cazi wrote it.'

'When?'

'Last year.'

'So shortly after we were invaded?'

'Hope, you see.'

Most of the time, Anton was overwhelmed by his realization of how alone they actually were, how vast the struggle of one small country, and with what disdain Britain and America regarded them.

'Britain cares about Britain,' he told Mara, 'but it loves sticking its fingers into other country's pies. King Peter might take British advice, but Tito won't so, if Britain backs a group of communist Partisans instead of the King of Yugoslavia, it will forfeit anything resembling the influence it used to have in Belgrade. If they help us, it will be because it will help them, and that help will stop, once they have what they want.'

'And what about America?'

'America hates communism. They won't help us. They'll pursue the Nazis, because Germany has caused two world wars and they can't allow that to happen a third time, but they'll have no interest in the Ustasha and they won't prosecute Italian war crimes. After the war, America will want to stabilize Italy, not prosecute it, because Britain and America see Italy as part of the West. Mark me, Mara, we are alone.'

CHAPTER THIRTY-FIVE

How she came to be with them on that night resembled her first efforts to be a Partisan, that initial journey to Drvar, when it seemed as if there was no place for her. Since then, she had learned that for a Partisan, discipline came second only to sacrifice for their homeland, with the concept of *self* trailing behind, the dinghy that would be hauled in when everything was over. She had been told she must remain in the camp and she would accept that, but, at the last minute, Branko the bard had been pulled out with what they suspected to be typhus, and Mara was hopeful. She was as tall as many of the men, and strong now, much stronger than that green girl who had shown a fledging interest in the role of women. She could see her way better by night than many of them and she was a proven runner. She could keep up when many of the smaller women could not. So, while a rash spread insidiously over Branko's famished body, Mara was added at the last minute to the unit with Anton, Nikola and their group of men, their hoard of explosives, timers and detonators, who were setting out to bomb the railway line carrying bauxite to Sarajevo.

Bauxite was the ore from which aluminium was refined, and the Germans needed it for aircraft production. Not having any bauxite mines of their own, they had bought it from other European countries like France. With the onset of war, they took whatever they needed from the countries they occupied, particularly from the mines near Mostar, west of Foča. The ore was then sent north to Sarajevo on the narrow-gauge railways built in the days of the Austrian empire, until the line that served the mines became a favourite target for Partisan attacks. While it was being repaired, the ore was loaded onto ships at Gruž, the port of Dubrovnik, then sent north up the Adriatic to Trieste. On the way, it was duly bombed by the Allies, so then it was back to the railways.

The railway itself was a feat of Austrian engineering, as its various sublines wound all over Bosnia by forests and mountains, over crevasses and rivers, in and out of the Dinaric Alps, an analogy of the Partisans themselves, who spent many nights blowing it up. They knew that dynamiting a bridge, of which there were many in mountainous Bosnia, could hold up an entire army, and destroying the railway lines achieved two things. Firstly, it deprived the enemy of raw materials and, secondly, it allowed the capture of the trains themselves and anything that was transported in them.

It should not be imagined that the Germans took all this lying down. Methods to secure the all-important sources of aluminium occupied time and resources, and further impressed upon the high command the importance of wiping out the high percentage of Yugoslav troublemakers, who refused to be occupied peacefully. They set aside an entire infantry division, the 718th, for this purpose. Comprising nearly 18,000 men, artillery, communication, medical services and tanks, it outsized the small black figures hopping on and off railway lines in the darkness as a dinosaur compares to a mouse. But, hampered by size and darkness, as one British report stated later in the war, there wasn't much they could do, and the railway continued to be destroyed, repaired and destroyed again.

'I wish I had a tank,' thought Anton, 'just for once, to deceive myself into believing that might is right.'

He couldn't decide whether Mara's inclusion in the group pleased him or not. Whilst the thought of her being close added that slim scrap of comfort to his tense and lonely days, he still thought, as he had from the beginning, that she was too eager to place herself before a danger she didn't fully comprehend. By this stage, he really thought she would have grasped it, but she was eight years his junior and he let it pass, because of her youth.

They were no longer men and women but shadows flitting forward, rifles slung upon their shoulders, grenades hanging from their belts. Those who carried the heavier explosives and timing devices had walked on ahead. Darkness, and around them a deep silence. No sound except for the raindrops on the leaves. Even the dogs were quiet. No roosters here. Farms a long way off. The rain that had held off all day, had precipitated as night fell and was now falling steadily, turning the ground beneath their feet into mud. Anton trod lightly, but nevertheless sunk well into it. Soft wet earth, cold feet and drips down the back of his neck. He couldn't clearly make out the features of the man in front of him, but he sensed Mara squelching forward just beyond. Like an animal, his senses had heightened. This was how the night had transformed him.

Silhouetted by clouds, the trees stood out above. He raised his eyes and thought that the night was not so black, although the moon was on the wane. Even on the darkest nights there always remained some light at sea, and the longing to return to it wrenched him hardest whenever he looked at the clouds. The waves ought to surge and swell at his feet. The wingspans of the great sea birds should soar over the

349

face of the water, just as he remembered them. The sharp-crying gulls, his familiar beacon as he came into port, would gather and swarm as the submarine approached. But tonight, having looked for the ocean to guide his steps, he found only earth at his feet and his way was as impenetrable as charcoal. The single railway line towards which they headed passed, in places, very close to the edge of the hill, and he imagined that the faintest sense of the sea came to him on the breeze that played at its base, but the Adriatic was a hundred kilometres to the south. The cliff, the trees, and the night air were playing tricks on hm. The salt tang, if salt it was, had come from his deep desire to be close to the water. Last night he had dreamed that he saw the land collapse from the Adriatic to the mountains of Bosnia and the sea thunder in, to hurl itself against the granite ruins. But what if he should be killed this night? Would he lie in his cold grave dreaming forever of the sea, like the young partisans of whom the poets spoke? Or would his heart fly back to the water?

You won't be able to keep me in the grave. Not like those others.

They had been walking for about three hours and he guessed that, by the time they had set the charges, the dawn would not be far away. The railway passed over a small stone bridge and continued on into the valley, while the track itself lay towards the base of the pine forest that skirted the final hill, where the trees had been partially cleared to provide access. They were descending and had already passed through the denser woods. Anton saw that the pines, though broad and strong, grew farther apart towards the tracks and did not provide sufficient cover for the Partisans to let down their guard. The railway track rushed around the bend from the dark forest like a stage coach along a haunted highway and then disappeared in the opposite direction. A single siding, the only point at which two trains might pass, was a long way back, and they had picked these two kilometres to dynamite just above the drop into the trees to the valley floor, at the point where the train and the track were at their most vulnerable. The Germans had only recently repaired it, a considerable amount of trouble given the precipice and the difficulty of approach.

The night was their ally, yet it pressed around them, and the soft mist blanketed their way, turning trees into statues and the underbrush into lakes of gossamer. Anton was again aware of Mara, just ahead. He imagined her warmth, saw, through the blur, the rise and fall of her shoulders; he watched as she turned her head towards a scurrying sound of the night. She had helped him to understand her and now he knew what she was thinking. She was thinking of Aleksandra dreaming beneath her mound of leaves, of Boško, to whom death had come too quickly for such a vigorous young man, of Slobodan clinging to life for the sake of his father, and of Jana. This evening, she had told him that she dreamed she had opened her shirt to him in the night and woken to find his face pillowed against her breasts, sleeping so heavily that when they roused him to commence the march, he had looked around him, confused. Thinking it over now, she said, she couldn't tell what was real and what wasn't, and it was only the confusion that had given him away. This was intimate speech and a measure of how things had progressed between them, that she could tell him so much. Don't wait until tomorrow when they might both be dead.

But what if they weren't dead? Then what? He could no longer imagine a world without Mara there to tease him and irritate him and dream soft wet dreams, like the leaves. What would evenings be like without her, or long patrols like this, where once he would have been alert and now he just felt lonely? Could he be happy on those sultry summer mornings in the woods by the river without the expectation that she might seek him out? Could he look forward, with any fulfilment, to an endless future on his own? Although modesty had never been one of his strong points, he had to admit that even he didn't have the answers. He did not understand himself anymore. He'd never picked girlfriends like her. Yet, upon reflection, he had always enjoyed talking to her, although he hadn't realized it when they'd first met and neither of them had been Partisan material. Was he in love? He wasn't certain what being in love actually was, but how else could he explain this restlessness he felt? In lust? Yes, but were not all men in love and in lust to varying degrees?

Ahead of them, Nikola was focussed on his task. He knelt down and put his ear to the track. He shook his head. The troop spread out around him, to the right and the left, preparing to destroy the track for a kilometre each way. From his utility belt, Nikola produced a small trowel and began quietly to lecture the troop concerning Newton's third law of motion.

'An equal and opposite reaction,' he whispered, 'won't happen if you place the dynamite *there*.' Nikola indicated the top of the hardwood sleeper, upon which rested the railway track, and then he commenced digging a trench beneath it. 'Placed *here*,' he thrust the stick of explosive into the trench. 'It will ensure an opposite force from the ground equal to the explosion, dislocating the track. Fair enough?' A whispered chorus responded and Nikola followed the instructions up with a further muffled bluster about how to set the detonators. 'Now go thou and do likewise! Every fifty metres, for a kilometre each way. I'll give you thirty minutes.'

Wordlessly, the men dispersed to lay the explosives Nikola's way while Nikola put his head again to the track.

'Not yet,' he said.

The black locomotives that hauled the ore-filled freight carriages were monstrous enough in the confines of the city stations, chafing at the bit, chimneys puffing and billowing, spewing from every pore the vast industrial stench of the empire that had created them. They needed coal for the furnaces and water for the boilers, and their oversized wheels reared above the level of the platform. Anton always imagined them about to explode, and he recalled the relief when the leviathans were finally out in the countryside, where they could plunge and roar at will. But this night in the wild mountains, a train would be an iron monster emerging from nowhere into an abyss of rolling track and then disappearing back into the darkness. Armoured for the threat they anticipated, raging because they were German.

For a third time, Nikola laid his ear to the track.

'It's coming,' he said.

Like a row of dominoes, the Partisans dropped one after another from the tracks and slid down the slope into the forest. Anton had counted one, two, he saw Mara jump, three, four, then it was his turn, his feet slipping and sliding through the undergrowth, and the slim trunks passing in a row of black shadows before his eyes. As the slope flattened, he scrambled for purchase in the mud. By now, he could hear the locomotive approaching, a sound muted by distance but growing steadily, a soft roar, a lush and plentiful surge into an onslaught of pressurized steam. Because his sense of distance was distorted by the night and the surreal sense of their actions, he experienced a fleeting fear of an approaching apocalypse, which he tried to suppress. He ran faster as the approach of the train became imminent and he glimpsed the light on the front of the locomotive, but could not accurately determine his margin of safety.

Then they heard the charges exploding up and down the line and, for a moment after, it seemed as though nothing untoward would happened. The train continued at the same speed, and apparently in the identical direction, around the bend. But then, like a string that had released a rock, the fiery engine swung out in a straight line far over the valley, thrust forward by its own momentum and pinioned as if it were a hovering eagle, then began an almost leisurely descent. Only when half a dozen carriages were off the rails did it twist and plunge, all the while spinning clouds of smoke and vermillion sparks that sprayed above the forest as it fell. Behind, the remaining armoured cars left the rails as a series of black walls and then swept downwards until, in its agony, the entire train struck the forest floor with a groan like some monstrous human.

Anton had been looking for Mara in only a half state of mind after the tension and excitement. From way behind, he heard shouts around the wreck and knew that they must hurry with all speed, for the enemy would know that, as usual, guerrilla activity meant Partisans not far away. They glided into the forest, keeping their heads down in the undergrowth. Passing through a tight gully in the forest floor, in the absolute blackness, someone behind him had reached out to take hold of his shirt as a guide and he assumed, without breaking their silence, that it was Mara. He didn't stop to consider that, as she had jumped first, she should have been in front of him, nor did he ponder the intricacies of touch, that she had never held his shirt before. Is that how she would hang on, if it were indeed her? Wouldn't she be gentler? Was the strength in the touch behind him an indication of her fear or her excitement? Were these the things that she was feeling, or merely relief that it was all over?

So that, when they had moved out of the gully onto higher ground and he turned to check that the hand clinging on to him was, in fact, hers, he decided that it was his estimation of touch that was wrong. It was not Mara who held him, but one of the boys, breathing heavily, wanting the touch of an older man to calm him. Anton looked around. As he had anticipated, the dawn was not far away. The deepest hour of the night, when even the night creatures were silent, was passing. Soon he would be able to see. Yet, where were the square shoulders that were recognisably hers, the head, clever and alert, and with it her gift for languages that made her always turn to listen to whomever was speaking?

With her absence, Anton remembered something that she had been frightened of. She had had a portent, had she not? He drew one quick breath. He put a hand to his chest. Think. There had been sixteen in the party. In the darkness, he could count six ahead of him. He stopped. Seven. He waited until those following him had passed. He counted six. Two missing. Then from the rear, he heard a patter of feet and his heart leapt, but it was only another boy. Fifteen, including him. He waited. No more coming. Surely, in the darkness he had missed one, and that one could only be Mara. He pushed past everyone until he had reached the front of the line and then stopped and counted their silent figures again.

Fifteen.

Black despair. Endless, cold life in the years ahead of him and a heart wrapped back in its shroud. But no, he would not waste time interpreting his feelings. Instead, he would ask questions that symbolised hope.

'Nikola, have you seen Mara?'

Nikola paused in his march to address Anton's anxious voice, scanning the group carefully, counting the same numbers as Anton had just done.

'Everyone, search for Mara,' he said quickly.

The short night of late spring was bleeding away. Dawn could not be far off and already, the eastern sky had bleached. The leafy gutters of sticks and stones and night creatures ran rich with reddening water. The night, which had made the forest classless, was separating its elements, and the trees were beginning to stand apart so that the air

355

between them could be roused. The warmth of the sun would thicken it and bring to life the clouds of insects. Reptiles stirred in the undergrowth and waited for the sun. The upland plains beyond the tree line yawned off their slumbers. The living forest, which had sunk in the small hours into its quietest repose, was returning to life. It was a change of state, damp to humid, mist to precipitation, but, for the two men chilled from the night, the ice of fear.

From out of the dark, Nikola's features firmed and delineated. He sent the other men on without them and began to speak rapidly.

'Could she have fallen?' he asked.

'I saw her jump. She should have been ahead by now.' Anton paused. 'She was worried about someone.'

'Ah! Talk while I search, would you? If that someone has taken her, he just can't just proceed randomly. There has to be a trail, a plan, a destination, to make sense of what he has in mind.' Nikola scouted around with his nose to the ground. 'After the rain, there would be footprints in the mud where he has turned, hands that wiped the drops from the leaves, a scent... if only I had the dogs... what if it was the Germans?'

'No,' replied Anton, 'not from the train. Mara was with us afterwards as we hurried away, when we were too distracted to notice.'

'Then whoever has her was down here with us.'

'Yes, perhaps; not far away.'

'There still has to be some indicator.'

'Some indicator could belong to anyone, Nikola. Anyone's boot. Anyone's hand.'

Nikola brushed away the branches that overhung the path, stooped down and inspected the wet ground.

'No, keep looking. There has to be some sign that it was not one of us. Who was the man that killed Jana? Was this the same man who was seen on the outskirts of the camp? If you were him, what would you do?'

'I wouldn't go back the way we had come, for fear of meeting us, and I would take care to obliterate my trail so that the enemy couldn't find me.'

'But he *is* the enemy, so he won't do that.'

'And he will have Mara with him, so we can expect to find double the disturbance and no evidence that he has tried to hide it. Keep looking.'

'So we don't look there. And yet, he has followed us, has he not?' persisted Anton. 'Can there be some parallel path to the one we had taken?'

'Then she is surely still with us and not so far away, for consider, Anton, how long has it been?'

'Since I saw her? A quarter of an hour.'

'Then two kilometres at the very most. Probably less, given that she would have resisted. It is a simple matter to determine the direction. You haven't heard a motor? A truck? A bike? No, neither have I.'

For such a big man, Nikola took care not to disturb evidence, so that Anton, accustomed to iron hulls, marvelled at him. Each leaf he restored carefully to its place. He was gentle with every spider web, retracting it lightly to enable the spider to retreat. Where his boots trod, he checked first for evidence of Mara and other living things. And while he did, Anton saw the lines of grief etched into his face, saw how weary he was.

But Nikola saw further than these trivial things. He looked deep into Anton's soul.

'Lift up your heart,' he said. 'She can't be far away.'

CHAPTER THIRTY-SIX

There was a long trail that they had followed earlier that
night, near a bank of ferns lying so low to the ground that
they caught the morning sun last of all the undergrowth. At
the touch of its light they burst into radiance, and for an instant, were vivid and alive before their green carpet trailed
away and a path opened up from where they ended. Two
other paths led from this first one, one passing right, across a
small water course running down the hill and the other left,
at the commencement of a slight incline. Five metres along
this second path, Nikola stopped. There were many foot
prints in the damp earth, but Nikola knelt beside two in particular.

'Here,' he said. He laid a finger on the prints. 'One has
gone up here heavily and the second is on its toes. No heel
print, you see. He's dragged her around him on his outside,
and it looks like he was running when he did it.' He fingered
a small bunch of bruised leaves, wiped clean of raindrops.
'She's grabbed the leaves and he's tugged her off them. Her
hand has touched these others as she went.' He increased his
pace, his eyes always upon the ground.

The single lane rose more steeply up the hill—a goat
track, a thin, worn path. Much of it remained overgrown—a

358

history, perhaps, of a very old thoroughfare that had fallen into disuse, hence its narrowness, and only recently had begun to be trekked again. As they ascended, the path became strewn with small boulders, so that Anton had to leap upwards and over them. Beside him, he heard Nikola's hard breathing and his boots scraping the gravel. Through the trees, the sky appeared white now; the grey had fled, and in the east the soft underbelly of the clouds was blushed with pink. With the new day, they heard the trill of the first morning birds.

Nikola stopped, a finger to his lips. He pointed down. Scrape marks. Desperate feet had damaged the bark of a young elm, and beside it, a tussock of grass was bent at an unnatural angle. He turned in, passed the damage, right and around the trunk, treading quietly, a hand to his chest to quell his breathing. No longer the signs of a struggle in the bushes. Shortly they must find her. Anton's heart began to thud hard against his ribs. Surely the fiend who had taken her could hear it! Strange how still the organ had been during their ascent, almost purposeful, and only now, the anticipation that was driving it might give them away.

Some distance on, as far as he could throw, the dawn had silhouetted a group of boulders that were shaped into a house-like angle, the size of a car, with two boulders between them forming a triangle, barely sheltering a space from the sky, black for an entrance, but going nowhere. It merely afforded a protected flat area, too far for him to see and, in the shadows, too dark. That there were two figures there, however, was apparent. Something in their ligature had broken the silence, the morning no longer possessed its holy calm and, in this place of dread, no birds sang. A black space beneath a vault of rock, wherein one laid the dead.

A terrible burst of fear gripped him, and he began to run towards the boulders that formed the gaping tomb and, as he gained pace, one of the figures moved. It reached down and dragged at an arm, wrenching a second body from the dirt, easily discernible as Mara by her height. There was the brief report of a pistol; the air of a single shot stung their cheeks and a bullet struck the soft bark of a tree behind them.

Anton stopped. Here was not her death, which he had feared.

And Mara had seen him.

'Anton!' she shrieked. She was dragged away and her foot vanished into the vault.

Nikola put out a hand, pulling Anton behind a tree. 'Stop! He has the advantage. He'll shoot you.'

'But he'll be miles away.'

'He can't move from there. See that ledge? He can't go over it; he can't go up—we'll see him.' He uncovered himself into the light and, assuming a position of assertion, called out, 'You are cornered, young man! Reinforcements are arriving at any minute. Walk forward with your hands up.'

At the tone of command, a figure unfolded itself gracefully from the shadows, and Anton was reminded at once of Michelangelo's *David,* accustomed to looking out forever over everything that was lovely. He was quite the most beautiful young man Anton had ever seen, who was accustomed to the sons of labourers and farmers and had never rated beauty very highly. The man had perfectly symmetrical features, a fresh, open face, clear complexion and pearl-white teeth. His fine brown hair was cut short at the front instead of the long fringe most men wore, so that it accentuated the hair's slight wave. It was more than possible to conceive of him as a child who'd retained the innocence people admired, though grown into the body of a man. Even the briefest morning beard only added to his attraction, and the entire effect was ageless, like the statue in marble he resembled. He looked forgivable, because he was admirable.

But in one hand he held a pistol trained on them, and he had evidently been in the act of undressing for, with the other, he began to button up his trousers.

'You cannot comprehend,' he began in a musical voice that was pleasant to hear, yet held a weariness worthy of the stage, 'the interlude that you have interrupted. Hail the conquering heroes! I curse you, yet I salute you because you wanted Mara that much. Fellow sufferers, you have my sympathy. She's not as cocky as she used to be, so maybe she'll treat you better now, on the principle of judging a society by how it treats its weaker members.'

He gave an entitled snort and lowered a fond gaze upon Mara, shaded on the ground within the structure.

'You see, my darling, I found you, didn't I? And you thought I wouldn't.'

At first Anton could not see her but there was a pile of her clothes flung to one side, as if hastily torn away and coming to rest at Miroslav's feet. Through the throbbing silence of the dawn bushland and his thundering heart, Anton heard her give the faintest groan of shame and roll away. Only about twenty metres separated them now, and he moved out from the protection of the tree with his eyes on the gun.

Nikola began to walk towards Miroslav, talking as he went.

'You appear to have chosen a poor spot for your intrigue, for I can easily see that you have nowhere to run. One more shot from you will bring the might of the German army down around your ears and mine and, as I fancy capture is not in our best interests, may I suggest we settle this in a more civilized fashion?'

'You said you had reinforcements,' insisted Miroslav.

'I do,' agreed Nikola. 'But the Germans will reach us first.'

'I work for the Germans, you fool!'

'And you're happy to explain that to them, in the middle of nowhere? I think I would rather be out of here myself. What is it you do, precisely?'

'And why should I tell you that?'

'Well, I thought it might please you,' said Nikola reasonably, still walking forwards. 'I can tell that you have a bright future ahead of you and it strikes me that a young man who claims to be working for an enemy the rest of us fear is in more of a position to be mindful of that than I am.'

Miroslav stared at him, and then he started laughing.

'Flattery is the oldest trick in the book.'

'Now who said that?' smiled Nikola.

Miroslav still laughed. Such talk from such a man at such an hour! He bent down and scratched one leg when suddenly Anton kicked dirt in his face.

Anton saw Nikola ignore the pistol, run around the cursing young man and fall to his knees where Mara lay. But, even as Miroslav swung around to fire, Anton had seized the hand that held the gun and, pushing it up, began to wrestle the weapon from his grip. As he did so, his shoulder collapsed.

Miroslav gave a peal of laughter, like a school boy, and easily pushed aside the compromised arm, yet Anton nevertheless clung onto his shirt with his hand.

'Old war wound?' asked Miroslav. 'Not that side then?'

Because Anton appeared crippled on the right, Miroslav was unaware of the power he had developed in his left arm and, whilst still holding the shirt, Anton dealt Miroslav a crushing blow across his face that dislocated the jaw and paralysed him with a blast of pain.

Anger suffused the beautiful features.

'How dare you hit me!' he cried. 'Do you know who I am?'

'I don't care,' returned Anton.

Margaret Walker

He was not surprized by the distraught *objet d'art*, for art did not interest him. He turned towards Mara. With Nikola's assistance, she was resembling, in some measure, the woman with whom he had left camp six hours before, but already scars were forming to conceal the hurts. But weren't they all wounded, weren't they all scarred? She had become like one of them now, just another casualty. Yet, even as Nikola began to dress her, Anton rejoiced that she was alive.

Nikola had finished with her trousers and shooed away the morning breeze that in its innocence had soothed her naked skin. With his help, Mara had put both arms in her shirt and, although several buttons were torn, enough remained for her to cover herself. Secure by his side, she had even discarded part of her despair, when Miroslav, that inimitable creature, idly pointed his pistol and shot Nikola in the chest. As arbitrary as all his actions, it gave him a feline satisfaction. He smiled, for its very randomness captivated him and he did not stop to contemplate why he did it. He was peeved. He was offended. He felt like it. His jaw hurt. In fact, the dislocation was very painful, but the outrage hurt a great deal more. So it was perhaps his pride that demanded restitution and this accounted for the action.

Following the pause of perplexity at the penetration of the bullet through his soft tissue—for the pain had not yet commenced—Nikola put out a hand to avoid collapsing across Mara's legs and fell instead from his kneeling position to a point of rest at an angle by her feet, so that his supporting arm landed across her lower legs and his face lay upright, gasping for air. An artery near the lungs had clearly been severed, for a burst of bright blood shot up twice from beneath his clavicle and then settled to a steady flow of blood, pulsing down his chest and into the dirt. Miroslav beheld it with dismay.

'That was inelegant,' he said, massaging his jaw and observing the tangle of arms and legs. 'I expected better of him after all his fine talk.'

Mara pulled her legs from beneath the arm and bent across Nikola's face, with her shirt shielding him like a curtain.

'Nikola!' she cried. She tore at her hair. 'Oh, dear God, Nikola!'

It was at this point, when there was still a spark of hope and it seemed to her that, if he could breathe he might live, that Miroslav dropped his gun and, dashing her aside, pulled out his switchblade and slashed Nikola across both eyes. Though blinding was a Ustasha speciality, yet the action was completely unexpected, and no one had seen the knife. In his impulsive glee at having an opponent so obviously at his mercy, Miroslav remained briefly above Nikola, fascinated by the torture he had inflicted upon his prone adversary who, having lain silently after the bullet entered his chest, was unable to suppress a groan, partly of pain and partly of horror.

Hating herself, Mara turned away, for there was something much more terrible in blinding than in death and it tore at all her ideas of what it meant to be brave. Yet, had she seen what Anton could see from above her, she might have recoiled at the grinning demon and been unable to move at all.

Anton did not hesitate. It was clear to him that Miroslav was mad, and neither insanity nor blindness frightened him. He smartly collected the discarded weapon and, having disabled Miroslav by kicking him in the groin, he stopped the festival of delight by shooting him once through the forehead. It was a well-aimed shot and there was no doubt that it had killed him, though for an instant the raised knees twitched before lying still.

Margaret Walker

Anton knelt beside Nikola and gathered his head and chest in his arms that he might breathe, but to no avail, for it was clear that the Montenegrin was dying. His face, still flushed from the run up the hill, began to whiten perceptibly. As his lungs filled with blood and the red-flecked foam spattered his lips, Mara started to weep.

'Nikola,' asked Anton gently. 'Can you hear me?'

'Yes,' Nikola replied, so softly that he seemed to speak only to himself while his blood stained the grass and his breathing stuttered, stalled, began again, wore down, quieted and waited. Two minutes, three minutes. No more time. Mara looked at his eyes, cruelly pierced, and challenged her fear. She moved closer and watched, remembering all of him.

He was whispering to himself.

'Time to go, boys.'

Already he had commenced his journey. He had put out the lamps, laid the bar over the double front doors, turned the key in the lock, and now there was little else to do but pick up his bags and depart. Lying motionless in Anton's arms, he was moving away from them. The quietening voice, the barest of rhythms, gave some indication of the distance he had already travelled.

'Nikola, I don't understand,' said Mara, who did understand, who realized that he saw beyond himself. Knowing this, she tried to get him to stay anyway, while his chest barely rose and his voice faded until it was nothing more than a murmur. 'Nikola, where are you going?'

'I see....'

'Yes. What do you see?'

'I see crowds running through Jerusalem. I see a young man covered with blood. I see boats pulled up on a far shore.'

'Nikola, wait.' But it seemed that he no longer knew her, that her entreaties were unheard and in vain. And she doubted herself, so she said, 'We can get you home,' when it was clear that they couldn't.

Yet, at the very last, Nikola recognized her—the air of that final breath, blown towards her, without explanation. Just something she felt. She raised his hand to her face. He traced its contours faintly and she let the hand drop to his side. She listened to him when there was barely a voice to hear.

'Mara, comrade partisan, I am home.'

Until finally the great chest was still. She knew he had gone, yet she remained, waiting by his body, feeling his warmth, slowly cooling, reminding herself to remember.

Anton laid him on the ground and took Mara's hand.

'It's dangerous, Mara. We have to go.'

They folded Nikola's hands upon his chest so that anyone who discovered him might know that he had been loved. Then they kissed him and left him there.

When they had gone an hour, they saw a party of Germans investigating the train wreck and were forced to skirt a longer way back to the camp, so that the trip took over five hours. Mara clung to Anton and wept silently for all she had lost that night. But here was the new day that had risen with no knowledge of these events and as little care, and she thought what a heartless thing was a new day, until she realized that it was only innocent and didn't mean it. Anton felt her warmth beside him and was comforted by her, this funny girl who had made him laugh at a time in his life when he thought that laughter was something only other people did.

And when they finally arrived, they heard that Slobodan had died that night, just after they'd left on patrol.

CHAPTER THIRTY-SEVEN

The question of marriage had eventually dawned on Anton. He was still land-locked, as he termed it, approaching thirty-three, and had, once and for all, rejected the idea that Mara was just the most recent in an extensive list of girlfriends of a fleeting and extrinsic nature. There weren't too many women who had managed to pierce his armour of emotional self-sufficiency as she had done, and he simply couldn't imagine a world without her there, to tease and irritate him, and possibly even love him.

He had sat down on a number of hollow logs recently to contemplate what he would be surrendering if he asked her to marry him, and whether it would be worth the cost. He pictured himself in a variety of scenarios, all domestic and none relevant to his present situation. He couldn't help it. All he had was his previous experience to guide him, without wars, without malnutrition, when he had a roof over his head instead of forests and mountains. Perhaps he was being too mechanical about it? He just knew that, unless he could secure a legal bond between them in these troubled times, he might lose her, and that was what it seemed necessary for him to avoid. He had let the other girlfriends go without regret but, with Mara, that action seemed unimaginable.

Through Forests and Mountains

What about her feelings? He got up and sat on another log. A brood of termites ran out into the sunshine and he paused to observe them scurrying back into the dark—back into the familiar. He himself did not feel familiar at all. He felt troubled. He had been launched into a new world, quite without regard to regularity. He liked things to be regular and suddenly they weren't. When had the trouble started? Last month? Last week? The morning he had put his life on the line, simply because she had not been there beside him when he needed her to be?

No, no, no, he thought, the problem was bigger than that. Did Mara want to marry him? He knew she had been stalked by the boyfriend and that the terror culminating in her capture had wounded her. Scars like that did not lightly fade away. He could never place himself in her position, but many of the other young women had been assaulted in the course of the war. Mara was not without true empathy within the Partisans.

He couldn't pretend to be pure himself, and he was simply not poetic about physical things. If Mara had problems with the physical side of marriage (being a realist, he did not think this was unlikely) he would find a way around it—go through his list, be patient and work out what to do to solve problems as they occurred. But he wouldn't create problems that weren't already there.

So he went to visit the commissar.

Josip Cazi assumed a solemn face and recited the lecture Anton expected: that the cause of the National Army of Liberation was too acute for romance. That while the Germans and the Italians, the Ustashas, the Hungarians and the Bulgarians still controlled Yugoslavia they had a fight ahead of them. That they had long ago given up hope of support from Moscow, and that snippets of a suggestion that Britain might have heard of the Partisans were barely giving them hope of

368

Allied support. That they had no food, no clothes, no ammunition. On and on went the melancholy story. Marriage was not high on anyone's priority now. Anton listened with resignation. *Yes, yes, commissar, I know all that.*

The commissar paused and Anton waited until the mechanics of the man's brain were reflected in his face and fell into a pattern that might indicate some hope. But no, off he went again, and Anton remained before him, beside the ubiquitous tree trunk, studying the twitch of that muscle behind the eye and the way his head swung to one quizzical side, as he had noticed it did before he composed a poem about love.

'However, I understand,' Cazi resumed finally, 'That you have only two loves in your life, Anton—the sea, and this young woman you rescued. Being of a romantic nature myself, I cannot, in all fairness, deprive you of both.'

Hope.

So the commissar went away and thought about it, and came back in enough time to save Anton from Despair, but not quickly enough to delay the expression of righteous Anger.

He found Anton pacing the riverbank until he had worn a track in the track that was already there, and hurling pebbles so far out into the stream that, had it been rubber, they would have bounced back and hit him in the face.

Really, had he not been a model captain? He had done nothing but consider the needs of others, and the one time he asked something for himself amidst the calamity in which they lived, his indiscretion had been pointed out to him with the logic of a textbook. Worse, the commissar was well aware that he knew all this, yet he had rattled off his sanctimonious liturgy anyway. What Anton most resented out in these woods was being deprived of the privacy to express his feelings. But his feelings didn't matter, Cazi had

*just assured him. All that mattered was defeating the ene-
my. I know, I know, I know! And, to be truthful, his feelings
hadn't mattered to him before he met Mara, either. He
would have been happy to fight in their absence, for, to this
day, he had never met a man who discussed his heart openly. But, more than anything else, he was upset because he
had no desire to sleep with anyone but her. It was almost as
if sex and emotions went hand-in-hand, which he knew was
ridiculous. So, it was beside the point that Mara, a modern
girl from a good family and educated, would never consent
to sleep with him unless he married her, and it all felt depressingly like the onset of middle-age. But what if she said
no? Then there'd be no more sex. Ever. Damn, damn, damn!
How had it come to this?*

At this point in his musings, he looked up to see the
commissar crunching through the undergrowth in his direction.

'Yes, commissar!'

And, as Anton finally ran out of verbal ways to express
how he felt and fell back on the physical, the commissar enquired, 'Does *she* want to marry *you*?' as formally as if they
had been waiting in front of the priest.

'I don't know!' Anton confessed and thumped his injured
shoulder.

Cazi inclined his head and asked politely, 'How's the
shoulder?'

'My shoulder's fine.' Anton ran a hand through his hair
with the flightpath of a Spitfire.

'But you want to marry her.'

'Yes!'

'The Supreme Partisan Command is rather severe on
these matters, Anton. We mustn't lose our focus.'

'I am focussed. Can you speak with them for me?'

'Of course.' The commissar was a romantic man, despite the time and place. 'You know I would want the same thing for myself, under different circumstances.'

'I appreciate that.' Very businesslike.

'It has to be marriage?'

'I've done the other. I can't lose her.'

'And it does seem hard to deprive you of both your loves.'

'You think I love her?'

'No one wears their heart on their sleeve like you do, Anton.'

'I'm sorry I'm that obvious to you, Commissar.'

So Josip Cazi spoke persuasively to the powers-that-be, adding that happiness was likely to improve everyone's performance, and they gave their permission for Anton to marry Mara in a brief civil ceremony.

Anton's planning for the event was progressing reasonably well (he thought) when one day, about three weeks into the procedure, it occurred to him to ask Mara her opinion. It wasn't that he hadn't intended to ask her if she wanted to marry him. They were good friends, but he hadn't yet found the right time in his preparations into which he could slot the question.

He discovered her late one afternoon, helping the off-duty nurses with their reading. The horror of her abduction had faded by that time but not gone altogether, and he noticed that she started when he approached before relaxing, once she saw that it was him.

'Mara,' he announced in front of the assembled group. 'When is it convenient to speak with you?'

'Now,' she said as if a word or two were no trouble in the world. The girls around her looked up with interest, particularly when Anton added. 'To speak with you alone.'

Thinking that he meant that the plans for tomorrow's patrol had to be changed or that they were short of ammunition again, or that one of the horses had thrown a shoe, and could she keep the home fires burning while he sorted the problem, she tidied her books into a neat pile and replied, 'You can't ask me now?'

'No,' he said simply, because he wasn't a creative talker.

He started rubbing his shoulder again. Nerves, they said. Well, he wasn't nervous now, or was he? One of the girls nudged another. This started a chain reaction of knowing smiles, in which everyone joined except Mara. Finally, she realized that something was on Anton's mind.

'Go, Mara,' said a nurse.

'Yes, I think you'd better,' added another.

'You can return when I'm finished,' said Anton. It was a sideways remark rather than a sentence. He was starting to shuffle his feet as well as rub his shoulder. He just wanted to get out of there with her and do what he came to do.

Off they went and found a further tree. It was a particularly nice tree that summer's day, an old oak with spreading limbs and an ocean of soft green to wash over them. They went around the back, where there were two roots to sit on, one for him and one for her. A fish jumped out of the river and the falling drops of water sparkled in the declining sun.

Anton came straight out with it.

'I have spoken with the commissar,' he began, 'who has given us permission to marry. If you'd like,' he added.

'Oh!' said Mara and put a hand to her lips. 'Oh.'

Anton got up, rubbed his shoulder and shuffled his feet again, dug his hands into his pockets and waited for her to say something else. When she didn't, it was obvious, even to him, that her mind had not been on love when he had interrupted her reading lesson.

In an effort to emphasise to her the uniqueness of the privilege granted them, he said, 'They don't generally allow it.' Still no reply. He added desperately, 'The commissar's re-

372

Margaret Walker

ply ran along the lines of what he thought would be in my best interests, or rather, you understand, our best interests.'

'I understand,' said Mara.

'What he meant was, I can't go back to sea, so...'

'Marriage might be a sweetener?'

'Well, yes, I expect you could put it like that. You wouldn't like the life of a navy wife, Mara. We're away for months.'

She started to laugh—her thoughtless girlish laugh that had so often wounded him—in his misery, it sounded like that now. He felt lonelier than ever. He was aware, by then, that he'd hadn't properly considered his approach, and had blown all his hopes of getting her that little bit closer to him for a longer time, instead of always being part of an army on the move, not knowing what might happen tomorrow.

Where would they be sent? When would he see her again? What sort of struggle against the Axis powers might it be for him, if he no longer had access to his heart? Or hers? If only he could start again and ask her properly in a way that any young woman would like to be asked. But had he? No, he had not. He'd just done it his way, as usual.

But she stopped laughing and looked up at him fondly.

'Of course, I'll marry you, Anton,' she said. 'You saved my life, but I like you anyway.' She got to her feet and kissed him. Nothing world shattering, just a lovely kiss on his lips. 'What would I do if you weren't here?'

He couldn't say a thing. Every word he thought of got stuck in his throat. So he brushed a hand through his hair again and turned her so that they both faced the river, and put his arms around her.

They stood silently, until night began to fall and the frogs came out. Their croaking chorus alerted the bush telegraph, and the Partisans waiting upstream paid close attention. By the time Anton and Mara arrived back at camp, everybody knew. Whether it was, indeed, the frogs that had told them,

373

they would never reveal, except by sly glances. Typical peasants.

THIRTY-EIGHT

No amount of encouragement from Tito could produce supplies out of a hat. There was no more food in the mountains of Eastern Bosnia and the shortage of ammunition had become critical. Terror of the combined German, Italian and Ustasha forces arrayed against Partisan farmers, the political agenda of the Partisan Command, and confusion created by the fluctuating allegiance of the various Chetnik groups that deterred Serb Partisans from attacking Serb Chetniks led to political coups. Under enemy pressure from the north, Foča was captured and the Ustashas stayed behind in East Bosnia to commit atrocities against Serbs and Jews. Tito took the First and Second Proletarian Brigades to Montenegro, to support the fighters there against the Italians, and the Chetniks who were fighting the Partisans with the aid of British resources.

And this was how, amidst all the confusion, Anton ended up back where he started.

The End

About the Author

Margaret Walker

Margaret Walker is a teacher. She has a Bachelor of Science degree from the University of Sydney and diploma in Education and Professional Communication. Her short stories have been published in Australia and England.

A keen historian, Margaret loves research and has a life-long fascination with the Balkans; her birth mother came from the former Yugoslavia. She has her husband to thank for an interest in modern languages. *Through Forests and Mountains* is her second novel.

If You Enjoyed This Book Visit

HIS MOST ITALIAN CITY

BY

MARGARET WALKER

WWII, Italian Fascists, Italian Resistance, Austrian submarines, sea stories , engagements at sea

Fascist Italy 1928.
Trieste, once the port of the Austrian Empire, has become Italian. As fascism strives violently to create a pure Italy along its streets, Matteo Brazzi is forced to choose his loyalties with care.
When his office is bombed, the police are baffled, but Brazzi knows who committed the crime, and he knows why.
Though he is no seaman, he can easily identify the dark shape that disappeared into the Gulf of Trieste that dramatic night and, as he escapes to Cittanova in Istria, the mysterious vessel follows him down the coast.
Brazzi has successfully exploited fascism to protect himself - many people would call him a traitor - but he's only ever had one real love. Now Nataša is dead and Brazzi owes his share of the blame.
Too soon he discovers that not even Mussolini can save him from an enemy who is bent on revenge.

PENMORE PRESS
www.penmorepress.com

TheClose to the Sun

by
Donald Michael Platt

WWII Fighter pilots, Air war over Europe. German Fighter aces, American Fighter Aces, War in Europe . Air War over Russia. German politics during WWII.

Close to the Sun follows the lives of fighter pilots during the Second World War. As a boy, Hank Milroy from Wyoming idealized the gallant exploits of WWI fighter aces. Karl, Fürst von Pfalz-Teuffelreich, aspires to surpass his father's 49 Luftsiegen. Seth Braham falls in love with flying during an air show at San Francisco's Chrissy Field.

The young men encounter friends, rivals, and exceptional women. Braxton Mobley, the hotshot, wants to outscore every man in the air force. Texas tomboy Catherine "Winty" McCabe is as good a flyer as any man. Princess Maria-Xenia, a stateless White Russian, works for the Abwehr, German Intelligence. Elfriede Wohlman is a frontline nurse with a dangerous secret. Miriam Keramopoulos is the girl from Brooklyn with a voice that will take her places.

Once the United States enter the war, Hank, Brax, and Seth experience the exhilaration of aerial combat and acedom during the unromantic reality of combat losses, tedious bomber escort, strafing runs, and the firebombing of entire cities. As one of the hated aristocrats, Karl is in as much danger from Nazis as he is from enemy fighter pilots, as he and his colleagues desperately try to stem the overwhelming tide as the war turns against Germany. Callous political decisions, disastrous mistakes, and horrific atrocities they witness at the end of WWII put a dark spin on all their dreams of glory.

PENMORE PRESS
www.penmorepress.com

Historical fiction and nonfiction
Paperback available for order on line
and as Ebook with all major distributers

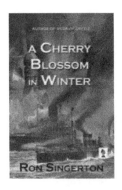

A CHERRY BLOSSOM IN WINTER
BY
RON SINGERTON

The -Russian Japanese War – Before the Revolution
 As the 20th century dawns, Japan is a rising power at odds with determinedly expanding Russia. In Moscow and St. Petersburg, aristocrats advance their political interests and have affairs as factory workers starve. Young Alexei Brusilov, son of an ambassador, accompanies his father to Japan and there falls in love with the daughter of a Japanese war hero. Amid the rising storm of revolution at home, Alexei returns to St. Petersburg to become a naval officer. A deadly rivalry with another cadet, a dangerous family secret, and friendships with revolutionaries imperil his career – and his life. Years later, Alexei finds himself aboard ship as the rusting and badly out of date Russian fleet is sent half way around the world to fight a modern and determined Japanese Navy. Will Alexei live to see his love again, or die under the blazing guns of the fast moving enemy cruisers?

PENMORE PRESS
www.penmorepress.com

Penmore Press

Challenging, Intriguing, Adventurous, Historical and Imaginative

www.penmorepress.com

Lightning Source UK Ltd.
Milton Keynes UK
UKHW012353231222
414383UK00001B/22